TARGET

TARGET

Brian Freemantle

This title first published in Great Britain 2000 by
SEVERN HOUSE PUBLISHERS LTD of
9–15 High Street, Sutton, Surrey SM1 1DF.
Originally published in 1980 as *Misfire* under
the pseudonym of *Jonathan Evans*.
First published in the USA 2000 by
SEVERN HOUSE PUBLISHERS INC of
595 Madison Avenue, New York, N.Y. 10022.

British Library Cataloguing in Publication Data

Freemantle, Brian, 1936–
   Target
   1.   Suspense fiction
   I.   Title
   823.9'14 [F]

   ISBN 0-7278-5550-6

Printed and bound in Great Britain by
MPG Books Ltd, Bodmin, Cornwall.

For Shirley. And Derek, too, of course.
With love.

INTRODUCTION

The preliminary events culminating in the various operations described in this book — and the operations themselves — are entirely fictional. All the characters are fictitious too, and any resemblance to actual persons, either living or dead, is purely coincidental.

However, there does exist in a certain central African state — although not that identified in this book — a complex with control over an area of 100,000 square kilometres, in which lives a native population of approximately 250,000 people. The company owning this complex draws its shareholders from West Germany. Its function is to build and launch, at a cost of £35,000,000, a spy satellite for any Third World country prepared to pay for such a device.

Although initially supported by a West German government research grant, the complex became a political embarrassment to Chancellor Helmut Schmidt after Soviet protests at the United Nations labelled the installation a cover for Western military operations in Africa. To monitor the activities of the complex, the Soviet Union positioned two spy satellites over the area.

The presence of the installation was fully disclosed in Great Britain by the BBC's current affairs programme *Panorama* in October 1978. That same month, a peace agreement was signed between Israel and Egypt. Immediately after the signing, Israeli Prime Minister Menachem Begin said: 'It's a revolutionary change in the situation in the Middle East.'

Egyptian President Anwar Sadat added, 'Nothing must be allowed to imperil the start that has been made.'

In January 1979, Leonid Brezhnev, General Secretary of the Soviet Communist Party, chairman of the Praesidium of the Supreme Soviet and Marshall of the Soviet Union said during an official interview: 'On the whole, over the last couple of years, there have been few encouraging moments, to be frank, in Soviet-American relations. Speaking quite candidly, I will tell you that very often we are hard put even to understand Washington's persistent desire to seek advantage for itself in the disadvantage of others. All this has, indeed, been tried — on more occasions than one — by American politicians in the cold war period. However, objective reality led the United States to conclude that it was necessary to co-operate with the Soviet Union, particularly in preventing nuclear war and in settling conflict situations in various parts of the world. Our reciprocal will to act precisely along these lines was then recorded in the relevant documents which we in the Soviet Union highly value and in which we continue to see a good basis for a durable and lasting turn for the better in relations between the USSR and the USA.'

BOOK ONE

I have no spur
To prick the sides of my intent, but only
Vaulting ambition, which o'er-leaps itself
And falls on the other.

William Shakespeare, Macbeth.

CHAPTER 1

The previous night had been bad — one of the worst he could remember — so Peterson was not surprised that Lucille was still heavily asleep. He still went quietly into her room, anxious not to disturb her. She lay on her back, mouth open, snoring. She'd tried to get her dress off, but had become entangled with one strap off the shoulder and the other in place and then apparently collapsed backwards, unable to bother further.

Peterson knew he should have checked when he came home. Had he not been so completely absorbed with the current crisis, he would have done. But it still wasn't a very satisfactory excuse: it rarely had been.

Gently he lifted her legs fully into the bed and pulled up a sheet to cover her one exposed breast. He realized she was dribbling and when he turned to the side table for a Kleenex to sponge her chin he saw that she had upset the glass. He looked down to the carpet, but there was no liquor stain. She stirred at the movement against her face and he stopped, apprehensively. Her make-up was patched and lined and in sleep her face had an oddly collapsed look, like a child's coloured balloon the day after the party. Poor Lucille, he thought, poor darling. He paused, turning to put the dirty tissue into the waste basket, aware for the first time of Paul's graduation picture lying flat upon the side table. It must have been her attempt to stand it there that had upset the empty glass. He picked up the frame, gazing down at the photograph. There had been nothing flaccid or collapsed about her face then. She looked bright and eager and vibrant with happiness — and pride. Certainly there had been everything to be proud of that year. His appointment as Director confirmed, Paul's graduation as *magnum cum laude* and the vacancy awaiting him in one of Washington's most prestigious law firms and Beth, still with her teeth in braces, but already showing the roundness of womanhood in her long white dress, promising to be even more academically brilliant than her brother.

Two years, he calculated. What had happened? What in God's name had caused them to disintegrate into what they were now: a wife who slept every night in an alcoholic stupor, a cult freak daughter somewhere on a commune refusing to respond to any name but 'Y', and a son who seemed to enjoy the embarrassment he caused as the capital's foremost advocate for decriminalizing the drug legislation and defender of the underprivileged.

Washington, Peterson supposed. It was certainly the social brawl that had shown Lucille the way to anaesthetize herself against her disappointment. But Washington wasn't the only cause — not even the main one. It was him, Peterson accepted. He had allowed it to happen, by imagining that examination results and Phi Beta Capa badges meant adulthood.When they had needed him, he hadn't been available. He'd been at the head-quarters at Langley or the White House or at the National Security Council or in some embassy in some foreign capital, the dynamic chief of the world's most effective intelligence agency, not intelligent enough to realize the effect of his neglect upon his family.

Lucille whimpered in her sleep, a pained sob. She turned, thrusting the sheet away and carefully Peterson covered her again. The movement caused his watch to show, warning him how soon his driver would be arriving. Because of the crisis, Peterson had ordered him an hour earlier than normal. He'd been awake before dawn and wished now that he'd summoned the car sooner. He was anxious to learn what had come in overnight.

He went back to his own room to prepare himself. He frowned at the word, recognizing it as appropriate. That was what he did; prepared himself. Like an actor applying the make-up for a particular performance, James Peterson every day adopted the carefully rehearsed role. He chose a discreet tie to accompany the discreet suit, selected a matching shirt from among those still crisp in their laundry cellophane and took from its accustomed drawer the duster specially placed there to give his already gleaming shoes a final buff. He surveyed the completed effect; overall it was one of competence. That's what he was, Peterson thought — competent.

Apart from Paul's occasional, slightly endangering outbursts in the *Washington Post* or the *Star*, the shambles of Peterson's personal life was carefully kept behind the triple-locked front door of the Georgetown brownstone. Publicly — and that was what mattered in Washington — he was regarded throughout the capital as someone who had reorganized and run the CIA with a competence and ability far beyond that shown by at least three of the Directors who had preceded him. Not once had he submitted a faulty foreign analysis to the President or the National Security Council; not once had an operation been initiated or sanctioned and later become a diplomatic embarrassment.

Through the window he saw the black, armoured limousine pull into the kerb, the bodyguard leaving through the front passenger door even before the vehicle came to a halt. Peterson straightened, as if trying to attain some stature and breathed deeply, a small, almost inconspicuous man packaged for the world outside.

Two years without a failure, Peterson calculated again. He'd been lucky, he accepted realistically — but always competent. And now that record, the only thing left in which he had any pride, was endangered. He knew little more now about what was happening in Africa than he had done when they were first warned of the installation and then confirmed its presence with satellite reconnaissance. Less, in fact. What had occurred since they had started investigating had increased rather than lessened the mystery. A month before it had been an uncertainty; now it was approaching priority proportions. And the Russian involvement only added to the worry. The President wouldn't like the presence of the Russians.

Peterson heard the doorbell chime and immediately left the room, before the maid could call up and possibly awaken Lucille. The woman was waiting as he descended the stairs, the door already open.

'Mrs Peterson isn't feeling very well,' he said.

'No,' she said expectantly.

'She'll probably stay in bed, until lunchtime at least.'

'Of course.'

They knew their lines very well, thought Peterson. Another performance. He nodded to the guard, following him out to the waiting car. The glass shield separating the driver from the back seat was lowered and when the car began moving Peterson raised it, indicating that he didn't want any conversation. For several moments he stared out, as the limousine slowly made its way out of the ghetto of the Washington élite, but as soon as they entered the city proper he turned back inside the car. The *Washington Post* and *The New York Times* were already laid out waiting, and beyond them was the foreign news digest which was prepared throughout the night and made available for him every morning, an exact copy of that prepared for the President.

Irrationally — which was unusual because Peterson was not an irrational man — he felt a stab of impatience at having to wait until Langley to discover what he really wanted to learn. He grimaced at the feeling, irritated by it; at this stage it would be ridiculous to permit that sort of anxiety. Knowing it would be equally ridiculous to expect it, he still went through the newspapers and then the digest seeking any reference to the part of Africa about which he was scheduled to brief the President that morning. There was nothing.

He went back to the newspapers and then the overnight round-up, reading them this time for their proper purpose. Peterson had an encyclopaedic yet analytical mind, capable not only of total absorption but also of immediate recall, and by the time the limousine turned off into the CIA complex deep in the Virginia countryside, he knew he was sufficiently briefed for any discussion that might arise during the day.

Walter Jones was already waiting when Peterson entered the office, knowing that the Director would expect him to be there.

'Anything?' demanded Peterson, immediately.

'Not enough,' said his deputy. Jones was a balding, scholarly-looking man who affected tweeds and a pipe which he always appeared to have difficulty lighting. They had known each other for fifteen years and Peterson regarded him as one of the few good friends he had in Washington. Frequently he envied the man's unencumbered life as a bachelor.

'What?'

'They'd already buried Brinton by the time our people got from N'Djamena ... it's customary apparently, because of the heat.'

'I know that,' said Peterson, impatiently.

'They managed an exhumation,' said Jones. He indicated Peterson's desk, turning his mouth distastefully, 'There are the pictures. Poor bastard.'

'Nothing apart from a crocodile attack?'

Jones shook his head. 'They weren't equipped for a proper autopsy, of course. But that was all that was obvious. He'd been terribly mauled.'

'What about Jenkins?'

'Still nothing,' said the deputy.

'Did they enquire?'

'As best they could, without wanting to cause any undue interest. There wasn't a trace.'

'When was his last radio contact?'

'Two weeks ago.'

'Anything on the emergency frequency?'

'We've had a twenty-four hour monitor established for over a week. There hasn't been a thing.'

'They were both good men.'

'The best,' agreed Jones.

Peterson picked up the photographs. 'So we can't believe that this ...' he frowned at what they showed, '... or whatever has happened to Jenkins is an accident. Or carelessness.'

'No, definitely not.'

'OK,' accepted Peterson, leaning across the desk to talk the problem out. 'We've discovered a perfectly bona fide consortium of West German companies, all with links or association with rocket research and development, who have apparently established an installation in the middle of an under-developed African country and would appear to be building a communication satellite ...'

'So far, so good,' agreed Jones.

'And so far, no illegality,' continued Peterson. 'The indications are that they intend to lease out at a very high price access to and usage of the satellite, wherever they place it ...'

'Which creates a political problem,' interjected Jones.

'Political,' seized Peterson immediately. 'But that's still all it is. So why have two of our operatives been eliminated?'

'That's the big one,' said Jones. 'If that hadn't happened, I'd have said all we'd got was an irritation. Now we've got to find out why.'

'And who,' said Peterson. 'The consortium might be constructed to avoid tax, but every member is well established and respected, not just in Germany but throughout the world. They don't *kill* people.'

Peterson once again took up the photographs of what remained of the agent whom they had infiltrated in through the Cameroons the previous week.

'Jesus!' he said softly.

'Hope to Christ he was dead first,' said Jones.

Peterson thrust the pictures aside, turning to the file that had been taken from the security room and laid in readiness on his desk. 'Does the President have a copy of everything?' he asked.

Jones nodded. 'There are some fresh satellite shots, although they don't add much.'

Peterson opened the folder. The Chad border with Libya, Sudan, the Camaroons, Nigeria and Niger had been superimposed, for ease of discussion. Peterson isolated Lake Chad, then the capital N'Djamena, and then, to the north, the huge complex.

'No sign of any rocket yet?' he demanded, not bothering for the moment with the detailed analysis.

'No,' said Jones. 'But that doesn't mean much. Anything would be kept in a silo until the last minute.'

Peterson was bent forward over the analyst's report of the space-satellite photographs of the installation. He looked up suddenly, his finger marking the spot at which he had stopped reading on the second page.

'From the silo dimensions,' he said, as if he found the information difficult to accept, 'they estimate the rocket size capable of lifting a nuclear pay-load into orbit.'

'Just the capability,' said Jones, cautiously. 'Our intelligence talks only of a monitoring satellite.'

'You've ordered the people back from N'Djamena?'

Jones looked at his watch. 'They're due at Andrews airbase in about four hours.'

'I want them brought here immediately.'

'I anticipated that,' said Jones. He fumbled to get his pipe ignited. There was a lot of flame but nothing happened.

Peterson finished the photographic analysis and sat back in his chair.

'So our only remaining hope is Williams,' he said.

'It would appear so.'

'Is he maintaining contact?'

'On the button,' said Jones. 'He hasn't missed a transmission yet.'

'When's he next due?'

'Six tonight, our time. According to the last message, he should have reached the installation by then.'

'What about the Russians?'

'Nothing more than you already know.'

'They've put a satellite over it, like we have?'

'Unquestionably,' said Jones.

'We can't be left behind on this.'

'I know,' said the deputy.

Peterson braced his hands against the desk, a prelude to a decision. 'What would happen', he said, 'if we put out an all-stations call to anyone with a double agent to try to discover how much the Russians know?'

Jones regarded him doubtfully. 'Odds on that Moscow would find out and realize how badly we're doing.' He appeared surprised at the question.

Peterson nodded, accepting the warning. 'So they might make a mistake ... give us a lead we haven't got.'

Jones remained doubtful. 'It's risky,' he said.

'But justifiable,' said Peterson. 'They might just do something silly, through over-confidence. Maybe it's time to start considering insurance options. I want it done.'

The Director reached out again for the pictures of the agent who had supposedly been killed by crocodiles. 'Let's hope Williams has more luck than this poor son-of-a-bitch,' he said.

'Yes,' agreed Jones. 'Let's hope.' His pipe flared at last and he sat back in a billow of smoke. And let's hope this Russian lure isn't a cock-up, he thought.

The earliest satellite pictures had made it possible for a map to be drawn showing almost to the metre the size and the position of the installation, so Edgar Williams estimated he couldn't be more than a mile away. Maybe two at the most.

He knew he had not been the first sent in, so it was logical to deduce that the others had been seized and probably killed. He had proceeded very carefully, sacrificing speed for caution, aware of the importance of the mission and determined to succeed. The nearer he got, the more difficult it had become. The jungle petered out into scrubland and the scrubland gave way to savannah; the previous night he had had to retreat for the protection of trees and undergrowth.

He was awake early, waiting for the first light of dawn, gauging it the best time to move. Through the field-glasses he could see the observation towers. His training had begun with a Green Beret attachment in Vietnam and so he was an acknowledged expert in jungle movement. If he attempted to approach through the grassland, he would leave the wake of an ocean liner. Which meant that he had to find a path. This took him an hour, time well spent, because when he finally located a trail it was clearly one created not by humans, but by animals. He started out cautiously, in the initial stages risking his head above the brushline to check that he was not leaving any indication of his progress.

The tortoise shell came first, and had he not by now been travelling at a crouch he might have missed its significance, dismissing it as nothing more than the skeleton of a chelonian. But he was almost on all fours, with his face comparatively close to the ground, so he saw the spike protruding from where the reptile's head would have been. It would be poisoned, he knew, recognizing the witchcraft symbol; he had been briefed very fully by African experts before leaving Washington. Cautiously turning it over with the tip of his knife, he saw that it had been carefully stuffed with unguents and red seeds. One side of the shell was marked with white, the other with red. Part of Williams' equipment was a radio fitted with a transmission device, enabling him to send messages at least thirty times the speed of normal relay, thus reducing the risk of detection by any listening device. He described his findings, unknowingly initiating a later operation, then depressed the despatch button, clearing the information in less than thirty seconds.

Over the next half mile, he identified three more shells, one with the white and red covering turned upwards, so that even if he had been walking upright he would have seen it. Soon afterwards he came upon the hyena figure, roughly fashioned from clay and with the feet inverted in the usual manner of the occult throughout Africa. For a man who had been schooled in Vietnam, where ground sensors had been made in the form of grass stalks as early as 1972, it was an almost inconceivable mistake for Williams not to recognize them as easily as he had done the witchcraft talismen, but then he had existed for a week with little more than three hours' sleep a night, his nerves were tense with anticipation as he grew closer to the objective and the muloi figures of the tortoise and the hyena had actually lulled him away from any thoughts of scientific detection.

Their approach was very quiet — much better than his. But then they were Africans and used to the savannah. He was aware of them only when they wanted him to know of their presence and when they emerged he reacted well, pretending that he was stooping to recover a dropped water-bottle and greeting them in French, knowing it to be the second language of the country, and confident that their ability to speak it would be insufficient for them to detect any fault in accent or pronunciation.

'Observation des oiseaux,' he said. He carried papers stating that he was an ornithologist attached to the World Wild Life authority; they also provided, for any casual examination, an explanation for the cameras, binoculars and even the radio he carried.

There was no response. At least twenty Africans were grouped around him, their faces devoid of any expression.

'L'oiseau,' he tried again, as if he imagined they had misunderstood. 'Je suis un observateur scientifique.'

The blow came not from the point of the spear but the shaft, so that the wind was driven from him and he doubled up, gasping with pain and surprise.

Intense though the agony was, he still managed to depress the despatch button and transmit the account of the latest witchcraft symbols. He operated the emergency switch, relaying a repeating signal from which Langley would know he had been identified, seconds before the second blow, across the back of his head this time, sending him into the blackness of unconsciousness.

His first impression, upon recovery, was of skin irritation and he realized that there were ants and other insects covering him. He tried to shift, to dislodge them, and became aware that he was tethered to the ground, spread-eagled between four stakes and secured to allow some movement in both his arms and legs but to prevent him from freeing himself.

Shadows from the savannah grass told him it was already late, perhaps an hour before sundown; he would not have expected to be unconscious for so long. He strained upwards, lifting his head from the ground and shaking it as wildly as he could, trying to unsettle the things crawling and sucking at him; the ants were even exploring his nose and he had to snort to free them from his nostrils.

Staked out as he was, it was difficult for Williams to obtain any view except that of the increasingly darkening sky, but he forced himself up again, screwing his head around at the sound from behind. An animal stood at the water-hole, statued with the immobility that comes just before flight — squat and tusked. Some kind of pig, he guessed. He was suddenly conscious of the sounds all around him as the jungle stirred with the movement towards the drinking place, and he opened his mouth and screamed a wild, almost insane howl. The pig burst away in immediate fright and he yelled again, knowing it would keep them off for some time. But he would grow tired, Williams knew. And the animals' thirst would increase, making them braver.

'Help!' he screamed again, his voice breaking with the beginning of panic, because he knew there was no one to hear him. 'For God's sake help!'

He twisted again, towards the water. One animal hadn't been frightened off. It had settled comfortably upon its haunches, with the patience of a carrion hunter. It was a hyena, Williams saw. Waiting.

CHAPTER 2

General Dimitri Petrov was sparsely tall, well over six feet, and fine boned, his features more Western than Slavic. His hair had gone completely white overnight during the horror of the Stalingrad siege, and what had looked unusual in his youth now gave him a courtly, patrician appearance. It was an impression he cultivated. His bachelor apartment within the shadow of the KGB headquarters in Dzerzhinsky Square was lavishly equipped with a stereo system for his enjoyment of both Russian and Western music. The walls of his study were lined on three sides by classics in French and English, both of which he read fluently, as well as Russian originals.

He imported French wine for his table and Western cloth for his civilian suits and his uniforms. He preferred the quality. His position accorded him automatic seating at the Bolshoi; he was one of the few in the ruling élite of the Soviet Union who used the privilege for genuine enjoyment rather than for a demonstration of their power.

Petrov still went regularly to the Bolshoi, despite what had happened with Irena. In fact, not to have gone would have heightened the suspicion among those who opposed him in the Soviet hierarchy. A man constantly involved in secrecy, Petrov knew he had kept their affair discreet, but inevitably there had been rumours. It was fortunate that the opposition to him at that time had not been as concentrated as it was now, so that the innuendo had never grown into a positive accusation that he had assisted in her defection. Poor Irena, thought Petrov. Poor Valentina, too. It had been a bizarre period in Petrov's ordered, regimented life — a madness. He had loved, passionately, his wife. And loved, with equal passion, Irena. She hadn't wanted the affair, in the beginning. She had talked of the betrayal of Valentina and hated the lies and the deception — and then, he thought, she had grown to love him as much as he had loved her.

She had been selected as principal dancer for the Bolshoi's tour of America. Petrov could still remember — and he had to remember, because to have kept newspaper cuttings would have been dangerous — how she had been honoured and feted in the West. He could remember, too, the numbed, disbelieving shock of her defection.

It had been almost six months to the day after Irena had slipped away from the final triumphant performance in California and sought asylum from the American authorities that Valentina, always so bright and so vibrant, had been given a diagnosis of terminal cancer. Six months later she had died.

Petrov knew that Irena Sinyavsky had not defected because of any ideological doubt. She had fled rather than continue in what they both knew to be an impossible triangle and now they were separated by five thousand miles and two separate cultures.

In the beginning, when the shock and remorse at Valentina's death had eased, Petrov had sometimes thought of trying to contact Irena. But he had never done so. Even his position couldn't have protected her, had she returned. To imagine the controller of the KGB marrying a defector was an absurd, laughable fantasy, as inconceivable as his following her into exile. But he missed her, just as he missed Valentina. He had almost completely reconciled himself. No one else knew of his aching loneliness. Certainly not the critics. They would have liked to have known, of course, because it would have presented an advantage and the opposition within the Politburo were increasingly seeking advantages over him.

Because his existence depended upon such knowledge, Petrov was aware of the criticism, not of the brief, insoluble tangle of his marriage, but of his life-style. It was not difficult to appreciate their misunderstanding. His grandfather had been a nobleman attached to the court of Nicholas II, with estates at St Petersburg and Moscow and Perm. It was simpler for them to believe that the way he lived represented nostalgia for the past, rather than to remember how truly revolutionary his ancestor had actually been.

Petrov was alert to the dangers of the talk about him, but not frightened by it. Providing he remained efficient — and he knew himself to be overwhelmingly efficient — then it could only be malicious gossip. Which was why Africa worried him. He should have had more success by now and the Politburo committee knew it. Petrov hunched forward over his hand-tooled leather desk, sifting yet again through the photographs and satellite pictures, as if another examination might give him the solution. Although he had the appearance and behaviour of an aesthete, Petrov was really a man of calloused emotions and he regarded without any revulsion the shots of the two agents who had apparently starved to death. There was a great deal of animal damage, but it was still possible to see how emaciated they had been allowed to become before being cast into the jungle. Both practically skeletons. They must have been subjected to severe dehydration to achieve that state in so short a time. Both of them had come from one of the best of his deep penetration units and were agents who should have been able to find food and water in the middle of the Sahara desert, let alone in a jungle teaming with wildlife. He moved on to the photograph and report of Laventri Malinkov. He had personally briefed Malinkov before sending him in, could still recall the controlled confidence of the man and his own subsequent conviction that they were going to penetrate the complex and discover the truth about it.

'Irretrievable', the psychiatric report said. Only three days earlier they had isolated the drugs that had taken Malinkov's reason, before he had been set down for their discovery in N'Djamena. Petrov turned to the photograph. Malinkov gazed out with empty, unfocused eyes, his tongue lolling between slack lips. It could have only been a challenge — or maybe a warning — for them to have reduced the man to that catatonic condition with the sulphur-based drugs that they knew the Soviet psychiatrists used upon the dissidents incarcerated in the Serbsky Institute.

Petrov got up from the desk and wandered over to the window. His office was at the back of the rambling Lubyanka, on the top floor from which he had an uninspired view of other office blocks. They must be very confident, to behave like this, Petrov thought. Very confident indeed.

He sighed, reluctantly turning back into the room, aware that it was time for the interview. There was a dressing-room off his main office, with a full-length mirror set into the door. He studied his reflection critically for several moments, adjusting the tilt of his cap and the shoulder setting of his topcoat before descending into the basement garage where his driver was waiting. His car was recognized as an official vehicle and the streets cleared for the short drive to the Kremlin.

Sergei Litvinov was waiting, as Petrov knew he would be: the man would imagine a psychological superiority. In confirmation of the thought, the man appointed as liaison with the committee gave a shift of impatience, as if Petrov had kept him waiting.

'Noon,' reminded Petrov, refusing to recognize this stupidity. As he spoke, some distant clock began chiming the hour.

'Thank you for being on time,' said Litvinov. He was a pince-nezed bureaucrat with thinning hair. There was even the inevitable pen in the pocket of the jacket. Petrov decided that the man would have been a very minor clerk before the revolution.

'I have been asked to give an account to the Politburo,' announced Litvinov.

'Yes.'

'The reports are insufficient.'

'Yes,' agreed Petrov. 'It's gone very badly.'

'We didn't expect that,' said Litvinov.

'We underestimated,' confessed Petrov. He knew Litvinov was one of his strongest critics.

'*You* underestimated,' corrected the man.

'Yes,' admitted Petrov.

'Is there thought to be any West German government involvement in this?'

'Only indirectly,' said Petrov. 'They are aware of the consortium, as they are of the companies which form it; all of them have been involved at some time or other on government defence contracts. But the whole operation appears to be one of private enterprise.'

'To build a rocket which is available to any country without the research facilities or time to manufacture their own?'

'As far as our knowledge goes, yes.'

'How far does our knowledge go?' seized Litvinov.

'Not far enough, I'm afraid.'

'I am afraid, too,' said the clerk-like man, turning the expression. 'I am very much afraid that we are on the edge of a whirlpool, being drawn in towards the centre.'

Petrov frowned at Litvinov's verbosity. He wondered why he felt it necessary to talk like that; perhaps it was something that clerks always did, like carrying pens and pencils in their outside pockets.

'We will discover more,' he said, trying to force some confidence into his voice. He didn't think he had satisfied the man.

'Our satellite pictures don't show the degree of construction upon any one rocket?'

'No,' said Petrov. 'But there are several silos.'

'Will they be spy satellites? Or nuclear?'

'There appears to be the capacity for both,' said Petrov. 'But the difference is really academic — we can't allow either.'

'What about the Americans?'

'They've attempted to infiltrate, as we have.'

'With success?'

'I don't think so.'

'But you can't be sure?'

'No,' conceded Petrov. 'I can't be sure.'

'It would be embarrassing to lose anything more to the Americans, wouldn't it?' demanded Litvinov.

Petrov made no immediate response, caught by the ambiguity of what the other man had said. Was it clumsy phrasing? he wondered, or a hint that Litvinov knew about his involvement with Irena? To over-respond would be a mistake, he decided.

'Yes,' he said. 'Very embarrassing.'

'What are you going to do about it?'

He didn't know, Petrov realized. He felt a tinge of uncertainty, a rare sensation for him.

'Attempt to discover more from Germany,' he said. 'Until we have better information, there's little point in risking additional people on the ground.'

'We're in a bad position, aren't we?' pressed Litvinov.

'At the moment, yes.'

'I want it improved,' insisted the politician. 'I want us to know everything about that installation and I want a guarantee that we are not lagging behind the CIA.'

'I understand,' said Petrov. He found it difficult to show respect to the other man.

'How much time do we have?'

'I don't know.'

'This isn't going to make a very satisfactory report.' Litvinov stared at Petrov, enjoying the confrontation. 'We want more,' he demanded. 'Much more. We want it quickly and we want it without the degree of failure that you've shown so far.'

Petrov glared back at the challenge, meeting the man's eye and refusing to be intimidated. 'You'll get it,' he promised.

'We'd better,' said Litvinov, determined to be the one who ended the exchange.

Litvinov clearly saw the affair as the opportunity he had been seeking — the opportunity to bring about Petrov's downfall.

The two Russians sat at the far end of the gay bar, from where they had a good view of the West German Defence Ministry employee they knew to be Otto Bock and Jurgen Beindorf, an eighteen-year-old clerk in an export office. To prevent approaches from anyone else, the Russians feigned interest in each other, one sitting with his arm loosely around the other's shoulders.

'Arguing,' said the larger of the two.

His companion nodded, looking down the bar. 'Love never runs smooth,' he said.

Bock was pulling at Jurgen's sleeve, but the youth was shrugging him off, moving his body in time to the music from the jukebox. After several moments, the older man got up from his bar stool and confronted the youth, gesturing angrily; Bock appeared embarrassed. Again Jurgen shook his head and Bock paused for a moment as if making a decision, then turned and hurried away.

'Our lucky night,' said the large man, 'even if it wasn't for poor Otto.'

They both moved without haste along the bar until they got to the boy. They made their approach obvious and he smiled — he was very handsome.

'Hello,' he said.

'Hello,' said the small Russian. His German was perfect, without a trace of accent.

'Noticed you earlier,' said Jurgen. 'Like it here?'

'Not much,' said the larger man. 'There's a much nicer club. We're just on our way.'

His companion allowed just the right amount of hesitation. 'Like to come?' he invited.

'Lovely.'

The Russians had a BMW parked almost directly outside. The smaller man got into the driver's seat and the other into the back with the German boy. The Russians had already reconnoitred the club area of Bonn and reached the alley very quickly. Jurgen appeared to become aware of the danger at the last moment and tried to yell but the larger man had been sitting with his arm around his shoulders and now gripped the nerve cluster near the boy's collar bone, immobilizing him with pain.

'Please,' said Jurgen. 'Please don't hurt me.'

He was crying.

The smaller man was waiting by the rear door and he hit the youth as the other man thrust him out. Jurgen crumpled, breathless. Carefully — because they didn't want to mark his face — the taller one supported him while the smaller man hit him repeatedly in his stomach. Jurgen was unconscious surprisingly quickly, so they lay him in the back of the car to recover. It took almost an hour. One of them smoked, listening to a Beethoven concert on the car radio; the other put on the interior light and read a German language edition of *Time* magazine.

Jurgen groaned back to consciousness. He remembered where he was and tried to scramble away, hunching himself against the far seat and crying out again at the pain from his bruising.

'We want to show you something, Jurgen,' said the smaller man. He held out some photographs and the youth screamed out in horror, putting his hands to his eyes.

The bigger man reached over the seat, forcing Jurgen's hands away so that he had to look.

'It's acid,' said the other Russian, conversationally. 'See how his nose has gone and all that scarring. And he's blind, of course. We're going to do that to you, Jurgen. We're going to do that to you unless you end your association with Otto Bock. *We* want him. You understand?'

'Oh yes, please yes. For God's sake, let me go.'

'End it,' insisted the Russian. 'End the friendship immediately.'

Jurgen nodded dumbly.

Six miles away in the residential area of the West German capital, Otto Bock, unaware of how he was about to be manipulated or of the effect that it would have upon him, stalked into the living-room of his apartment without any greeting to his wife.

'Do you want supper?' asked Gretal.

'No.'

She frowned at the abruptness. 'What then?'

'To be left alone.'

Gretal turned away to hide her reaction to his attitude. It was the work, she tried to convince herself. Otto worked far too hard and if he were not careful, it would make him ill.

CHAPTER 3

The others were already assembled when James Peterson entered the Oval Office. He paused just inside the door, recognizing them one by one and assessing from their presence how seriously the President regarded the situation. It was very serious.

'Glad you're here. Come in, come in,' greeted William Fowler. It was a practised, insincere folksiness. Fowler was a tall, gangling man who had thrust his way to the Presidency with the single-minded ruthlessness with which his forefathers had established the largest cattle holding in Texas; he was nostalgic for the frontier life and fond of boasting how his grandfather had pursued three cattle rustlers into Mexico and lynched them all from the same tree. Lobbyists for the National Rifle Association had rarely known a more receptive Executive when any anti-gun legislation was proposed.

Henry Moore, who sat in a chair to the left of the presidential desk, was a plumply indulgent senior partner in a New York legal firm who had taken leave of absence to serve as Secretary of State. It was no secret in the capital that he regretted the decision, particularly now that his absolute authority had been eroded by the appointment of Herbert Flood as foreign affairs adviser. Flood was a stooped, bespectacled lecturer from Harvard who still adopted the attitude of an academic: the crumpled sports jacket, wool shirts and loafers were practically a uniform. It was a calculated deceit, Peterson knew. Since his arrival in Washington, Flood had developed an intense ambition and whatever happened in the next election, he had no intention of returning to any Massachusetts university. Without having any positive grounds for the belief, Peterson didn't think Flood respected his ability. He was certainly unsure about Flood, but like all Washington professionals he took care to conceal the attitude.

Peterson went to the chair indicated, carefully placing his

brief-case beside him and straightening his trouser crease.

'You got a can of worms for us this time,' said the President.

'It would seem so,' said Peterson.

'Have we got in yet?' demanded Moore.

'In the car on the way here I got a call that our third man was in trouble.'

'Dead?' asked the President.

'Probably,' said Peterson.

'What the hell!' erupted Fowler. 'That makes three, in under two weeks.'

'Yes.'

The President turned to Moore. 'What do the Germans say?'

'That it's a legally established consortium of recognized companies working outside the laws or jurisdiction of Bonn and apparently doing nothing illegal.'

'They won't interfere in any way?' asked Flood.

Moore frowned at being asked a direct question by anyone other than the President. 'They say they have no cause.'

'I want Bonn leaned on,' insisted Fowler.

'I'll take it as far as I can,' said Moore, 'but I doubt that we will be able to make them do anything effective. So far there *is* no illegality.'

'Have we gone back to source?' asked Flood, staring intently at the CIA Director.

'On several occasions,' said Peterson. 'The Israelis say they can't learn anything further. They're as worried as hell at the prospect of a spy satellite over their territory.'

'The information came from them in the first place,' pointed out Flood.

'Only that they believed there was an installation somewhere,' qualified Peterson, irritated at the other man's attitude of constant criticism. 'They didn't even know which country; it took a satellite to identify Chad.'

'What *do* we know?' demanded Flood. He managed to infuse sarcasm into the question, anticipating the limit of Peterson's knowledge. Henry Moore was right in disliking the man, decided the CIA Director.

Peterson lifted the brief-case to his lap, taking out the

information clip that had been prepared in anticipation of the query. 'It would appear to be a highly technical, well built, very modern installation,' he said, glancing between the men and the notes upon his lap. 'It's large, something like eighty thousand square kilometres. It has its own air strip and they apparently use helicopters as well as aircraft. The satellite pictures show a very extensive and elaborate communications section, including radar. The consortium, BADRA, is registered in Bonn and formed from six German rocket-related companies. The function in their prospectus is given as the development of advanced communication systems. They appear to have survived the '79 fighting between President Malloum and the guerillas of Hissene Habre. And the religious genocide the same year between the Muslims and the Christians ....'

'So everyone is on the take?' interrupted the President, as if to confirm some private impression.

Peterson smiled bleakly. 'Seems that way,' he agreed. 'The company are to pay the government $40,000,000 a year, from the date of the first successful launch, for the right to be there, though I don't expect it to go into the economy of the country.'

'Why can't we bribe our way in?' demanded Flood.

'There's no trouble getting into the country,' said Peterson, patiently. 'It's entering the complex.'

'We're sure it *is* rocket construction?' said Moore.

'We've identified at least six silos ... there could be more. Our analysts are positive about them — they are unquestionably for rocket storage.'

'Our intelligence is poor,' criticized Flood.

'I know,' said Peterson, accepting the rebuke. 'It's proving more difficult than I expected it to be.' He paused. 'The Soviets have involved themselves,' he reminded, 'and like us they've put a satellite over the complex.'

Fowler looked first to Moore, then to Flood. 'Any point in attempting some sort of consultation?'

'Too early,' said Moore at once. 'We'd be approaching from a position of weakness and if the Soviets realized it, they'd screw us.'

'I agree,' said Flood, reluctantly. 'We need more intelligence.'

'I don't like this,' said Fowler. 'I don't like this one goddamn bit.'

Everyone remained silent, none wishing to be the first to make a suggestion and risk being wrong. The President looked towards Peterson. 'I want you in personal control,' he ordered quietly. 'I don't care what it costs or what it involves, I want it stopped. I'm not having some shit-kicking country getting access to any sort of rocketry and risking the balance of power we've established.'

'*Me*!' said Peterson, bewildered. 'What about the Operational Director?'

'*You*,' insisted the President. 'This is big — too big. You're the man at the top.'

Peterson knew the Secretary of State and the foreign affairs adviser were as surprised as he was at the decision. They would have appreciated Fowler's reasoning, though, just as he had. If the affair were big, then any scapegoat had to be correspondingly important. William Fowler, President, was prepared to take a fall-back position, and James Peterson, CIA Director, had been put into line to protect him from all the crap.

'If that's your wish,' said Peterson, allowing the doubt to show. 'It's a little against standard practice.'

'I don't give a damn about standard practice,' said Fowler, angrily. 'I want you in personal control, at all times.'

'I understand,' said Peterson, tightly.

'Glad you do,' said Fowler. 'I want to be kept fully informed; I shall be available at any time.'

In the car going back to Langley, Peterson again closed the glass partition between himself and the driver. It had been a bad performance, he conceded to himself. One of the unwritten dictums of Washington politics was that a person did not show his doubts, and Peterson knew that he had just failed to observe it. The President's edict worried him. Of course, as Director, he would ultimately be responsible for whatever happened in the name of the Agency. He would expect that. But the President's decision established a personal link, removing any room for manoeuvre. So he wasn't allowed any mistakes. He sighed and checked the time. Lucille would be awakening now. He looked towards the car telephone, wondering whether to call her. Better to wait, to give her more time. If she were up, she'd still be in a bad way.

He summoned Walter Jones the moment he entered his office.

'The President has put me in personal charge,' he announced.

'You're not an operational man,' said the deputy immediately.

'I made that point,' said Peterson. 'He insisted — a presidential order.'

'Insurance, in case it goes wrong,' judged Jones.

'Yes,' accepted Peterson.

'I'm sorry,' said Jones. 'That it happened that way, I mean.'

'So nothing must go wrong.'

'No,' agreed Jones. 'Nothing must go wrong.'

'Anything from Williams?' demanded Peterson anxiously.

'Nothing,' said the other man. 'We've tried constantly, since the emergency alert. His radio is out.'

'So that's that?'

'It would seem so,' said Jones. 'Your son came through, on the private line.'

'Paul called here!' Peterson had always discouraged any personal intrusion from his family; lately he'd come to regard the distancing as some sort of protection.

'Said it was important.'

'Sorry you were bothered,' apologized Peterson.

Jones looked at him curiously. 'It was no bother,' he said. 'He wants you to return his call.'

Peterson made an impatient gesture. 'What about the people coming back from Africa?'

Jones looked apologetic. 'Plane's developed trouble in the Azores,' he said. 'No chance of them getting here tonight.'

'Damn,' said Peterson bitterly. He looked steadily across the desk at his deputy. 'We're on the line over this.'

'I realize that.'

'It's not just the President. That bastard Flood is playing politics with us, as well.'

'Are we going to mount another operation in Chad?'

Peterson considered the question, staring down at the picture of the mutilated body of the first agent.

'No,' he said positively. He saw Jones looking at him in anticipation of some alternative proposal.

'It could lead to a mistake,' explained Peterson cautiously. 'After today's meeting at the White House, we can't risk mistakes.'

'I suppose not,' accepted Jones.

'We'll have a strategy meeting once the people get back from the Azores,' decided Peterson. He saw the other man frown at the twenty-four hour delay before any fresh action.

'I want every appointment and commitment in which I might be involved delegated for the next two months,' Peterson hurried on, trying to convey the impression of activity. 'And get back to Israel: see if they've come up with anything more.'

Peterson wondered if his deputy was aware of how frightened he was.

'I'll see to it,' said Jones doubtfully. He rose, to return to his own office. 'I put your son's number on the pad,' he said at the door.

Alone again, Peterson sat staring at the notation, undecided. It was two months since they had last talked, nearer three. Inevitably, it had ended in an argument. He dialled the number. Paul answered immediately, as if he had been anxious for the call.

'Still keeping the free world safe?' he said. It was a friendly attempt at humour, not sarcasm.

'You wanted me,' said Peterson, refusing the lightness.

'I'd like to meet you.'

'Why?'

'It's important.'

'I'm very busy.'

'You always are.'

'What is it?'

'Important.'

Why couldn't he go some way towards meeting the boy? Paul had made the first approach, tried to be friendly.

'When?'

'How about tonight?'

He ought to remain in the office, Peterson thought. But for what? The people who'd recovered the body of Brinton weren't getting back until tomorrow. And he could easily do everything else during the afternoon.

'The Hay Adams,' selected Peterson. He was taken past the hotel on the way home; it would mean a fairly short delay.

'Do they admit people in jeans?' asked Paul, trying again to reduce the hostility between them.

'I don't know,' said Peterson, refusing his son again. 'I don't wear them.'

'Perhaps you should,' came back his son, his temper going at last. 'They keep your balls up under your chin, where everyone can see them.'

'Do you really want a meeting?'

'Yes.'

'Six then.'

'All right.'

'Don't be late.'

'I'm being fitted with difficulty into the schedule?'

'I'm very busy.'

'So you said. I won't be late.'

Peterson determined that tonight he would try, really try. He would permit the boy as much time as he wanted and avoid any dispute. And not patronize him — treat him man to man. More than that, even. He would reach out, try to restore what had once existed between them. It was past one, he noted. Time for Lucille. She answered almost as promptly as their son had done, expecting the contact. Time for yet another little performance.

'How are you?'

'Fine.'

'You were sleeping when I left.'

'Thank you for not awakening me.'

The make-up would be repaired by now. The hair would be perfect, even though she was about to visit the beauty parlour. The afternoon dress would match the afternoon coat and she would have toning shoes and handbag. In the afternoons, the Washington women were always at their public best.

'So you're all right?'

'Of course,' she said, too quickly. 'Why shouldn't I be?'

'No reason.'

'So it was a stupid question?'

'Yes,' he retreated. 'I'm sorry. Have you had any lunch?'

'I wasn't hungry.'

'Please try something.'

'I don't feel like it.'

'I thought we'd stay in tonight ... eat at home,' said Peterson.

'There's a reception, at the French embassy.'

'I don't want to go,' he said wearily.

'It'll be fun.'

'I'm tired.'

'I'm not.'

'We'll talk about it tonight. I might be a little later than usual.'

'Why?'

'A late meeting.' He wouldn't tell her about Paul. Not until after they'd met, anyway.

'I *want* to go to the reception.'

'Later, I said.'

'I won't let you down.'

'I didn't say you would.'

'You're frightened that I might embarrass you.'

'Don't start, Lucille.'

'I didn't start it.'

'You're threatening to.' There would be a glass by the phone, he knew.

'What time?'

He hesitated, remembering the decision not to hurry the encounter with Paul.

'Seven,' he said.

'The reception is at seven-thirty.'

'I said we'd talk about it later.'

'And I said I wanted to go.' There was just the slightest blur in her voice.

'I love you,' he tried desperately.

She laughed at him, disbelievingly. 'How would I know that?' she demanded. 'When was the last time ...'

'Stop it!' he demanded. He wondered if the maid was in hearing.

She laughed again. 'Embarrassed, James?'

'I must go.'

'Of course. The World to protect.'

'I'm very busy.' Why did the truth sound so much like an excuse? he wondered. He had said the same words so often that they were practically meaningless.

'It was kind of you to call,' she said formally.

He started to speak and then stopped himself. The time for arguing was long past.

'Don't ...' he started, halting immediately. 'Let's have a pleasant evening,' he added lamely.

'Don't what?' she challenged.

'Nothing,' he said.

'Don't what?' she insisted.

'You were disgusting last night,' he blurted. He hadn't meant to say it, but now that it was out he was glad; perhaps his distaste would shock her and make her realize what was happening.

'So it's not embarrassment. It's disgust?'

'Yes.'

'Have you ever thought how much you disappoint me?'

'Yes I have,' he admitted, honestly. 'And I'm deeply sorry.'

The answer momentarily silenced her. 'Isn't it too late for that?' she demanded.

'I hope not.'

There was no response from the other end of the line.

'Lucille!' he said, anxiously.

'What?'

'It went quiet.' She was crying, he knew.

'I'm sorry,' she said, thickly.

'It's not too late. Honestly it isn't.'

'I don't really want to go to the reception.'

Peterson felt the hope flare through him: it was stupid, he knew, as stupid as his premature anxiety in the car that morning.

'I'd like to stay in,' he repeated.

'You won't be late?'

'I promise.'

'I'm sorry,' she said.

'Sorry?'

'For last night. And all the other nights. I know it's not your fault.'

His meeting with Paul would be something for them to talk about that night; would the boy actually come home with him? That would be rushing things, decided Peterson. Better to effect a gradual reconciliation.

'Have a quiet day,' he said, finding the euphemism at last.

'I will,' she promised.

'I love you,' he said.

She didn't laugh this time. 'I love you too,' she said.

Had it not been for the war, which changed so many careers, it was unlikely that Dimitri Petrov would have entered his country's intelligence service. When he was scarcely in his teens he was playing chess at near Grand Master level and even now, to relax, he sometimes went to the Academy and challenged the world champions. His winning average was very high. At a chessboard he regarded himself as a pragmatist and it was a philosophy he carried with him to his desk within Lubyanka.

The accepted treatment of operatives who were discovered to be double agents was liquidation. But Petrov rarely did anything in the accepted way, which was why he had survived for so long. A man anxious to impress Washington as much as Moscow could be a useful conduit for the dissemination of false information and Petrov's tendency was to maintain the agents and use them when the need arose.

He had alerted every embassy, not just throughout Africa but in Europe and Asia as well, for any intelligence concerning the Chad installation, so the enquiry from Paris would have come to his attention anyway. Petrov was immediately curious because Michel Levebre, who worked at the Elysée Palace, was a known informant of Washington. Within four hours, a message had come from London, this time reporting the interest of a junior official in the Canadian trade mission in Britain who was also an accepted double. Petrov smiled the smile of a chess player who recognizes his opponent's gambit and has a defence prepared to nullify it.

The expression did not last for long. It was comforting to know that the Americans' desperation was such as to make them take the risk of making enquiries, but it did little to overcome the immediate problem. He stared down at the photographs of his mutilated agents, remembering the meeting with Litvinov and his inability to present any acceptable proposition for discovering what was happening in Africa. The idea was slow to formulate and even when he had accepted it, Petrov remained still at his desk, considering first the dangers and then the moves and counter-moves that the proposal might precipitate. The possibility of disaster would be appalling, he realized, particularly with the opposition he was encountering from Litvinov. But properly explored, the advantages would make it worthwhile.

CHAPTER 4

Peterson tried to clear his mind of the forthcoming meeting with his estranged son. During the afternoon, working with Jones, he initiated cables to all their stations throughout the world making the Chad installation a matter of urgent priority. Although there were parts he almost knew verbatim, he once again went right through the file that had so far been assembled, seeking anything that he had missed and becoming increasingly depressed at the absence of any proper, workable intelligence.

Shadows were already patterning out over the Virginia countryside when he left Langley for the journey back into Washington. He had given himself plenty of time, determined not to keep Paul waiting. Because of some quirk in the traffic flow, they completed the journey faster than usual and he arrived at the Hay Adams fifteen minutes early. He lingered momentarily in the panelled lobby, then walked on through into the bar. Like many people associated with a drink problem, Peterson severely curtailed his own alcohol intake. He ordered a beer and after it was served took only a token sip.

Paul was early; he appeared disappointed at not arriving first. He smiled hesitantly and halted leaving some distance between them, seeming unsure how to greet his father.

'Thank you for coming.'

'You said it was important.'

The boy hadn't worn jeans after all, Peterson noticed. The trousers and jacket were smartly pressed and the hair, which had been shoulder-length when they last met, was much shorter now. Had it not been for the drooping moustache, he would have looked like the young executive he had left college to become. When the waiter returned, Paul ordered a coke.

'How's mother?'

'No better.'

'She should have treatment.'

'She won't accept the problem. I've taken advice: they've got to *want* a cure. It can't be forced upon them.'

'Perhaps I should drop by.'

'She might like that. Better to give her a warning, though.'

'I've heard from Beth,' Paul announced suddenly.

Peterson had reached forward for his glass, but now he stopped, looking to his son.

'When?'

'Yesterday.'

'Where is she?'

'Arizona. Near a place called Tonalea.'

'A letter.'

'Yes.'

'How is she?'

'Hard to tell.'

'Did you bring the letter with you?'

'No.'

'Why not?'

'It wasn't particularly coherent. You wouldn't have learned anything from it.'

'So she's *not* all right.'

'I think she wants out,' said Paul.

'Did she say so?'

'She said she'd call me, soon. Wanted to speak to me again.'

'I thought the commune she had joined severed all family ties ... a new family in place of the old.'

'They do,' agreed Paul. 'That's why I think she wants to come home.'

Would Lucille stop drinking, if they were a family again? It would be too much to expect the girl to settle at home, but there could be an apartment in Washington at least. She would be close enough for them to look after her. Would she be ill, undernourished by whatever crazy diet was supposed to bring them closer to the full understanding of life? Or mentally disorientated by the quasi-religious crap she had been fed?

'Do you know what I think?'

Peterson looked up at his son's question. 'What?'

'That she'd guess I'd contact you.'

'So?'

'She's asking for help, Dad.'

'But of course ...'

'If you went to Tonalea, I think she'd come home with you.'

Maybe two thousand miles, Peterson estimated; probably way out in the boondocks, taking at least a day, perhaps even longer to find. Four days at least.

'I could send people ...' he started, but again Paul cut him short, leaning across the table and seizing his arm for emphasis.

'Dad! We're talking about Beth, your daughter ... my sister. Not some mission for airborne cavalry or a Green Beret squad.'

'I can't get away from Washington, not at the moment.'

Paul sat back, his face fixed. 'I'd forgotten,' he said. 'You're busy.'

'It's not possible, not at the moment,' insisted Peterson. He wouldn't fight with the boy; he'd control his temper, whatever the provocation and keep the encounter as amicable as possible.

'Jesus!' said Paul.

'It's something very important,' said Peterson.

'It always is.'

'I mean it.'

'I would have thought Beth was pretty important.'

'That's trite, and you know it. Why can't you go?'

'Because it's not me from whom she's asking forgiveness.'

'Did she say that in the letter?'

'She hinted it.'

'She knows I'd forgive her.'

Paul thrust himself back into the chair, as if his exasperation made it difficult to form the words. 'How the hell can we guess what she knows, after the sort of life she's been living?' he demanded. 'You know the psychological damage these cults can cause. She's made the effort, Dad. She's made the first approach. Now we've got to go to her.'

'I told you I can't. Not at the moment.'

'Bastard.'

How far had they moved apart, for Paul to call him that? And for him not even to be moved to any hurt or anger?

'I'll send some people,' he repeated.

'Do that,' said Paul. 'And you'll drive her so far into the bullshit society in which she's involved herself that we'll never see her again. Why do you think she quit in the first place?'

Peterson looked at his son, wanting the answer.

Paul saw his father's need and shook his head in astonishment. 'Because it was always *people being sent*,' he said. 'It was always an anonymous driver or a polite assistant or a maid. It was never *you*. Don't you know why she split for these stupid communes? Because ridiculous though they are, she was *noticed*. She was treated as a person, not a possession which had to be protected and occasionally dusted but not bothered about too much.'

The waiter returned, hopefully, but Peterson shook his head.

'Maybe in a week or two,' he said, doubtfully. 'Maybe I could get away then.'

'And maybe in a week or two she will be pregnant or tripping on mescalin or drinking cyanide, because some half-assed messiah has convinced her the world is coming to an end.'

'Don't you think I care!' erupted Peterson, angry at last. 'Don't you think I know any one of those things is possible and that it frightens the hell out of me.'

Paul smiled at the outburst, unconvinced. 'Then do something about it,' he said. 'Forget about being the button-down Superman, for as long as it takes.'

They were talking in circles, decided Peterson. 'Will you let me know when she calls?'

'Why?'

'Because I'd like to know.'

'I don't believe you.'

'Tell her that I love her ... that I want her back ....'

'Tell her yourself.'

'Please!'

'You make me sick.'

'I want ...' Peterson stopped, bewildered by the appearance in the bar entrance of Walter Jones. The Deputy Director saw him and approached smiling. 'Sorry to intrude,' he said.

Paul looked at the two men. 'Was he on schedule?' he demanded cynically of his father, looking at his watch. 'I'd no idea my time was up.'

'I don't understand ...' frowned Jones.

'Forget it,' said Peterson irritably. 'What is it?'

'Something I thought you would want to handle personally,' said Jones, glancing around the open bar with the awareness of how easily they might be overheard.

'Right now?'

'I think so.'

'It's quite an act you've perfected,' sneered Paul. 'Is there a dance as well?'

'This is my son,' Peterson said, in belated introduction. 'Walter Jones, my deputy.'

Jones extended his hand. Paul stared at it before taking it, briefly.

'I really am sorry to intrude,' repeated Jones.

'We'd finished anyway, hadn't we Dad?' said Paul.

Peterson stood, but didn't immediately move away from the table.

'Tell me when she calls?' he asked.

'Maybe.'

'I meant what I said ... about wanting her back ....' He stopped, looking with embarrassment towards Jones. '... about loving her,' he finished.

'Shouldn't you get along,' said Paul. 'The bad guys might be winning.'

Peterson walked out without any farewell, Jones trailing behind him. They both got into Peterson's car, the vehicle in which Jones had arrived following empty behind.

'I was lucky the motor-pool managed to locate your driver so quickly,' said Jones.

'There's been contact from Williams?' anticipated Peterson.

'No.'

'What then?'

Jones glanced towards the glass shield, ensuring it was fully raised. 'The Russians,' he said.

Peterson turned fully towards the man sitting beside him. 'It worked!' he said.

'I'm not sure.'

Peterson frowned. 'What do you mean?'

'From Dimitri Petrov himself.'

'I don't believe it!'

'Neither did I. Before coming to get you I checked it, fully. It seems genuine.'

'How?'

'Through the embassy in Vienna.'

'Who knows?'

'Our resident in Vienna, obviously. Cipher clerks. And us.'

'Nobody else?'

'No.'

'We'll keep it that way.'

'Of course.'

Through the windscreen, Peterson saw the direction sign to Langley briefly illuminated in the car headlights. As the vehicle turned off the highway towards the complex, he remembered his promise to Lucille: seven, he'd said. From the dashboard clock he could see it was seven-thirty.

'Shit,' he said, to himself.

'What is it?' asked Jones.

'Nothing,' said Peterson.

Four thousand miles away, near an African water-hole, the patient hyena rose at last. The leopard, who had attacked first, followed by the lioness and her two cubs had not left a great deal, but there was still sufficient to have made the vigil worthwhile.

CHAPTER 5

From the window of his office David Levy could gaze out over the olive grove from which legend had it the cross had been fashioned for Christ to carry to Calvary. Far to the right, but still identifiable from the disordered thatch of trees on the hillside above it was Yad Vashem, the memorial to the six million who had perished in the holocaust. He could also just pick out the roof, designed after the cover of the reed basket in which they had been discovered, of the museum housing the Dead Sea scrolls, with their still readable account of Jewish guerilla opposition to Roman occupation. Why was it, wondered Levy, that all monuments in Israel were to tragedy?

The Mossad chief was an almost unnaturally short man, but very broad and barrel-bellied from an inherited appetite for Polish dumplings and flour-thickened stews. He was fiercely proud of being a sabra but sometimes regretted that his Israeli birth had denied him the era of his father, who had escaped the Nazi destruction of Warsaw to become a leader in the Irgun Zvai Leumi movement which had fought against the British in 1948. The Zvai Leumi had been the genesis of the Mossad; Levy's career had seemed predestined. His pride in his birth was matched by his pride in the service he had created with such painstaking care. Without greater financial resources, the Mossad did not have the scope of the CIA or the KGB, but Levy believed that what they lacked in material they compensated for in the quality of their operatives. He meant it when he said he would match any one of his people against three from either the American or Russian services. His critics accused him of arrogance, but then his critics accused him of many things — to his complete disinterest. One of the strongest accusations against him was that he was refusing to adjust to the times, a man too accustomed to conflict to be able to accept the possibility of peace. It was an unfair charge; Levy appreciated the advantage of a secure border with Egypt but was too objective to overlook the remaining problem of a million dispossessed Palestinians, or a Jerusalem which was as much a holy place to Muslims and Christians as to Jews, or the fact that none of the Arab States had supported the Sadat initiative. He'd let the politicians toast the celebration in champagne and Moslem orange juice and keep his service as vigilant as ever.

It was a vigilance which had paid dividends in Africa. Neither America nor Russia had known about it, despite all their spies in the sky and their aerial monitoring.

Levy pulled the file towards him, flicking through the photographs and the accompanying analysis which the Americans had provided, gazing down at the pictures for a long time and finally settling back into his chair, staring blankly through the window to the olive grove beyond.

The dossier had every indication of being complete; Peterson had even supplied details of the deaths of his own deep penetration agents. But there should have been more — much more. He smiled, remembering the American assurance of full liaison. He had not believed it, from the moment the undertaking had been given.

He thrust aside the American file, turning to his own reports. The information was very weak; by themselves each account amounted to little more than a rumour. But assessed as a whole it became clearer; America would certainly think so. The source for the Damascus account would be Palestinian. Probably the same from Benghazi; Libya was as much a sanctuary for the guerillas now as Syria. Iraq was more likely to be a government leak.

Levy arranged the fact sheets before him, as if he were physically attempting to make a pattern. Would Peterson's assessment be the same as his? It would be impossible to guess with absolute accuracy, until there was next personal contact between them. Asked to bet, Levy would have offered odds of sixty to one.

He assembled the agents' intelligence in the order in which it had come into the Mossad and then spent more than an hour creating a covering message. It occupied less than half a folio, but Levy scrapped several attempts, determined to get the text exactly how he wanted it.

'I invite your own independent assessment,' he wrote in the concluding paragraph to Peterson. 'But from the information available, I would certainly connect this as yet undefined Middle East activity with what is taking place in Africa. I draw your particular attention to the coincidence in phrasing between what came from Baghdad and from Damascus. In each case, the threat is of "spectacular demonstration". What else can this mean, measured against the atrocities to which we have been subjected in the past?'

Satisfied at last, he summoned a secretary with instructions that it should be ciphered and then transmitted to the Washington embassy, for transmission to Langley.

It was almost completely dark by the time he went back to the window; it was impossible to see the trees above Yad Vashem. Monuments to tragedy, he thought again. Of one thing David Levy was quite determined. There were not going to be any more — not while he was in a position to prevent them.

The Vienna residency had been Richard Brownlow's first foreign posting. He had been attached to the American embassy for six months, had seriously misinterpreted the purpose of some government changes in neighbouring Czechoslovakia within the first weeks, and was frighteningly aware that this inexplicable approach from the Soviet Union could ruin his career if he made the slightest mistake. Jones' response to his report — to bring him home on the first available aircraft and then ferry him by helicopter directly to Langley — had increased his nervousness, and he entered the Director's office damp with perspiration. It was the first time he had been in the Director's presence; Peterson was a much smaller man than he had expected. He appeared out of proportion for the desk and high-backed chair in which he sat.

Jones had ordered Brownlow's recall from Vienna within an hour of receiving the man's report, long before setting out to locate the Director in Washington. There had still been a four-hour wait, for the aircraft to arrive from Europe, and they had occupied their time studying a complete profile of the KGB chief and considering Brownlow's assessment in view of his record. Peterson had hoped that Lucille would accept his apology during the first telephone call. When he had called a second time, after an hour, she had been drunk.

'Sorry to drag you back so hurriedly,' greeted Peterson.

'I understand,' said Brownlow, hand hovering near his mouth. The man bit his nails, Peterson noticed.

'Tell me again about the approach,' instructed the Director.

'There was a reception last night, at the Austrian Foreign Ministry,' said Brownlow. 'Usual sort of thing ...'

'You'd formally accepted an invitation?' interrupted Peterson.

'Yes.'

'So the Russians could have checked you were going?'

'I suppose so,' agreed the younger man. He felt uncomfortable from the perspiration and realized that he'd lost five hours flying back across the Atlantic — in Vienna, it would be four in the morning. He felt exhausted.

'Did it appear to be a planned approach?' asked Jones.

'Not at first. Milhailov wasn't wearing his uniform and I didn't immediately recognize him as the military attaché.'

'So what happened?'

'Milhailov is a ski-buff. We started out talking about the snow this year. It wasn't until later that I became aware he'd led me away from where anyone could overhear the conversation. As soon as he achieved that, he mentioned Petrov.'

'How?' demanded Peterson. 'What were the exact words?'

'That he had been instructed to get an approach through to you, suggesting a meeting.'

'He stipulated a meeting?' pressed Jones.

'Yes.'

'Where?' said Peterson.

'That was for you to suggest.'

'He mentioned me by name?'

'Throughout the conversation.'

'So you're not interpreting innuendo?' pressed Peterson, remembering the Prague mistake. 'It was spelled out.'

'Absolutely,' said Brownlow, miserably aware of the reason for the question. 'He mentioned Petrov and you by name and talked of a meeting.'

'It was definitely Milhailov?' asked Jones, suddenly.

'I checked the photographs,' assured Brownlow. 'Even obtained one taken by the official photographer at the reception that night. I've brought them with me, for comparison. But it's Milhailov. I'm sure of it.'

'How am I to respond?' asked Peterson.

'That wasn't discussed,' said Brownlow. 'Through Milhailov, I presumed.'

'Was any mention at all made about Africa?' he asked.

'Nothing. A matter of extreme concern affecting you both was what he said.'

'They could be screwed up just as badly as we are,' suggested Jones.

'Liaison isn't unknown,' said Peterson, distantly. 'There was contact during the Bay of Pigs towards the end. And when the U-2 went down.'

'You're surely not thinking of responding!' said the deputy, incredulous.

'Why not?'

'Because it's a trap, that's why not. It's got to be.'

'But I thought of it first,' reminded Peterson.

'It would be too dangerous,' said Jones, adamantly.

'Not if we started out with that expectation in mind. And did it better.'

'I thought Africa was the problem.'

'It is. A very big problem. That's why insurance wouldn't be a bad idea.'

'It's too dangerous,' insisted Jones. 'It introduces a complication we don't need.'

'Or maybe a way out that we *do* need,' said Peterson. He went back to Brownlow. 'What did you tell Milhailov?'

'Nothing positive,' said the man. 'He asked if I'd make a report and I said I would.'

'Shouldn't it be a presidential decision?' pressed Jones, concerned about the way the Director's thoughts were moving.

'He wouldn't agree, not after this morning's discussion with Moore and Flood.'

'*Surely*, after this morning's discussion, it should be the last thing to consider. The risk would be appalling.'

'What response has there been, from any station anywhere, to the message we sent out this afternoon?' demanded Peterson.

'Nothing,' admitted Jones.

'Not even Bonn?'

'No.'

'What about the Israelis?'

'Nothing,' said Jones again, uncomfortable with the argument.

'And we've lost Williams?' persisted Peterson.

'There's no body. But I'm sure he's dead,' agreed the deputy.

'So we're screwed,' judged Peterson. 'We need an out and Petrov might provide it. Properly planned, it would only take a couple of days.'

Perhaps as long as it would have taken him to go to Arizona to get Beth back. Paul had been right; it would be far too risky for anyone other than himself to go there.

'You wouldn't expect Petrov to come here?' said Jones.

'Of course not.'

'So you'd go to Europe!'

Peterson smiled at his deputy's continued amazement. 'It would be seen as a concession ... create a false sense of security. And you're forgetting something.'

'What?'

'A ballet dancer named Irena Sinyavsky.'

'There was never any proof,' insisted Jones. 'She never mentioned him — not once.'

'But there are three pictures of them, together at various Bolshoi functions, before she ran.'

'Receptions,' qualified Jones. 'With dozen of people.'

'By itself, not enough,' conceded Peterson. 'Combined with other things, it might fit perfectly.'

'Where would you meet him?'

Peterson returned to Brownlow. 'What's wrong with Austria?' he said. 'That's neutral enough.'

'Would you want me along?' asked Jones.

Peterson shook his head. 'You'd be needed here. We've got to guard our backs.'

'What about the President?'

'Not yet,' said Peterson. He'd set it up first, so that it was foolproof. The President had been quick enough to arrange his own let-out. Now, Peterson decided, it was his turn. He became aware of the fatigue pressing down upon Brownlow.

'I'll get a military aircraft to take you back from Andrews first thing in the morning,' he said. 'Tell Milhailov I accept. Say Vienna would be acceptable to me, but that I must know more about the problem he believes to be our mutual concern ....'

The younger man tried to straighten in the chair.

'You'll need a squad with you,' continued Peterson. 'Photographic, electronic surveillance ... everything necessary for an entrapment. I want it all in place when I arrive.'

They didn't consider he'd made a mistake, Brownlow realized, and was relieved.

Peterson leaned across to the man, to emphasize what he was saying. 'I want Vienna sewn up tighter than a drum. I want to know the moment Petrov arrives, what he does, who he does it with ... I want to learn more about him than he knows about himself. You got that?'

'Yes,' said Brownlow, nervously.

'Now go and get some rest,' ordered Peterson. 'You've got a hell of a lot of work to do.'

Jones waited until the man had left the room and then turned back to the Director.

'You leaving it to him?' he said.

'Of course not,' said Peterson, surprised at the question. 'I want another group sent in, tonight. They're to know of Brownlow's instructions so they don't get in the way, but they're to work entirely independently.'

'I still don't think you should do it.'

'If I think it's getting too dangerous, I can always abort it,' said Peterson, confidently.

'Providing you realize where the danger is,' said Jones, guardedly.

It was almost 2 a.m. before Peterson finally got back to Georgetown. Lights were on throughout the house and none of the curtains were drawn. Peterson went slowly in, going from room to room in search of Lucille and carefully closing doors and extinguishing the lamps behind him. He found her in her own bedroom, apparently peacefully asleep. He smiled down at her, relieved. It was not until he got close that he saw she had vomited on to the pillow and then rolled into it sometime during the night. He got a flannel and towels from the bathroom and gently sponged her clean. He pulled away the stained pillows and replaced them with more from the linen closet. She half wakened, when he had practically finished, and smiled crookedly up at him. Her throat moved when she tried to speak, but nothing came. Finally she gave up and was asleep again very quickly. He kissed her softly, and went through into his own room, aware for the first time of his tiredness.

He was convinced that the practical advantages of meeting Petrov far outweighed the dangers, grave though they were. No matter how evasively or reluctantly the Russian behaved, Peterson was sure he could gauge the degree of the Soviet knowledge of the events in Africa. He would still keep it from the President — for the time being at least — until he had compromised Petrov. Then it could be presented as a coup. And then Fowler would approve of it.

Tired though he was, Peterson still found sleep difficult. Had Paul's assessment about Beth been right? It would be wonderful to have her back in Washington, where he could care for her — properly this time, giving her the attention she had wanted, the need for which he had failed to appreciate. It *might* be possible to get to Arizona in two or three weeks, he thought. Then again, it might not.

CHAPTER 6

Peterson, who ate from a diet sheet which did not allow any calories at the beginning of the day, drank several cups of breakfast coffee, and then, with nothing to do until his wife arose, wandered into the study he never used. Once he had meant to read all the books, he remembered, running his hands along the orderly arrangement of titles and authors. Just as he had meant to do so many things. Once. There was a display table behind the proper desk, with the Yale pennants and the sporting photographs and even a signed picture of the Korean war aircrew. He picked it up, gazing down at the innocent, unformed faces, surprised at the difficulty he had recalling men he'd regarded as the sort of friends for whom he would have given his life. He'd been very young then; he hadn't learned how to be properly afraid, or ever believed that any harm, real, painful, damaging harm could come to him. It had seemed like some game that he'd always been convinced he would win. It would have been different, he supposed, if he had been a soldier. On the ground he would have come close to death, seen the gaping wounds and the torn limbs and the lifeless bodies. Even then, he didn't think he would have conceived any danger to himself. Too young, he thought again.

He concentrated upon the picture, trying to remember the day when it had been taken and the occasion on which they'd all signed it. It wouldn't come, any of it. Only Hibbert had tried to keep in touch, sending Christmas cards with pictures of his wife and kids and invitations to Seattle, and for a time he had maintained the contact, even promising the visit that had never materialized.

Apart from Walter Jones, he didn't have any friends now. He had thought of Lucille as his friend, at the beginning of their marriage. But it had been an impression that faded. Some men made their sons into friends — but not Peterson, even when he'd done the things that fathers were supposed to do, like going on weekend hunting trips or to football matches. And now the boy called him a bastard and meant it. He sighed, replacing the wartime photograph. How strange it was that people regarded him as successful.

He had taken the ritual conversation with the maid beyond its usual exchange, knowing that Lucille would need to be warned of his presence in the house. She entered the study freshly made up, her hair carefully in place. Only the tinted spectacles gave a clue to how she was feeling; perhaps she wore them to conceal the redness of her eyes, rather than to prevent any discomfort the light might cause.

'I didn't expect you to be here.'

'I wanted to talk to you. I'm sorry about last night.' Once, he thought, they'd kissed each other in the mornings.

'You stayed here, to tell me that?'

'No. Something else.'

'Can I get you some coffee?' she asked.

'I've had some. You go ahead.'

'I don't,' she reminded him. 'Just juice.'

'I'd forgotten. I'll come to the kitchen with you.' It was a forced politeness; why were they so nervous of each other?

She regimented a selection of vitamin pills alongside the orange juice glass.

'You should eat something,' he said.

'Later.'

She began taking the pills, choosing them as if the order in which she swallowed them mattered. She was very careful about picking them up, so that he wouldn't see any shake in her hand.

'It must be important.'

'What?' he said.

'Whatever it is you want to say. I can't remember the last time you stayed away from the office, on a working day.'

She was still beautiful, he thought. Not pretty, as she had been when they first married or even as she had been in the photograph she had tried to place upon the bedside table. More mature now, but still very attractive. Perhaps there was some pinching around the eyes, hidden behind the elaborate frames of her spectacles, but there was no thickening of her figure despite the increasing neglect. Would she stop drinking if some physical signs began to show? She had always been a vain woman, he thought, without malice.

'I might have to go away.'

'Oh.'

'Not for very long. A few days, perhaps.'

She was regarding him intently, expecting more.

'I'm worried about you, Lucille.'

'Worried?'

'You know what I mean.'

'I don't.'

He bent his head away from her stare; it would be pointless to argue. As pointless as it had been with their son.

'I saw Paul yesterday.'

'I know.'

He looked up. 'How?'

'He called.'

'What about?' asked Peterson, anxiously.

'Just to talk.'

'He asked me how you were,' said Peterson.

She waited for him to continue.

'I told him not very well,' he said.

'Why did you tell him that?'

'Because I don't think you *are* well.'

She finished the final vitamin pill, like a child apportioning the favourite sweet until last. 'I feel fine,' she said.

'You're an alcoholic.' He hadn't meant to say it, any more than he had meant to argue. The accusation came in a normal, almost casual tone and for several moments she did not appear to have heard him. He saw that the hand holding the orange juice glass was white with tension.

'I'm not,' she said at last. Her voice was perfectly controlled, as his had been. They could have been discussing the weather.

'I want you to get help, Lucille,' he said. It was not going as he had planned.

'I said there's nothing wrong,' she insisted, with just a slight rise in her voice. 'Nothing at all.'

'I don't want to go away and leave you like this.'

'Like what?'

'You know what I mean.'

'I don't.'

'There are places ...' he started out again. 'Proper clinics ...'

'Asylums.'

'Of course they're not asylums,' he said, trying to curb his exasperation. 'Proper hospitals. Why not talk to someone, at least?'

'There's no need.'

Should he tell her of Paul's belief that Beth wanted to come back home? No. It might only be an interpretation of an incoherent letter. To raise hopes he could not fulfil would do more harm than good.

'We could see our own doctor.'

'No.'

'Why not?'

'I don't want to.' There was a trace of petulance in her voice.

'It couldn't do any harm.' He saw her look quickly at the wall clock. Had they gone past the time when she normally made her first drink? Her hands were moving nervously.

She stood up, abruptly, then appeared unsure why she had done so. 'I'm not seeing any doctor or going to any clinic,' she said. 'Because there isn't any need. There's nothing wrong with me.'

'Last night I found you lying in your own vomit,' he said, conscious of her wince. 'I can count, for God's sake; you're getting through a bottle of vodka a day in the house alone, without taking into consideration what you drink outside.'

'I could stop, if I wanted to,' she said.

The discussion was becoming as formalized as his daily conversations with the maid, Peterson thought.

'I don't believe you,' he said. Would she respond to some sort of challenge to her will-power? It was probably too late for that.

'I just don't want to,' she continued, as if she hadn't heard him. 'Being sociable, that's all.'

'When was the last time we were invited to anybody's home for dinner?' he demanded, trying to get through to her. 'Or that anybody has accepted an invitation here?'

'When was the last time you would have been able to guarantee your attendance?' she tried to fight back.

'We're being avoided, Lucille,' he said desperately. 'People don't want you in their houses because they don't want the possibility of a scene.'

'I don't make scenes!' she shouted, at last.

'Two months ago you broke up a dinner party at John Sinclair's,' he reminded her. 'It took three of us to get you into the car. You were disgusting.'

She stood with her back to him, refusing to accept the reminder.

'That was the last time we were invited out,' he went on relentlessly. He thought she was crying, but when she turned he saw that he had been mistaken.

'Let *us* give a party,' she challenged.

'We can't, not yet,' he said.

'Too busy?' she said, seizing his favourite expression and imagining she had gained an advantage in the argument.

'I said I had to go away. I'm not sure how long it will be.'

'Where?'

'Europe.' Could he take her with him? Immediately he realized the impracticality of the idea. He would not be able to control her drinking, not all the time. And he would be taking an incalculable risk in accepting Petrov's approach anyway; Lucille would be too great an additional burden.

'So there it is,' she said. She looked again at the clock. 'Have you a lunch engagement?'

'No.'

'It's the second time you've looked at the clock in five minutes.'

'What's that supposed to mean, for Christ's sake?'

'Past first drink time, Lucille?'

She tried to stare him down, but her look wavered. Defiantly she went to the cupboard and with her back to him mixed vodka, vermouth and ice into the shaker. There was a pathetic eagerness in her movements.

'Do you want one?' she said.

'No.'

'I don't need it,' she said, trying to maintain the defiance.

Peterson didn't respond.

'But I'm damned if I'm going to have you tell me what to do.' She gulped at the drink, half emptying the glass.

Peterson felt a surge of pity for her — and annoyance at himself. He had handled it appallingly, as he did everything connected with his family, and as he was now, with the President.

The maid appeared at the kitchen door, to tell him that his car had arrived.

'I won't be late,' he said.

'Like you weren't late last night?'

'I've apologized for that.'

'I could make dinner,' she said.

'I'd like that.'

'What time?'

'I'll be here by six-thirty. I promise.'

'Fine.'

'Please try ...' he started, stopping immediately.

'What?'

'Nothing.'

'What were you going to say?' she demanded.

'Try not to drink too much today.'

'I'll do what I damn well like.'

The maid was probably somewhere in the passageway, able to hear, thought Peterson, standing.

'Six-thirty,' he said again.

'All right.'

The newspapers and the digest awaited him in the car, laid out in the usual orderly fashion. By now they were out of date, Peterson realized. He still read them with his customary absorption, irritated that he had wasted the morning. Illogically, he felt he would have missed something by not having been in his office at the proper time.

Walter Jones was waiting for him at Langley, stoking the perpetually difficult pipe.

'Well?' demanded Peterson, before he'd even removed his hat and coat.

'Something interesting from Jerusalem,' said Jones. 'Levy thinks it's got some connection with Africa.'

The Mossad message was uppermost on the material set out

upon his desk. Jones concentrated upon his pipe while Peterson read.

'Spectacular demonstration,' quoted Peterson, looking up.

'Could be unconnected with Chad,' said Jones, cautiously.

'Then again, it might be,' said Peterson. 'What have you done?'

'Cabled every station in the Middle East, in case one of our people pick up something the Mossad didn't get.'

'That's unlikely,' said Peterson.

'Still worth the cables.'

'I agree,' said Peterson. 'How about Germany?'

'That too.'

Peterson nodded. 'That's where we're going to have to begin,' he said positively.

'How?'

'I'm not sure yet.'

'Still going to see Petrov?'

'Yes.'

'It doesn't have the right feel about it,' said the deputy.

'It's only a meeting.'

'You should tell the President, at least.'

'It would mean refusal,' said Peterson. 'I've got to get the timing right.'

The Deputy Director's pipe went out and he abandoned it into the top pocket of his jacket. 'You've certainly got to get the timing right,' he said, heavily.

'When does Brownlow get back to Vienna?' asked Peterson, subduing the irritation at the other man's perpetual caution.

'Four this afternoon, our time. Even if he manages contact with the Russians straight away, I don't imagine there'll be a report tonight. Both surveillance squads will be in position by mid-evening.'

'Good.'

'I wonder what the hell is *really* going on?' said Jones, with an intensity that surprised Peterson.

'Whatever it is, it's making us look pretty damned stupid at the moment.'

'Let's hope it stops here,' said Jones.

'It will,' said Peterson, confidently.

'The remains of Brinton and Williams have arrived at Andrews,' said Jones. 'Will you go to the funeral?'

'If I'm back from Vienna. If not, it'll have to be you.'

'I thought I'd go anyway. I've arranged for you to see the people who came back from Africa after lunch.'

Peterson nodded, rising at the reminder of the time. He and Jones ate together in the executive dining area. In anticipation of his encounter with the Russian, Peterson used the time to debate with his deputy everything that had occurred since their attempted entry into Chad. The meal and the discussion ended at the same time and Peterson sat back, satisfied. The entire operation so far was perfectly indexed in his mind. The men who had gone to N'Djamena to retrieve Brinton's body had been given explicit instructions not to attempt any approach to the complex, and so Peterson's meeting with them was a formality, providing him with nothing more than he had learned already from their cabled reports.

After the debriefing, Peterson remained alone in his office, wondering at the uncertainty he felt. It was the inactivity, he decided. He wanted to be doing something, making decisions and initiating actions, but until he'd met Petrov the operation had to swing in limbo. *That* was a criticism, if one were to be made.

He leaned back, considering his decision about Vienna. It *could* go wrong, he accepted, realistically. And if it did, it was conceivable he would lose his job. He smiled, confronting another question. Would it really matter? There was always a board-room place or a directorship for an ex-CIA Director, so money would never be a problem. It might mean normality again; time to spend with Lucille and the children. No more presidential breakfasts or middle-of-the-night telephone calls or bullet-proofed limousines or the gut-churning fear that once, just once, he might make a mistake. A mistake like agreeing to meet a Russian in a mid-European capital.

Twice during the afternoon he attempted to call his son but got the answering service on both occasions. He left a message for Paul to call him, but there had been no contact by the time he left the CIA headquarters. Peterson had been very careful about the time; it was just six-fifteen when the limousine pulled up outside his house.

He hesitated, uncertainly, just inside the door, listening for any sounds of activity. The maid, who did not live in, would have left hours ago. There was movement from the kitchen and Peterson went towards it hopefully. Lucille turned at his entry, her smile rigidly in place.

'Home the happy warrior,' she greeted. She enunciated very clearly, with no blur in her voice.

'Six-thirty,' he said, reminding her of a promise kept.

'Pot roast,' she said, 'and pecan pie.'

Peterson hated pecan pie and thought she knew it, but he said, 'Marvellous.'

She came towards him, carefully, as if she were trying to walk along a straight line, and offered her face to be kissed. He put his lips against her cheek. Vodka didn't smell, he remembered. There was a trace of vermouth.

'Shall we have wine, to celebrate?' she said.

'Celebrate?'

She breathed out heavily, challenging him to find the alcohol on her breath. 'If you're going to do it, do it properly,' she said, aware of his check.

'I'm pleased.'

'You sound like a teacher I had at high school.'

'I really mean it. Thank you.'

'Told you I could do it.'

'Please don't drink while I'm away.'

'I shall, if I want.'

'Not so much. Please.'

'I can control it!'

There was a danger of his being more occupied with Lucille than with the African affair, thought Peterson suddenly. The feeling surprised him, bringing a burn of embarrassment. Wasn't that how it should be? No, he decided, immediately. For an ordinary person, perhaps. But his job did not allow him to be ordinary. For the power, the prestige and the money, he had offered a sacrifice. Like the commitment of Faustus, it was too late now to attempt to withdraw from the bargain — no matter how much he regretted it.

The pot roast was undercooked and the pecan pie as sugared as he had known it would be. Lucille drank nearly all the wine and then, determined to make up for her daytime abstinence, she demanded brandy. It was still an improvement upon her usual intake.

'Is it important?' she asked, after they had finished their meal.

'What?'

'This European trip.'

'Extremely important.'

'It's a long time since we've been to Europe together,' she said, as if she had been aware of his earlier thoughts.

'How about a vacation?' he said, suddenly eager. 'When I've cleared this thing, why don't we try to get away for a while together?'

She looked at him uncertainly, someone expecting disappointment.

'Where?' she said.

'You can choose.'

'Anywhere?'

'Your choice,' he assured her.

Lucille smiled at an inward thought. 'It seems to have been so long,' she said, distantly. 'It would be nice.'

'Why not start planning, while I'm away? Get some brochures.' It would be activity, Peterson thought; something other than a vodka bottle to hold her attention.

'Maybe,' she said, still seeming suspicious of the conversation.

'You could make the reservations,' he said, trying to infect her with his enthusiasm. 'Surprise me when I get back.'

'All right,' she accepted. 'There's no restriction on money?'

'None.'

'Wouldn't it be nice?' she said.

'Yes,' he said, too quickly, misunderstanding the remark.

'If Beth could come,' she completed. 'And maybe even Paul.'

'She might,' said Peterson, anxiety moving ahead of his caution. 'Perhaps I could persuade Beth to come.'

Lucille replaced her brandy bowl, gazing at him. 'What do you mean?'

'We could invite her at least,' said Peterson, trying to evade the curiosity.

'Are you in contact with her?'

'No.'

She was looking at him with her head tilted to one side, in the disbelief of early drunkenness. 'You in contact with her?' she repeated. 'You know what my Beth is doing?'

'No!' insisted Peterson, with a different urgency now. 'It was a passing idea, nothing more.'

'I want her back, James,' said the woman. 'I want Beth back. Why can't you get her back for me? Aren't you almost as powerful as the President himself?'

'Stop it, Lucille.'

'Why can't you?' she said, gripped now by the thought. 'Why can't you get Beth back?'

It was no more possible than getting Lucille into a clinic to treat her drinking, thought Peterson.

'Get her back for me, James. Save her for me.' Embodied in the plea was an aspect of his wife that had been missing for so long.

'I'll try,' he promised.

'When you've time?' she demanded, erecting the barrier again.

'I mean it,' he said. 'I promise.'

'I want us to be a family again,' said Lucille, letting the desperation show. 'I want us to be normal.'

Would it ever be possible? It was much later when he realized that Lucille expected him to sleep with her. He tried and failed to remember the last time; it had to be months. With it came another realization. He didn't want to. He tried to avoid the embrace at her bedroom door, but she seized him eagerly, pulling his face towards her and kissing him messily. He tried to respond and became frighteningly aware that Lucille had no attraction for him.

'Don't go to your own room,' she said. She was almost begging.

'You're tired.'

'I'm not.'

He entered hesitantly, conscious of the outburst that any continued refusal might cause. She attempted the coquette as she undressed, but was too unsteady on her feet to make it work, tottering dangerously; he felt very sad for her.

They lay side by side, untouching, but more conscious of each other than they would have been had there been any contact.

'I'm sorry, James. For what I am.'

'It'll get better. Everything will get better.'

'Oh Christ, I hope so.'

It became so quiet that he was aware of the sound from his wrist watch.

'I love you, James.'

'I love you.'

'I didn't mean this to happen. It just ... happened. Oh shit.'

He felt out for her hand and she took it, anxiously.

'You *do* love me, don't you?'

'I told you.'

'Say it again.'

'I love you.'

'Show me then.'

'I'm very tired, Lucille ... exhausting day.' He said the words and hated himself as he spoke them.

'Oh my God!'

'I'm sorry.'

'You're sorry!' She began to cry at almost the same time as he did.

It was a long time before she became conscious of it, and she tried to control her sobbing, as if she were frightened of making any mistake.

'James!' she said, disbelievingly.

Peterson wanted to blow his nose but remembered the tissues were on her side of the bed; he scrubbed the sheet over his face.

'Sorry,' he apologized again.

'You've never cried before. Not in all the years. Not once.'

'Didn't mean to.'

'Do you hate me?'

'No!' he said, forcefully.

'What then?'

'I'm very frightened, Lucille.'

Now she moved, reaching out for him and he went to her at last, grateful for her comfort.

'Of what, darling?'

'So many things. Just frightened.'

'Can I help?'

'No.'

'I never could,' she said, without any bitterness.

'I'm not sure, any more,' said Peterson, trying to explain and failing.

'I *don't* help, do I?'

'It's not your fault ... nothing's your fault.'

'Is it so important, to be the Director?'

'Yes.'

'Couldn't you do without it?'

'I've never thought about it,' he lied. 'I don't think so.'

'Poor Jamie.'

'I didn't want it to do this to us ... everything that's happened.'

'It has.'

'I know.'

'So what are you going to do?'

He shrugged against her, an uncertain movement.

'You shouldn't blame yourself for everything,' she said.

'It's because of me ...'

She rested her free hand against his cheek, stopping the self-pity. 'Go to sleep,' she said tenderly.

'I'm sorry,' he said. 'So very sorry.'

'Go to sleep,' she repeated.

Petrov sat considering the reply that had come from Vienna, intrigued at the speed with which Peterson had reacted. So the CIA *were* encountering as much difficulty as he was; it was good to get the confirmation.

Petrov accepted that he was taking a very great risk. Above all else, Litvinov must not learn that he was considering crossing to the West. Petrov was sure the Praesidium member suspected his involvement with Irena; he would interpret a crossing as confirmation and mount an immediate purge. Petrov shuddered at the thought, smiling at the unexpectedness of the reaction. He had not considered himself so unnerved by Litvinov's opposition.

Irena would have been debriefed in America, Petrov knew — and knew just as surely that she would have said nothing about their relationship. So there was no danger of that becoming a

weapon. Peterson would be imagining that he was involving himself in a horrifying risk, yet at this stage Petrov knew himself to be
far more exposed than the American. It was fortunate there was no
way Peterson could learn of it. There *could* be an argument for
informing Litvinov — the whole Politburo committee even. But it
would be exchanging one problem for another; better to wait, until
he had an advantage over Peterson that he could use, if he had to.

And there would be an advantage, soon enough. They appeared
to have a common aim so some sort of co-operation appeared
logical. Africa appeared a difficult problem, which meant the
possibility of failure — and if he hoped to survive a failure, then he
was going to need a substantial excuse. Ideally, Peterson would
become an ally, for as long as it took. But as well as being a
pragmatist, Petrov was a realist and knew that things rarely
worked out ideally. As a scapegoat, he considered the Director of
the CIA substantial enough.

It did not take long to prepare the cable of acceptance to
Peterson's suggestion that the meeting should be in Vienna: he'd
cross from Czechoslovakia, Petrov decided. It would not be
difficult to create a reason for visiting Prague and he could be in
and out of Austria before Litvinov or anyone else realized he had
left the Czech capital.

Petrov pulled Peterson's dossier towards him. Already he knew
the biographical details by heart, so he ignored them, concentrating upon the photograph. It was a bland, official-looking portrait
showing nothing but the image of the man. What would he really
be like? Would he be able to dominate the meeting, as he intended?
He shifted, the discomfort similar to his earlier feeling at the
thought of Litvinov discovering that there was to be an encounter.
It was always possible, he realized, that Peterson would dominate
him. That was an unsettling thought.

CHAPTER 7

There was only one response to the Middle East cables, an hour
before Peterson was due to leave Langley for his meeting with
the President. Elaboration was demanded, automatically, but
Peterson knew there was insufficient time to provide additional
information, even if it were available, before he went to the White
House. It did not matter; linked with what they had received from
the Mossad, it indicated progress, which was important. It also
justified the trip to Europe. For a man who rarely did anything
irrational, Peterson was taking a considerable risk in delaying the
information to the President. The most constant criticism in the
past, some of it convincing enough to cause the dismissal of
Directors, had been that the CIA regarded itself beyond the
restrictions of the Executive, a government within a government.
And that *had* been the attitude, far too often. But never under
Peterson; this was the first time under his Directorship that he had
actively considered any action which could be construed in such a
way. He had meant what he had told Lucille; he was very
frightened.

To reduce any later accusations of deceit, Peterson knew he had
to minimize everything he kept back from the President, to the
point where misunderstanding rather than falsehood might be
argued. It meant that Fowler had to know about Europe, only not
about the actual purpose, and in such a way that it would be able to
withstand later examination.

Fowler was alone when Peterson entered the Oval Office. His
first reaction was surprise. Relief followed quickly. The meeting
would be recorded, obviously; it was the customary practice. So
Fowler would always have a transcript to call upon. But he would
not have any witnesses.

'How's it going?' demanded the Texan.

'Slowly,' said Peterson, aware that he would have to be cautious of every word. 'But I think there's some activity in the Middle East.'

'Shit,' said the President, whose folksy affectations extended to cursing.

'The Israelis have picked up rumours throughout the area, from Libya to Syria. Nothing substantial, but two agents have reported talk of a spectacular demonstration.'

'What about our own people, for Christ's sake?' demanded Fowler.

'There was some information this morning,' said Peterson. Thank God, he thought. Fowler had many dislikes, one of which was having to rely on sources other than their own.

'What?' said the President.

'Our man in Benghazi reported a lot of government activity there. The Defence Minister was in Bonn, two weeks ago. He was known to have returned, but he hasn't been seen for the past three days. There's talk of his being in Africa.'

'Son of a bitch!' said Fowler slowly. 'Gadaffi!'

'He's got the money,' said Peterson.

Fowler nodded. 'When you think about it, he'd be the obvious person. Yet I'm slightly surprised, considering the foul-up with Amin in Uganda.'

'I think what happened in Uganda makes it even more logical,' argued Peterson. 'Gadaffi lost face there and made himself a laughing stock in the Arab world by having to pay a ransom for the Libyan soldiers who had been seized. He'd make an enormous recovery as the Arab with a listening post over the very heads of the Israelis, after the Egyptian peace settlement.'

Fowler nodded at the assessment. 'You're right,' he said.

'And Chad has got a common border with Libya. It would be impossible to monitor completely any contact between them.'

'It couldn't be worse,' said Fowler. 'Can you imagine what Gadaffi would do with a spy rocket in the Middle East!'

'The Israelis couldn't allow it,' said Peterson.

'I don't see they're in a position to stop it,' said the President. 'But sure as hell somebody has got to. Have you told Jerusalem?'

Peterson shook his head. 'Not yet. We only got the cable a couple of hours ago. And I'd like to know more.'

'They'd have to take some sort of punitive action,' said Fowler reflectively.

'Yes.'

'And we're pledged to help them, in the event of any aggression.'

'It's hardly that,' said Peterson.

Fowler snorted, cynically. 'That's how every Jewish voter in America would regard it,' he said. 'You stick to intelligence and I'll stick to politics.'

Peterson looked down, so that the President wouldn't see his reaction to the cynicism. It was a farmyard existence, he thought, thinking back to his bedroom collapse in front of Lucille. Why was it so important to him?

'I thought I'd go to Europe,' announced Peterson, looking up to meet the President's stare.

'Why?'

'That's where the key is, in Bonn. We're getting nowhere in Chad.' No provable lie so far, he judged.

'How long for?' asked the President. He liked the security of having his senior people around him.

'A few days,' generalized Peterson.

'Just Bonn?'

'Providing nothing else comes up while I'm there.' That would be perfect, if there were any subsequent enquiry.

'We've got people there,' said Fowler, in weak protest.

'A personal visit is always more successful.'

'We're going to have to walk on eggs over this,' said Fowler, reflective again, and Peterson realized the President's mind was locked on to politics rather than logistics. It was proving easier than he had expected.

'Yes,' encouraged the Director.

'We daren't be seen taking any obvious offensive action,' continued Fowler. 'Since Iran, we're far too dependent on Libyan oil.'

The Persian collapse had been another CIA disaster that he had escaped, thought Peterson. Would he be as fortunate with this? 'Israel would be the only target for whatever Libya plans,' he said. 'It could escalate into another war.'

'We should have had Moore and Flood in on this,' said Fowler. 'I think there should be a fuller meeting.'

'I want to plan the trip properly,' said Peterson hurriedly. The others might question him more deeply about his intentions in Europe, Flood particularly. Aware of the President's hesitation, Peterson added, 'I don't think we should waste any time.'

Fowler nodded reluctantly. 'You're probably right,' he said. 'I'll want twenty-four hour contact.'

'Of course.'

'Another thing.'

'What?'

'Let's not tell the Israelis, not yet. I don't want any cowboy and Indian stuff, like they did in Entebbe.'

'We might need them,' cautioned Peterson. 'As I said, they've got a very good organization, particularly in the Middle East.'

'I know, I know,' said Fowler, with just a trace of impatience. 'But let's make quite sure. There'll be plenty of time for them, when we've decided what to do.'

'All right,' accepted the Director.

'We could be brought into confrontation with Russia over this,' said Fowler. 'It's a bastard.'

'If there's a flare up in the area then the danger is there,' agreed Peterson. Should he tell the President of the Russian approach? If it achieved nothing more, the Vienna meeting would enable them to gauge Moscow's reaction to what was happening. It was too late, he decided: to reveal it now would show the intention of dishonesty.

'So we've got to get it right,' said the President urgently.

'Yes.'

'No mistakes,' emphasized Fowler, staring intently across the table at him. 'No mistakes whatsoever.'

'I realize that.'

'I hope you do.'

Peterson recognized that it was warning time. He wasn't the only person talking with the awareness of the tape recordings, another confirmation that he was the obvious sacrifice if things went wrong. Had it been that knowledge that had caused him to cry against Lucille's shoulder?

'I do,' he assured the President.

'Daily contact,' repeated Fowler. 'Remember, the buck stops here.'

'I understand,' said Peterson. He thought Truman had managed more sincerity in the original remark.

'And remember what I said before. Anything, to stop it. I'm not concerned about manpower or costs. Whatever it takes.'

'I'll remember.'

There was still no response from Benghazi when Peterson got back to Langley, but a full dossier had been decoded from Vienna. Jones was waiting with it in Peterson's office.

'Petrov identifies Africa,' read Peterson.

'Yes,' said Jones.

'Agreement in less than twenty-four hours,' said the Director, bent over the summary. 'Petrov wants to move as soon as possible.'

'Which shows either that they're as badly placed as we are,' said the deputy, guardedly, 'or that they're ready for us.'

'Still think it's a set-up?'

'I think it's the likeliest explanation. Did you tell the President?'

'No.'

'I think you should have done.'

'He'd have vetoed it. You know that.'

'When will you go?'

'Immediately.'

'There's a plane available.'

'I'll go to Bonn first.'

'Cover?'

'Yes.'

Jones indicated the dossier. 'There's already evidence,' he said.

'I know. We'll keep it to the minimum.'

'Brownlow says he's confident of picking up Petrov.'

'He'd better be.' Peterson went back to the Vienna report. 'It doesn't say where Petrov wants to meet.'

'We've got two safe houses there,' reminded Jones.

'Petrov wouldn't come to them any more than I'd go to one of theirs.'

'You can't use the embassy,' said Jones. 'The President would learn of it almost immediately through the State Department.'

'It's hardly likely that he'd come there, either, is it?' said Peterson.

'You'll be as exposed as hell.'

'Yes,' agreed Peterson.

'Do you really think it will be worth it?'

'I shan't know, until we've met.'

'What if meeting Petrov *is* a waste of time?' questioned Jones, objectively.

'Bonn isn't entirely a cover,' said Peterson, ignoring his subordinate's question. 'We've invested a lot of time and money in Germany over the years and I want a better return for it than we're getting at the moment.'

'But we're inevitably going to have to go back to Africa.'

Peterson didn't reply immediately. 'Yes,' he said, after several moments. 'I suppose we are.'

'Shall I start selecting some men?'

Briefly Peterson recalled the photographs of Brinton and Williams. 'Yes,' he said reluctantly.

Paul's call on the private line, an hour after Jones had left his office, surprised Peterson; momentarily he had forgotten the messages he had left on his son's answering machine.

'Thank you for calling your mother,' said Peterson.

'She seemed all right to me.'

'You got her early in the day. And yesterday she tried.' Very much, Peterson thought.

'So?'

'So I don't think she can sustain it, without help.'

'Have you suggested it?'

'Yes,' said Peterson. 'She won't consider it. But that wasn't the sort of help I was thinking of.'

'What?'

'I've got to go on a trip.'

'Arizona?' said the boy, too quick in his excitement.

Peterson hesitated, anticipating the reaction. 'No,' he said. 'Not yet.'

'Not yet?'

'I promised I'd try.'

'When you can fit it in!'

'Will you try and call your mother often?' Peterson pressed on, determined not to argue. 'Maybe even visit the house.'

This time it was Paul who paused before replying. 'You're sure it's necessary?'

'I wouldn't trouble you if I didn't think so.'

'It isn't any trouble.'

'You'll do it then?'

'Of course.'

'She would appreciate it. So would I.'

'How long are you going to be away?'

'I don't know. Not more than a few days, I hope.'

'Will it be possible? Arizona I mean.'

'I said I'd try.'

'But that's not saying you will.'

'I'll try! Have you heard any more from her?'

'No.'

'She might have called, when you were out.'

'There's the answering machine,' reminded his son. 'And I'm staying around the apartment, just in case.'

For the first time, Peterson became aware of his son's concern at how the family had split apart. The knowledge hurt him as much as his confession to Lucille had done.

'At the moment there's something that's making it difficult for me,' said Peterson. 'But when it's over I mean things to be different, Paul.'

'If you give me a moment,' said his son, 'I'll remember the movie in which I heard that.'

'I mean it,' said Peterson, ignoring the cynicism. 'We'll get Beth back.'

'I'll keep in touch with mother,' said the boy, the disbelief sounding in his voice.

'Thank you. I'll call in a few days.'

'I'll be waiting,' said Paul. 'Let's hope Beth still is.'

Dimitri Petrov surrounded himself with fifty men, experiencing no difficulty in infiltrating them into the Austrian capital on false documentation. The Sacher is the best hotel in Vienna and within an hour of his registration, Brownlow and the second team of which he was unaware had Petrov under surveillance.

Petrov had purposely allowed himself three days before the scheduled confrontation. On the first night he went to the Vienna State Opera at the Opernring and decided that the acoustics had indisputably been improved by the rebuilding after wartime destruction; he dined at the Drei Hussars. The following afternoon he happily paid the blackmarket price for the performance at the Spanish Riding School of the Lipizzaner horses, which he had always wanted to see. How perfect it would have been with Irena beside him, he thought.

The night before the encounter with Peterson, the KGB chief remained in his room, preparing himself. Did he have enough to offer? It was difficult to decide, without any idea of what Peterson had to exchange. Despite the gravity of the reason for their meeting, Petrov was looking forward to it. He stared down at the photograph of Peterson; the American did not look the sort of person who enjoyed life very much.

Petrov had found a Mahler concert on the radio and was preparing for bed when the message came from Bonn. Otto Bock had started taking a new way home from the West German Defence Ministry. It took him right past a gay club, but so far he had not stopped. He would, Petrov thought, confidently.

Ironically, Bock's route took him down Poppelsdorfer Allee and past the Hotel Bristol in which Peterson was studying the reports and photographs of Petrov's enjoyment of Vienna. It was good, the American decided. The Vienna pictures alone would be sufficient to cause Petrov embarrassment in Moscow. Peterson decided to update his files upon Irena Sinyavsky, in case he had to make more problems for the KGB chief. To create the impression that Petrov was considering crossing to join his defector mistress would be a smear big enough to bring him down.

CHAPTER 8

The Russian's suggestion that they should meet in a public restaurant initially surprised Peterson. Then he accepted it for what it possibly was: neutral territory. He responded carefully, of course. Even before he left Bonn, he instructed Brownlow to check it thoroughly and waited for the assurance that the Frances Karna was one of the best restaurants in Vienna — and certainly without any links to the Soviet service — before accepting. Having received the guarantee, he still proceeded cautiously, putting the restaurant under observation twenty-four hours before his arrival in Austria, installing a concentrated team of men throughout the day of the intended meeting and ensuring that at least three tables were reserved for his people, to provide protection within a few feet.

The encounter was scheduled for eight, but Peterson had decided to wait at least forty-five minutes beyond that time, to give his people time to make certain that no operation was being mounted by the Russians, with him as the victim: he calculated that an abduction squad could be across the Czechoslovak-Austrian border from Vienna in a little under three hours. It was an unlikely extreme, Peterson accepted. But not unthinkable.

While he waited for the final assurance, Peterson reflected upon his stop-over in Bonn. His bureau there should have got more, much more. Perhaps in no other country in Europe, given the opportunities that had existed there after the war, had the CIA concentrated more money, effort and time upon intelligence gathering. Yet they had failed almost completely to infiltrate BADRA. The consortium was layered like an onion from parent companies to subsidiaries to nominees and bank directorships, which finally disappeared into the tax anonymity of the Swiss Banking Corporation in Zürich. The directors whose names they had uncovered had been investigated with a thoroughness with which Peterson could find no fault: all of them were lawyers or accountants, accepting the post as a business commitment, for which they were being paid a statutory fee, qualifying the company for establishment within West Germany but taking no part in its running or control. There were accommodation addresses in Bonn's Konrad Adenaeurplatz and in the Schierker Strasse in West Berlin, both staffed by attractive secretaries of Teutonic efficiency who promised to pass on any enquiries to their superiors and who kept their words; through a legitimate but CIA-financed company they had instituted an approach for television relay equipment and within three days an apology was sent on a BADRA letterhead with a Zürich postmark, saying regrettably that this was not the sort of technology with which the company was associated.

Attempts to discover more about the West German government involvement had proved even more disappointing. Through the CIA's paid informants within the government there was enough confirmation that there *was* some relationship and that it was governed by the Foreign Ministry. When their man within the Ministry attempted to discover more, he encountered a security classification for which he did not possess the necessary clearance and from which he immediately withdrew, frightened that he would be exposed.

Careful not to say anything which could later be construed as naïvety, Peterson had nevertheless, during his conversations with the President, tried to minimize the setbacks from the security of the American embassy communications room. From Fowler's responses, it was obvious that there had been several meetings with the Secretary of State and the foreign affairs adviser since his departure from Washington, and that Chad was now considered a problem of priority importance.

He talked at much greater length to Walter Jones, hoping that something might have arrived at Langley in his absence. From Jerusalem David Levy had sent two cables, the second stronger than the first, requesting some reaction to the information the Mossad had supplied. And the latest satellite photograph showed one of the silos with its covering removed; as far as the analysts could ascertain, the container was empty.

'There's something else,' Jones had said, in the last conversation before he'd embarked for Vienna.

'What?'

'I've been invited to a cocktail party.'

'By whom?' Peterson knew that his deputy wouldn't waste his time with gossip.

'Herbert Flood.'

'He'll try to make you his man,' Peterson had predicted. 'Not immediately, of course. But that'll be the final approach.'

'I know.'

'Fancy being Director?'

'I haven't thought about it.'

'That'll be the promise. I suppose he's even got the influence to make it happen. Fowler seems more impressed by Flood than by the Secretary of State.'

'What shall I tell Levy?'

'Let him have the pictures of the open silo. Stall about our confirmation from Libya.'

'He's getting impatient.'

'Let him!'

He shouldn't have allowed the irritation of that reply, reflected Peterson, when he finally received clearance from his people outside the restaurant and set out for the short journey from the Intercontinental Hotel. It was comforting to know his deputy would soften the response, guarding him against any reaction. Still irrational though, but it was the frustration of what he was trying to do, Peterson decided. More than frustration; nervousness. The sort of nervousness that had sent him weeping into Lucille's arms. He thought back to the foreign affairs adviser's attempts to infiltrate the operation through Jones. Flood *would* promise Jones the job; he was the sort of man who believed that everyone was motivated by the need for ultimate power, as he was.

'Is it so important, to be the Director?'

Had he answered Lucille's question honestly? To say yes had been automatic; he had been more embarrassed by the tears than conscious of the question. So what was the answer: the proper response, not the one that sprang immediately to mind? It had taken him twenty years to achieve it; twenty years of political infighting and sycophancy and preparation. And having got it, it had cost him his family. Yet he still wanted it. He wanted the money and the respect and the chauffeur-driven cars and the instant, unquestioned reaction from an army of men as highly trained and efficient as any general had ever led into any war.

The car stopped in Frances Karnerplatz but Peterson remained in the seat.

'We're here, sir.'

'Yes.'

The moment of commitment, he realized, with a sudden jerk of nervousness. The moment from which — much later — he might become a legend within the Agency. Or at which he might, as Jones feared, be making a bad error.

'Anything the matter, sir?'

'No.'

He got out of the car, looking around the narrow street to see if he could locate the men who had been assigned to protect him outside the restaurant. He could not; had it been possible, they wouldn't have been doing their job properly.

He went slowly into the building, nodding at the greeting from the receptionist on the ground floor and then following her up the winding stairs to the first-floor dining-room. He ignored the tables at which his people were sitting, wondering where the Russians sat: Petrov would certainly have placed people there, as he had done.

Petrov was waiting at a table set slightly aside, with the protection at one side of the buttress of a small alcove. Even though, from the biographies and photographs, Peterson knew almost as much about the man as he did his own family — perhaps even more — he was still surprised at the first sight of the KGB chief. His first impression was how unlike a Russian Petrov was.

Peterson stopped, a few feet from the table. Now that it was happening, he found it difficult to believe that he was about to confront the man he was supposed constantly to oppose. Petrov had risen, too, and appeared halted by a similar thought. Petrov smiled hesitantly, then offered his hand. Peterson moved nearer, accepting the gesture. He wanted to laugh but didn't know why. Nervousness again, he supposed.

'Sorry I'm late,' said Peterson. It sounded facile.

'You had to be sure, of course.'

'Yes.' Peterson was intrigued by the apparent forthrightness: Petrov's English was very good.

'I did the same,' admitted Petrov. He smiled, nodding in the direction of the curtained windows. 'There must be quite a crowd out there.'

'It was fortunate there was no misunderstanding.'

'I gave very strict instructions.'

A waiter approached, enquiringly.

'I've gone straight into some Austrian wine,' said Petrov. 'The red is really very good. What would you like to drink?'

'Wine will be fine.'

'Sure? Have anything you want.'

Petrov had assigned himself the role of host, thought Peterson. He wondered who would pay at the end.

'Wine,' insisted Peterson.

Petrov poured it himself, handing the glass to the American.

'To a very unusual meeting,' toasted the Russian.

'Very unusual,' agreed Peterson, sipping the drink. It was like a social reunion of friends who had been apart a long time: quite different from what he had expected.

'I'm surprised you accepted,' said Petrov.

'I'm surprised you proposed it.'

'Let's hope neither of us will regard it as a mistake.'

'Let's hope.'

There was none of the awkwardness that Peterson had anticipated in the opening sparring; Petrov had the ability to put a person very much at ease. Peterson realized he would have to be cautious.

'I don't think my government would approve of such an encounter,' said Petrov, smiling.

Peterson did not immediately reply, momentarily taken aback

by the honesty. Was it honesty? Or an invitation from Petrov for him to give himself away?

'You haven't told them?' said Peterson. If it were true, then the sightseeing dossier had even greater value.

'No. Have you told your President?'

Petrov would recognize any evasion immediately, Peterson decided, and the whole meeting would be ruined.

'No,' he said. It was like trying to swim in the deep end for the first time. Suddenly he had the worrying feeling that Petrov was better at it than he was.

'So we're both equally exposed,' said Petrov.

'Are we?'

'Don't you trust me?' asked the Russian.

'No,' said Peterson, immediately. 'Do you trust me?'

'No.'

'You'll have had photographs taken of us, sitting here together, by now,' anticipated Peterson.

'Yes,' admitted Petrov. 'Have you?'

'Yes.'

'I hope your people enjoy their meal. The food here is excellent.'

Peterson smiled, openly. Petrov was a disarmingly easy man to like. He examined the Russian, admiring the cloth and cut of his suit. Petrov reminded him very much of the American senators who had been in the House for a long time and conducted themselves like elder statesmen.

'The wild boar is first class,' continued Petrov, 'or maybe the venison. With red cabbage, of course. And the mushrooms in batter are a superb hors d'oeuvre — it's an Austrian speciality, you know.'

Peterson sat back, letting himself be patronized, but unoffended by it. The waiter had returned, aware of their attention to the menu.

'The mushrooms,' agreed Peterson. 'But after that I'll take a plain Schnitzel.' He had been neglecting his diet during the trip.

Petrov frowned, very slightly. 'Should have chosen the boar,' he insisted.

'This meeting is very unusual,' repeated Peterson.

'Yes.'

'So you must be very worried?'

'Very,' agreed Petrov. 'My government too. Yours?'

'Deeply concerned,' admitted Peterson. Already the meeting had proved worthwhile; the President had wanted intelligence and he was going to get it. Fowler would have no reason for criticizing him, for agreeing to the meeting.

They paused, while the mushrooms were served.

'I've lost three men,' said Petrov.

'Three also,' matched Peterson.

'Only in movies do legally constituted, properly constructed companies or consortiums go around killing people,' dismissed Petrov.

'Somebody is,' said Peterson.

'That's the mystery,' agreed Petrov. 'I can hardly remember an operation which has continued for so long with my knowing so little.' He lifted his fork. 'Aren't these mushrooms delicious?' he said.

'Very good,' agreed Peterson. 'What are you proposing?'

'Co-operation.'

'An exchange of information?'

'More than that,' said Petrov.

'What?'

'A combined operation.'

Peterson pushed away his plate, unable to continue the pretence of eating. Petrov was taking the initiative away from him.

'Why not?' demanded Petrov. 'We're faced with an unknown situation in Africa, which we can't allow to continue. My people don't want a confrontation, wherever it may occur. And I don't believe yours do either. Aren't our aims the same?'

'I suppose so,' said Peterson. He realized that Petrov didn't know where the confrontation might take place.

'Then why not?' repeated the Russian.

'I don't know that the President would agree.' said Peterson, doubtfully. Any joint incursion which went wrong could be blamed publicly upon the Soviet Union, he thought.

'If it were successful, he might.'

'But there's no way of predicting that.'

'Which would make it our responsibility.'

They paused again while their plates were cleared and the next courses arranged. Petrov indicated the wine and asked for a fresh bottle to be opened.

'You're not drinking,' he complained.

Dutifully, Peterson took up his glass.

'It would be a large-scale operation,' said Peterson, thoughtfully.

'We've got the facilities,' said Petrov.

He would need at least the tacit support of the President, decided Peterson. Would Fowler consider the possibility of making the Soviet Union scapegoat for any fiasco sufficient compensation for the risk?

'What would the benefits be?' asked the American.

'Lack of duplication is the most obvious,' said Petrov. 'Full sharing of information another.'

He could certainly do with the information, thought Peterson. Yet Petrov appeared unaware of the Libyan involvement.

'I'd have to consider it,' said Peterson, guardedly.

'Did you have any luck in Germany?' asked Petrov.

Peterson remained silent for a moment. The shock affect of Petrov's sudden announcement was carefully calculated, he decided. He had been unaware of any observation. So he didn't have the advantage he had imagined over the Russian.

'Not enough,' he said.

'That's where it will have to be, in the first place. Not Africa,' said Petrov.

'Yes.'

'I have an entry into the Defence Ministry. At a sufficiently high level. And an idea of how it might enable us to get into the installation in Chad.'

The Russian was stage-managing the evening very well, conceded Peterson. He finished his wine and Petrov immediately refilled the glass. Peterson decided he had had enough.

'Any confrontation will be in the Middle East,' disclosed Peterson. If Petrov felt there was nothing to be achieved, he might withdraw and Peterson didn't want that now. He was suddenly excited by the proposal. If a joint operation worked, then it would be worthwhile. If it didn't, he had the chance to damage Soviet prestige in Africa. And there was still the potential personal damage to Petrov. 'I think I know the country involved,' he added.

'Can you make a decision tonight? Or do you need to consult in Washington?'

'I need to consult.'

'There may not be a lot of time.'

'I'm aware of that.'

'One of the silos has been uncovered.'

'We've seen that too.'

'We think it's empty.'

'So do we.'

'Duplication,' pointed out Petrov.

'Yes,' agreed Peterson.

'How long would you need, for a decision?'

Peterson considered the question. 'Forty-eight hours,' he said.

'What method of communication shall we use?'

'It seems to have worked well this way, so far,' said Peterson.

'All right. If it comes to fruition, we'll have to work very closely together?'

'Yes.'

'I might enjoy that.'

'It would only be for this one occasion.'

'Naturally,' said Petrov.

'I admire your service,' said Peterson.

'I admire yours,' said Petrov.

'Can I pay for the meal?'

'It was my invitation,' refused Petrov. 'You really should have had the wild boar.'

'Next time.'

'I hope there is one.'

'I'll make some contact, whatever the decision, within two days.'

'It won't be easy ... convincing them.'

'No.'

'Sometimes it's easier working in a totalitarian state.'

'But not often.'

'No,' agreed Petrov. 'Not often. It depends how you adjust.' In another of his unexpected statements, he said 'Gadaffi can't be allowed to disrupt the Middle East.'

'You knew then?'

'Yes. I wanted to see if you would hold back. You should try to convince your people.'

'I will,' said Peterson, meaning it.

'Brandy?' invited Petrov.

Peterson hesitated and then said, 'Thank you.'

The Russian gestured, with just a hint of irritation, so that the waiter left the decanter upon the table. Peterson swirled the liquor around the bowl. 'We're supposed to be enemies,' he said, as if he were surprised at the realization.

'Why?'

'Opposing sides, at least.'

'Yes. It seems ridiculous, doesn't it?'

'There's field level contact, of course,' said Peterson.' I suppose it's inevitable, operationally, that paths sometimes cross.'

'I encourage it,' conceded Petrov. 'Don't you?'

'I choose not to know.'

'That might be the reaction of your President.'

'I hope it is.'

'What will you do, if it isn't?'

'I can't discuss that with you. Not yet,' said Peterson.

'I haven't any good ideas, apart from some pre-emptive strike which can't work without the risk of the Soviet Union losing prestige or leverage throughout Africa,' said Petrov.

Peterson accepted that he would have to be constantly upon his guard against the insidious effect of the other man's apparent honesty. He didn't even expect Walter Jones to be as open with him as Petrov appeared to be.

'I hope we can work together,' said Peterson.

'You really should have had the boar,' the Russian repeated. 'It was delicious.'

Many people were to be affected by the first ever, very civilized encounter between the Director of the American Central Intelligence Agency and the head of the Soviet Komitet Gosudarstvennoi Bezopasnosti in one of Vienna's better restaurants.

In Moscow, Gerda Lintz, a serious minded, bespectacled brunette who was learning to enjoy her transfer to the KGB from the Soviet space exploration headquarters at Baikonur, stared with appreciation around the unshared apartment that her position gave her, and wondered if she would satisfactorily carry out whatever function might be assigned to her. She then settled herself into an easy chair to enjoy Goethe in the original German.

In Washington, Michael Bohler decided that at last, as far as security would permit, he would have to write to his parents in Milwaukee to try to convince them that his departure from the Johnson Center at Houston, so soon after his transfer from the complex at Cape Canaveral, did not constitute a demotion, but was merely a sign of the attempt to adjust to America's reduced space commitment. It would be difficult explaining that his new function in Washington utilized his qualifications as a physicist: he decided to write the letter in German, knowing that even after forty years they still had difficulty with any other language.

Vladimir Makovsky resented his transfer to Leningrad, although he was aware there was no protest he could make. He had passed every examination with top marks, and in the physical tests he had achieved almost optimum rating. He knew the reason for his relegation from Moscow, the stigma that would adhere to him throughout his career in the KGB. By now, he had stopped trying to argue against the disadvantage of the transfer, the implication that he might not be a true Communist. He hated the clerk-like job in Leningrad and the clerk-like mentality of those all around him. His grandfather had not really been a very devout Orthodox priest: he'd frequently been drunk on vodka and had even fathered two illegitimate children. But there was little he could do about it. It was in his dossier; the stigma was marked upon him.

Henry Blakey was extremely grateful to God for preventing him from becoming a priest, even though a parish might have been pleasanter than Washington. He only expressed his gratitude in prayers, of course, because he didn't think that other people would understand. But God would. Henry Blakey prayed quite a lot. Not as much as in the seminary, because there prayer had been a ritual rather than a choice, but still more than most. He thanked God for giving him the courage to face his frailty, to realize that strong though his belief might have been, he still lacked the absolute courage to commit himself completely. He thanked God, too, for sparing him from the untenable vows of celibacy. He couldn't imagine life without Jane and Samantha. Sometimes he wondered if God would understand the apparent dichotomy of the career he had chosen, having abandoned the priesthood. But then he remembered that God had spared him the mistake of attempting to become something for which he was not spiritually equipped and could only conclude that He had meant him to join his country's security service. It was, after all, a form of guardianship.

Oleg Sharakov, who proudly boasted that his father had been one of the guards upon Tsar Nicholas at Ipatiev House in Ekaterinburg and often hinted that the man might have been involved in the assassination, guessed from the lack of information from Moscow that the agents he had trained to such a high level at the KGB jungle warfare school on the outskirts of Odessa had failed in their African mission. This would cast doubts on his own abilities. The irascibility had grown with the days, until he knew that his judgement was being affected, but still he was unable to lift the pressure from the recruits. If those he had trained for Africa had failed, then it meant he had not been strict enough. He drove the newcomers to the very point of exhaustion and brought them to their feet at bayonet point. When a twenty-year-old, whom he had initially considered to be the one with the highest potential, collapsed on the ground in tears, Sharakov had smashed the pistol butt into his face, unmoved at the sound of the nose splitting and walked away, leaving his adjutant to dismiss the assembly.

Hank Bradley had the feeling of having lived too long. He was some kind of a legend perhaps, but that meant fuck all apart from the occasional Green Beret reunions. As each year passed 'Nam became that much more of a memory and the reunions that much more difficult to organize. He now felt like the one the elephants had forgotten to tell, on their way to the graveyard. It was a ridiculous attitude, he knew, for someone just forty-five years old one of the youngest colonels ever to achieve the honour and to be seconded with rank, privileges and prestige to the Agency, with offices in Washington as well as Fort Worth. But he could not avoid it: he had been born out of his time, Bradley decided. He should have been a fourteenth-century knight, able to involve himself in perpetual warfare. He blinked at the thought, recognizing the effect of all the whisky. He sniggered, and from beside him there came an answering laugh of misunderstanding. The Washington hierarchy would have his balls, if they knew what he was doing at this very moment, Bradley decided. But he had another use for them. He turned drunkenly on to the whore beside him and she closed her eyes and arranged the smile, for the practised expression of ecstasy, wondering why he still wore the army dog tags, which tickled her chin. Probably like so many of them, he had never grown up.

In Chad, a woman whose beauty was rarely appreciated because of the uniformity of her dress, her rejection of make-up and the severe way in which she wore her hair, calculated that the heat of the sun was finally safe and moved the sunbed out on to the patio of her quarters. She was aware of the attention of the few Africans working in the grounds and suspected too, that some of the European men would be secretly studying her, surprised and maybe even excited at the briefness of her bikini. For their benefit, but apparently unconsciously, Hannah Bloor pulled down the bra, so that it barely covered her nipples. The revised launch date was just a month away, she recalled, thinking back to that morning's briefing. Everyone had worked with an admirable dedication; she wondered if it would all go satisfactorily.

In Washington, Herbert Flood listened patiently to the

President's analysis of what was happening in Africa, Peterson's report from Europe and Walter Jones' brief from Langley that morning.

'Are you sure Peterson is the right person for the job?' asked Flood, when Fowler had finished.

'What?'

'Peterson,' repeated Flood. 'Are you sure he's up to the job?'

'He hasn't made a mistake so far,' pointed out the President.

'But he's not achieved a great deal, has he? This could be a disaster and we're not in any position to oppose it.'

'What are you suggesting?' asked Fowler.

'Nothing,' said Flood, appearing surprised at the question. 'Just felt the point was worth making.'

CHAPTER 9

Peterson should have gone first to Georgetown, if only for a few moments. But he might have caught Lucille on the first drink of the day and they would have argued. Or she might have wanted to talk and extended it for longer than a few moments, shortening the time available for his briefing from his deputy on what had happened over the past four days. And he needed to be fully informed; as completely briefed as possible, in fact. From the White House reaction to his mid-air contact from the aircraft communications centre, Peterson knew he had guessed correctly; Chad was category one priority. The President had agreed immediately to a three o'clock meeting.

It would be over by four, thought Peterson confidently; he could still be with Lucille earlier than normal. He would warn her by telephone, so that she would expect him and not be embarrassed by any surprise arrival.

He experienced a strange unease, going into the sprawl of Langley. It had happened once before, on the day when his Directorship had been confirmed. He had regarded it then as excitement, plus the uncertainty from not knowing how long he could hold down the job, after the failure of those who had preceded him. Now there was no excitement, just uncertainty — enormous uncertainty. He was anxious about the President's reaction to what he had done, and to what he still hoped to do. If Fowler chose to regard the Viennese meeting as deceit, the Directorship could be taken away from him that day. Even if the President accepted it without any immediate challenge, it was still going to be difficult assembling a convincing argument for liaison.

Peterson had liked Petrov, and wanted to believe the man. But balanced against that attitude was the constant awareness that as genuine as the approach had appeared, it could still be a trap.

The Soviet Union, either directly or through its Cuban satellite, had been working to increase its prestige in Africa for over a decade. He had an assessment file inches thick of Moscow's fear of the Chinese presence in Tanzania, Somalia, Ethiopia and the Yemen. Russia needed a convincing demonstration of its friendship throughout the continent. What better than to lure the United States into some kind of covert action against an African state, even one considered as minor as Chad, and then disclose it just when it would be impossible for the Americans to withdraw without positive identification?

Peterson had asked Jones to be waiting from the car telephone, so the deputy had laid out on his desk all the material that had come in on Chad while he had been in Europe. It looked thin, thought Peterson, as he entered the office.

'Summarize it for me,' he asked.

'Very little,' responded Jones, immediately. 'Most important is another aerial photograph, of the opened silo ...'

He indicated the picture and Peterson stared down, frowning.

'What is it, for God's sake?' The open crater was only just visible, through charred and blackened surround.

'Test firing,' identified Jones.

'An actual missile?' Peterson looked up, concerned; please God don't let me be too late, he thought.

Jones shook his head. 'We don't think so. Just a fuel test.'

'Can that be done, without any sort of projectile?'

'Apparently,' said Jones. 'It could also have been to try some sort of firing mechanism. There would have been a dummy container, but it would either have incinerated on the spot, or just risen a few hundred feet into the air; our people say that in rocket terms it's like firing a blank to test the mechanism of a gun.'

'So something is going to happen there soon?' demanded Peterson.

'That's the obvious interpretation,' said Jones.

'The only one. What else?'

'Levy seems to be becoming increasingly irritated. Clearly thinks we're holding out.'

'Have we shown him the satellite stuff on the silo?'

'Yes.'

'What does he expect, miracles?' said Peterson, irritably. 'If his service is so damned good, why hasn't he achieved more?'

'He's asked for a meeting.'

'He's in Washington?'

'He wants to come.'

'When?'

'Immediately.'

'I suppose we've got to agree. We might need them.'

'I'll contact him then?'

Peterson hesitated a moment, then said; 'Yes. Anything from our own sources in Libya?'

'Nothing,' reported Jones, shortly. 'The Defence Minister appears to be back; our people can't get any confirmation of an African visit. There's something, though ...'

'What?'

'The campaign against you appears to have been started.'

Peterson felt the burst of apprehension, almost a sensation of physical sickness.

'When?'

'Difficult to date,' said Jones. 'The rumours just appeared to be there.'

'How strong?'

'All over Capitol Hill.'

Peterson nodded slowly, in growing appreciation. 'If Flood prepares his ground work cleverly enough, any disaster in Africa will be CIA responsibility with no blame at all attaching itself to a foreign affairs adviser.'

'That's my reading,' said Jones.

'How was your cocktail party?'

'Pleasant. But formal. No invitation to choose sides.'

'It would have been too soon,' assessed Peterson. 'He would want to sound you out first. And there would be a danger, at this stage, in associating himself too closely with the Agency.'

'What about Petrov?' asked Jones at last.

For thirty minutes Peterson talked, welcoming the rehearsal for his interview that afternoon with the President. The deputy sat unmoving, for once not even bothering with the difficult pipe.

'You were right to go,' conceded Jones at the end of the account.

'It's useful to know Moscow are as badly placed as we are.'

'I hope the President agrees.'

'What about the suggestion of a joint operation?' asked Jones.

Peterson shrugged. 'Appears genuine, but really it's impossible to say ...' he glanced again towards the picture of the fire-seared silo. 'I'd like to do it,' he confessed, suddenly. 'We've got to do something and do it bloody quick!'

'Jesus, it would be a risk!' said Jones, as if the enormity of the idea had just registered.

'Do you think I haven't considered that?'

'Will you tell Flood?'

'Not directly. The President will, probably. That's what he appointed the man for.'

'Flood will veto it,' predicted Jones.

'Maybe not,' said Peterson. 'Think it through ... consider the leverage it would give him, if things go wrong.'

'What if it goes right?'

'Then he'd have lost out anyway. He's got nothing to lose.'

'We have,' reminded Jones.

'Yes,' agreed Peterson sincerely. 'We have.' Appearing to have been reminded of something, he said, 'Let's get an up-to-date dossier on Irena Sinyavsky. What she's doing, how she's living, any contact with ballet ...' Peterson paused. 'Maybe even a phone tap.'

Jones frowned across the table. 'That's illegal.'

'So's jumping a red light,' dismissed Peterson. 'I'd like to monitor her calls for a week or two.'

'Why?'

'We can prove Petrov was in the West,' suggested Peterson.

'Yes,' said the deputy, with growing awareness.

'Irena Sinyavsky lives in the West,' said Peterson.

'There wasn't any proof,' insisted Jones. 'At the debriefing she denied all knowledge of him.'

'Innuendo would be enough,' said Peterson. He coughed, appearing embarrassed. 'There's something else,' he said. 'Something personal.'

Jones waited curiously.

'In Arizona,' said Peterson, 'somewhere near a town called

Tonalea, there's one of those freaky communes ... you know the kind of stuff. Some sort of stud in leather and chains convincing a lot of kids he's God and that it's all right for him to screw as many as he can get his hands on ...'

Jones was nodding, his curiosity obvious now.

'I don't know its exact location. But I want to. I don't want any direct approach. I don't want anyone aware we're even interested.'

'What's it about?' asked Jones.

'Beth.'

'Beth?'

'My daughter.'

'Oh,' accepted Jones. 'You don't want to involve the FBI? Or the police?'

'No. Entirely self-contained.'

'What do we do when we locate it?'

'Nothing,' said Peterson. 'Just try to establish if she's there. But not if there's a risk of anyone learning of the enquiries. I don't want her to run.'

'OK,' accepted Jones.

'And Walt ...'

'What?'

'Thanks,' said Peterson again. 'It's good to know you're at my back.'

Jones appeared surprisingly discomforted by the gratitude. 'Haven't said I won't become Flood's man yet,' he said, trying to turn it into a joke.

'Would you like to be the one going to see the President this afternoon?'

'Christ no!' said Jones fervently and Peterson believed him.

Peterson went to the White House feeling an even greater apprehension than that he had felt earlier in the day. The rumours, that were obviously being created by Herbert Flood, frightened him. Politically, Washington was the smallest village in the world: as the Middle Ages had believed in witches, the capital believed in gossip. He had known men in Congress or the Senate totally ruined by an innuendo no stronger than that being voiced about him. Whispers became fact and suggestions hardened into doubt;

he would have to be cautious against over-compensating, like so many tried to do, worsening his position before those who would now be watching him with particular interest, anxious for indications to support Flood's campaign.

Peterson was early, but the appointments secretary was standing at his desk, apparently eager to hurry him into the President's office. Fowler rose from his chair as Peterson entered and the Director saw with immediate relief that the man was alone.

'Damned glad you're back,' said Fowler. 'Didn't like having you so far away.'

Criticism or a casual remark? wondered Peterson. He would have to be careful of such nervousness. It was the sort that generated mistakes.

'I think it was a very worthwhile trip,' he said.

'It had better be,' said the President. 'Let's have it.'

The tapes, remembered Peterson. 'May I ask you something, Mr President?'

Fowler, who had been returning to his chair, turned to him enquiringly.

'Could we walk in the Rose Garden?'

A politician less astute than Fowler would have reacted to such an apparently bizarre request with the surprise it deserved, but the man showed little response. He remained by the side of the desk for a few minutes, appearing to consider the question, and then said, 'Might it be a good idea?'

'Yes.'

'Of course,' agreed Fowler. He led the way through the French windows and out into the arbour. He got some way from the building before turning.

'Well?' he demanded.

Peterson felt a sudden wash of fear, strong enough for the briefest impression of actual dizziness.

'Well?' repeated the President, with the first hint of impatience.

Peterson began to speak, fighting against a flurry of words because he knew it would disclose the doubt he felt at what he had done. He decided that there was no point in explaining it as if there were a need for a defence, and instead he recounted the meeting as factually as he was able, consciously avoiding any words or expression which might be construed as his personal reaction to Petrov's suggestion. Aware that a good liar tells as few lies as possible, the only falsehood Peterson attempted was the circumstances of Petrov's approach, which would have revealed the intention before he left Washington.

The fear returned the moment he stopped talking. Fowler stood before him quite motionless, his face blank of any expression, the stance of someone shocked into disbelief. Then he said: 'Holy Mother of Christ!'

'Yes,' said Peterson. 'It's difficult to accept, isn't it?'

The President looked back towards the Oval Office.

'Thank you for your suggestion to come out here,' he said, his very first reaction taking into account his own political safety.

There may be a chance, thought Peterson. The uncertainty stayed with him.

'You took a very great risk,' said the President.

'I was as careful as possible.'

'It was still a risk.'

'But worthwhile,' insisted Peterson. 'We know now the extent of the Soviet concern from an unimpeachable source.'

'Worthwhile,' nodded Fowler. Then, heavily, he added: 'Just.'

The President remained looking at him, very steadily. Peterson stared back, his face expressionless. This was the moment, he thought — the time for any challenge or accusation.

Instead Fowler said: 'What about this idea of a joint operation? It's a trap, isn't it?'

Peterson felt the tension begin to go. 'I had Petrov under observation from the moment he arrived in Austria and got some reasonable material for a smear dossier, if that becomes necessary. Why couldn't *we* use their presence on any incursion as insurance protection?'

'The law states that the President has to approve any covert action,' he said.

'And under the Hughes-Ryan amendment I must go through eight separate congressional committees,' said Peterson, 'which means a total of 163 legislators and 41 staff members. It would be impossible to prevent a leakage.'

'The test firing indicates something pretty soon?'

'Yes,' said Peterson.

'What about Germany?'

'We couldn't stop it from there by ourselves,' said Peterson. 'Not in the time that seems to be available.'

'But the Russians have got an entry that we haven't.'

'So Petrov claims.'

'If he's ahead, why doesn't he do it alone?'

'We couldn't sit back, in the expectation that the Russians would succeed,' pointed out Peterson.

'No,' accepted Fowler.

'So there'd be a chance of our ruining it by trying to run some sort of parallel operation, whatever it might be.'

The President stared at him, doubtful. 'That isn't a very strong argument,' he said.

'It's the only one I have.'

'The Secretary of State won't like it,' predicted Fowler. 'Or Herbert Flood.'

'No.'

The President fixed him once more with a direct look. 'You took a hell of a chance,' he said again.

Peterson felt the renewal of unease. 'I purposely avoided consultation,' he said. 'Had anything gone wrong, I didn't want any risk of your involvement.'

Not quite a lie, Peterson thought. Not quite the truth, either. The President was examining him, quizzically.

'That was thoughtful,' said Fowler.

Had there been suspicion in his voice? If there were going to be outrage, it would surely have come by now.

'It seemed a sensible precaution,' he said.

Gesturing Peterson to remain where he was, Fowler strolled away towards an arrangement of rose trees, hands clasped loosely behind his back, head forward upon his chest. He stopped, unaware of the flowers, and began absently stubbing his toe into the border, gradually creating a groove. It was almost ten minutes before he returned to where the Director was standing.

'If you sought congressional approval, it would take weeks, even if there were no leaks,' he said.

'We haven't got weeks.'

'You've told me everything?' Fowler demanded, hinting the suspicion which the Executive always felt for the CIA.

'Yes,' said Peterson, immediately.

'Do you think we need to go in?'

'You said yourself we've got to do something.'

'If we are going to by-pass Congress, then I can't know of anything officially.'

Peterson felt the stir of a different sort of concern. 'I suppose not,' he agreed. He was being further abandoned.

'I've got to come out clean, if the shit hits the fan.'

'I understand.'

'This part of our meeting never took place. We just walked in the garden, reviewing the facts that exist so far.'

'Yes,' agreed Peterson.

Fowler suddenly looked down at the Director's clothing, as if trying to locate the bulge of any pocket recorder with which Peterson might have been trying to protect his future.

'What about the Secretary of State? And Mr Flood?' asked Peterson.

'That is my problem; something about which you've no need to know.'

'All right.'

'If it goes wrong ... publicly wrong, I won't make any move to save you.'

Again Peterson felt the sweep of dizziness. 'I wouldn't expect it,' he said.

'You would,' disputed the President. 'But I wouldn't do it.'

The election at which Fowler would be attempting a second term was only two years away, remembered Peterson; it was almost time for the man to begin his campaign. He was obviously planning it carefully.

'I'm to go ahead?' asked Peterson.

'You're to do everything and anything you consider necessary to take out that installation,' said Fowler. 'I've already made that clear, on several occasions. In front of witnesses.'

'Yes,' remembered Peterson. The man was a consummate professional.

'It frightens the hell out of me,' admitted Fowler, with an

M.—D

unexpected smile. 'You poor bastard.'

'We are working to turn any disaster into a Russian responsibility,' repeated Peterson.

'You'd better plan to,' said the President, sincerely. 'You'll need your hand over your balls all the time. Even if the Russians mean everything they've said, they sure as hell don't intend to be left holding any can.'

'I know the problems,' said Peterson.

Fowler shook his head. 'No you don't,' he insisted. 'None of us can guess this thing through.'

Fowler straightened, taking Peterson's arm to lead him back towards the Oval Office. 'Let's go inside and talk about Africa,' he invited.

So posterity — or any investigation — would have its proper record, recognized Peterson.

Back where their conversation was being recorded, Fowler and Peterson talked their way through an apparently fresh review of the Chad complex and the Director's visit to Germany. Twice, Peterson realized, the President repeated the instruction that everything had to be done to abort whatever might be planned there. Would he be able to turn that into some sort of explanation for what he was intending to do if there were later any congressional enquiry? Perhaps, he thought. Realistically, he doubted if anyone would believe him naïve enough to be so lacking in understanding. The interview ended with the President appearing forcefully to remind Peterson of his concern, with orders to keep in constant contact.

Peterson crumpled in the back of the limousine taking him past the sentries and then out through the high barred gates. Easier than he had expected, decided Peterson — far easier. But he was hardly in any better position than he had been before the President knew. He'd merely swopped one potential catastrophe for another.

Fowler would not do anything to curb his foreign affairs adviser's rumours, even if he had ever considered doing so. It would be useful protection for him, if the American and Russian liaison were to become known. The President had been right.

None of them could think it through with any hope of an accurate prediction. There was only one certainty at the moment: his exposure. It was like playing Russian roulette with a fully-loaded machine gun.

He had warned Lucille of the time he expected to be home before leaving Langley, and although he was fifteen minutes early she was standing in the hallway as if she had been waiting for him.

She stared past him, anxiously, and Peterson realized she was completely sober.

'Where is she?' said the woman.

'Who?' Momentarily, Peterson was bewildered.

Lucille came back to him. Her face began to break into an almost childlike expression of disappointment.

'Beth,' she said. 'Where's Beth?'

'Who told you?'

'Paul came. Stayed. Showed me a letter.' Her words came jerkily, as if she had difficulty in assembling her thoughts.

'I'm trying to find her, Lucille,' he said, reaching out for her hands in a gesture of reassurance. 'I'm having her traced, wherever she is in Arizona.'

'Why didn't you go? I thought that's where you were!'

Despair was etched very deeply into her voice. She made the questions an accusation.

'I was in Europe,' he reminded her. 'I told you.'

'Thought you were going to surprise me ... bring Beth back.'

Had the alcohol affected her mind? he wondered, caught again by the childishness.

'I'll bring her back,' promised Peterson. 'I'll find her and bring her back and we'll be a family again.'

Lucille gazed around, as if she were seeking something. Then she moved towards the kitchen. So that's where she keeps the vodka, thought Peterson.

Because of the priority of the cables, the CIA Resident in the US embassy in Benghazi began spending heavily among his informants. Just twenty-four hours before he was due to depart, he learned of the Libyan courier's visit to Zürich. He liaised with the embassy in Berne, so that when Muhammed Talil stepped off the aircraft, he entered a surveillance operation involving thirty people. The Libyan went straight to the Baur au Lac, on the Talstrasse.

Talil enjoyed the foreign visits because they freed him from the Islamic restrictions that the President had imposed upon Libya after the overthrow of the Shah in Iran. Talil was in the bar within an hour of his arrival, in conversation with an exciting-looking brunette. She disclosed during dinner that she was a buyer for a West German diamond firm, lonely on her first visit to Switzerland, a cover which would not have withstood too much scrutiny but which had been the best the CIA had been able to come up with in the time available.

Talil persuaded her to go to a club, but they were both disappointed by its dullness and the Libyan was impatient anyway, because he was certain the woman would come to his room with him. She put the apomorphine into his drink as he was settling the bill and the stomach cramps began when they were in the lift at the Baur au Lac. The first spasm gripped him as they got to his suite. She helped him to the bathroom, dampening a towel for his head as he clutched over the bowl, unable to stop the violent retching. It had been a strong dosage and he was soon too weak to protest effectively when she called the hotel doctor. The physician arrived very quickly and excluded her from the bedroom while he carried out his examination. The girl was able to copy with the Minnox camera every document in Talil's brief-case before the doctor emerged to tell her that he suspected a burst ulcer and was moving him to hospital.

'Are you his wife?' he asked the girl.

'A friend.'

The doctor nodded, understanding. 'He seems very concerned about a brief-case.'

The girl looked enquiringly around the room. 'This must be it,' she said, as if aware of it for the first time.

CHAPTER 10

Otto Bock convinced himself that he had tried very hard. And not just because of Gretal and the children, but because of the danger of his position, which he recognized with frightening clarity. Yet like a child reaching out for a candle flame it has been warned might burn, he could not stop himself. It might have been easier had he not been so upset, but Jurgen Beindorf's unexpected behaviour had been terribly cruel. He thought they had been friends, real friends. He closed his eyes, shuddering at the memory of the boy's rejection, the sneers and the laughter: it had been horrible, truly horrible.

Bock remained in his office near the Defence Ministry computer room long after most others had left, staring at the telephone upon his desk. To call his wife and utter the lie would be the first step, putting the thought into some sort of determination. That wasn't quite true, Bock remembered. Every night now for a week he had driven home by the circuitous route which took him past the club where they gathered. But he had never stopped; the first night, he had not even looked towards it.

He snatched the phone up, hurrying with the number before common-sense overcame his desire. Bock, who was the senior computer programmer for the Ministry, frequently had to stay late for some sudden crisis involving his country somewhere in the world, so the woman accepted without question that this was just another such occasion. She was to eat without him, Bock said. And apologize to the children that he would not be home until they were in bed.

He passed out through security with a perfunctory, yet efficient examination, offering his brief-case for scrutiny at the final check. There were some within the Ministry, certainly at his level of clearance, who resented the intrusion, but Bock regarded it as a necessary imposition. In recent years there had been far too much leakage of information into the Eastern bloc: traitors were even discovered among respected employees.

He drove slowly, still attempting to keep his mind clear of any positive intention. If there was not a parking space available, he would drive on. If there were too many people grouped around the door, he wouldn't stop. There was a meter free almost opposite. A discreet light burned, from which it was just possible to read the sign. There was no one at the entrance. Bock braked, turned off the ignition and remained in his seat. In the office, he had gazed at the telephone; now he studied his hands, gripped against the wheel so tightly that they hurt.

He moved at last, trying to imagine some reluctance that wasn't there. The receptionist was polite and friendly, discerning his embarrassment: his lack of membership was not a problem. He completed the form with the carefully selected alias, which was accepted without challenge, paid his twenty marks and within ten minutes was through into the main room. A long bar ran along the wall to the left, the lighting behind it subdued and unobtrusive. There were books set into a far wall and tables of various sizes arranged around a small dance area, illuminated by soft candles. Hidden in an alcove, a quintet was playing slow music and on the dance floor several couples were moving, close together.

Self-conscious about remaining within the immediate visibility of the entrance, Bock went impulsively to the bar. The barman came to him immediately and without thinking Bock ordered a whisky. As his eyes adjusted to the lighting, he saw that nearly everyone was dressed very conservatively in subdued suits. There were just a few in jeans and those who had affected women's clothing had done so by wearing tailored trouser suits.

'Hello.'

At first Bock didn't respond.

'Hello.'

He looked cautiously to his left. Slim, neatly dressed, his blond hair closely cropped and not even a ring to hint at any flamboyance.

'Hello.'

'I haven't seen you here before.'

'No.'

'So you're nervous?' It was a kindly question, not an accusation.

Bock sniggered, confirming the impression. 'Yes,' he said. 'Very.'

'There's no need to be.'

'Probably not. But I can't seem to help it.'

'Can I buy you a drink?' invited the blond man.

'I was about to ask you.'

'Let's not argue about it,' said the other man. 'You're not in any hurry to leave, are you?'

'No,' said Bock. 'No hurry at all.'

'Then you can buy me a drink later on.'

'I'd like that.'

'Why don't we move to one of the booths, away from all these bright lights?'

Bock smiled, gratefully. It had really been so much easier than he had expected. Already it was difficult to believe that he had cried over Jurgen's rejection. Too old, Jurgen had said. But he was not too old. His new friend was about the same age as Jurgen, but nicer — far nicer.

'Yes,' Bock accepted. 'Let's go to one of the booths.'

'Glad now that you came?' said the man, as they moved away from the bar.

'Very much,' said Bock.

'My name is Klaus,' said the new friend.

'I'm Otto,' said the computer chief.

It was typical of Petrov's professionalism that having had his meeting with the CIA Director he went ahead with further proposals and did not wait for Peterson's response. If Peterson agreed, then it meant that he, Petrov, was that much further ahead in any joint action they decided upon; if Peterson refused, then he had not wasted any time.

There is nothing within the Soviet Union beyond the influence or attention of the KGB and during this period of leadership Dimitri Petrov had fully utilized the facility. Very early in his directorship, he had decided to use it to provide himself with a particular type of operative — someone who would not normally have been considered suitable for intelligence work but whose technical ability fitted them for a specialized assignment which might be the only one in which they were ever involved. There were some within the Praesidium, Litvinov foremost among them, who argued against wastefulness of manpower and accused him of empire building. The events in Chad and his decision, three years earlier, to take Gerda Lintz from Baikonur was a complete answer to any criticism about the system, and when the problem in Africa was resolved, Petrov thought he might argue it before an open meeting to prove his critics wrong. Then again, he might not. It might be interpreted as nervousness in the face of the opposition — bad psychology.

He pulled her file towards him, examining the photograph which was on top. The spectacles and the functional way she wore her hair — strained back into a bun at the nape of her neck — gave her a severe appearance which was misleading. With a different coiffure and clothes chosen for their style rather than for their practicality, Gerda Lintz would have been an attractive woman. The Director at Baikonur had described her as an excellent physicist, with an apparent knowledge and expertise extending far beyond what would have been expected in someone of thirty-five. After her transfer from Leipzig to Moscow University, she had always been among the top five in any class she attended and had graduated with honours. Petrov turned back to her biography, noting her birth at Falkensee and the fact that her move from Leipzig had not come until she was eighteen. Would the fluency of her German have suffered in the seventeen years she had spent in the Soviet Union? He would have to have her returned to East Berlin for assessment before attempting to infiltrate her into the Chad complex. Unbeknown to her, the woman had been under close observation for the preceding week and Petrov noted that there was no record of any sexual involvement, either male or female. He was glad. He was always frightened of personal interests conflicting with the complete attention necessary for any operation.

It would have been unthinkable to put her within the installation without providing some sort of exterior support, which meant another deep penetration attempt. Petrov sighed, still not completely sure about the decision he had made. The three men who had already attempted to reach the site had been described by their jungle training instructor as the best graduates he had. And each had been caught. Which meant that there had to be somebody better. The only person who fitted that criterion was Oleg Sharakov, their instructor.

Petrov began reading the second dossier, frowning down at the uncompromising face of the commando school head. Petrov had never met Sharakov, but it was a familiar face. He had only been a boy at the time, but he could still remember all the other faces like it, in the final horrors of Stalingrad, when the veneer had cracked and the animalism had taken over. The survivors had been the first to accept the necessity of cannibalism, to stay alive. There had been two instances of recruits dying under Sharakov's tuition, Petrov saw, and another had been crippled. Sharakov himself had fought as an adviser against the British in Aden and again in Angola and distinguished himself in both operations.

Sharakov was the only man, Petrov decided finally. He would allow him to select his own unit, once the operation had been fully explained to him. And he would delay, for a few days at least. Just in case there was the hoped-for response from the Americans.

The decision made, Petrov pushed aside the files. That of Gerda Lintz fell open at the section containing her photograph and Petrov smiled, caught by a thought. It was in his power to have photographs of anyone in the Soviet Union, the world even. Yet he could not have the one picture he wanted, because to have possessed it would have been dangerous. He had actually resisted taking Irena's defection folder from the records, in case Litvinov discovered a clerk's listing of its withdrawal. There had been a photograph there, Petrov knew. Several. Why not? It would be a chance in a million of Litvinov ever learning about it.

CHAPTER 11

Peterson knew the argument with Paul had been his fault. He had raged on the telephone accusingly without allowing the boy to speak of the second letter from Beth, but he had found it impossible to apologize. Even though the second note had been more coherent and the wish to return home made plainer, Paul should still have waited until he got back from Europe and kept it from Lucille.

She had become so drunk and then so deeply unconscious when she realized that he hadn't brought their daughter home with him that at one stage Peterson had even considered getting her to hospital, frightened she was suffering from alcoholic poisoning. Hospitalization would have to come, Peterson realized: probably very soon. He supposed he could commit her, even if Lucille refused her consent. Somewhere as discreet as possible. Peterson sighed at the thought; no matter how discreet, the news would be around Washington within twenty-four hours, something more for Herbert Flood to use in his campaign. Peterson thought he might wait a little longer, to see if Lucille could control the drinking, as she boasted she could. Certainly on the few occasions that she'd tried, she had appeared able to manage it.

Peterson looked up at his deputy's entry. There was a broad smile on Jones' face, but it faltered at the sight of the Director.

'What is it?' asked Peterson.

'You all right?' said Jones.

'Of course. Why?'

'You don't look well.'

'Tired,' said Peterson. 'Still a bit jet-lagged. You seem pleased.'

'We got a break!' said Jones, triumphantly. 'At last we got a break.'

'What?' demanded Peterson urgently.

'Trapped a courier in Zürich,' said the deputy. 'It was a

combined operation, involving our people in Libya and Switzerland. Managed complete access to what he was carrying.'

'And?'

'Libyan government authorization for the payment of $20,000,000 in gold to a numbered account of the Swiss Banking Corporation in Zurich.'

'Twenty million!' exclaimed Peterson.

'Libya are buying all the time available, for six months,' said Jones. 'Effectively, it's *their* satellite.' He offered the Director the folder. 'Everything is there,' he said. 'Arab originals, as well as the translations.'

'It's worse than we thought,' judged Peterson.

'There's something interesting,' said Jones.

'What?'

'It appears that BADRA want a physical transfer of the money.'

Peterson frowned up. 'Trucked, you mean? What's wrong with a paper transfer?'

Jones shrugged. 'No idea. That's the only inference from the documents the Libyan was carrying.'

'Any knowledge of our access?'

'We don't think so.'

'Wonderful,' said Peterson, sitting back expansively. It was the first break-through in a fortnight of frustration. 'Send congratulation cables to Libya and Switzerland.'

'Already sent, in your name,' said Jones.

'This is the information we wanted,' said Peterson, positively, patting the papers before him.

'It would seem so,' said Jones.

'What about Levy?' said Peterson.

'Confirmed his appointment from the embassy this morning. He's part of some Israeli government delegation, apparently.'

'For what?'

'Aid.'

'What about Vienna?'

'Brownlow has made contact, passing on our agreement to Petrov of full co-operation and suggesting the positive planning meeting you proposed. There should be a reply sometime today.'

'It will mean another trip to Europe,' said Peterson. He

wondered who would care for Lucille. He would have to apologize to Paul.

'I prepared a file of people to send into Chad,' said Jones. 'You asked me to, remember?'

'Of course,' said Peterson, too sharply. Why should Jones believe he might have forgotten?

The deputy stared across the desk, his face unmoving.

'I need to know exactly what you want.' The tone of his voice and the time it took him to speak, after Peterson's reaction, showed Jones' surprise at the rebuke.

'Several things,' said Peterson, anxious to cover the awkwardness between them. 'Petrov thinks he can infiltrate somebody into the complex. So we'll need expertise. And I want a computer run on any operative with qualifications involving rocketry or missiles or anything that would give him the cover of a scientist ...'

'Right,' said Jones, making a notation on the pad he carried.

'Witchcraft,' said Peterson, in sudden recollection.

'What?' said Jones.

'Williams' report, on the day he disappeared,' recalled Peterson, sifting through the dossiers upon his desk until he came to the one that dealt with the third agent they had sent to penetrate the installation. He scanned through the closely typed sheets, finally stabbing his finger against the page.

'Here ...' he said. ' "Tortoise-shell symbol, with poisoned barb",' he read aloud. ' "Tortoise-shell, painted red and white. Hyena image, with inverted feet ...".' The Director looked up at the other man. 'Witchcraft,' he said again.

'I thought the Chadians were either Moslems or Christians,' said Jones.

'Doesn't matter, in Africa,' said Peterson positively. 'Beneath the top layer of whatever belief they're supposed to have, there's still the belief in witchcraft. And BADRA seem to be utilizing it ....'

He indicated the page upon which the symbols were listed. 'That sort of stuff would keep any curious native away far more effectively than reinforced wire.'

'So?' asked Jones.

Peterson sat back in his chair, gazing over his deptuy's head and

speaking more as the speculation came to him than in any formalized proposal.

'Efficient and self-contained as they obviously are,' he said,
'There must be some need to use the local population, either for
labouring work or for obtaining a limited supply of provisions.
Might be useful, if we could arouse some opposition from among
the people?'

'How?'

'A priest,' said Peterson. 'A priest who could explain that
mishaps were happening because of witchcraft ... witchcraft
stemming directly from the BADRA complex. And *ensure* that the
Africans know it!'

Jones nodded, smiling. 'It's a great idea,' he said.

'Worth a try,' said Peterson. 'Find out for me if we've anyone
who could properly employ the cover. Denomination needn't
matter, particularly.'

Jones made a further note. 'Anything else?'

'We sent in three deep penetration people working solo, and lost
them all,' said Peterson, reminiscing again. 'And so did the
Russians. So solo operations won't work.'

'What then?'

'A unit,' decided Peterson. 'The sort of platoons that the Green
Berets established in Vietnam, able to remain undetected in the
jungle until they were needed, living off the land, equipped and
trained to carry out one punitive action, if the occasion arose.'

Jones regarded Peterson doubtfully. 'They'd have to be damned
good,' he said. 'It wouldn't be easy, staying undetected, no matter
how much jungle training they got.' Peterson suddenly noticed
the photograph of the blackened silo lying on his desk. He picked
it up, holding it so Jones could see.

'If this is a guide, they won't have to stay there long,' he said.
'But I want them to be more than just damned good. I want them
to be the best.'

'How many?'

'Decision really for the unit commander,' said Peterson. 'Maybe
ten. I don't think it should be more.'

'I'll choose the commander first then?'

'Yes,' said Peterson. 'And remember: I want the best man

available. After Vietnam, there should be enough to choose from.'

Jones smiled, pleased at last at the positive decisions coming from Peterson. He had been afraid, in the past few days, that there was some substance to Herbert Flood's innuendo.

'Need we communicate to the Russians the sort of things we're considering?' he asked.

Peterson pondered the question. 'Let's see if we've got the right people available first,' he said, cautiously. 'If we're working with them, then it's really going to be *joint*. I want to match them, man for man, expert for expert. There's no point in giving them an idea they may not have had and then find that we haven't got the properly qualified agent while they have.'

Again Jones smiled. Peterson was once more operating with his old efficiency.

'When will you go back to Vienna?' asked Jones.

'Depends upon Petrov's reaction. As soon as possible, I would imagine.'

Peterson realized he would have to contact Paul sometime during the day: he wondered when he would have time.

'So you want the plane kept in readiness?'

Peterson nodded. 'And the same number of people I took with me last time.'

'Still not absolutely sure about Petrov?'

'As sure as I'll ever be,' said Peterson. 'But I don't intend taking any chances ...'

He hesitated, remembering his commitments throughout the day. 'Summon a conference,' he said. 'I shan't be able to, so I want you to address them. Their sole function has got to be guarding my back. Understood?'

'Understood,' said Jones. 'Sure you don't want me along this time?'

'Flood would want to know what the two top men were doing away together,' said Peterson. 'And I think you're more valuable here, as liaison man.'

'Christ, we're going to be exposed if this goes wrong,' said Jones, voicing the constant concern.

'Yes,' accepted Peterson.

The intercom upon his desk buzzed and Peterson depressed the receiver. David Levy had just passed through the entry gate.

'We ran the traces you wanted,' said Jones, at the door.

Peterson looked up from the paperwork before him.

'Irena Sinyavsky has tried to bury herself in Hartford, Connecticut. She's changed her name and runs a ballet school. Involved with a guy in real estate.'

'How involved?'

'Seems their friends expect them to get married. Nothing's fixed.'

'Anything else?'

'Our people have found the commune in Arizona,' reported Jones. 'Still no identification of Beth. It's difficult, not being able to make any direct approach. They're having to hang around Tonalea, trying to get into conversation with people they think might be making provision runs from the place.'

'How long do they think?'

Jones shrugged. 'Impossible to say.'

'Thanks,' said Peterson.

Before the Mossad chief's entry, Peterson reassembled the files in the order in which they had been arranged for him and put them into a side drawer, so that his desk was empty when Levy entered the room. Peterson stood to greet him, studying the Israeli. A comparatively short man himself, Peterson was conscious of stature. In most people Levy's lack of height would have made him appear almost dwarf-like, but that was not the impression the Jewish intelligence chief conveyed.

The man's bulk compensated, Peterson supposed, but that wasn't the only thing that covered the disadvantage of his size. One gained an immediate awareness of the man's personality, so forceful that it made him appear taller than he actually was.

'Good to see you again, David,' greeted Peterson, moving across the room with his hand outstretched. Levy appeared to consider the offer, then responded. Peterson led him away from the desk, towards an area of the office where easy chairs and a couch were arranged for informal discussions.

'Is it good to see me?' demanded Levy.

Peterson allowed the curiosity to show on his face. 'I don't understand.'

'There are many things I don't understand,' said Levy awkwardly.

Peterson put himself in the chair facing the Israeli and let the smile leave his face.

'So we're not going to waste time with any forced politeness?' he said.

'I think we're too adult for that,' said Levy.

'Well?' demanded Peterson, curtly, matching the other man's demeanour.

'Almost a month ago, I gave you information from which it became obvious that a very real threat existed in Africa,' reminded the Israeli. 'And now there's every reason to believe that the threat could be centred around my country.'

'We've no confirmation of that yet,' said Peterson. 'But don't let that stop the hypothesis.'

Levy splayed his fingers, ticking off points.

'The information about Chad came from us,' he listed. 'The information about Germany came from us. The information about Libya came from us ...' He lowered his hands. 'And we've got nothing back, in return.'

'You've got satellite photographs ...' began Peterson, but the Israeli cut him off, impatiently.

'Don't patronize me, Peterson. You're supposed to head the most effective information-gathering machine ever created. Are you asking me to believe that in three weeks, all you've done is to manage the most basic aerial reconnaissance and confirm what we already knew!'

'Yes,' said the CIA Director, simply.

'I don't believe you.'

'That's got to be your misfortune, not mine,' said Peterson, refusing the other man's aggression. 'You *didn't* tell us about Chad. You told us about a vague rumour which it took time to confirm and locate the country concerned. You guessed at some German involvement, which needed to be established. You sent rumours about Libya, which required confirmation. And since when has the Mossad trailed around behind the coat-tails of another service, prepared to let them do the work!'

Levy was momentarily silenced by the force of Peterson's

reaction, a man unused to having his arguments disputed.

'I don't think you're being completely honest with me,' Levy complained, his arrogance temporarily curbed. 'We set out talking of complete co-operation and exchange of information.'

'We did not,' rejected Peterson. 'We agreed upon mutually convenient liaison, which is exactly what you've been getting. I have informed you of every single item of information that has been appropriate. Are you going to turn over every report that's come into you from your agents? Show me your paths of enquiry and sources of information?'

'Something like that,' retaliated Levy.

Peterson regarded the squat man apprehensively, confused by the answer. 'What?' he said.

'Your analysis must be the same as ours, about that firing picture,' said Levy. 'Whatever is planned there is pretty near completion. We're not going to sit around and wait for it to happen: if Israel had done that, it would have been pushed into the sea years ago.'

'You only succeed with an Entebbe operation once,' said Peterson.

'It depends how good you are,' said Levy, the confidence re-emerging. 'I'm a general. I'm prepared to sacrifice three hundred men to save three million.'

'What if it failed?' tried Peterson, anxiously.

'We cannot afford to fail,' said Levy, the arrogance open now. 'So we rarely do.'

Peterson got up from his chair, filling the silence with movement.

'Would you like a drink?' he invited.

'No.'

'Coffee?'

'No.'

Peterson continued to move about the room, debating the response before making it. Any operation that he and Petrov might mount would be problem enough, confronting just the difficulties that existed in Chad. A separate Israeli operation would make success inconceivable.

He turned back to Levy. 'I don't want you to mount any operation,' he said.

Levy appeared speechless for several seconds and then he laughed. '*You* don't want it!' he challenged.

'No,' said Peterson. How much could he avoid letting the other man know?

He returned to the easy chairs, sitting down to face the Israeli again.

'I'm trying to set up an operation,' he began, carefully. 'At the moment none of the details are finalized. It is for that reason that you haven't already been told of it. If there is to be any chance of success at all, then we've got to have the benefit of surprise. It won't be easy: they've already killed three of my men, so they're alert to our attempts to discover what's going on. If you try to set up something independent from us, then you'll ruin everything.'

Peterson stopped, reviewing what he had said. He had revealed nothing, he realized gratefully.

For the first time since the meeting had begun, Levy smiled. 'Let's do it together,' he suggested eagerly.

Oh God, thought Peterson. Soon there would be more people involved in the incursion than in the European landings of World War II.

'No,' he said.

'Why not?' demanded Levy.

'Because we might fail,' improvised Peterson desperately. 'And if we do, then there will need to be men ready and prepared to make another attempt.'

Levy regarded the American doubtfully. 'If the first attempt failed, what chance would the second have?'

'It would have to be made,' argued Peterson, gauging an advantage in the argument.

'Perhaps,' said Levy, unconvinced.

'Already they're test firing,' reminded Peterson. 'There'd be no time ... no time at all ... to prepare something else if we didn't succeed. You'd have to be moving within hours.'

The Israeli was unconvinced, Peterson knew. Anxiously he went on: 'We've positive confirmation of Libya.'

'Definite?' demanded Levy. Excitement replaced the uncertainty.

'Yes,' said the Director. 'We know details of a gold transfer ... something like $20,000,000 ...'

'You've got to be joking!'

'Libya is purchasing complete access to the satellite for six months.'

Levy's face hardened. 'When's the transfer?' he demanded.

'The day after tomorrow.'

'What are you going to do about it?'

'I've made no plans yet,' admitted Peterson, honestly. 'I've only got the intelligence in the last hour.'

'I'd like to handle it,' said Levy.

It wasn't a major concession, decided Peterson. In fact, it was peripheral, but it would at least give the Israelis the impression of involvement.

'Agreed,' he said.

Levy smiled, gratefully. 'We're very worried about the danger in Chad,' he said.

'So are we,' admitted Peterson.

'The point will be made to President Fowler, by the people I'm with,' said Levy.

'And they will get from him the same assurance of concern that I've just given you,' said Peterson. He had averted a problem, he realized suddenly. And without too much compromise. There *would* be the need for some Israeli commando attempt, if the American-Soviet operation failed. And any difficulty with the gold shipment might give them a little more time.

Levy rose, extending his hand. 'I would not like us to fall out because of this,' he said.

'Neither would I,' said Peterson, accepting the gesture.

'We'll keep in close contact?'

'You've my word,' repeated Peterson.

'It must not be allowed to happen.'

'It won't.'

'I wish I felt more confident.'

'We'll stop it,' insisted the CIA Director. I hope, he thought.

Peterson travelled towards his White House meeting with the President, encouraged by the encounter with Levy. Ironically, the awareness bothered him; until recently, he realized, he would not have needed the reassurance of such omens. It was a fuller meeting than his last encounter with Fowler. Henry Moore was in the chair he seemed to regard his own as Secretary of State. Flood, crumpled and unkempt, sat opposite. Did they look at him with more attention than usual, he wondered, as he entered the room. Flood seemed particularly intent. Peterson was unsure whether the fatigue and worry upon which Jones had remarked had left his face.

'Still not exactly a surfeit of information is it?' Flood attacked immediately.

His report had preceded the Libyan news, Peterson realized. The foreign affairs adviser would suspect that he had held the information back, in order to make a dramatic announcement.

'We've positive confirmation that Libya is to purchase six months' satellite time from BADRA,' said Peterson, quietly.

Fowler jerked up from his desk and Flood turned, so that he could see him more easily.

'Why wasn't it in the report?' demanded Flood, irritated at having been exposed by his aggressive greeting.

'It only came in a few moments before I left Langley,' said Peterson. He had read the complete file on his way to the White House and summarized for them the interception of the courier and what they had learned from the contents of his brief-case.

'Good piece of work,' congratulated Fowler.

'Thank you,' said Peterson. It would go a long way to diffuse Flood's attacks.

'So now we know the problem,' said the President.

'And it *is* a problem,' said Flood. 'It'll mean a war in the Middle East.'

'I've seen the Israelis this morning,' said Fowler, generally. 'They said they were worried, and now with every reason.'

'I met the Mossad Chief, Levy,' said Peterson.

'Did you tell him about the Libyan confirmation?' demanded Flood, sharply.

'Yes.'

'That was stupid,' attacked the foreign affairs adviser. 'You should have sought presidential permission first.'

'I judged it necessary,' said Peterson, refusing to give way under the man's renewed pressure. 'The transfer is only forty-eight hours away.'

'They're going to intercept it?' said Moore, critically.

'It gives them involvement,' said Peterson. 'It'll have to be an open operation and there's always the risk of failure. I didn't want any of my men caught up in an embarrassing diplomatic situation.'

'I think the Director made the right decision,' supported Fowler.

'We've received a lot of help from the Mossad,' elaborated Peterson. 'It was important to reciprocate.'

Flood was regarding him curiously. 'You keeping something from us?' he asked.

'No,' lied Peterson.

'We've a little leverage to prevent the Israelis becoming too difficult,' said Fowler, coming to the CIA chief's rescue. 'They've sought a commitment from me for another one hundred M-60 tanks, a guarantee of oil shipments at an unfluctuating posted price, pegged for two years, and a positive aid programme amounting to nearly a billion dollars in addition to what they already get.'

Peterson breathed out noisily, an exaggerated expression of surprise.

'Clever bastards, aren't they?' conceded Fowler, begrudgingly.

'It's a strong demand, even before we knew it was Gadaffi,' said Moore.

'But it's a bargaining position,' came in Flood, immediately, trying to make the other man appear diplomatically naïve.

'Only if we accept it as such,' fought back Moore. 'We're the ones in control: we set the rules.'

'Right,' agreed the President, responding predictably to any argument from a position of strength.

Flood picked irritably at a fleck of skin against his thumbnail, knowing that the Secretary of State had outmanoeuvred him. Peterson sat easily in the chair, content for the other two men to squabble. It took the pressure off him.

'And we *are* in control,' continued the President, smiling with satisfaction at the others sitting before him. 'While they believe we're even considering their demands, they're not going to do anything that might screw their chances.'

He was looking at Peterson as he spoke. The Director responded with just the slightest movement of his head, indicating his appreciation of the pressure.

The discussion continued for a further half an hour, ranging over every aspect of the African complex but coming to no fresh conclusions. Peterson got away without any further determined questioning from anyone. From the car he called Langley and learned from Jones that there was nothing sufficiently important to take him back to CIA headquarters. With the glass between himself and the driver raised, he telephoned Paul's number, but only got the answering machine. He replaced the instrument but then took it up again after a few minutes consideration and dialled the number for a second time. When the indication came for him to dictate his message, Peterson said, haltingly: 'I want to say I'm very sorry for what happened last night ... it was my fault ... all of it. And I deeply regret it. I'm having to go away again, probably very soon. I'm having Beth found and when that happens, I'll go to get her ... of that you have my word. I want the family together again and not forever at the point of destruction. And I fear it will be destroyed if your mother doesn't get some permanent care. I'm going to arrange that, too. But while I'm away I would like you to return home, to stop her drinking herself to death ....'

Peterson was increasingly aware of the difficulty in talking. He swallowed, pulling his hand across his eyes to clear the blurred vision.

'Please Paul,' he stumbled. 'Please help me. There isn't anyone else ....'

Peterson found Lucille slumped in a living-room chair, eyes glassed over. She appeared unaware of his entry. Today she hadn't even bothered to make up and her hair was birds-nested in disarray. The glass had fallen from her hand and lay in her lap, and the dampness was spread across her skirt. Peterson couldn't tell whether she had spilled the contents or wet herself.

He was moving forward to clean her up when the telephone rang. Petrov had welcomed the agreement: he would be in Austria the following day for a second meeting.

Bock was humming as he drove towards his new friend's apartment, feeling a contentment he hadn't known for a long time. Seven months, he reminded himself. Klaus was far nicer than Jurgen — more understanding, too. He did not want to go to the sort of brassy bars or noisy, smoky clubs that had always appealed to Jurgen. It had been Klaus' suggestion that they eat in his apartment tonight, rather than go out anywhere.

Bock stood against the back wall of the elevator, tapping his fingers impatiently against the metalwork. The apartment key was already in his hand when he emerged on the tenth floor.

A meticulous man, Bock had turned to ensure that the apartment door was properly closed behind him and so he had come some way into the room before he realized Klaus was not alone. Bock smiled, nervously. The other two men seemed different from Klaus: with the first twitch of despair, Bock thought they reminded him of officialdom.

'What is it?' he asked, baldly.

The man to Klaus' left grinned, but it was not a pleasant expression. He stretched out, offering something to the Foreign Office official.

'Look at that picture, Otto,' he invited. 'You've got a birthmark on your bum!'

CHAPTER 12

After receiving Petrov's message, Peterson had fixed a tightly scheduled day, intending to leave Andrews airbase in the afternoon. He booked a six a.m. alarm call, but was awake at dawn anyway. It was complete wakefulness, not a gradual arrival of consciousness and he recognized the tension. He was not surprised by it or even concerned; such nervousness was natural, making him properly alert. And he would need to be properly alert, until it was all over. He did not get up immediately, but lay in the comforting warmth of the bed, thinking through the arrangements he had made the previous night and trying to anticipate anything he might have overlooked. The breakfast meeting with the President should be over by nine, which made Langley possible by ten. That gave him the morning to approve Jones' preparations and then, hopefully, enough time to contact Paul before his scheduled departure for Europe.

He had tried twice, after speaking to the White House and then to Jones, to get through to his son. On both occasions, he'd got the answering machine and each time had repeated the plea he had made from the car, just before his arrival home the previous night. Peterson sighed, pushing back the covers; he was unsure what to do if there had been no response from the boy by the time the plane was scheduled to leave.

A quick, precise man, Peterson had an established routine for most things, even his morning toilet. He had showered, shaved and dressed and was packing the first of his three suitcases by the time the alarm call came. He finished packing by six-thirty and went, as he did every morning, to Lucille. The curtains were drawn, darkening the room against almost all the light, so that it was only just possible to isolate the shape of things within the room. She seemed to be sleeping quite easily, with none of the troubled, jerky movements she sometimes had. He started to go

into the room and then stopped. What was the point? For whose
benefit did he make these morning visits, perhaps to cover her
with a displaced sheet or brush away some wisp of hair? It was
certainly not for Lucille, who always remained unaware of him. It
was an act, accepted Peterson — another part of the preparation
that began every day. Abruptly he turned away from his wife's
room, quietly closing the door.

He had his cases in the hallway by the time the maid arrived,
promptly at seven. There was the customary exchange about
Lucille remaining in bed and then a slight extension of the
parrotted conversation when she saw the cases. A brief trip, he
said, wondering if it would be.

He was at the White House by seven-thirty. Fowler was waiting.

'Do you want breakfast?'

'Not really,' said Peterson, gauging the President's reluctance.

Fowler led the way out for another Rose Garden conversation,
listening as intently as he had done on the first occasion to the preparations that Peterson had made for his return to Austria for the
planning meeting with the Russian.

'It's going to be a sizeable operation,' predicted Fowler.

'Yes.'

'We're taking a big chance, ignoring congressional approval.'

I'm taking a big chance, thought Peterson. 'There's really no
other way,' he said.

'Congress won't accept that, if they ever discover what's been
done.'

'Let's hope they don't discover it.'

'Sure you can keep it secure?'

'From whom?' asked Peterson, presciently.

The President nodded at the question. 'Lot of gossip, up on the
Hill.'

'So I've heard.'

'Doesn't make any of this easier for you.'

'No.'

'I want you to know you have my full and complete confidence,'
said Fowler, with his politician's sincerity.

'Thank you, Mr President,' said Peterson. Until it became
political for the man to adopt another stance, he thought. The

President's attitude had forced him into the risk in the first place.

'Tell your deputy I want daily liaison.'

'I will.'

'Who's going to be in overall control?'

'Sir?' queried Peterson.

'Of the operation in Africa,' elaborated Fowler. 'You? Or the Russian?'

'We haven't got to that stage yet,' said Peterson.

'I don't want an American contingent under any Soviet command,' said Fowler.

'No,' accepted Peterson.

'I'm insistent upon this,' said the President.

'We're matching them, operative for operative. The command decisions will be joint, too.'

'How long will you be away this time?'

'I'm unsure,' said Peterson.

'I'll help all I can,' said Fowler. 'Without getting into any actual involvement.'

'I appreciate it,' said Peterson.

'Try not to become distracted by the gossip.'

'I'll try,' said Peterson. Just as he would try not to become distracted at the thought of a wife drinking herself into insanity or a daughter becoming some sort of religious groupie.

'My full confidence, remember.'

'I'll remember.'

Peterson was at Langley earlier than he had expected, but Jones was already there.

'We've got a man who trained to be a priest, one of the highest decorated officers to come out of Vietnam, and a scientist who's worked at Cape Canaveral as well as the Houston Space Center,' reported the deputy, offering the dossiers.

'Sounds impressive.' Jones was proud of his selection, Peterson realized.

'I think it is. Will you brief them?'

Peterson considered the question, calculating the time it would take. If he couldn't raise Paul by telephone, he would have to go either to his apartment or his office.

'No,' he said. 'I'll leave it to you.'

The surprise on the deputy's face was only momentary.

'What did the President say?' asked Jones.

'I had his full support and he'd try to counteract Flood's rumours.'

'Bullshit,' judged Jones.

'Convincingly said though.'

Jones indicated the files on the operatives. 'Shall I tell them it's a joint operation with the Soviet Union?'

'Only the soldier,' decided Peterson. 'He'll have to know, because he's got to select a unit that will be most affected by what's going to happen. The others can wait, until I'm ready.'

Jones picked up one of the folders. 'The man who nearly became a priest is called Henry Blakey,' he said, reading from it. 'I wonder if he'll have any religious objection to impersonation.'

'Override it, if he has,' ordered Peterson. 'I don't care how you do it, but bring him into line if he gets awkward.'

'Nothing fresh from Arizona,' said Jones.

'It's taking a long time.'

'She could have left.'

Paul had said the second letter had been posted four days before, remembered Peterson. 'I don't think so.'

'Lunching?'

Peterson shook his head. 'One or two personal things to settle before the plane,' he said. 'I'll be at Andrews by three. Get me either there or in the car.'

Again there was some indeterminate reaction from Jones. 'What's wrong?' challenged Peterson.

'Wrong?'

'You seem surprised.'

'Nothing. Really,' assured Jones.

Peterson had told his driver to remain at the main entrance. A fine, persistent rain had started, shrouding the countryside in greyness. Peterson shrugged his coat around him, hurrying into the car. Jones had every reason for surprise that he was not personally briefing the people they intended moving into Africa, he reflected as the vehicle moved off. There would be subsequent meetings with all of them, at which the final instructions would be given, but he *should* have conducted the initial interviews.

Personal control, the President had said. Not said — ordered. For the first time he was ignoring an instruction. It seemed he was doing many things for the first time.

Peterson knuckled his eyes, confronting the fact; he had put his family before his commitment to the Agency. To what purpose? Was it possible, really possible, to help Lucille? Or rebuild bridges with Paul? Or recover Beth, from whatever Godforsaken existence into which she had plunged herself? Perhaps Herbert Flood was right. Perhaps he had lost his grip. How Flood would use what he was doing today, just hours before flying off on probably the most important operation to effect America for a decade!

Peterson had never been to his son's office and was bewildered by it. He was used to lawyers working in corporate partnerships with secretary-thronged suites behind glass-fronted, marbled entrances. To reach Paul's room in the clap-board building near the Greyhound bus depot, he had to pass along an uncarpeted corridor from which each door offered a different business: pest control and office cleaning to the left, abortion advice and small stockholder investment advice to the right. There was a sour smell of uncleared garbage, cooking and urine.

Paul occupied what had originally been one room but was now divided into two by a reeded glass partition. Along the wall of the outside section, filing cabinets stood with their drawers half-open. Facing it was a file table and some half-empty library shelves; some back numbers of *Rolling Stone* appeared to occupy one space. There was an unsteady, plywood desk in the centre of the room, holding an old, upright typewriter, a defiant daffodil in a coffee jar and a wire basket no longer able to contain all the papers, which leaked over the edge and on to the table. The girl behind the typewriter was bubble-haired, wore steel-framed spectacles, no make-up and was shapeless beneath layers of jumble-sale clothing.

'Hi,' she said brightly.

Beyond the secretary, Peterson saw Paul talking into the telephone. His son watched him enter, without expression.

'Can I help?' said the girl.

Peterson came back to her. 'I'd like to see my son,' he said politely.

The girl looked from Peterson to Paul and then back to Peterson again.

'Oh,' she said. She seemed embarrassed by Peterson's presence, reaching out to restore the spilled papers into the wire tray. 'Didn't expect you,' she said.

'No.'

She was about to speak again when Paul replaced the telephone. He remained behind his desk, making no effort to get up to greet his father.

'Have you an appointment?' he called, through the half-open door into the second half of the room.

Peterson walked across to it, unwilling to shout over the girl's head.

'I apologized,' he said at the door.

'It was very moving.'

'I meant it.'

'Sure,' said Paul, with his usual disbelief.

'I'm going away,' said Peterson.

'But not to Arizona.'

'No, not to Arizona,' said Peterson. 'But I've had the commune there located. As soon as I'm positive Beth is there, I'll go to get her.'

Paul gazed steadily at him for several moments. 'Yourself?' he said.

'Yes.'

'Christ, I wish I could believe you.'

'I'll get her,' repeated Peterson. 'I give you my word.'

'You have before,' reminded Paul. 'Something more important nearly always comes up.'

'This time it won't.' Was that an undertaking he could keep, Peterson asked himself, worriedly.

'You could have telephoned to tell me,' said Paul.

'I didn't come for that. I came about your mother.'

'She's bad,' accepted Paul. The antagonism had left him.

'I want to give you power of attorney, so that you would be able to authorize any treatment which could become necessary while I'm away.'

Paul frowned. 'What are you talking about?'

'I'm not suggesting that it *will*,' stressed Peterson. 'It's just a precaution.'

'How long will you be away?'

'I don't know.'

'I didn't think she was *that* bad.'

'She's been very much worse, since the disappointment with Beth.'

Paul moved, an uncertain gesture. 'I'm sorry about that,' he said.

It was very difficult for his son to apologize, Peterson realized. Perhaps as difficult as it had been for him to do the same thing.

'It's done now.'

'I gave her no reason to believe that was what you were doing.' said Paul. 'I told her to *stop* her drinking ... for her to realize there wasn't any reason any more. That Beth didn't want to stay away any longer.'

'I know. She doesn't think as clearly as she once did,' said Peterson. Hurriedly, he added, 'Sure Beth wouldn't come home with you?'

Paul took a very worn piece of paper from his inside pocket, frowning down to find the place he wanted. ' "... tell them I'm sorry. Tell Daddy I want him to come and get me ... to come home ...." ' read the younger man.

He offered his father the note. The handwriting was spiked and uneven, completely different from the orderly exercise books Peterson remembered from her bedroom homework. The paper appeared to have been torn from an accounts book; on the reverse side there was a jumble of figures, arranged in a haphazard calculation. The answer was wrong, Peterson saw. It was a very brief letter, but coherent; three paragraphs of apology and then the plea for forgiveness.

'She hasn't called?'

'Not yet,' said Paul.

'Tell her I'm coming,' said Peterson, swallowing heavily. 'When she does, tell her I'm coming.'

'You mean it?'

'I've promised.'

'I'll tell her.'

'Will you take the power of attorney?'

'Do you think it's necessary?'

'Yes.'

Paul nodded, shouting beyond his father for the girl to come into the office. It only took a few minutes to dictate the formalized document and, despite the appearance of the secretary and the typewriter, a perfect copy was produced very quickly. The abortion adviser and the office cleaning manager were summoned as witnesses; from their behaviour, it was obvious it was a regular function for them.

'I hope I won't have to use it,' said Paul.

'So do I,' agreed Peterson. 'If you want to get any message to me, call on the private office number. Walter Jones will pass it on.'

'I couldn't know where you're going to call direct?'

Peterson shook his head. 'I'll be contacted faster through the Agency.'

'Wouldn't it be nice,' said Paul, distantly.

'What?'

'To be a family again.'

'We're going to be,' said Peterson fervently. 'Believe me, Paul, it's going to happen!'

Walter Jones felt exhausted but happy: it was unfortunate that Peterson had not conducted the briefings personally, to have appreciated how good the choices had been. Jones had attempted to remain quite objective — critical even, to identify any doubts or problems now rather than later, when it would be too late. Each had conducted himself far better than the Deputy Director had hoped. Of the three, Jones had been most impressed with Michael Bohler which is how it should have been, because Bohler's was to be the most difficult part in the proposed operation. The security file assembled without Bohler's knowledge had commented quite a lot upon the man's sexual activity and it was easy to see why he had so much success with women. Blond, fair-skinned, yet without the bulk that so often marked people of German heritage, Bohler had an utterly misleading ambiance of helplessness about him, which Jones knew many women found attractive. He supposed a psychiatrist would call it a mothering complex. But there had been no helplessness when it came to the man's ability. When there had been questions, he had shown the concern Jones had anticipated as appropriate, yet not a nervousness he would have judged as dangerous. There had been a separate, technical interview before his encounter with Bohler and from the report of the experts, Jones noted that no gaps had been found in the man's knowledge.

Henry Blakey's hesitation at impersonating a priest had been predictable from someone who had spent six years in a seminary and Jones had not worried about the initial objections. He had prepared his argument, stressing that the dangers could run as high as another Middle East war and a confrontation between the US and the Soviet Union, and gradually Blakey had lost his reluctance. The regret would not be a hindrance in what he was being called upon to do.

Jones had expected less questioning from Bradley. Even though a colonel, the man was used to military discipline and the acceptance of orders from superior officers. The shocked, near-angry response to the announcement that he was expected to work with a Soviet penetration force was as predictable as Henry Blakey's instinctive objection to passing himself off as a priest. Throughout a military career spanning more than two decades, Bradley had been conditioned to regard Communism as the creed of the enemy. Any reaction other than outrage would have been unnatural. Once the surprise had passed, every argument that Bradley had put forward had been constructive. The man had insisted upon the need for joint training and stressed the difficulty of split command and communication, operating in two languages. It had been the longest of the three meetings, but Jones had anticipated that, too. He was satisfied Bradley had left the room as committed as either Bohler or Blakey.

He checked his watch, calculating that Peterson had been airborne for two hours. Knowing the wavelength of the CIA plane to be secure, he didn't bother to cipher the message; to anyone else it was meaningless anyway. 'All absolutely satisfactory,' Jones cabled. He wondered if Peterson had yet consulted the dossiers that had been made available upon the aircraft.

The private telephone had an unlisted number and did not pass through the switchboard; few people had access to it. When it rang, Jones looked at it in momentary surprise.

'Walter Jones?'

'Yes,' said the deputy. 'Who is this?'

'Flood,' said the caller. 'Herbert Flood.'

CHAPTER 13

When the idea had come to him, Peterson had hesitated, wondering if the Russian would become irritated or even suspicious at the theatricality of the meeting spot, but Petrov had accepted without any objection. When Peterson entered the Volksprater, Petrov was already there, waiting. Peterson was purposely late, to give his photographers the opportunity of picturing the Russian with the funfair background.

'Traffic,' apologized the American. 'I'm very sorry.'

Petrov shrugged. 'They made a film here once,' he said. '*The Third Man*. It was very good.'

'I know,' said Peterson. He set out towards the booths and the Russian fell into step beside him.

'I'm glad we're going to work together,' said Petrov.

'I hope it's successful,' said Peterson. And he *did*, he decided. He wouldn't enjoy exposing the Russian if things went wrong. He wondered how the Irena file was progressing.

'It will need very detailed planning.'

'Yes.'

'And complete liaison.'

'Of course.'

They hesitated near the giant ferris wheel; Petrov was perfectly silhouetted.

'It used to be the biggest wheel in the world,' said the Russian, staring up. 'That was in the film, too.'

Peterson wondered if his surveillance had been identified; there seemed the vaguest trace of mockery in the Russian's attitude.

Petrov turned away from the attraction to face the other man fully. 'If it stands any chance of working, we're going to have to trust each other,' he said. 'Any suspicion we feel will permeate down to whoever we put into the field. And that will make it impossible.'

'You're right,' said Peterson. Petrov *was* suspicious. Quickly he continued, 'I was honest with you at the restaurant. If things go wrong, I might try to turn the relationship to my advantage, if I think it necessary to do so. And I accept that you will attempt to do the same. But until that moment, which I hope to God never arises, I'll work openly with you.'

'No cameras?' demanded the Russian.

'No cameras.'

'No tapes?'

'No tapes.'

Petrov offered his hand upon the agreement. He gazed beyond Peterson into the crowd. 'It'll free a lot of people from rather boring surveillance,' he said. It was an assured smile this time.

'Same as the restaurant?' queried Peterson.

'Of course,' admitted Petrov. 'In many ways, I've more to lose than you.'

'I think the danger is about equal,' said Peterson.

They began walking between the booths again. There was the smell of open air sausage cooking and children scurried between them; they had green tabs upon their lapels and Peterson guessed they were part of an organized school party. He couldn't remember having taken Paul and Beth to a fair. He supposed he must have done sometime.

'Have you discovered a way to infiltrate the installation?' asked Peterson.

'Not completely,' said Petrov. 'Maybe three or four days.'

'How?'

'We've found a homosexual in the West German Defence Ministry computer room,' said Petrov. 'His clearance is sufficiently high for him to have access to all the programmes. And to use any cross link between that and the computer that BADRA use.'

At that moment, Peterson realized that he was being forced into a subservient role. 'He could introduce biographies of both our people?' he anticipated.

Petrov nodded. 'And then we can send them to Chad as government officials, secure from any official enquiry from the complex. And intercept any checks made upon them.'

'Will he do it?'

Petrov seemed amused at the doubt. 'We've softened him just sufficiently,' he said. 'Do you have a scientist?'

'Already selected,' said the American. 'German-speaking, of course. You?'

'Her name is Gerda Lintz; she's a brilliant physicist.'

'A woman?' queried Paterson.

Petrov smiled sideways. 'In the Soviet Union we arrived at the equality of sexes a little earlier than the West,' he said. 'We put one in space, remember?'

'It isn't a Russian name.'

'She's German-born; that's why I've selected her.'

'I think field back-up is essential, despite the people I've already lost,' said Peterson.

'Of course.'

'I thought ten.'

'That would be about right,' agreed Petrov. He recalled the uncompromising face of Oleg 'Sharakov. 'I think there's going to be a problem of command here,' he said.

'I couldn't put a company of American soldiers under Soviet control,' said Peterson.

'Nor could I agree to American supremacy.'

'We'll have to brief them very thoroughly.'

'No matter how thorough, there'll still be difficulties,' predicted the Russian. 'An army unit can't be commanded by committee.'

'On this occasion it will have to be.'

'We'll have to retain tight control from outside,' said Petrov.

'That won't be easy.'

'More difficult for me than for you,' said the Russian. 'We don't have any countries in the area sufficiently friendly to allow the sort of access I'd need.'

'I wasn't thinking about a country,' said Peterson, moving quickly to secure the advantage for himself.

'What then?'

'A ship,' said Peterson. 'We'll need some fairly sophisticated electronics.'

Petrov appeared to consider the suggestion. 'If you were established in the Gulf of Guinea,' he said, debating the idea with himself, 'I could keep in contact from Odessa. We've a large communication centre there, to monitor the Mediterranean.'

This would give *him* command status, realized Peterson, with a sudden flare of excitement. The President would see it as a positive coup.

'It would seem a good enough arrangement,' said Peterson. He tried to make it sound insignificant.

'Could you put a vessel there?' said Petrov.

'Yes,' said Peterson. Petrov hadn't realized, thought the American.

'Let's agree upon that as the communication link,' said Petrov. As he spoke, the Russian turned, and for a moment Peterson thought he had belatedly realized the concession and was going to change his mind. Instead Petrov shook his head very slightly and said nothing.

They came to the end of the avenue of booths and turned left along an intersection. There was a sudden snap of firing from a shooting gallery and Peterson jumped involuntarily. He quickly looked sideways at Petrov, embarrassed at such a reaction among so much noise. The Russian appeared not to have noticed.

'Is that all you're thinking of — a deep penetration unit and someone inside the complex?' asked Peterson, wanting to move the conversation on.

Petrov turned to him again. 'What else?' he said.

Peterson hesitated, feeling another bubble of satisfaction, this time at being able to improve upon the planning. He tried to curb it, cautious of over-confidence. It was going extremely well. Patiently he explained the witchcraft symbols that Williams had discovered and the idea of introducing a phoney priest into the area.

'That's good,' said Petrov immediately. 'That's very good.'

The supremacy had switched, Peterson decided: he was leading the planning now.

'You've got a man?' queried Petrov.

'Yes. He trained for several years to be a priest, before joining the Agency. Will you be able to find someone?'

'Of course,' said Petrov, immediately. He seemed to realize the quickness of his reply and smiled again, awkwardly this time. 'But I'd have difficulty in providing the proper cover,' he admitted.

'There's a Catholic charity which the Agency completely supports financially,' said Peterson. 'Cover will be easy.'

'Between us,' said Petrov, reflectively, 'we control a very impressive degree of expertise.'

'And power,' expanded Peterson. 'It's a thought that might upset some people in my administration.'

'And certainly within mine,' said Petrov, remembering Litvinov. It was almost time to seek protection and inform the Politburo. It wouldn't be an easy encounter.

Petrov stopped again, facing the American.

'If everything works, I want to reach an undertaking with you,' he said.

'What?' asked Peterson.

'All records of this association destroyed.'

Peterson gazed at the other man. 'You'd trust me, to provide everything?'

'You'd have to trust me. We've both of us gone too far now to be completely safe.'

'Agreed,' said Peterson. 'I'll make everything available.'

'I give you my word, in return,' said Petrov, sincerely.

Petrov didn't mean it, Peterson knew. Any more than he did.

'BADRA are receiving a gold transfer tomorrow,' disclosed Peterson. 'In Zürich.'

'You intercepting?'

'The Israelis.'

'Would there be any point in exposing the interception, so that the Jews were seized?' suggested Petrov.

Peterson considered the idea, gauging the advantages. 'We've no reason at the moment to draw attention away from ourselves,' he said. 'Surely better to let it go ahead and create some confusion in Libya and Chad.'

'Gadaffi will replace it easily enough.'

'But it will make them nervous.'

'You're right,' accepted Petrov. 'Let's not interfere.'

They came to the big wheel again and once more Petrov stopped, gazing up. 'I've never been on a thing like that,' he said.

'It's boring, I believe,' said Peterson.

'There would be a marvellous view of Vienna.' He turned to the

American. 'Why not?' he said, grinning.

Even though he saw it as another advantage, Peterson still felt self-conscious following the Russian into one of the glass booths. If there was a need to use the photograph later, they could erase his presence from it, Peterson thought, as the attendant secured the safety bar across their laps. It shuddered upwards, swinging upon the pivots as other cars were filled behind them. As they got higher, Peterson stared around, identifying St Stephan's cathedral and the Schönbrunn palace in the old part of the city, and nearer at hand the Nazi-built anti-aircraft tower in the Augarten which had defied all city attempts at destruction.

'My God,' said Petrov. 'If my people could see me now!'

They might, thought Peterson.

'What about briefings?' said Petrov, turning back inside the cabin.

'We maintain safe houses here in Vienna,' said Peterson.

'We have one nearby, at Melk.'

'Why don't we alternate?'

'Fine,' agreed Petrov.

Unexpectedly, the wheel stopped at the very apex of the turn and the booth swung back and forth again.

'In the film,' said Petrov, 'Harry Lime threatened to kill his friend, just about now.'

'I remember.'

'But he didn't. And then later the friend killed him.'

'I hope we haven't made a mistake,' said Peterson.

'So do I.'

The wheel heaved into motion and they began going down to earth again. He'd achieved a lot, Peterson decided.

Otto Bock hunched in the window seat of the apartment, hands clutched around his body, as if he were in physical pain. He was perspiring but still felt cold. He shivered, unwilling to return to the bedroom for a robe. He knew the danger had always been there, but never imagined that it could happen to him; to other people, perhaps, but never to him. The self-pity swept over him. It wasn't fair. He'd done nothing wrong, nothing to be ashamed of.

He hadn't hurt anyone, not like Jurgen had hurt him. Or caused any embarrassment or scandal. He tried to quieten himself, to rationalize the problem. It could be worse, he supposed. There could have been money demands, which he couldn't have met. Or the request for classified documents, which would inevitably have led to his detection and arrest. He supposed the computer details were secret, but he didn't think of them in the same way as papers.

There had to be a dozen people, maybe more, with clearance as high as his; there would be no way that what those dreadful men wanted him to do could be traced back to him, once he had done it. He had no choice, Bock realized. If he didn't want his job and his family destroyed, he would have to do what they told him. The shivering increased and he began to cry, his shoulders heaving with the sobs. Because of the weeping, he didn't hear Gretal enter the room; she was behind him, with her hand against his back, before he knew of her presence. He jumped, at first startled and then annoyed.

'What is it?' she said.

'Nothing.' He didn't have a handkerchief so he tried to dry his face in the sleeve of his pyjamas.

'You're crying.'

'No.'

'You are,' she insisted. 'What's the matter? Are you ill?'

'I said it's nothing!'

'Shall I get a doctor?'

'Leave me alone.'

'Come back to bed.'

'I don't want your bed.'

'I didn't mean that,' she said pointedly.

He started to cry again, careless of her knowing. Why did it have to be him? Why couldn't it have happened to somebody else?

CHAPTER 14

Israel apportions a third of its annual budget to defence expenditure and therefore regards the holding of a substantial secret, foreign bank account which denies income to the country not only as illegal but almost traitorous. Accordingly they give their currency control inspectors wide ranging powers. They work closely with the Mossad, hence David Levy's knowledge of the illegal Zürich account of Menachai Levitsky. Head of one of the country's leading diamond firms, Levitsky travelled extensively, both to South Africa which supplied the uncut stones and to Europe and America, which purchased the finished, polished products. Frequently the transactions were in cash and unrecorded. This made it difficult for an accurate official check on his exact income and therefore comparatively easy for the establishment of the Zürich account. But despite pressure from the control commission, Levy had refused to make any move against Levitsky. Instead he had used his superior authority to prevent any prosecution whatsoever. Unlike his government, Levy looked for an advantage beyond monetary income and realized he had found it even while he had been sitting in Peterson's office, learning of the gold transfer from Libya to BADRA. Within an hour, from the communications room at the Israeli embassy in Washington, he had initiated a check upon Levitsky's whereabouts and when the reply came, almost immediately, uttered a silent prayer to his continuing good fortune. Levitsky was on a trade mission to the United States, using a ninth-floor suite at the Waldorf Astoria as an office. It had only taken a further hour to have Jerusalem telex the full details of Levitsky's operation and by mid-afternoon, Levy was in central Manhattan, accompanied by four other Mossad operatives, two of whom were his personal bodyguards. Levy, a consummate professional, had decided upon his approach before encountering the diamond merchant. And immediately he saw Levitsky he knew it to be the correct one. Levitsky was a soft, crinkle-haired man who wore three diamond rings, a cologne which perfumed the room and had an ego to match his portly, six-foot figure. His outraged protests at the accusation were irritatingly rehearsed and Levy bullied him into collapse, shouting details of the $350,000 account into the man's face and then reciting the penalties that existed if he appeared before an Israeli court. Levitsky, who was not a fool, recognized the qualifications through his fear and eagerly demanded the compromise.

The sums of money in which Levitsky habitually dealt meant that it was quite common for him to use after-hours banking facilities, and the Manhattan branch of the Credit Suisse had already alerted Zürich when they arrived at the branch. Because the instructions came from New York and were verified on the telex machine by the name and personal number of the American assistant manager, there was no query from the Swiss headquarters. At the very moment when Levitsky's orders began to be received in the Credit Suisse cable room, the three agents whom Levy had ordered into Switzerland before leaving Washington and upon whose presence Levitsky was insisting at all stages of the gold shipment, were arriving in Zürich. Another of Levy's Washington messages had activated the Israeli embassy in Berne, so the account at the Swiss Banking Corporation to which Levitsky was making his transfer had been opened by the time the Credit Suisse enquired.

Shortly after Levy had escorted the diamond merchant back to the Waldorf Astoria the telephone call came from the operatives in Zürich, confirming that the Banking Corporation had accepted the instructions of the Berne depositor and those of Menachai Levitsky to allow the three observers to accompany the shipment to their vaults.

'Thank you for your co-operation,' Levy said, moving with his companions to leave the diamond merchant.

Levitsky blinked, still unaware of the use to which he had been put. 'I've transferred a quarter of a million dollars' worth of gold to an account that isn't mine,' he said. All the ego was gone, but it was still a muted protest.

'I know,' said Levy.

'But ... .'

'Which still leaves you a hundred thousand in the Credit Suisse account.'

'What will happen to the quarter of a million?'

'It's a fine without the necessity of a court appearance,' said Levy, lightly. 'It'll be transferred to Israel within a few days.'

'And that's the end of it?'

'That's the end of it,' confirmed Levy. 'Look upon it as summary justice and be thankful I let you keep something: I could have taken it all.'

Levy managed the early evening Swissair flight to Zürich. Aware that there would be little opportunity for rest in the coming thirty-six hours, he gave instructions against being disturbed, said he wanted no food and slept the seven-hour flight quite dreamlessly. The three men he had already established in Zürich were personally known to him, and he was confident that while accompanying Levitsky's transfer they would have acquainted themselves fully with the type of vehicle used, the security precautions adopted, the route followed and established the best place for interception.

It was dawn when Levy arrived in Switzerland. He got immediate diplomatic clearance and was at the Baur au Lac before it was properly light. The three men who had accompanied the gold shipment had been joined by a commando squad of thirty and the grenades, plastic explosive, radios and weapons which had been brought into the country in diplomatic bags had already been moved from Berne.

Levy split the commandos into units of ten, so that only the leaders were necessary in his suite, thus reducing the possibility of curiosity from the hotel staff.

The men who had been in Levitsky's bullion van had drawn duplicate maps of the route and established — from seemingly casual conversation with the Swiss Banking Corporation guards — that it was the one normally used. So rare was any attempted robbery that it was not considered necessary to vary the route. Levy noted the complacency and marked it as a factor in their favour. The normal journey was parallel with the lake's

Seefeld Quai along Bellerivestrasse, right into the one-way system in Ramistrasse at Bellevue Place, left and beneath the funicular railway on to Seiler Grabendstrasse and from there left again into Stampfenbackstrasse. The driver and front seat guard were secured in their bullet-proofed, wire-meshed cabs by a lock operated within the body of the van by the second guard. All carried pistols. There was a shotgun in the cab and another at the rear. In addition, shotguns were permanently mounted over the two rear wheels, to shoot out the tyres if anyone gained admission to the cab and attempted to drive it off. There were two independent radio systems, one medium, one long wave. Levy's men had obtained the transmission wavelength of each. They had also learned that the Swiss Banking Corporation open their bullion vaults twice a day, once just after eleven and again just before three.

'Good,' praised Levy. 'Very good indeed.'

He travelled the route twice in one of the four cars that had already been hired, then returned to the hotel for the final planning session. He ordered two more cars and two heavy duty vans, identical in colour and make. By eight a.m. squads had gone to the railway station bordering the River Sihl and to the tourist information centre at the Hauptbahnhof. Both carried smoke devices, plastic explosive charges and radios. By nine a.m. further groups were in readiness outside the Bank of Libya and the Swiss Banking Corporation in Paradeplatz and the main assault force was prepared to move towards the Kreuzstrasse intersection with Bellerivestrasse. At ten a.m. the Swiss Foreign Ministry received a routine application from the Israeli embassy in Berne to fly a Boeing 727 under diplomatic clearance from Zürich airport sometime during the afternoon; the agreement was given just as routinely.

There was no movement in the morning. Levy chafed at the delay, knowing it risked taking the edge off the readiness of his men. He occupied the time going to every squad, checking them personally, finding miniscule errors and criticizing them for it, wanting them to become irritated with him: it only needed one section to become complacent and the whole operation was endangered.

The bullion van set out for collection a little after one-thirty. Within ten minutes, every unit was notified. The van arrived at the Libyan bank promptly at one-fifty. A group of bank employees and guards was already waiting expectantly at the side entrance in an alleyway which could be completely secured by placing men at either end. The gold was packed in wooden crates, each fitted with rope handles. It was moved into the van on trolleys, ten boxes at a time.

Because of the earlier reconnoitering and their awareness of the route the driver was likely to take on the return journey, Levy was able to estimate to within three minutes the time the van would travel along Bellerivestrasse, parallel to the lake. He was two minutes out. Just before two-thirty one of the vans pulled out in front of the bullion truck and was separated from it only by another Israeli occupied car.

At that moment, Levy radioed instructions to the squads at the railway station and the tourist office. The railway station explosions were the more spectacular. The Israelis had placed one timed charge in a waiting-room and two people died when it erupted. A second ripped up the main Zürich-to-Geneva track, derailing a commuter train but fortunately causing no injuries beyond shock and minor cuts from broken glass. The third destroyed the signalling equipment for the entire station, producing a chaos that was to take almost ten hours to rectify. At the moment of the first explosion, the squad let off five smoke devices and then wrapped the red and white spotted kiffeya head-dress of Arab guerillas around their heads and ran screaming through the station concourse, firing the Uzzi machine-guns harmlessly into the air. They gained their waiting Mercedes quite uninterrupted and escaped without any interference.

Three people died in the tourist office explosion, one, ironically, a Jewish woman enquiring about return flights to Tel Aviv. The whole front shattered under the force of the blast and a gas main burst and then ignited, sending a spurt of flame twelve feet into the air and causing far more of a distraction than Levy had planned. The smoke was hardly necessary, but they released it anyway, causing traffic confusion immediately

Two Israeli cars were following the bullion truck. Four hundred yards from the Kreuzstrasse junction, one of them pulled out as if to overtake and the vehicle in front swung wide, apparently to prevent it. The second car braked at the moment of impact, expertly bringing the rear across the road, blocking it completely. Both drivers maintained the pressure upon their accelerators, so that the wings ground one against the other with a screeching, tearing sound of metal, locking both cars together. Immediately the drivers leapt from their cars and began a hysterical dispute.

The hired van preceding the bullion truck had been warned in advance by radio, so the stall was timed perfectly to coincide with the fake accident. The following Israeli car halted and the front-seat occupants got out, apparently to investigate. The bullion van had to stop as well. There were two Israelis still in the rear of the car, electronic jamming equipment unseen at their feet. Even before the bank guards imagined a need to use either, both their emergency radio frequencies were unusable.

The motorists wandered back from the stalled van, shrugging to the occupants of the bank vehicle in an invitation for patience.

The explosive devices had been developed by Israeli scientists to combat aircraft hijacking, particularly if the terrorist had locked himself somewhere within a plane. The effect was of an implosion, reverberating shock waves within a confined space and reducing anyone inside senseless. The grenade which the car driver placed against the cab window went off seconds ahead of the one which his companion placed against the rear of the van to incapacitate the unseen guard.

The van was already reversing, sweeping wide in the empty road and then coming up back to back with the bullion van. It stopped three feet away, but the opening of the doors prevented anyone on either Seefeld or Uto Quai seeing the oxy-acetylene equipment flare into life and then start cutting into the bullion door. It would have been difficult for the Zürich authorities to have responded, because by now they were convinced of a concerted terrorist attack. Every available policeman, ambulance and fire brigade appliance had been drafted to the area of the railway station and tourist office, and reinforcements were summoned by road from Winterthur and Wodenswil and by helicopter from Berne and Geneva.

The interior guard was recovering by the time the doors were opened, but he was still too disorientated to offer any resistance, even against the injection which was administered by the first Israeli to enter the vehicle and which rendered him unconscious for a further three hours. The same Israeli unlocked the front cab and the two guards there were injected, even though they were still unconscious.

Aware of the weight of gold, Levy had put eight men inside the van. They placed a roller track between the two vehicles and slid the gold across in hurried, one-to-the-other unison. The bullion was cleared in eight minutes. At the radioed alert, the arguing motorists four hundred yards away suddenly stopped shouting and sprinted towards the ambush. The decoy van emerged from Seefeld Quai, just as the vehicle containing the gold moved away. It crashed into the rear of the bullion van, causing a further obstruction. More smoke was released giving the impression of fire. The driver joined the motorists in the waiting car and drove unhurriedly up Kreuzstrasse and then right into Seefeldstrasse, keeping the gold van just in sight. They went straight to the airport, where Levy was waiting with the Israeli embassy customs clearance for the cargo.

By five p.m. it was loaded aboard the Boeing 727 and half an hour later the aircraft was cleared for take-off. Forty-five minutes earlier, responding to the alarm raised by the Swiss Banking Corporation, a police motorcyclist had managed to penetrate the congestion around the lake and discover the looted bullion truck. It was a further two hours before the size of the robbery was realized and sufficient police and forensic scientists could be moved to the scene. By then, the Boeing was clearing Italian airspace and in beacon contact with Tel Aviv.

Levy had already held a mid-air debriefing, congratulating the men on the complete success of the operation and now he sat in the first-class section of the aircraft, reflecting upon what had happened. It had been a very productive forty-eight hours, he decided; more than $20,000,000 into the Israeli exchequer.

Peterson had offered him the gold shipment as a sop, Levy knew. He wondered if the American Director would imagine he was content to remain on the periphery. He had always regarded

Peterson as astute: it would be a surprising error for such a man to make.

They ate at Duke Zeibert's. It was Wednesday and Herbert Flood was on the Scarsdale diet, so he ordered lamb. Jones, who was uninterested in food, took the same.

'I find weight's a problem in Washington,' confided Flood. 'A lot of good parties.'

'I don't go to many,' said Jones. The foreign affairs adviser intrigued him; it was difficult to believe there was so much ambition beneath that untidy, everyone's-favourite-uncle exterior.

'Should do,' advised Flood. 'Important to be seen around.'

'I'm not a politician,' reminded Jones.

'Nor am I,' said Flood. The inference was very clear that the omission was only temporary.

The diet denied Flood alcohol, but Jones had ordered scotch. He was aware of Flood studying him as he drank.

'That's another problem,' said Flood. 'Booze.'

'Hardly confined to Washington,' said the Deputy Director.

'Far too much drinking goes on,' insisted the former academic.

'You're probably right.'

'You're not seen around much,' said Flood and the deputy CIA director realized a check had been made upon him; he was irritated that he had not discovered it.

'I'm not particularly interested in the social scene,' he said.

'You're not married?'

'No.' It had been a very thorough check, Jones appreciated.

'Lonely life then?'

'Not really.' Jones wondered if Flood was trying to run a check on his sex life.

'How do you spend your spare time then?'

'Easily enough,' said the deputy intelligence chief. 'I read a great deal. I like opera, so I go to concerts. And I do my job; I don't work nine to five hours, you know.'

'Doesn't Washington excite you?' demanded Flood, in sudden urgency. He fashioned a cornucopia with his hand. 'It's all here,' he said. 'All the power.'

'I haven't thought about it,' said Jones, unhelpfully.

'You should,' urged Flood. 'With the proper ability and the right friends, it's possible to do very well here.'

'So I've heard.' Jones wondered if he was annoying the other man with his platitudinous replies.

'This Africa business is disturbing,' said Flood. 'It could create a lot of problems.'

'We're fairly confident we'll be able to contain it,' said Jones.

'*Fairly* confident isn't good enough,' said Flood. 'The President wants positive assurances.'

'I'm hopeful the Director will be able to give them, very soon.'

'Are you?' challenged Flood.

'Yes.'

'He's had a lot of time, already.'

'It hasn't been easy.'

'I hear suggestions that Peterson has got some domestic problems.'

'No more than most people.'

'That's not what I hear.'

'It's not affecting his work,' said Jones, loyally.

'I've never believed it possible for people to secure themselves in water-tight compartments, divorcing their private from their public life.'

'I suppose it's a matter of opinion,' said Jones, carelessly.

'With Peterson it's becoming a matter of record,' said Flood. 'I'm not impressed so far. Not impressed at all.'

Jones deliberately ordered cheesecake with whipped topping for dessert, hoping to irritate the other man. Flood refused everything but coffee.

'I'm sure the President will be satisfied in the end,' said Jones. The snub that it was the President and not Flood who had to be impressed was very obvious, but the foreign affairs adviser made no response.

'I think you've got the proper ability,' said Flood, picking up his earlier point. 'I think you could do with the right friends.'

'To achieve what?'

'A position to which you might be better suited than someone else.'

'I'm satisfied, the way things are.'

'You should never be satisfied in Washington; this place is fuelled by ambition.'

Jones pushed aside the dessert half-eaten; he hadn't enjoyed it and recognized it now as a juvenile gesture.

'Yes,' the deputy CIA director agreed. 'It's certainly that.'

'It's something more,' said Flood.

'What?'

'No place for losers.'

'No.'

'It's very dangerous, to become associated with losers.'

'I wouldn't know,' said Jones. 'I've never been linked with any.'

'There's a chance of it happening now.'

'Isn't that a premature judgement?'

'I don't know,' said Flood. 'You tell me.'

'I don't think so.'

'I wonder if Peterson would be as loyal to you.'

So did he, thought Jones. Immediately he became irritated at the doubt. Of course Peterson would have supported him.

'Don't screw your chances, Walt,' advised Flood.

Jones registered the Christian-name attempt and smiled, and the other man misunderstood the expression.

'Ours could be a very beneficial association,' said Flood. 'I could offer you a lot of administrative protection.'

'What could I offer in return?' He was still manipulating the other man, Jones told himself. He didn't mean any disloyalty to Peterson.

'What could the CIA offer!' said Flood, stressing the incredulity. 'I'm sure we could find something.'

A politician with the expertise and knowledge of the CIA at his disposal would be a very formidable figure in the capital, accepted Jones.

'It's been a very pleasant lunch,' he said. 'Thank you.'

'And an interesting one?'

'Yes, interesting too.'

'You should try the Scarsdale diet,' encouraged Flood, rising from the table. 'I've lost ten pounds and I've hardly entered the second week.'

'I don't seem to find the need to diet,' said Jones. 'I think I lose all my weight in nervous energy.'

'What have you got to be nervous about?' asked Flood at the door.

'Nothing, I hope,' said Jones.

CHAPTER 15

The monastery dominates Melk, an enormous, many-storeyed rectangle of a building, with outcrops of unexpected construction added haphazardly, so that courtyards and entrance areas jut out, like architectural potholes. Peterson frowned up at it as they drove by, momentarily awed by its size; a container for clerics, he thought.

'Quite a building.'

Peterson looked away at the assessment, towards Michael Bohler: they had been together less than two hours but already he was impressed. He'd made a note to congratulate Walter Jones upon the selection during their telephone conversation that night.

'Yes,' agreed Peterson. 'Quite a building.'

'Not much further then?'

'No,' said the Director. 'The Russian house is very near. Nervous?'

'Very,' admitted Bohler.

Peterson respected him for the honesty. 'It's right that you should be.'

Bohler talked looking down into his lap, almost as if he were reminiscing. 'I've often wondered how I would feel upon an assignment ... whether I'd be frightened or able to do what was asked of me. But I never conceived an operation in which I would be linked with a Russian.'

'It's not normal,' said Peterson. 'The circumstances demand it.'

'Are they prepared to co-operate ... as you are?'

'I think so,' said Peterson.

'Have you met her?' asked Bohler.

'No,' said Peterson. 'Just photographs. And the case records, of course. I've made yours available to them.'

'Are these the records I've seen?'

Peterson nodded.

'She looks a very severe woman,' said the scientist.

'Russians often do,' said Peterson. 'It's a national characteristic.'

'She appears highly qualified.'

'So are you. That's why you were chosen.'

'I hope I don't fail you,' said Bohler.

'So do I.'

Bohler grinned at the Director's response. 'I mean I'm not really a CIA agent ... not a proper one. I'm a little nervous I might not do the right thing.'

Peterson was not worried by the other man's hesitation. Indeed, he welcomed it: he had always been deeply suspicious of operatives who disdained danger and offered as many assurances as were demanded of them.

'If there'd been any doubt,' he said, trying to sound reassuring, 'you wouldn't have been selected.'

'That's not strictly true,' said Bohler and Peterson turned to him again, intrigued at someone who was prepared to argue so openly with him.

'What do you mean?'

'I'm the only one,' said Bohler, without any conceit. 'I know that. That's *why* I've been chosen: that's the extent of my ability.'

'You're very objective.'

'Isn't that how I should be?'

'Yes,' conceded Peterson. He decided that Bohler looked younger than his thirty-five years.

He was surprised to realize that it was someone like Bohler he had always imagined Beth marrying. He wondered whether she was still in Arizona.

The limousine skirted the monastery and came to a house so close that it could have been an outbuilding. It was well chosen, Peterson recognized. It was at the conjuction of two roads, with a view at least three hundred yards along each of them. There was open farmland on three sides, with sweeping fields upon which helicopters could have landed and taken off in an emergency without encumbrance.

'We're here,' anticipated Bohler.

'Yes.'

Petrov appeared at the doorway as they got out of the vehicle and Peterson was reminded of how the Russian had conducted their first meeting at the restaurant; once again Petrov had cast himself in the role of the solicitous host. Peterson turned sideways to the younger man. Bohler was staring at the Russian, but the expression was one of curiosity, not intimidation. Peterson realized that since they had been together, Bohler had shown him just the appropriate amount of respect; there had been no sycophancy.

'He doesn't look like a Russian,' said Bohler.

'No,' agreed Peterson.

'More like the sort of Englishman Hollywood was casting as a typical butler in those 1940 movies.'

Peterson smiled at the description. 'A very imposing butler,' he said.

'But still a butler.'

As they entered the garden, Peterson became aware of more vehicles and felt a momentary hollowness at the thought that, for the first time, he was about to enter a place that was entirely Russian-controlled. As if aware of the American's feeling, Petrov said, 'We're well protected. Both of us.'

'General Dimitri Petrov,' introduced Peterson. 'This is Michael Bohler.'

Immediately the American scientist thrust out his hand and Petrov gazed at it, unused to such familiarity. The hesitation was only momentary; he returned the greeting, gazing curiously over the younger man's shoulder to the CIA Director.

'Shall we go in?' the Russian invited.

It was dark inside the building and briefly Peterson found it difficult to focus. There was a short corridor leading into a main room. The furnishings were functional but limited — a table around which were grouped six chairs, a couch against the wall beneath the main window, a side table upon which were arranged bottles, glasses and a tray of food and two chairs bordering a fireplace. There was no fire and the house was cold; involuntarily, Peterson shivered. Petrov led the way forward, surer of his surroundings, and as he became adjusted to the room, Peterson saw that the woman was already there. She was standing by the fireplace, away from the window, so it was difficult to distinguish her features. She appeared to be standing stiffly, almost to attention. Peterson wondered if it was nervousness at what was being asked of her or uncertainty at being in the presence of her Director. At this stage it was more likely to be uncertainty, he decided; until they got to Africa, it would be difficult for either of them to foresee the difficulties. Petrov motioned the woman away from where she stood and she came towards the centre of the room.

'Gerda Lintz,' announced the Russian.

Peterson nodded, but once again Bohler reached out. The woman's falter was more marked than Petrov's had been: she started looking sideways, as if seeking some guidance, but Bohler spoke before she completed the movement.

'We're going to have to be friends,' he said.

She took his hand at last and although it was difficult to be sure, Peterson thought she was blushing.

'Let's sit down,' said Petrov.

'Your file is impressive,' said Petrov, speaking to Bohler.

'Thank you,' said the American. He looked towards the woman. 'It must have been fascinating, working upon your Cosmos series,' he said.

'Roughly comparable to your Vela programme,' she said. She had a soft voice and Peterson wondered if there were the trace of a lisp; would her German be as fluent as her English?

'We don't designate by that name any more,' said Bohler. 'Now it's a number reference.'

'We never used Cosmos as a programme identity.'

Peterson and Petrov remained silent, both aware that the two scientists were testing each other out, like prize fighters at the beginning of a bout.

'The test firing indicates preparedness for a launch,' said Gerda.

'Yes,' said Bohler. He spoke quickly, to anticipate her point: 'So it can't have been a normal research programme.'

'An established rocket, then?'

'That's the only inference. From the silo scorching, it must be solid fuel.'

'Isn't that the tendency among smaller rockets, with the development of new plastic-base compounds?' asked the woman, eager to score.

'We don't know the size of this rocket,' reminded Bohler, 'nor the stage of the technology within the installation.'

'High, I would have guessed,' said Gerda.

'It could be hybrid-engined then,' said Bohler. 'In America we've developed an engine working off liquid fluorine-oxygen oxidant mounted above a cylinder of lithium, lithium hydride and polybutadiene solid propellant, with the combustion chamber at the lower end.'

'With stop-start capability?' asked the woman curiously.

'Yes,' said Bohler. 'We can also vary the thrust by using a throttle to control the supply of oxidant flowing from the tank to the solid fuel.'

It was becoming ridiculously dark within the room. 'Couldn't we have some light?' complained Peterson, anxious to see the Russian scientist more clearly. Petrov made a movement with his hand and Peterson became aware for the first time of attendants in the room. A man pulled the curtains and then put on a series of side lights.

'There are drinks,' said Petrov, 'and some caviar.'

Peterson and Bohler shook their heads. The woman said: 'No thank you.'

There was a marked deference when she spoke to Petrov, Peterson noted.

'I know you've had a separate briefing,' said Petrov, talking again to Bohler, 'but it's imperative that there should be no misunderstanding, so I'll go over it again, even at the risk of repetition. Both of you are to be introduced into the complex as West German government officials, scientists attached to the Defence Ministry. You'll carry every accreditation document necessary and there'll be back-up precautions in Bonn: it's almost inevitable that there'll be a check from Chad.'

'What's the back-up?' demanded Bohler.

'Your biographies are being introduced into the Defence Ministry computer file: it's got a very high classification. Automatic verification would act as the best reference possible.'

'What about photographic verification?' asked Bohler. 'What would happen if there's a demand for our pictures to be wired from Bonn?'

'I've already considered that,' said Petrov. 'Pictures of both of you are to be filed, as well. The computer would produce the reference and your pictures sent quite automatically.'

'Will we know, if a check is made?' asked Gerda.

There *was* a lisp, decided Peterson. And she had blushed, too, asking a direct question of Petrov.

'Yes,' assured the Russian Director. 'Our man within the Ministry will be instructed to tell us .'

'Does he know the extent of his involvement yet?' Peterson asked.

Petrov smiled sideways at the other Director. 'Not completely,' he said. 'But he's agreed to introduce the biographies and once he's done that, he's increased his dependence upon our discretion.'

Peterson turned to Bohler and the woman. 'What have you deduced from the photographs of the site that you've seen so far?'

Bohler shrugged. 'Almost impossible to judge anything, merely from the size of a silo,' he said. 'Could be something as big as 4000 lb, like a MIDAS. Or as small as 500 lb.'

'The Vela rocket which America launched in 1970 weighed 500 lb,' said Gerda, appearing eager to support the other scientist. 'It had a 90 lb pay-load capable of detecting a nuclear explosion as far away as Venus.'

'Can we make an intelligent guess, working on the assumption that the satellite is to be positioned over Israel?' asked Petrov.

Bohler turned towards the woman, inviting her to respond.

'No,' said Gerda, immediately. 'For near static observation, I'd go for a geostationary orbit, but that involves a big rocket, to achieve the lift through the atmosphere. A smaller thrust would achieve a lower, polar orbit but that doesn't allow constant surveillance.'

'How much?' demanded Peterson.

'Three months, over a complete range of local times,' said Bohler. 'You can increase the cover, by gearing your rocket for sun synchronization.'

'What sort of monitoring would be possible?' said Petrov.

Gerda responded immediately and Peterson was aware that as

she became engrossed in the discussion, her reticence was diminishing.

'Again it's almost limitless,' she said. 'In the Soviet Union we bring our satellites back to earth after a certain period; in America, they eject a film capsule for lower air interception by conventional aircraft.'

'I don't imagine the satellite would be brought down,' said Peterson. 'And there would be no way Libya could expect to intercept ejected film.'

'Simple television,' said Bohler. 'The definition wouldn't be as good as high resolution still photography, but it would be adequate for whatever Libya wanted to learn about Israel.'

'How accurate can photography be?' queried Petrov.

Again it was the woman who answered. 'A camera with a definition of two hundred lines per millimetre and an effective focal length of ten feet would be able to distinguish a nine-inch wide patch of light against a dark background from an orbiting position eighty-five miles from earth,' she said.

'Christ!' said Peterson, unthinkingly.

'And from that low-level orbit, ground radio communications could be eavesdropped,' added Bohler.

'I would also expect it to have infra-red sensor devices,' said Gerda. 'The chief function is to detect heat changes. From an eighty-five mile orbit they could locate any sort of industrial development or factory, even if it were concealed underground; the earth heat level would disclose it.'

'And it can detect a sea temperature change as low as 0.5° C,' elaborated Bohler. 'Which means it can establish the passage of any submarine, because it creates a water-heating pattern.'

Petrov smiled at the dissertation. 'So now I hope you're convinced,' he said, to both of them.

'Convinced?' asked Bohler.

Petrov moved, to include Peterson. 'We've let the discussion cover things we both knew already, but for a very specific purpose. We wanted you to realize how important it is that whatever the device being constructed in Africa, it must not be allowed into orbit over the Middle East.'

Bohler smiled, unoffended. 'Very effective,' he said.

'I'd already realized the importance of the assignment,' insisted Gerda and Peterson looked intently at the woman, conscious of the stiffness. She had not liked being made the object of an exercise.

'What practical difficulties do you foresee, even before you get there?' demanded the American Director.

'The cover of Ministry officials should allow us access,' said Bohler, reflectively. 'Otherwise I doubt that we would even have got near the site; projects are run by carefully selected teams who become xenophobic about outside interference ... '

He turned to look directly at Peterson. 'From what you've told me already of the security, it's still not going to be easy.'

'But if you get near enough, it should be possible to sabotage?' pressed Petrov.

'A rocket or a satellite is a very delicate piece of machinery,' said Gerda Lintz. 'An infinitesimal miscalculation will cause it to malfunction.'

'And it must appear a miscalculation,' stressed Peterson, urgently. 'We don't just want to abort this launch; we want to create sufficient doubt about BADRA's ability to prevent Gadaffi or anyone else from ever considering buying time from them again. The failure must appear to be their fault, not the result of any obvious interference.'

Bohler unexpectedly addressed the woman in German. Peterson turned sharply, staring at the man. He was about to interrupt when Gerda responded in the same language and he felt pressure against his arm and realized that Petrov had leaned across to warn him against any intrusion: from the attention he was paying to the exchange, it was obvious Petrov understood the language. Peterson remained still, feeling slightly ridiculous. After three or four minutes, Gerda took pen and paper from her handbag and made a sketch: from what he could see, it appeared to be a drawing of differing orbital heights and space-window entries after launch. It was almost fifteen minutes before Bohler sat back in his chair. He looked across at Petrov and said, in English this time, 'I think I will have that drink now. Beer.'

Petrov made another gesture to his people at the edge of the room, looking all the time at the American.

'Fifteen minutes of highly technical discussion,' identified the Russian and Peterson realized the man had spoken for his benefit.

'Very technical,' agreed Bohler.

'To what purpose?' asked Peterson.

'Another exercise,' said Bohler, accepting the drink that was handed over his shoulder.

'Go on,' instructed Peterson.

'I learned German in America,' began Bohler. 'Admittedly it was the only language in the house and I maintained it when I went to college so it's fluent ... '

'So what's the problem?' intruded Peterson, concerned at what was happening.

'Gerda didn't leave Germany until she was seventeen or eighteen,' reminded Bohler. 'Her *technical* awareness and pronunciation in German is superior to mine.'

'Dangerously so?' asked Petrov, realizing the danger to which the man was alluding.

'Any doubt would be dangerous,' said Bohler.

'Do you mean you can't do it?' demanded Peterson.

'No,' said Bohler, immediately. 'But I don't think we should present ourselves on an equal, comparable basis. I think Gerda should purport to be the examining scientist, the expert.'

'And you?' said Peterson.

'Scientific liaison, the link between the laboratory and the diplomatic service; I'm more than adequate for that and if there were a mispronunciation or error then it would be easily explained ... '

He turned to look directly at Petrov. 'It won't mean any alteration to what you've arranged in Bonn.'

'It's not too late,' said Petrov. 'And if we're going to make the qualification, then it should be covered on your file.' The Russian smiled. 'You're a very astute man,' he said to Bohler.

Petrov turned to Peterson. 'It would mean an immediate change in what we're decided upon,' he said. 'It would appear to give Gerda superiority.'

Peterson considered the development, unsettled by it. Walter Jones should have discovered the weakness, before proposing the man for the assignment. But then so perhaps should he, during their discussion before the journey to Melk.

'You're sure of the risk?' he demanded from Bohler, unwilling to make the concession.

'It's very slight,' said Bohler, honestly. 'But it exists.'

'Then we should guard against it,' said Petrov.

'Yes,' agreed Peterson. 'We should guard against it.'

The success of the mission had to be the major consideration, more important than any misgivings. But he could not suppress the feeling of reluctance. 'The different status wouldn't exist in any private discussions or decisions between you,' he stressed, speaking to both scientists.

Bohler seemed curious at his chief's attitude. 'Of course not,' he said. 'It would still be a joint mission.'

'I think Michael is being very sensible,' said the woman. 'His technical pronunciation *isn't* as it should be.'

'All right then,' accepted Peterson, at last. He turned at a movement from Petrov.

'Why don't you and I take a stroll and allow these two to get to know each other better?' suggested the Russian.

Peterson hesitated, then stood, following the KGB leader from the room. It was the grey time of twilight, the sun's redness still sore against the sky and deep shadows marked out against the surrounding hills. From the direction of the monastery came the muffled, half-hearted sound of a bell; evening prayers, Peterson assumed.

'I thought it went well,' said Petrov.

'Yes.'

'Had there been any discussion between you of this technical ability?'

'No.'

'Then he's a remarkably well-adjusted young man,' praised Petrov. 'There aren't many men who would have done that, particularly not with a woman.'

'I suppose he is,' said Peterson, with growing awareness.

'I hope the other groups get on as well as these two appear to do,' said Petrov.

'That's unlikely,' said Peterson, objectively. 'Have you found a priest?'

'He's arriving tonight.'

'My man is already here.'

'So tomorrow it's an American rendezvous?'

'The Israelis intercepted the gold transfer,' said Peterson. They reached the conjunction of the two roads and turned back towards the house.

'I know,' said Petrov. 'Apparently it was brilliantly done. The authorities seem to think it was carried out by some dissident Palestinian guerilla group.'

'Levy's a clever man' said Peterson.

'I hope he won't become a nuisance,' said Petrov. 'This is going to be difficult enough as it is.'

Both Directors stopped, just inside the front door of the house. From the room in which they had left Michael Bohler and Gerda Lintz came the sound of laughter.

Peterson had not marked Bohler as a demonstrative man and so the enthusiasm in the car returning them to Vienna surprised the CIA Director.

'She's good,' said Bohler. 'An expert, in fact.'

'So are you.'

'I'm still impressed. She could be attractive, too. Doesn't seem to bother about her appearance.'

'No.'

'A national characteristic.'

'What?'

'That's what you called it, on the way here.'

'I'd forgotten. I meant what I said back there about it being a joint operation.'

'Were you annoyed at what I did?' demanded Bohler.

'Maybe off-balanced.'

'I felt it important.'

'You were right,' said Peterson. Bohler was unlike other operatives with whom he had dealt during his time with the Agency: Peterson was unsure whether the change was welcome or disturbing. It was past eight o'clock by the time they got back to the Intercontinental hotel in Vienna; there were two outstanding messages from Walter Jones in Washington.

'Bad news, I'm afraid,' said his deputy, as soon as they were connected.

'What?'

'Paul has had to have Lucille hospitalized: he thinks there was some sort of suicide attempt last night. Certainly she overdosed very heavily.'

'How is she now?' He would have expected to feel a stronger physical reaction to what Jones was saying but there was nothing, not even surprise.

'Out of any danger — Paul's had her transferred to a psychiatric wing. He wants you to come home.'

'I can't, not right away.'

'I warned him.'

'What did he say?'

'That he expected there might be some excuse.'

'Tell him I'll be back as soon as possible, within a couple of days, hopefully.'

'There's something else,' said Jones.

'What?'

'Beth isn't at the commune any longer.'

There had been five photographs in Irena's dossier, all of them in staged, theatrical poses to illustrate some production of the Bolshoi in which she had been appearing. Petrov had ensured that the file index had not listed the quantity of pictures and had taken the one which showed her face most clearly. As in the others she had been holding a professional stance, but it was still possible to see how beautiful she was. Five years, thought Petrov. How much would she have changed in five years? Did she think of him, wherever she was, as often as he thought of her? Or had she erased him from her memory — maybe even married and had children? There was a flare of jealousy at the thought. He replaced the photograph positively in his combination-locked brief-case, concealing it among some papers. The KGB chief realized he was allowing himself to become too immersed in nostalgia. The affair with Irena was over — finished. There could never be another meeting, another contact even. She had to be put out of mind, suppressed at least. What he was involved in now did not allow for any distraction. Petrov sighed; he felt so very lonely.

CHAPTER 16

The air conditioning at ground level was far less effective than underground, in the silo control room and laboratories, and Hannah Bloor gave a sigh of annoyance as she stepped from the lift. She suffered from the heat, and as soon as she felt the perspiration prick out upon her skin the irritation started. Instinctively she checked one of the frequent wall clocks. She had just enough time for a shower before her conference with the Director, Dieter Muller. She was surprised at the summons. There had been a meeting involving the whole team only three days earlier, at which they had reviewed the successful progress of the launch, and she was curious at the need for another so soon.

The installation had been designed in the shape of a giant T, with the laboratories and research rooms arranged along the main section and the recreation, rest areas and living accommodation in the crosspiece; the women's quarters were to the right, the men's to the left. She walked unhurriedly along the central corridor, her special laboratory shoes squeaking against the highly polished floor. They employed a large native staff and everything about her shone with an almost clinical cleanliness. The Director was strict about all things, particularly cleanliness; a lot of the scientists in the complex found it irksome, but Hannah admired the attitude. In a situation such as theirs, it was very easy to let standards drop. Once that started happening, efficiency went with it. Hannah regarded herself as a very efficient woman.

Hannah had one of the larger sets of rooms, befitting a Project Director. The living-room was separated from the bedroom by a dressing area, with the shower and bathroom leading off. Only in the living quarters did Muller allow any relaxation of tidiness, but Hannah's rooms were as neat and orderly as the most sterilized research chamber. They had the appearance of a freshly-prepared hotel suite awaiting the arrival of a fastidious customer rather than someone's permanent home. The only jarring note was the radio equipment. To live in the middle of the African continent yet completely cut off from it was an unreal existence, and the scientists and technicians adjusted in different ways. Some tried to read all the books they had always promised themselves to complete but had never before had time for; others became physical fitness fanatics or chess or backgammon enthusiasts. Hannah Bloor's pastime was her radio and tape recorder deck. It was mounted on the wall to make it as compact as possible, the recorder spools vertical rather than horizontal, and the VHF frequency was powerful enough for her to receive concerts with perfect clarity from as far away as New York or London. Muller shared her interest in music and occasionally joined her, if they knew in advance of a particular opera or performance; as far as anyone could remember, he was the only man who had ever gained admission to her living quarters and as he was almost seventy, it was disregarded within the complex. Hannah was aware of the rumours about her sexuality but unworried by them. She regarded the problem rather as she considered the effect of cleanliness upon efficiency: a romance might have created jealousy and that would have been an unnecessary complication in the life they led. And there was always the difficulty of ending it, without causing pain or bad feeling. She had decided it just wasn't worth bothering with. The situation was simplified by the fact that there was no man within the complex to whom she was attracted. Even so, it was an abstinence which in the early days she had found uncomfortable, because contrary to the gossip, Hannah was a highly sexed woman. It had got better, during the last few months; only occasionally did she sleep with her hand between her legs now.

She stripped off her laboratory uniform and underclothes, carefully placing them in the laundry basket and then gratefully got under the shower. Despite her discomfort with the heat, she ran the water warm, knowing that if she over-cooled her skin the perspiration would become worse once she dressed again. She didn't bother with a shower cap, plunging her head beneath the water jet; because of the heat, she wore her blond hair close-cropped. It was naturally straight and she knew that by brisk towelling and then combing, it would be perfectly in place by the time she entered Muller's office.

After ten minutes, she stepped from the shower, wrapped a towel around her and used another to wipe the steam from the full-length mirror. Satisfied at last with the reflection, she let the towel drop away and surveyed her body. She was a full, heavy-breasted woman and even though she had suppressed her sensuality she naturally looked there first, pleased that they held their shape without any sag. She was pleased, too, at the flatness of her belly; the food at the installation was very good, but Hannah ate carefully, determined not to put on weight. She moved closer to the mirror, intent upon her skin. She was deeply tanned, white just across her nipple tips and above her pubic hairline, but she found the eruptions that had started to itch in the bend of her elbow and beneath her left arm. Hannah had studied medicine for two years before abandoning a medical career in favour of applied physics, and realized that the blemishes were caused by a combination of the heat and the frequency with which she soaped her body; it was not unusual for her to shower four times a day.

She was at the Director's office five minutes before the appointed time, but he was waiting for her, expectantly.

'Always prompt, Hannah,' he smiled.

'I always think of lateness as rudeness,' she said. She had a soft, caressing voice, and until they had learned of her interest in classical music, people in the complex had thought she might be able to sing pop songs at the entertainments they sometimes organized. Hannah rarely attended, embarrassed by the amateurism of those taking part.

'Sit down,' encouraged the Director. Muller was a thin, almost cadaverous man. As fastidious about his person as he was about the installation he managed, he sometimes changed his suit during the course of the day and, despite the heat, customarily wore a waistcoat. His hair was white but very full, so that he appeared younger than he was. He was one of the people who suppressed the boredom of the place with exercise, which further decreased the impression of age; his face glowed pink, not from the heat but from health.

From their shared interest in music and the conversation that they had had in her rooms on his occasional visits, Hannah supposed she knew Dieter Muller better than anyone else in the complex; he maintained a reserve against close relationships, aware that his authority might be jeopardized by over-familiarity.

It had taken her a long time to realize that the perpetual tendency to boastfulness, regarded by some as irritating conceit, came from his disappointments. And he was a disappointed man, she knew. Deep within him was the remorse that a man learns to subdue after he has made an irrevocable decision that alters the course of his life. It must have been easy to have panicked, as Muller had panicked, in the closing stages of the war — to have imagined, even, that having been one of the German rocket pioneers could have meant arraignment at Nuremberg, on war crime charges. So Werner von Braun had gone to America, to the honour and excitement of NASA moon shot development and Dieter Muller had fled to Egypt among real Nazis whose politics and ethos he could never understand and whose company he didn't enjoy.

As slowly over the months, Hannah had pieced together his history, she had often reflected how sad it was that space exploration had lost such a brilliant, innovative mind. The youngest member ever allowed admission to the Verein für Raumschiffahrt — the German society formed to study astronautics before the war — he had been employed at Kummersdorf, south of Berlin, on the Army Weapons Department rocket research as early as 1935. It was there that he had first encountered von Braun, then only twenty but already chief designer. Muller had risen to become his personal assistant by 1939 when, from their new base at Pennemunde on the Baltic coast, the A-5 covered a test fire distance of eleven miles and, five years later, made possible the rocket that carried a one-ton explosive warhead to London.

After so many setbacks, Hannah felt that his boastfulness was excusable, just as she understood what was perhaps his greatest disappointment — the fear that this development was being taken from him by the greed of the BADRA consortium in Germany. It was probably his last chance to be recognized as the rocket genius that he was, but in order to earn that scientific acclaim, the satellite would have had to be utilized properly, as a communications vehicle of which many countries would make use. Muller was not a political man, but she was sure he could easily see the criticism that would arise from allowing Libya the monopoly.

'I'm surprised at the need for another meeting, so soon,' she said.

He smiled at her directness. 'Something has happened that I felt you should know about.'

'Not to affect the launch?' Her concern was immediately obvious.

He raised his hands, a placatory gesture. 'Don't become alarmed,' he said.

'What is it?'

'The agreement for the use of the rocket on which you have been working requires half payment to be deposited in advance, in gold.'

She sat nodding, head to one side in curiosity.

'The bullion truck was intercepted,' reported Muller, flatly. 'The money stolen.'

'Intercepted! But how?'

'I only know the barest details,' apologized the old man. 'It seems it was a very well-planned robbery; it was completely successful.'

'Who?'

'There are apparently some suggestions of Arab guerillas.'

'But why would they want to disrupt it?'

He shrugged. 'I don't know. There is so much I don't know.' That was the nearest she could remember him coming to criticizing the BADRA decision to entrust the security of the complex to the Libyans: in the three months since the Arab arrival, something approaching an army garrison atmosphere had been imposed upon the place. She wondered if Muller was becoming tired of the constant arguments with the Libyan officers about the degree of restrictions that should be imposed upon even the most senior scientists.

'Who knew of the gold transfer?'

'Very few people.'

'So there's a spy, somewhere within the company?'

'That's the logical conclusion. But in Europe. Here we remain very secure.'

'We can't be completely secure, if information of this degree was allowed to get out,' insisted the girl.

'I suppose you're right.'

'Are you sure it won't affect the launch? There's a limited window available to get the vehicle into space. I don't estimate more than five days.'

'I told you not to become alarmed,' reminded Muller. 'There's little risk of a postponement. There is no shortage of money — you know that. This time it will be a normal book transaction, with no physical transfer.'

Hannah frowned. 'I wouldn't have been surprised at some political protest once we had launched and it had become known who had bought the facility. But I would never have guessed at open crime!'

'It's very worrying,' the old man confessed. For once the carefully maintained ebullience left him; he looked very tired, she thought.

'Should I tell the team?' she said.

Muller turned down the corners of his mouth, a doubtful expression. 'It might unsettle them,' he warned. 'There's always a lot of tension, this near to a launch.'

The soreness in Hannah's arms began to irritate again: perhaps it was nervousness and not the overuse of soap, she thought, suddenly.

'The idea of an informant makes me uneasy,' she said.

'Everything will be fine, believe me,' encouraged the man. 'The launch will go uninterrupted and our reputation will be established in the Third World; this is going to prove a highly commercial venture.'

'I hope you're right,' said the girl.

'I will be,' said Muller.

She looked at him, sadly.

David Levy bustled across the wide approach to the Knesset and then entered the parliamentary building, head bent in concentration and oblivious of the Chagall murals that lined the walls. He went familiarly around the shell of the debating chamber towards the private offices. Even though he was recognized by the guards, there was still the formality of a security check: had there not been, Levy would have had the soldiers court-martialled.

From the Premier's rooms, there was a better view of the Dome of Scrolls than there was from his own office: Levy was staring out over them when Shimeon Weismann came into the room, flurrying between two secretaries.

'A moment, David,' said the man. 'Allow me a moment.'

Levy nodded, amused, as the Premier dictated a paperchase of memoranda, consulted an appointment diary and answered the intercom from a third assistant, refusing an immediate meeting with the leader of the Likud party. It was fully ten minutes before the activity was over and the office became quiet again.

'In my prayers I sometimes ask God to extend the day to thirty hours,' said Weismann, smiling. He wore an open-necked shirt, sports jacket and sandals. The Mossad chief wondered why Israeli politicians made such an affectation of casualness.

'I'd welcome the extension,' said Levy.

'It was a good operation in Switzerland,' praised Weismann. He smiled again. 'Just like intercepting pirate ships off the Spanish Main.'

'It went well,' agreed Levy.

'What else is happening?'

'Peterson and Petrov have had a meeting.'

'They've met personally!' Weismann came forward in his chair, not smiling now.

'In Vienna,' said Levy.

'I didn't expect that.'

'Neither did I.'

'You couldn't be mistaken?'

'I've had Peterson under observation since we provided the first information about the complex,' confessed Levy.

'What can it mean?'

'When we met in Washington, Peterson told me he was planning an incursion.'

'Surely you don't think they could be going in together!' Weismann was shaking his head, as if he found the whole thing impossible to believe.

'It would reduce the risk of one group getting in the way of another,' said Levy. 'But I agree it seems an unlikely idea.'

'Aren't we going in?'

'I've assembled a force,' said Levy. 'But it won't be as easy as Entebbe. I doubt that Kenya would allow us to refuel again.'

'What about South Africa?' suggested the Premier. 'They're very friendly to us.'

'I don't know that they'd want to become so openly involved.'

'Still no indication of a launch date?'

'None,' said Levy. 'All the assessments put it fairly near.'

'You're doing very well on this, David,' congratulated Weismann again. 'Very well indeed.'

'There's still a long way to go yet,' said the Mossad chief, cautiously.

CHAPTER 17

Otto Bock planned very carefully, determined to guard against any detection. As the controller, his presence within the computer room was unchallengeable, but he spread his visits throughout the day and even into the night, aware of the rota and systems check, but still wanting to insure against every danger.

There were two security checks when the user's name and purpose was noted in a ledger, one immediately inside the door and the other before access to the machines in which higher classified material was stored. Neither concerned him — they were for outside people coming in, not for someone already on the inside.

Morning was a bad time, he concluded. At the beginning of the day the volume of traffic and people seemed greater, increasing the danger of someone glancing idly at a computer window and seeing a file that might later be remembered if there were ever any enquiry. Early evening, he decided; before the change-over to the night staff, when the attendants and operators were tired and concerned only with going home.

Bock had rehearsed everything, so there would be no hesitation which might attract attention. Consequently he was irritated at the unexpected change in the instructions, isolating the man Bohler not as a scientist, but as someone involved in diplomatic liaison. It meant a slight change of programme, which unsettled him; in his apprehension, Bock was easily upset.

Both the personnel files and the BADRA records were located by a twelve-item letter and number block code and he memorized both before venturing into the computer room, so that nothing would have been found upon his person had there been a spot search. It did not happen often, but it was best to anticipate every eventuality.

The ledger clerk smiled familiarly at him as he emerged from his office. 'Late night?' enquired the man.

'Afraid so,' said Bock. His stomach was in turmoil and there was the slightest shake in his hand, but his voice showed no anxiety. 'Some suggestion of print-out deficiencies in African investment.'

'Only another half an hour for me,' said the man.

'I envy you — I think I'll be here late.'

An operator looked up politely as Bock approached, moving away from his bench to greet the controller.

'Complaints from above,' said Bock. 'Print-out deficiencies.'

'What do you want me to do?'

'Nothing,' said Bock. 'I'll handle it.' He wondered if the other man was conscious of the grease of perspiration he could feel easing down his face.

'Let me help.'

'No,' refused Bock. 'I'll do it. That's what I'm paid for.'

Bock selected a console at the end of a bank, to reduce the chance of being overlooked as much as possible. He turned on the machine but did not immediately ask for the personnel file; instead he logged on to the investment dossier that was the supposed purpose of his visit. Bock had rehearsed it this way to give others in the room the opportunity to become used to his presence, but recognized now that it was also a useful gap for calming his nerves. He worked for fifteen minutes, apparently making notes from the print-out, then glanced casually around the room. There were only two other people there; the operator who had offered to help already had his coat on and was in conversation with the security man.

At the moment of commitment, Bock began to tremble, his fingers vibrating against the keyboard in front of him. Abruptly, almost in a defiant gesture, he punched in his user's identification and immediately 'What file?' was printed out in the window. Bock hesitated, then demanded personnel. Three questions immediately appeared before him. Amend? Update? Insert?

Bock selected insert and the screen filled with something like an application form, insisting upon forename, surname, sex, security coding and clearance level and biographical details. Immersed in what he was doing, the shake went from Bock's hands. Only once did he mis-punch and have to erase. From the far end of the room he became aware of the shift change and looked up in time to see the departing operator gesturing towards him and shaking his head to the new man. By the time the nightman approached, Bock had completed Gerda Lintz's entry.

'Any problems?' asked the new operator.

'None.'

'Just call, if you need me.'

'I will.'

Bock waited until the man had gone some way down the room before recalling the woman's records, adding the automatic cross-reference to the BADRA file and the identity code for a photograph if one were demanded. Now surer of himself, it did not take Bock as long to complete the insertion of Michael Bohler and when he had finished he hesitated again, his finger hovering over the send key which would put both into the memory bank. The erase key was only two inches away; maybe nearer. His hand actually moved towards it involuntarily, and then Bock thought of Gretal and the boys and his twenty-five year career and his pension and he stabbed his finger down upon the send button. The screen went blank.

He was very wet with perspiration, Bock realized distastefully, crinkling his nose at his own odour. But he'd done it! He'd done it and he hadn't been detected and even if the BADRA file was seen to come up on his screen, there was an explanation for it. He was safe. He started the machine again, identified himself and then asked for the BADRA file by feeding in the numbered and lettered code. He had expected to see the name of the firm appear, but instead it came up with another code designation and Bock frowned, curious at the choice. There was just one word in his window — Overcrowd.

Covering himself against any print-out check, he fed in several questions linked with his listed reason for entry into the computer room, then added the cross-check references that he had already attached to the personal files of Gerda Lintz and Michael Bohler. There was no pause with the 'send' key this time; he thrust at it urgently, anxious to clear the screen and end what he was doing.

Bock slumped back into the functional but uncomfortable office chair, aware for the first time of a feeling of fatigue; there was a deep ache in his arms and legs and across his back, as if he had been involved in some strenuous physical effort. He heaved himself from the seat, walking slowly down towards the exit.

'Finished?' asked the night operator.

'Finished,' agreed Bock. And he had, he thought. He had done what the bastards had demanded and now he was finished with them. And he was finished, too, with dimly lit clubs and the uncertainty of strangers he couldn't trust. He would see a doctor, maybe a psychiatrist, and get help, to stop him wanting to do it. He had got to the very lip of disaster and managed to escape; he couldn't expect to be so lucky the next time.

He rinsed his hands and face in a washroom, carefully combed his hair and tried to suppress the unpleasantness of the perspiration with some cologne that he kept in a desk drawer. He had expected to feel frightened, going to the apartment in which he had confronted the men who had trapped him, but instead he was seized by a feeling of light-heartedness, light-headedness almost. He managed to get a Mozart concerto on the car radio and hummed along with the movement, tapping his fingers against the wheel in tiny conducting gestures. He could be home with Gretal in an hour: the meeting with his blackmailers wouldn't take more than a few minutes.

They had specified the appointment time and were waiting when he was ushered into the apartment by the man he had so stupidly thought would replace Jurgen Beindorf and who now practically ignored him. He hated Klaus — a far deeper dislike than he had felt for Jurgen. At least Jurgen had loved him once, no matter for how short a time. But Klaus hadn't. It had always been a trick.

'Everything go all right?' asked the larger of the two men, already in Klaus' apartment.

'Yes,' said Bock, tightly. 'The biographies are there, as you wanted them to be. And they're cross-linked with BADRA .'

'Excellent,' said the smaller man. He gestured to a tray of bottles. 'A celebration drink?'

'No thank you,' refused Bock. The light-heartedness did not extend to that degree. He felt very anxious to be away from these men and the apartment and go back home to his family.

'We've things to talk about,' said Klaus. 'You might as well have a drink.'

'What things?' A feeling of sickness settled in Bock's stomach and he began to sweat again, frightened that he might retch.

'These people won't be accepted in Chad unless there's the advice and the authority from the Ministry,' said Klaus, patiently. 'We've got to compose the proper sort of cable and anticipate the response, so that what you've done tonight isn't wasted.'

'No!' said Bock, in despairing protest, 'I've done what you wanted me to do. I won't do any more.'

'Yes you will, Otto,' said the big man. 'You'll do everything we ask. And we're going to ask for a lot more yet. Tonight was only the beginning.' He had been moving towards the drinks but turned at a sound from the German. 'Oh Christ!' he said, exasperated. 'Don't start crying again.'

It had been a bad connection and there were parts of the conversation with Paul that Peterson had had difficulty following. The hospital doctors were unsure whether it had been a deliberate suicide attempt as it was a common tendency for someone awakening from a drugged sleep to forget an earlier dosage. The alcohol wouldn't have helped the forgetfulness, but it had come dangerously close to strengthening the soporific. Certainly there had been no suicide note, just some travel brochures and plane departure listings for Puerto Rico. Peterson had winced at the reminder, recalling his promise to Lucille. A holiday anywhere she liked, he had said — money to be no consideration.

He had expected an argument from Paul at the announcement of Beth's disappearance from Arizona, but surprisingly there was no outburst. It was as if all emotion and feeling between them had gone, so that all that was left in the boy was a resigned acceptance of further disappointment.

'We'll find her,' Peterson had said, trying to sound encouraging. 'I've people working on it.'

'Sure.'

'I mean it: she'll be OK.'

'Sure.'

'I'll be home as soon as I can.'
'Yeah.'

Peterson set off for the second meeting with Petrov, irritated that he had not spent as much time as he would have liked studying the dossier on Henry Blakey. As the car became clogged in the congestion around St Stephan's cathedral, he confronted the feeling and became annoyed at himself. He knew the files off by heart, every one of them, so that wasn't the cause of his uncertainty. It was the family again — the awareness of his failure, but also of the way it distracted him from what he was trying to do as Director of the CIA. He frowned, caught by a further thought. Perhaps his discomfort was deeper rooted than that? Maybe he was afraid that the ineffectiveness of his private life was likely to cross the boundary and affect what he was trying to achieve in Chad? He thought again how Petrov had predominated at the meeting with the scientists and then of Michael Bohler's suggestion of being the subservient party in that part of the operation. There was common sense in the decision — logic, too. But the President wouldn't see it that way. He would think of it as being out-manoeuvred.

Peterson arrived a full hour before Petrov and his agent. Henry Blakey was already waiting, in an ante-room next to the one in which Peterson intended the meeting to be. The man rose as he entered, then stood waiting for some move from Peterson. The Director's immediate impression of the younger man was that of calmness. Michael Bohler's attitude the previous day had been similar, but in Blakey it appeared far more natural. With Bohler, there had been times when Peterson had suspected the man of forcing the demeanour.

'Sorry we couldn't come together,' said Peterson. 'I was unsure about a call from America.'

'I've only been here a few minutes.'

'Did Walter Jones explain fully what the operation was?'

'I think so.'

'How do you feel about working with a Russian?'

'Curious,' said Blakey, immediately.

'No reservations?'

'Some,' said Blakey, just as promptly, and Peterson noted the forthrightness.

'What?' he said.

'There's a great deal of pomp and ritual in the Russian Orthodox creed,' said Blakey. 'But there's quite a divergence between that and Catholicism, and we're supposed to be Catholic missionaries.'

'Exactly,' said Peterson. 'And missionaries work in the field, not in conducting high church services.'

'I felt it was a danger of which you should be aware,' said the man.

Peterson realized that he hadn't anticipated this problem. 'Thank you,' he said.

He moved further into the room, so that he was better able to see the other man. He remembered from the dossier that Henry Blakey was listed as middle height, but the slightness surprised him. It seemed a frailness, making the man appear smaller than he really was. He had fair, short-cropped hair and blue, untroubled eyes: aware of the examination, Blakey was not discomforted by it and once again Peterson noticed the calmness of the man. He would probably have made a very good priest. The Director wondered why he had changed his mind.

'You've studied the file on Vladimir Makovsky?' Peterson asked.

'All last night,' said Blakey. 'I couldn't adjust to the time change.'

'I hope to be able to allow you two or three days for getting to know each other, before you go in.'

'That should be sufficient,' said Blakey.

There was movement from the doorway and Peterson turned as the Vienna resident, Richard Brownlow, led the two Russians in. There was a moment of reserved cordiality as the introductions were completed, and then Peterson led the way into the room set aside for the meeting. It was much better furnished than the Soviet house in Melk. There were padded chairs at the table, but in front of the fire, which had been lighted and was throwing a pleasant warmth out into the room, armchairs had been placed around a low table upon which coffee and cups were already set.

Remembering the lack of interest on the previous day, Peterson had not bothered with food: he wondered if Petrov would see the absence as a criticism of his attempt at hospitality.

'The table or near the fire?' invited the American.

'The coffee is already there,' said Petrov, leading the way to the easy chair. Blakey and Makovsky seated themselves in facing seats, each intent upon the other, and Peterson was reminded of the shadow boxing in which the two scientists had engaged the previous day. The surrogate priests were quite different from each other, almost comically so. Makovsky was a dark-haired, broodingly tall, bulky man who appeared constrained even in an ample armchair — the sort of person in whose path crockery shattered. The Russian leaned forward for his coffee and jarred against the saucer, spilling some before he could lift the cup. He made a slurping noise when he drank. Peterson looked for some reaction from the other American. Blakey's face remained expressionless.

Peterson moved quickly to establish his supremacy over the meeting.

'You've both read the intelligence reports about the witchcraft symbols?' He addressed the Russian, already aware of Blakey's study.

'Yes,' said Makovsky. The Russian had a deeply resonant voice which matched his build.

'You are going on a disinformation mission,' announced Peterson. 'We want as much rumour and innuendo directed towards the complex as possible.'

'About what?' demanded Blakey.

Peterson paused. Then he said. 'Two days ago, American B52s and Soviet Tupalov aircraft began spraying defoliants over a wide area of the country around the installation ... ' He held up his hand, preventing Blakey's interruption.

'You'll also have defoliants,' continued Peterson. 'We want the crop destruction to be as widespread as possible. There'll also be poisons.'

'Poison?' queried Makovsky.

'We want the water-holes and any other drinking place used by animals treated.'

'Even on the limited scale that we would be able to achieve, the destruction of crops and animals would have a fairly serious effect,' said Blakey.

Peterson looked at the man sharply, aware of the protest in his voice and remembering Walter Jones' warning of the man's tendency to question openly. In the circumstances, it could be embarrassing.

'We *want* it to be very serious,' he said. 'We want to turn the local population against the complex.'

'So who will feed them?' persisted Blakey.

'A government which permitted the installation to be created there in the first place,' said Petrov.

'In Vietnam, defoliants were found to be the cause of some foetal deformation in pregnant women,' said Blakey.

'That was never proven,' said Peterson.

'To my satisfaction it was.'

Peterson shifted uncomfortably at the open challenge. 'It's not your satisfaction that's important,' he said. 'It's mine.'

'Won't the local population use some of the same water-holes as the animals?' said Makovsky.

'Yes,' said Petrov.

'So some people are to die, as well as the animals?' Unlike Blakey, the Russian's question was for clarification, not criticism.

'Yes,' said Peterson. 'There will also be other chemical preparations to cause temporary but not permanent illnesses.'

'What else?' demanded Makovsky.

'We'll monitor any climatic changes from the weather satellites,' said Peterson. 'If we're lucky enough to get any sort of cloud formation, we'll seed it with carbon dioxide and cause as much rain as possible. It might not be possible to achieve much this way, but we'll do what we can — spread the word about the weather gods becoming upset at fire in the sky, just in case.'

'Is that what they call it, fire in the sky?' asked Makovsky.

'Yes,' said Peterson.

'Poor, innocent bastards,' said Blakey. It was almost a private remark. It sounded like one of personal regret.

'If we succeed in what we're trying to do, then it will cost the minimum of lives,' said Peterson, patiently. 'If we fail and have to respond in some more direct way, an air strike for instance, a lot of people could die.'

'I accept that,' said Blakey.

'Then you must accept that what you are being told to do is to save lives, not just in Africa but possibly over a wider area in the Middle East.'

'It's a difficult logic to absorb,' said the American.

'It's the right equation, whether you can absorb it or not,' said Petrov, unused to such challenges and curious about them. 'We know the purchaser to be Libya, so it can only be directed at the Middle East. Are you aware how many people get maimed and killed in a war, even a short war?'

'I'm sorry,' apologized Blakey. 'I didn't mean to question the operation — not to the degree I appear to have done, anyway.'

There should have been more time spent with Blakey in preparation, Peterson realized. That would have been the moment for the moral questioning, not now. He remembered the brief time they had spent together in the ante-room and looked to the Russians.

'Your grandfather was a priest?' he demanded.

'Yes,' said Makovsky.

'But you never had any training?'

The Russian frowned, unsure of the direction of the questioning. 'No,' he said.

Peterson turned to Petrov, enquiringly. 'Don't we have the reverse of yesterday's situation?' he said. It might give him the opportunity to redress the imbalance created by Michael Bohler's honesty.

'Perhaps,' said Petrov, doubtfully.

Peterson went back to the younger Russian. 'If you were directly challenged on Catholic dogma ... some point of canon law or catechism, could you respond without any difficulty?'

Makovsky turned to Petrov for guidance, his face twisted with uncertainty at the question.

'Could you?' demanded Petrov, unhelpfully.

'I don't know,' said Makovsky awkwardly.

'Then you couldn't,' judged Peterson. He looked to Petrov again.

'So?' demanded the Russian.

'For the same reasons as those put forward yesterday, I think Blakey should appear the senior priest at least,' said Peterson.

'It would adjust the balance,' agreed Petrov.

'I was not thinking of the balance,' avoided Peterson. 'I was thinking of the success of the operation.'

'Of course,' said Petrov and smiled. He turned to Makovsky. 'At all times,' he said, speaking slowly and positively, 'the decisions between you are to be joint ones; neither has command over the other. But if there's ever any challenge to you as priests, then you'll defer to the American.'

For the briefest moment, Makovsky's face tightened but then the expression cleared. 'Of course,' he said. 'I understand.'

Petrov, who had tensed as if expecting the sort of arguments that Blakey had put against his Director, smiled again.

'Will we be entirely alone?' queried Blakey.

'You'll have radio liaison with people inside the complex and others outside,' said Peterson. 'You'll remain here together, for two days at least. At the end of that time, we want you behaving like two men who've trained together for years and who are friends.'

'There'll be a further meeting, before you go,' promised Petrov at the door. 'Until that time you stay here, together.'

In the ante-room in which Peterson and Blakey had first met, Petrov said, 'The biographical details are in the computer; apparently there was no problem.'

'It's beginning to look quite good,' said Peterson.

'Yes,' agreed the Russian. 'After so much difficulty, it's almost a surprise.'

Bohler had waited for the moment of relaxation, but it never came. Gerda remained courteous but always formal, as if she *saw* herself as the superior partner in the operation and was guarding against any familiarity. Almost immediately the two Directors had left them alone she had corrected him, insisting that from then on any conversation should be in German. She had responded politely but without humour to his attempts at lightness, refused wine with any of the meals, and during a walk they had taken through the fields bordering the house she had torn her skirt on an awkward fence, having refused to accept a helping hand across.

'Have I annoyed you in some way?' he asked, at dinner the second night.

'No,'

'You seem reserved.'

'We're engaged in a job, even here.'

'It wouldn't hurt to smile occasionally.'

'It might,' she said, seriously.

'What do you mean?'

'In a month, maybe two, it'll all be over.'

He shrugged, disconcerted by her attitude. 'I was suggesting a friendship, not a marriage.'

She smiled briefly, then immediately seemed to regret the expression. 'It's a job,' she said again.

'Nervous?'

'Very,' she admitted. 'Are you?'

'Yes.'

'I've been waiting for this moment, for a long time,' she said. 'And now it's arrived I don't feel at all as I expected to.'

'Nor do I,' confessed Bohler, remembering his conversation with the CIA Director.

'It doesn't seem ... ' she paused, trying for the proper word. ' ... real,' she completed.

'It'll seem real, soon enough.'

In the capital, fifty miles away, Peterson opened the door to Richard Brownlow and ushered him into the suite. The Austrian resident remained nervous, his nail-bitten hand close to his mouth even before he had sat down in the chair that the CIA Director indicated.

'The man's name is Bock,' reported Brownlow, hurriedly. 'Otto Bock.'

Peterson smiled, a self-satisfied expression. 'Excellent,' he said. 'Really excellent! What about the Russians?'

'Photographs of them all,' said Brownlow. 'Two appear to have been brought in from outside, Moscow probably. The one who set himself up as Bock's boyfriend is a chauffeur attached to the Soviet embassy in East Berlin.'

Peterson's expression widened. 'It couldn't be better, could it?' he said.

'It's a very complete dossier,' agreed Brownlow.

'You got off to a bad start with the Agency,' said Peterson. 'After that mistake in Prague, there was even some discussion of withdrawing you back to Langley ... '

Brownlow swallowed, uncomfortably.

' ... and now I want you to know that I'm glad we didn't,' took up the Director. 'You've done a magnificent job on this one. Truly magnificent.'

Brownlow's hand came way from his mouth and he smiled. It was the first time that Peterson could remember the younger man relaxing. He had crooked teeth when he smiled.

'Thank you sir,' he said.

'I'm going to see to it that a special commendation is attached to your file,' promised Peterson. 'I think you are going to go a long way with the Agency.'

'I'd like that, sir,' said Brownlow. 'I'm very keen on the job.'

Once, reflected Peterson, he had been too.

CHAPTER 18

Although he had anticipated the attitude, the degree of hostility between Colonel Bradley and the Russian soldier surprised Peterson. Even a formal greeting had appeared difficult for them and so far they had refused any direct conversation, always addressing each other through their respective Directors.

Both men seemed uncomfortable out of uniform: they shifted frequently in their seats and Sharakov kept smoothing his hand over his civilian suit, as if he needed reassurance that it was there at all. Peterson thought there was an odd similarity between the two men which went beyond the rigid, military bearing — hardness. Peterson thought irrationally that their skin would be tough and unyielding if he reached out to touch them. There was also another impression, which the American Director could not immediately identify, and when the thought came to him he frowned at it, unable at first to accept the description. But it was the word that fitted, he decided at last. There was a brutality about them.

The meeting was in the second of the American houses and quite unlike the others that had preceded it. Bradley and Sharakov sat tensed on opposite sides of the table. Both showed the proper deference when either Peterson or Petrov addressed them, but most of the time, although refusing conversation, they stared at each other as if expecting some sudden movement. Both Directors had adjusted their own demeanour, maintaining a curt gap of authority from both the soldiers and conducting the meeting as if it were a military briefing.

'For an operation of this sort, a split command is impractical,' protested Bradley, after the function of the deep penetration unit had been explained first by Peterson and then elaborated upon by Petrov.

'We're aware of the difficulties, but there can be no other way,' insisted Peterson. The man's unease extended beyond the Russian soldier, Peterson realized; Bradley appeared suspicious of everyone in the room.

'There should be an opportunity for a practice joint exercise, at least,' said Sharakov. His English was thickly accented.

'There isn't time,' said Petrov. 'You'll have to improvise whatever is necessary once you get to Chad.'

'Who makes the decision to move against the installation?' asked Bradley.

'We do,' said Peterson, immediately. 'There'll be a constant VHF radio link. There's to be no assault mounted until you receive our authority.'

'A joint decision?' queried Bradley, looking from one Director to the other.

'Yes,' said Peterson. 'A joint decision.'

He hesitated, uncertain whether to continue: the two soldiers were a weak link, he decided, suddenly nervous. 'Understand one thing,' he went on, 'and understand it very clearly. The success of what we are trying to achieve depends, on this one occasion, on our two countries working together. I know it's alien for both of you; perhaps more so because of your military training than for others who are involved. For the period of this assignment, you are to subjugate any dislike ... any differences ... everything, in fact, which might jeopardize that success ... .'

Bradley sat regarding him blank-faced and totally unmoved by the warning.

'Is that clear?' pressed Peterson.

'Quite clear,' said Bradley.

'Did *you* understand?' Petrov asked the Russian colonel.

'Yes,' said Sharakov, shortly.

'Then be aware of something else,' said Petrov, staring fixedly at the other Russian. 'If anything were to go wrong and subsequently be traced to any fault of yours through some stupidity about working together, then you would be answerable not to any military tribunal ... '

For the first time Peterson detected a change in the man's

attitude. Not fear, he decided. More an irritation at such a warning being given in front of him and Bradley. He was surprised Petrov had done it so openly.

Petrov ended the artificial pause. ' ... You would be accountable to me.'

'From me, there'll be no cause for complaint,' said Sharakov.

'Or from me,' said Bradley hurriedly and Peterson winced, first at the Russian's formality and then at Bradley's need to match the other man's assurance; it was childish, like counting sweets in a bag, to see who had the greater number.

'There's only one consideration,' said Petrov. 'And that's to prevent the rocket launch. Never forget that for a moment.'

'I won't,' said Sharakov. Bradley nodded.

Peterson stared at both officers: the warnings and the threats had achieved nothing, he decided. The distrust was too deeply ingrained in both men; their reaction to each other was instinctive. Thank God their presence was only for emergencies.

'Other deep penetration units were sent in,' he said. 'All failed.'

'Combined?' queried Bradley.

'No,' said Peterson.

'We both lost the same number of people,' supported Petrov. He looked again at Sharakov, who had trained them. 'They were your best people,' he reminded.

'Yes,' conceded Sharakov, uncomfortably.

'And they were detected,' said Petrov. 'There's logic in your combining.'

Both men reacted to the remark, each wanting to insist upon their ability to perform alone, but each held back by their respect for authority.

'They must have made small mistakes,' said Sharakov.

'It won't happen again,' said Bradley.

'It'll happen if you go on behaving as you are now,' said Peterson, suddenly exasperated. He stood, hand against the table, leaning across towards the soldier to emphasize what he was saying. 'You were transferred from the Army to the CIA for a purpose — this sort of purpose. Don't foul it up by your inability to adjust to circumstances.'

Now it was Bradley's turn to mirror the irritation at an open threat, as Sharakov had done before him. 'You've already made yourself very clear,' he said.

'And I expect in return a clearer indication that you fully appreciate what I'm saying,' insisted Peterson. He paused again; the words were ready but he was uncertain whether to utter them. Deciding it was necessary, he continued: 'This has the direct authority and backing of the President himself.'

'But it's clandestine,' said Bradley.

'Of course it's clandestine!' said Peterson, allowing the irritation. 'Would you expect an open invasion?'

Bradley appeared to yield under the pressure. '*Presidential* authority?' he said.

'Yes,' assured Peterson. He hoped Fowler would never learn of the over-commitment. He was aware of Petrov's attention and regretted the impulse to exaggerate.

'Any antipathy you show towards each other will immediately be visible to the units you control,' warned Petrov.

Unexpectedly, Bradley thrust his hand across the table towards the Russian. Sharakov stopped himself just short of starting away from the gesture. Instead he stared undecidedly at the American, then with seeming reluctance reached out and shook his hand. Peterson was aware of the tension going out to Petrov. He looked back to the two soldiers and their caricature of friendship. Was it genuine, he wondered, or merely a device to stop the haranguing? He had no way of knowing.

'Why did you join the CIA?' asked Makovsky.

'My father was in the OSS, which became the CIA after the war,' said Blakey.

'But you trained to be a priest?' There was as much disbelief as curiosity in the Russian's voice.

'Yes,' said Blakey. 'For almost six years.'

'Why weren't you ordained?'

Blakey smiled at the other man. 'I didn't think I was strong enough to become one. The Agency seemed the only thing available when I quit the seminary. My father used his influence.'

'You think being a priest is more difficult than what we're being sent in to do!'

'Oh yes,' said the American sincerely. 'Far more difficult. To be a priest requires real courage.'

Makovsky shook his head, unable to accept the immediate assurance. 'You'll change your mind before it's all over,' he said.

'I doubt it,' replied the American confidently.

CHAPTER 19

There was a bunk in the compartment aboard the CIA plane, already turned down in readiness, but Peterson ignored it, knowing that sleep would be impossible. He felt nervous, returning to Washington: more unsure than he had felt during any of the briefings in Vienna, even the unsatisfactory one with the two soldiers. There were causes enough, he accepted. For the past three days he had tried to put Herbert Flood's campaign out of his mind, but as his aircraft crossed the Atlantic he thought back to Walter Jones' account of the meal during which Flood had invited his deputy's disloyalty. He was determined to fight Flood but realized that at the moment he didn't know how. He sighed, changing position in his seat. Flood wasn't his major concern, he decided. He was anxious about how Lucille would be, in hospital. And about the President's reaction to what he had done. He knew he had achieved a lot but it seemed oddly insufficient.

He thought again of his forthcoming meeting with the President, anxious for further guarantees. Fowler had had nightly briefings, Peterson knew. And an hour before his departure from Austria, Walter Jones had confirmed that the *Arthur J. Grant*, a guided missile destroyer, was being diverted from NATO exercises in the South Atlantic to take up station as the communications vessel in the Gulf of Guinea. So that *must* indicate some approval for what he had done. Yet the unease remained as strong as ever.

Walter Jones was waiting for him at Andrews airbase and Peterson experienced an unexpected feeling of encouragement at the sight of the man standing beside the car, hunched in an overcoat that appeared almost too long for him. There was an air of dependability about Walter Jones.

'Thanks for coming,' said Peterson.

'Thought there might be a lot to catch up on,' said the deputy. He stood aside, for Peterson to enter the car first.

'What happened in Austria can wait,' said Peterson, immediately they had settled themselves and erected the glass screen. 'What's been going on here?'

'A lot of things,' said Jones. 'Some of which I'm not even sure of myself.'

'Like what?'

'Lucille's illness has been leaked to the gossip columnists. Described as exhaustion.'

'Bastard,' said Peterson, vehemently.

'Personal attacks are as strong as ever. The talk is of you being distracted by personal problems. I don't imagine it will be long before something appears in the *Post*.'

'What's the President's reaction?'

'He's said nothing about Lucille or the rumours. But I think he's frightened that he's over-committed himself in allowing us to go so far in Africa. Keeps talking of the law of congressional approval. I think he's frightened he could be impeached.'

'Is he going to back down?' Peterson turned anxiously towards his companion.

'Hardly be in character, would it?' said Jones.

'To survive, Fowler would change character easily enough,' predicted the Director.

'Don't show any lack of confidence,' advised Jones. 'He wants to know he's done the right thing, without risk of failure.'

'That won't be easy,' said Peterson, honestly.

'Easy or not, I think it's necessary.'

'I've got to oppose Flood,' said Peterson, positively.

'How?' demanded Jones. 'You're due aboard the missile destroyer in three days.'

Peterson turned, to stare across the car again. 'You could appear to accept Flood's offer,' said Peterson, slowly. 'We might learn which way the attacks were coming.'

'We might,' said Jones, doubtfully.

'It would mean exposing yourself,' said Peterson. 'If Flood found out what we were attempting, he'd make you a target as much as me.'

'I realize that.' Jones was staring out of the window, as if unwilling to meet Peterson's gaze.

'It would be asking you to take a big risk,' agreed Peterson.

'Isn't that the business we're in?'

'There's a difference.'

Jones looked into the car, smiling. 'What do you want me to do?'

Peterson felt a sweep of relief. 'Protect me while I'm away,' he said eagerly. 'We've as many media outlets as Flood, probably more. Let's start to counter the stories ... plant innuendo of our own ... .'

He frowned, at a sudden idea. 'Have we ever run an investigation on him?'

Jones shook his head, doubtful again. 'There'll be his security clearance file, of course.'

'Get it,' ordered Peterson. 'Use it as the starting point. Look into his academic background, societies or organizations he might have joined at college. He might play the hawk now, at Fowler's prompting, but I bet there'll be the usual period of college liberal. We might even be able to find some Communist affiliation ... .'

'He *is* the country's foreign affairs adviser,' frowned Jones. 'Sure you want to take it this far?'

'Yes,' said Peterson. 'I want to take it this far. The son-of-a-bitch declared war, not me.'

'I'm sorry about Beth,' said Jones.

'Any leads?'

The deputy shook his head. 'When we couldn't trace her there, I had the local police pick up a couple of boys from the commune, hassled them a bit for vagrancy and marijuana possession. They said she just took off, without any warning. Didn't say where she might be heading.'

'What about the ballet dancer?'

'Complete dossier,' said Jones. 'Photographs, lists of all associates, bank records, transcript of telephone conversations ... .'

'Any way we can tie her in with any Russian links?'

'Corresponds with two other dissidents, one who escaped on a later ballet tour.'

'Good,' said Peterson. 'Very good. Does the President expect you to be with me?' he asked his deputy.

'Yes.'

'I want to thank you, Walt,' said Peterson. 'For this family business ... and the risk you're taking with Flood.'

'Let's hope it all comes out right,' said Jones briskly. He always appeared uncomfortable at any display of gratitude, thought Peterson.

Once again the appointments secretary was standing alongside his desk, as if impatient for Peterson's arrival. The ambivalence about which Jones had warned was obvious the moment Peterson entered the Oval Office. There was a wariness about Fowler, as if the man had cause to be suspicious of them. Peterson had always taken the Texan's exuberance to be phoney, calculated to create the impression of a permanently genial temperament. There was certainly no cordiality tonight: instead the greeting was one of reserved formality. Peterson wondered if Fowler would regret the decision to have Walter Jones in on the conference.

'Mr Director,' greeted Fowler.

'Mr President,' responded Peterson.

'A thoroughly successful trip?'

'I think so, sir,' said Peterson. He looked towards the French windows, leading out on to the Rose Garden. Was Fowler going to let this meeting be recorded, for any subsequent enquiry?

Fowler was aware of the look. 'It's a cold night,' he said.

'Not too cold,' encouraged Peterson.

The President rose almost abruptly, thrusting his way through the doors ahead of the two CIA men. Peterson's impression was that Fowler was irritated at the subterfuge. He followed the man into the garden, waiting until Jones had caught up before giving a complete account of what had occurred in Austria, stressing the supremacy he had managed to attain.

'Sure we're not being set up by the Soviets?' asked Fowler, immediately the Director had finished talking. There had not been a meeting between them when the President had not expressed this fear.

'Not at this stage, anyway. And we've covered ourselves.'

'Sometimes,' said Fowler, 'I think with my gut. And I'm beginning to get a gut reaction that we're over-committed on this.'

Peterson felt a sudden burst of anger at the man's changed attitude, at the play-acting of security and the personal commitment he was being called upon to make, with so little open support.

'Shall I abort it then?' he demanded, in open challenge. He wondered if Fowler would appreciate the danger he had created by including Jones in the briefing; it meant there was going to be a witness to a presidential decision. And covert actions *had* to be presidential decisions.

'I didn't say that,' insisted Fowler.

'It would still be possible,' said Peterson, unwilling to allow the other man to evade the responsibility.

'You sure it can succeed?'

'That would be an impossible undertaking to give,' said Peterson, not taking care to hide his irritation. 'We've tried to anticipate every obstacle. And largely as the result of Soviet assistance, we're confident of infiltrating two people into the installation: we're in a lot better shape now than we were a week ago.'

'We're breaking the law, you know,' said Fowler, suddenly.

'It would be difficult to work within it, in these circumstances,' said Peterson quickly. He wondered if Fowler realized his mistake: he had admitted complicity before a third person. He looked at Jones, unsure of his awareness. The deputy gazed back at him, his expression without comment.

'If we withdrew, would the Russians go on without us?' demanded the President.

'Unquestionably,' said Peterson, prompt again.

'Could they screw us on our involvement so far?'

'Probably,' said Peterson. 'If we feared that strongly enough, we'd have to foul their efforts so that it was provably a Soviet incursion.'

'And if we did that, the installation would survive and the Libyan rocket would be launched?'

'Yes.'

'We don't have a choice,' said Fowler.

'So you don't want me to abort?' demanded Peterson, insistently.

'No,' said Fowler.

If Jones remained loyal, he had some sort of defence, decided Peterson. He hesitated at the thought about his deputy: there had never been a vestige of suspicion through which he could doubt the man. He smiled at Jones, who moved his mouth slightly in response. One of the closest friends, thought Peterson: perhaps *the* closest.

'They go into the complex tomorrow,' said Peterson. 'I'll be the communications link, from the destroyer.'

'The Soviets didn't argue.'

'There'll be constant liaison between us.'

'I'm surprised.'

Peterson realized that he would been too, had he not spent the previous three days with Petrov. It had been very easy to work with the man.

'What about your wife?' demanded the President, suddenly. 'Won't you want to spend some time with her?'

'She's getting the best care possible,' said Peterson. 'There's not a lot I can do, at this stage. By the time she's due for discharge, I shall be back here.'

Fowler nodded. 'Sorry to hear of her problem,' he said.

'Thank you.'

Fowler looked beyond the Director to the deputy. 'Appreciated the briefings of Mr Jones, while you were away,' he said.

'Thank you,' said Peterson again. The praise was as much for the Agency as for the man, he decided. And was therefore a congratulation for him, as well.

'Still got my full support,' said Fowler.

'I'm grateful for the assurance,' said Peterson, sincerely.

'Don't let me down.'

'I don't intend to,' promised Peterson.

'Just wish I could get rid of this gut feeling,' said Fowler.

The Director of the clinic was named Richard Harrap. Surprisingly, although Peterson realized there was no logical reason for the surprise, he appeared hardly older than Paul. He was a heavy, athletic-looking man, with sports pennants and group football photographs around his office supporting the impression. They talked initially in the man's office and then in an antechamber to the common room where there was a two-way mirror through which it was possible to watch the patients without their being aware of the attention. Peterson felt discomforted by it, as if he were a Peeping Tom. There were about twenty people in the room, more than half of them grouped in an annexe in front of a television set. Lucille sat apart from them, reading a magazine. Occasionally she glanced up, apparently distracted by some response from the viewing group. She appeared relaxed and looked very well — not at all what Peterson had expected.

'We've conducted a medical examination, of course,' said Harrap. 'There's some liver enlargement.'

'What does that mean?' asked Peterson, with abrupt concern.

'If she doesn't drink again, nothing very much,' said the doctor. 'Fatty tissue is the most obvious sign of cirrhosis.'

'How long would you have her stay here?'

'The full treatment takes three months,' said Harrap. 'She's got to be brought around to the mental attitude of not wanting to drink.'

'What can I do to help?'

'Just be here,' said the doctor. 'The worst part of the recovery is the awareness of how badly they've let themselves go. They've got to be constantly convinced that they still have the love of people who matter to them.'

'It might be difficult, in the next week or two,' said Peterson.

He was conscious of Harrap's attention. 'Couldn't you re-arrange your schedule a little?'

'No,' said Peterson. 'It's impossible.'

'I see,' said the doctor, stressing the disappointment in his voice.

'Just a couple of weeks,' repeated Peterson, awkwardly.

'Your son's been very good,' said Harrap. 'He hasn't missed a visit.'

'Can I see her now?'

'Of course. Do you want to go in there or have her taken back to her own room?'

Peterson's face flickered with distaste at the dispassionate way the doctor was referring to Lucille. 'Is one better than the other?'

'Psychologically, the communal room is better. It shows you're not ashamed of her in front of people whom she's now having to regard as friends.'

'Is that what she thinks? That I was somehow ashamed of her?'

Harrap smiled at the naïvety of the question. 'It's never as easy as that to discover a reason, Mr Peterson. Alcoholism is a psychological disease, latent in many people, like a tubercular bacillus.'

'I'll see her in the communal room,' he decided.

'It'll be best if a nurse warns her first.'

'I'll wait in the corridor,' said Peterson. He wanted to accord her some privacy, to prepare herself.

It was fifteen minutes before a nurse came to fetch him. Everyone in the room turned as he entered; there only seemed to be one other visitor — a woman visiting a man. They sat close together near a window, their knees touching.

Lucille was in the same chair that he had seen her occupy from the viewing-room. Her hair seemed freshly combed and as he approached she pulled at her skirt, trying to straighten some imaginary crease. He stopped some way short of where she was, not knowing what to do.

'Hello,' she said.

'Hello.' Why did there seem to be embarrassment between them? He was reminded of the dinner she had prepared, just before he had gone away. That hadn't worked, either.

'It's nice to see you.'

'I've been away.'

'Paul told me.'

Peterson remembered Harrap's warning that she would be afraid he was ashamed of her. He should show some affection, he thought. He went forward again, bending as he reached the chair, and kissed her on the cheek. She smelt very clean and fresh, with only a trace of perfume.

'How are you?'

'I feel fine.'

'Good.'

'You look tired,' she said.

He felt it, Peterson realized. He should have attempted some rest on the plane. 'I've been busy,' he said, immediately regretting the words.

She smiled, but it wasn't a sarcastic expression. 'Always so very busy,' she remembered.

'The doctors seem very nice.' Would Harrap still be watching them, through the two-way glass, wondered Peterson somewhat uncomfortably.

'They say it's an illness.'

'Yes.'

'And that I'll always have it. That I'll have to learn never to drink again.'

'I know.'

'I don't think that will be difficult. Not sitting here, thinking about it, I mean. I don't know what it'll be like outside.'

'I'll be there to help,' he said, immediately.

'Will you, Jamie?' Again there was no sarcasm.

'Yes,' he said and meant it. It was his fault she was here, just as Beth was his fault. He wouldn't fail her again. Or his daughter, if he could locate her.

As if aware of his thoughts, she said: 'Since I've been in here ... able to understand things better ... Paul has told me all about Beth.'

'She's gone from Arizona,' said Peterson.

'She'd be back here with us in Washington if you'd been able to go.' Just as there had been no sarcasm, there was no recrimination.

'Yes,' he said.

'Or if I'd been able to go.'

He frowned up at her. 'It's not for you to reproach yourself,' he said urgently. 'Nothing was your fault.'

'I wasn't a lot of help though, was I?'

He extended his hand towards her and she snatched at it, as if she had been waiting for the gesture. 'Lucille,' he said. 'Beth didn't leave because of you or become involved with the people she has because of you. If anyone is responsible, then I am.'

'Will you be able to find her again?'

'Of course,' lied Peterson, remembering Harrap's warning about encouragement and confidence.

'Will you go to get her this time?'

'Yes. This time I'll go immediately to get her back,' he said. What would happen if it occurred when he was on a destroyer somewhere off the coast of some godforsaken African country?

'Promise me, Jamie.'

'I promise,' Just as he had done before, on more occasions than he cared to remember.

'I *can* do it, you know,' she said suddenly, and for a moment he was confused, unsure of what she was talking about. 'Not drink,' she said, seeing his difficulty. 'I really don't want to. And that's after only two weeks.'

'Of course you can do it,' he said.

'If you help me,' she said.

'I've said I will.'

'Do you mean it?' she said. 'Do you *really* mean it?' Her grip against his hand was so tight it hurt.

'I really mean it,' he said.

CHAPTER 20

Dimitri Petrov's decision to seek a meeting with the full Politburo cabinet had been consciously thought out. The importance of what he was attempting provided cause enough, but that was not the predominant reason for the request. The KGB chief was determined to bypass Sergei Litvinov. Petrov was convinced that through the liaison official, the account would have been presented as grounds for the purge for which his critics had waited so long.

And Litvinov had guessed at the manoeuvre, Petrov decided. For almost an hour, he had sat to the left of the three men, attempting to listen expressionlessly as Petrov patiently recounted everything that had happened since they had become aware of the Chad installation from satellite surveillance. Litvinov had been unable to control the tic beneath his left eye. From previous encounters, Petrov knew it to be a nervous response to being beaten; it pleased him to have upset the man.

The silence stretched on for a long time after Petrov had finished talking.

'I find it very worrying,' said the chairman, Boris Dorensky, at last. Dorensky was an overweight, bespectacled man who had wielded power within the Soviet Union since Krushchev's regime. He suffered from angina and his ill-health was the subject of frequent speculation in the Western press, to whom his importance within the Politburo had only just become obvious.

Litvinov moved hurriedly to take up Dorensky's lead. 'I have already reported on several earlier occasions on the outline of this problem,' he said. 'During those reports, I made no secret of my concern at what I considered to be the unsatisfactory way the problem was being handled.'

'There has been proper reason for occasional contact with the US in the past,' said Dorensky, 'but this is active co-operation.'

'There should have been consultation before a decision of this magnitude was taken,' said the third member of the cabinet. Ivan Borrosuba was a thin, aesthetic man whom Petrov considered the most cultured of the group; he knew that Borrosuba saw himself as the natural successor to the leadership of the KGB.

'There was a need for speed,' said Petrov. 'Every indication from the satellite photographs is that a launch is near.'

Dorensky gestured towards Litvinov. 'An official was appointed to liaise over the matter,' he said. 'What delay would have been caused by informing him fully of what you intended?'

Again Litvinov intruded. 'Isn't the truth of the matter that you feared immediate rejection and sought to work without the knowledge of people to whom you had a duty to report?'

'No,' said Petrov. 'That isn't the truth of the matter at all.' He felt very relaxed. Litvinov's determination to oppose him was making it much easier than he had anticipated. The Cabinet sat looking at him expectantly: they were all hostile, Petrov decided.

'Without American liaison,' said Petrov, 'we would not have got the confirmation that the purchaser was Libya and that it was the Middle East where the danger existed.'

'And America would not have been able to infiltrate the complex,' argued Litvinov. 'Why couldn't we have kept that to ourselves?'

'Because it would not have been safe,' said Petrov. He stopped, determined to expose Litvinov as far as possible.

'Safe?' queried the man.

'Does the Soviet Union want another conflict in the Middle East?' said Petrov.

'Of course not,' said Dorensky.

'But can we risk any relationship we have with the Middle East nations by being seen to interfere openly with the affairs of an Arab country, even one regarded with the suspicion that Libya is?'

'No,' said Dorensky. He was speaking guardedly now, curious at the points that Petrov was establishing.

'Any more, surely, than we can appear to be attempting to influence affairs in Africa, particularly with the penetration that the People's Republic of China is achieving?'

'Is there any point in this elementary display of political awareness?' demanded Litvinov, attempting sarcasm.

'Every point, Comrade Litvinov,' said Petrov, patronizing now.

'Every point in the world.'

Again he waited, forcing the question from his opponent.

'What?' said Litvínov. At last he was beginning to appear uncomfortable.

'Gerda Lintz is entering Africa under West German documentation,' said Petrov, speaking carefully so that nothing would be missed by the Cabinet. 'All trace of her ever having been transferred from Leipzig to Moscow University is being erased. Not that there is any way of the West discovering it anyway, but her name has been removed from any record at Baikonur, as well. Vladimir Makovsky is going to Chad under the auspices of a Roman Catholic order financed by the Central Intelligence Agency. There is no trace of his name ever having been on any records held by the KGB or of his residency in Moscow or Leningrad. Similarly, there are no longer any records in existence of the jungle training school near Odessa run by Oleg Sharakov or of the ten-man unit he is taking into Africa ... .'

Dorensky was smiling now, sitting back expansively in his chair.

'The communications for the attempted sabotage are being conducted from an American guided-missile destroyer on station in the Gulf of Guinea,' continued the KGB head. 'On board will be the Director of the Central Intelligence Agency ... '

' ... You've been very clever, Comrade General,' praised the chairman.

'If all or any part of our attempted incursion goes publicly wrong, then there is nothing at all establishing Soviet involvement that we cannot satisfactorily explain,' said Petrov, determined to finish. 'For every accusation made against us, we could leak through the Western media outlets we control enough convincing proof that people being identified as Russians were in fact Americans introduced to embarrass us.'

'Ingenious,' supported Borrosuba reluctantly,

'Comrade Litvinov?' invited the chairman.

'I congratulate you,' said the liaison man frigidly.

'I'm glad not to have disappointed you,' said Petrov, enjoying the moment. He hoped he would not have to do this to Peterson; he genuinely liked the man. Would Peterson have established a similar sort of campaign against him? Unquestionably, decided Petrov realistically.

EPILOGUE

Because of the distances they had to travel after the incursion, both groups of soldiers left forty-eight hours before either the scientists or the imposter priests.

One of the storms which are so frequent over the Azores had broken just before Hank Bradley had concluded his briefing and he had to shout to make himself heard over the thunder.

'Any questions?' the colonel had demanded.

'Tell me you're kidding,' a man immediately before him had said. Richard Banks was a squat, bullet-headed career soldier, proud at having risen to the rank of marine sergeant.

'No,' Bradley had replied. 'I'm not kidding. For quite a while there aren't going to be many laughs.'

The Tupalov had refuelled in mid-air, so they had been airborne for several hours. The ration trays lay discarded around them, the Russians had arranged their packs and were mostly asleep. At the rear, Sharakov could see the glow of a cigarette. He had decided that there was a simple way to resolve the problem of a split command. If the American colonel were to die, then he would automatically assume leadership as the most senior officer in the field.

Michael Bohler and Gerda Lintz flew from Bonn. He became aware of her nervousness soon after take-off. He instinctively reached out to squeeze her hand reassuringly.

'It'll be all right,' he said.

She took his fingers anxiously and he became curious at her touch. She looked up, aware of his attention.

'Just friends,' she reminded.

'Sure.' But maybe something more, he thought.

Henry Blakey and Vladimir Makovsky flew from Rome. The cassock kept catching between the Russian's legs and he walked awkwardly, like a small boy who had wet himself and had sore thighs.

'Will I have to wear this damned thing when we get there?' he said.

'No,' assured Blakey. 'It wouldn't be practical. Maybe not even the collar.'

'Thank God for that,' said Makovsky.

'You're supposed to believe in Him, not blaspheme,' corrected the American.

'I'll try to remember,' said Makovsky.

BOOK TWO

We have seen
Good men made evil wrangling with the evil
Straight minds grown crooked fighting crooked minds
Our peace betrayed us; we betrayed our peace
Look at it well. This was the good town once.

Edwin Muir, *The Good Town*

CHAPTER 21

Michael Bohler had seen the watchtowers just before the driver's warning that they were approaching the complex, and the nervousness that he had felt ever since the landing at N'Djamena worsened. He looked across the vehicle at the girl. Gerda was staring fixedly ahead, refusing to respond to his attention. She was very pale and still appeared wilted by the airport heat, even though they had been travelling in the refrigerated air-conditioning of the Mercedes for over an hour. He made to reach across but she pulled away, refusing the intimacy she had allowed during the flight. He turned from her, gazing out of the car again.

Everything seemed bleached and crushed by the heat. He could see the necklace of islets along the edge of Lake Chad and occasionally there were cattle and goats. They seemed to move very little, as if the effort of grazing was the most they could manage. The villages through which they had passed had been smaller than he expected: encampments of four or five mud and rush huts, each with a palm and rush lean-to providing shade. The women at their pots had watched without expression as they had swept through, but the children had risked the choking swirl of red dust to run after them, shouting and screaming.

The BADRA complex had been constucted away from the lake's flood plain and Bohler was conscious of the car climbing up through the savannah grasses; once, very close to the road, they suprised a colony of giraffes feeding from some trees. They immediately started away in long-legged flight, trailed by two skittering babies. Bohler looked at Gerda again, expecting some response, but she seemed oblivious to everything around her.

Although he knew the size from their satellite reconnaissance, the area covered by the installation still surprised Bohler. The ground was comparatively flat, yet from the perimeter it was impossible to see anything of the main buildings. The approach road was dominated by a watchtower, and far away to the east Bohler could just detect another, not forming part of any corner of the surrounding wire but introduced into the fencing to provide continued surveillance. The protective fence was fine mesh, rising for about fifteen feet and topped with barbed wire. Before they had got through the strip of land that had been cleared in front of it Bohler had isolated the junction boxes and leads from which it was obviously electrified. He studied the cleared area intently — the savannah had not just been cut down. The earth beneath had been ploughed and then raked, creating a dusty area maybe six hundred yards across. From the watchtowers, the track of anyone crossing would be immediately visible. Bohler wondered if the clearing was mined.

The entrance construction was elaborate. There were guard-rooms on either side, and concrete obstructions were arranged between them so that it would be impossible for any vehicle to go through at speed; the driver had to ease his way through the dog's leg at little more than a walking pace. Bohler watched the guards as the car number was checked against a record sheet and their faces compared with the photographs which were attached to clip-boards. The ordinary security officials were clearly African, but in the guard-room he could see people of different nationalities. The officers and soldiers were mostly Arabs and as the car began moving forward, he saw one of them go to a telephone, obviously warning the main building of their arrival.

As the car passed through the control point, Bohler leaned forward, using the Mercedes mileage gauge to judge the distance to the installation. It was three miles before there was any sign of construction and when it came Bohler squinted, despite his sunglasses, at the sudden harsh whiteness of the buildings.

There had been an attempt at creating some sort of garden approach along the driveway, but only near the buildings had it really succeeded. Here sprinklers had been installed and appeared to be in constant operation, producing a sudden flare of green lawns which skirted the complex. Climbing plants were being trained up some trellis work and immediately outside the entrance there was a fountain attempting to convey an impression of coolness with its perpetual play of water.

The glass of the windows and doors was smoked, so Bohler could not distinguish the man waiting for them until he and Gerda had made their way through the double-doored entrance. They stopped immediately inside, momentarily disorientated by the shade and then Bohler saw the man approaching, smiling.

'I am Dieter Muller,' he said, 'The Director here. Welcome to my establishment. I think you'll find it interesting.'

As he shook Gerda's hand, Bohler wondered if the name and description would be sufficient for Langley to trace any record in their files.

He took Muller's hand, conscious of its dryness and therefore of his own perspiration.

'I'm suffering from the heat,' he apologized.

Muller continued to smile. 'It's always the immediate problem,' he agreed. 'Quite often the constant extremes of air-conditioning and climate cause some respiratory problems.'

Behind them Africans were bringing their luggage from the Mercedes.

'I thought you'd probably like to shower and change, then we might talk again,' invited Muller. 'Dinner perhaps.'

'That would be fine,' accepted Bohler.

Muller solicitously took Gerda's arm, leading her along the wide corridor.

'A good flight?' he enquired.

'Tiring,' said the woman. 'I always find it very difficult to rest on aircraft.'

Bohler had been concerned from her attitude in the car that the nervousness would show, but there was no indication of it in Gerda's response.

'How long do you think you will remain with us?' said the Director.

Bohler looked across sharply. The question had been asked of Gerda, and appeared to be nothing more than the continued politeness, but Bohler wondered whether he should intrude. Before he could speak, Gerda was responding.

'I've been asked to prepare a thorough report,' she evaded, easily. 'So it really depends how long it takes to assemble.'

They reached an intersection.

'Women to the right, men to the left,' guided Muller. He indicated the men carrying their luggage. 'They'll take you to your rooms and I shall expect you in an hour.'

Bohler waited just inside the lobby while the African deposited his bags and then as soon as he had left, began a close examination of his quarters. To his right, a door led to the bathroom. On the other side of the lobby was wardrobe space and the main room was designed to be a living area during the day with a divan that converted into a bed at night. Bohler was surprised at the television set — video cassettes, he presumed. The air-conditioning was beneath the window and he turned it to high. He unpacked his clothes quickly, leaving the case containing the radio until last. It was a very elaborate portable, with VHF as well as medium bands and a directional aerial. It had a solid, sealed case to guard against any close examination and each of the outside dials and switches performed the function ascribed to them. Only when the controls were pulled out in a particular sequence did the radio that formed the undetectable core of the set become activated and link him with Peterson on the missile destroyer. Momentarily Bohler stared at the set, wondering whether to record the information about Muller and the perimeter precautions. Later, he decided: there was still the meeting with the Director. Instead he located a Munich station with only minimal interference and carried the set with him to the bathroom to hear the news broadcast.

Bohler was out of the room again within thirty minutes. As he walked back towards the main part of the building, he saw Gerda approaching in the opposite direction and smiled. She responded wanly. He reached the Director's suite ahead of her and stood waiting outside until she reached him.

'All right?' he said, quietly.

'Much better,' she said.

'Good.'

'Sorry about earlier,' she said, looking directly at him. 'It suddenly came to me, what we're trying to do. I got very frightened.'

'Me too.'

'I don't think it's going to be very easy.'

'No.'

They stood staring at each other. Even with her practical hair-
style and spectacles, she really was a very attractive woman.

'We'd better not keep the Director waiting,' he said.

'No,' she said again.

He led the way in. Muller was already waiting at a table upon
which drinks had been arranged. It was an L-shaped room, the
desk, filing cabinets and working area separate from the long
lounge. Beyond where Muller sat there was another larger table
already laid for a meal. The fading sun flashed off the crystal glass
and an African was fussing around the settings, rearranging small
pieces of silver.

Seeing Bohler's attention, Muller said: 'We try to live as well as
possible.'

'And seem to succeed,' said the American.

The Director smiled towards Gerda. 'More comfortable now?'

'Yes,' said the woman.

Muller indicated the bottles. Bohler took whisky but Gerda
insisted upon mineral water. Muller was drinking from a half
bottle of wine.

'It takes some adjustment,' said the man. 'If you've any thoughts
of sunbathing, leave it until the late afternoon.'

'We've come to work,' said Gerda and Bohler was aware of her
increasing confidence.

'I'm not surprised at this visit,' said Muller, unexpectedly.

Bohler was instantly attentive. 'Why not?' he encouraged.

'The attempted interference,' said Muller, as if the answer were
obvious.

Bohler held the other man's eyes, not trusting himself to look at
Gerda. 'There was concern, naturally,' said the American; it was
ambiguous enough to prompt the Director further, he thought.

'It's natural that the government *should* be concerned,'
continued Muller. 'Is there any indication who stole the money?'

'Not when I left Bonn,' said Bohler. If the old man was prepared
to talk so openly so soon, why no mention of the attempted entries
into the complex itself?

'Your security here seems very efficient,' said Bohler, taking the
opening.

'The strictness is a recent innovation, since the Libyan

involvement,' said Muller. Imagining an opportunity for conveying criticism back to people in authority, he added, 'I'm afraid there are many instances where it's too rigidly enforced. They seem to regard themselves as being separate from any control from within the establishment.'

The army officers at the gate, recalled Bohler. Could Muller be unaware of the attempted penetration?

'It surely frees you for more important considerations?' said Bohler.

'This is *my* establishment,' insisted Muller. 'I like to be responsible for every part of its working.'

Bohler was suddenly conscious of the other man's pride. And surprised at Muller's ready acceptance of them. Bohler had anticipated some hostility. He was sure that neither Peterson nor Petrov had guessed the advantages of intercepting the bullion shipment, which would provide a reason that Muller could accept so readily.

Muller turned to include Gerda in the conversation. 'The Project Director is a woman,' he disclosed. 'Hannah Bloor. I thought you'd be too tired tonight, so I've arranged a meeting for tomorrow.'

Another name for Langley to check, thought Bohler. He was glad he hadn't rushed into a transmission. There was no reason why there should be any monitoring within the installation, but it made sense to keep interceptible broadcasts to the minimum.

'I look forward to it,' said Gerda.

Muller finished his wine and looked towards the table. Bohler and the girl rose, following the old man. Immediately a team of Africans came in through an unseen side door. There was paté, with truffles, venison and strawberries; the wine was Moselle.

'It's all imported,' said Muller, as they began eating. 'We buy a few vegetables locally, but not much otherwise.'

'How many Africans do you employ?'

'Maybe two hundred, within the complex,' said Muller. 'But since the German office agreement to allow the Libyans to take over security, there's been an increase of about another two hundred, for perimeter duties. They've got their settlements outside and come in every day.'

'You don't agree with the Libyan involvement?' demanded Bohler openly, assessing Muller's feeling from his previous remark.

'No,' said Muller shortly. 'It was perfectly adequate before their arrival.'

Bohler was about to attempt to take the conversation further when the Director turned, pointing behind him. 'This is why I like to eat at this time of night,' he said. 'Isn't it spectacular?'

It was a few minutes before complete sunset. Already the savannah and jungle beyond were thickly black, a stark contrast to the blood red of the sky which flared up to reflect the occasional scudding cloud. As they watched floodlights suddenly blazed on, obviously operated by a time-switch, and the effect was destroyed.

'Another Libyan innovation,' said Muller, seemingly annoyed.

'I hope our visit won't cause any serious inconvenience to the progress of the project,' said Bohler.

The Director shook his head. 'It's been a splendid programme,' he said. 'We'll launch on the schedule established eighteen months ago.'

Realizing what Bohler was attempting to learn, Gerda said: 'There's always the unexpected.'

'Not with Dr Bloor in charge. It will be a week from now, I promise you.'

Peterson should be more than pleased at the progress on their first day, thought Bohler. Muller's latest indiscretion was as worrying as it was informative; it gave them a very tight deadline to which they had to work.

'What are your window vacancies?' asked Gerda.

Muller smiled. 'Four days, at least. Maybe five. But as I said, with Dr Bloor in charge it will launch exactly on time.'

The Director turned back to Bohler. 'Will there be any need for you to communicate with Bonn?'

'I don't think so,' said the American immediately. 'My instructions are to visit and then to prepare a report on my return.'

'I hope you won't be bored here,' said Muller, polite again. 'I'm afraid the insects from the lake marshes make the swimming pool uncomfortable, despite the insect lamps. There are film shows on most nights of the week and a fairly active sports club — they've even tried boating on the lake, but it hasn't proved very successful. Now our new security regulations discourage it.'

'I'm surprised that any sport is successful in this climate,' said Bohler, happy to relax momentarily into pleasantries.

'It's possible,' assured Muller. 'And the gymnasium here is air-conditioned. I use it a great deal myself.'

Bohler was not suprised to learn that Muller was a health fanatic; the man's appearance suggested fitness. It meant he would have to extend the age assessment beyond sixty when he sent the description to Langley.

'I'll remember that,' said Bohler.

'Throughout your stay here I shall be available to you both whenever you feel it necessary,' offered Muller. 'Quite obviously no part of the establishment is out of bounds to you, but as a courtesy gesture I would appreciate your asking Dr Bloor or any other project leader for permission to enter their work areas ...' He smiled. 'As I'm sure you've discovered before, there are ways in which scientists sometimes resemble orchestral conductors in temperament.'

Bohler and Gerda smiled with the old man. 'Of course,' said Gerda. 'As my colleague said earlier, we don't want to do anything that will inconvenience any of your work here.'

'How many projects do you have under development?' said Bohler. He spoke as if concentrating upon his coffee cup, a man temporarily eluded by a fact he already knew.

'Only Dr Bloor's anywhere near completion,' said Muller, perpetrating the error of pride. 'But there are four other rocket proposals in various stages of development.'

'So the success of the current programme will act as an advertisement and you will be partially prepared should there be heavy interest as a result of it.'

'Exactly,' smiled Muller. 'The consortium decided there was a positive advantage in forward planning.'

'A wise decision,' said Bohler.

Muller shifted and Bohler anticipated the move. 'We've occupied enough of your time,' said the American. 'I'm sure we're keeping you from something more important.'

Muller grimaced at the exaggeration. 'I regard your visit as important,' he said. 'But there are certain routines which have evolved, even at night.'

They hesitated in the corridor outside. Bohler realized there would be an advantage in having Gerda with him, to provide some warning if there were an unexpected approach while he was making a transmission.

'My room,' he said, moving towards it before she could make any protest. He stopped after several steps, turning back to where she stood. 'Please,' he said.

Doubtfully, she caught up with him and they walked side by side towards the male section of the complex.

'That was astonishing,' she said, digesting what they had learned.

'He was very proud,' agreed Bohler.

'Thank God.'

'Can he really be ignorant of the killings?'

'I believed him,' said the girl.

'It would make sense,' said Bohler, with growing conviction. 'It would be unthinkable for any private organisation, certainly with the respectability of those involved here. But from an army unit, it would almost be a natural reaction.'

'I was surprised at Muller's openness,' said Gerda. 'And by the fact that he doesn't appear to control the security.'

'It surprised me too.'

'Let's hope the openness remains.'

'And that Hannah Bloor is equally forthcoming.'

With so much information to transmit, Bohler made notes and then checked them with Gerda, to ensure that he'd remembered everything. With Gerda attentive at the door, he made his recording, played it back for sound level and clarity and then sent the speeded transmission. It took forty-five seconds. Even if there were any listening devices, Bohler was confident he would have evaded detection.

He relaxed back in his chair, smiling across the room at her.

'In three hours we discovered more than they had managed in more than three weeks,' he said, proudly.

She smiled back, at his attitude. 'It went well,' she agreed.

'You don't have to stay by the door any more,' said Bohler. He readjusted the radio for its more usual function and selected some music. Hesitantly, Gerda came further into the room. He indicated the chair opposite his and she sat down.

'What's your room like?' he asked.

'Duplicate of this,' she said. She sat on the very edge of the seat.

'Why do you wear your hair like that?'

Automatically she raised her hand to the bun and he smiled as she blushed.

'I'd better get back to my own rooms,' she said.

'Why?'

'I've got some things to do.'

'What?'

'Don't be ridiculous,' she said.

'What's ridiculous?'

'This play acting.'

'We're here for a purpose ... a job to do,' he mocked.

'We *are*,' she insisted. 'Let's not forget it.'

'I'm not forgetting it,' said Bohler. 'I've just finished a very good day's work.'

She smiled again. 'I'm sorry,' she said. 'I'm not being very good company am I?'

'I'm still nervous, too,' he said.

'But concealing it far better than I am.'

'You did well enough with Muller.'

'I didn't find it easy.'

He stretched across for her hand. She didn't try to move it.

'We're going to do it!' he said, encouraged by their initial success and trying to instil some confidence. 'We're going to do it, fly away from here in glory and everything else they've planned will be unnecessary.'

'I don't really think you believe that,' she said, serious again.

'Most of it,' he insisted.

'Thank you for trying to be kind,' she said.

Without consciously making the decision to do so, he stood, leaned across the narrow gap and kissed her. She didn't attempt to avoid him but neither did she respond, remaining with her hands along the armrests, her body tense.

He felt embarrassed, moving away from her. Women weren't usually so unresponsive to him.

'I wish you hadn't done that,' she said. Yet she didn't appear offended.

'It's impossible to become pregnant that way,' he said, trying to lighten the mood.

'It's an unnecessary complication.'

'It needn't be.'

'That *is* ridiculous.'

'Sorry,' he said. 'I forgot you were in charge.'

'You mustn't mock me.'

'Play acting,' he reminded her.

She stood, a determined movement. 'I'll see you tomorrow.'

He rose, walking with her to the door. As she was about to leave, Bohler said, 'You didn't quite manage it.'

She paused, turning back. 'Manage what?'

'To stay absolutely frigid,' he grinned. 'You closed your eyes.'

Peterson was uneasy aboard the warship — claustrophobic, almost. But he recognized that the uncertainty was not caused by the constriction of space; it was because he was trapped aboard a vessel in the middle of a sea, hopefully in control of the operation but with no way of monitoring what was happening back in Washington. And a lot would be happening, with Herbert Flood's guidance. How lucky would Jones be trying to find some compromising aspect of the man's past? There would be no way he could find out aboard ship — cause for further uncertainty.

Peterson did not think the officers had noticed the attitude. The captain, a fresh-faced, eager-to-prove-himself-capable New Englander named Tom Riley, was obviously very flattered to have the CIA Director on his ship and the feeling had spread through the command. Soon after being airlifted aboard by helicopter from the American airbase in the Azores, Peterson had noticed the respect and instinctively capitalized upon it. There hadn't been the suspicion that Peterson had feared over the sealed orders from Washington informing Riley that there was to be direct communication with a Soviet installation at Odessa; rather it seemed to have impressed the man even more.

Peterson had been allocated the quarters of the Executive Officer, David Hilgare. The man had moved his uniforms and working clothes from the cabin but left the personal belongings and Peterson felt intrusive. On top of a small bureau there was a photograph of a shining-faced, blond woman with a bubble-haired child cupped in her arms. Peterson wondered how she would cope, with her husband away at sea for so long. Did she keep vodka in a kitchen cabinet? Would Hilgare have to search for a neglected child in a few years' time?

Peterson turned at a movement in the curtained doorway and saw Riley.

'I think you'd better come,' said the Captain. 'There's been a message.'

Peterson hurried from the cabin behind the other man, reaching out for the support bars. They seemed greasy to the touch; since he'd been aboard, Peterson had never felt properly clean.

For the size of the ship, it was a surprisingly large communications room, because it formed part of America's nuclear capability. When Peterson entered, Hilgare was standing beside two operators, as if guarding against any attempt to decode the message. The transcription machine had been brought aboard in Peterson's helicopter and assembled on a work-bench near the ship's computer.

Hilgare indicated a wire spool. 'Arrived about ten minutes ago,' he said. 'Nobody's touched it.'

'Thank you,' said Peterson. 'I'd like it fitted for replay and then the room cleared for a few moments.'

One of the operators fixed the spool and then followed the other three men from the room. Peterson ran Bohler's message through to a duplicate tape that would play at an ordinary speed and then sat back, listening to the first day's account from inside the complex. He listened twice, to assimilate the information completely, then snapped the machine off, feeling the depression lift at the thought of what had been achieved in such a short time. It was premature to make such plans, but Peterson decided to have

Bohler personally thanked by the President when it was all over. The man had performed magnificently.

Peterson had always regarded the murders as the biggest mystery: he now sat tapping a pencil against his teeth, accepting Bohler's assessment of the simple answer. He smiled, as another thought came to him. The Libyans might have been effective against a single, unarmed operative, but they'd provide little opposition for the groups led by Bradley and Sharakov, if the need arose for an incursion. The CIA Director felt another stir of satisfaction. Having been so difficult for so long, it appeared possible that the operation might be resolved far more easily than he had anticipated.

Peterson found the radio operators on the bridge, with Riley and Hilgare. The Executive Officer stayed where he was and the Captain and the two other men followed him back into the radio shack. Peterson decoded what was applicable about the perimeter protection and identity of the security controllers for transmission into the field, to Bradley and Sharakov, then composed a larger message for Washington, containing everything that Bohler had sent and adding his own interpretations and assessment. Finally he had Bohler's message sent in its entirety to Petrov in Odessa. Peterson waited until everything had been cleared, so it was almost three hours before he left the radio room; he felt tired and hot as he followed Riley back to his cabin.

'Successful?' queried Riley.

'Incredibly so,' said Peterson. 'Far better than I could ever have hoped.'

'I'm glad,' said the Captain. 'Pity these ships are dry.'

'Too early yet for any celebrations,' said Peterson, cautiously.

Two and a half thousand miles away, near the Georgian port of Odessa, Petrov sat studying what had arrived from the American warship, nodding as the American had done a few hours earlier at the completeness of the report.

Petrov decided to send the American message intact, confident that immediately it arrived, Litvinov would attempt to smear it in front of the Politburo. There was a meeting scheduled within two days, which allowed just the right amount of time for the man to commit himself. And then Petrov would send the duplicate account he had monitored from the telemetry satellite which, unknown to the Americans, he had had positioned over the complex to intercept all transmissions between Bohler and the American destroyer. This proved that the CIA Director had adhered strictly to their agreement and withheld nothing.

Petrov began moving from the communications room towards the sun-washed verandah. With unconscious irony he decided it was comforting to know that he could trust Peterson.

CHAPTER 22

They had changed the cassocks in N'Djamena, but Makovsky appeared just as uncomfortable in the priest's collar, and constantly straightened and twisted his neck, running his fingers around the inner edge as if it were too tight. They *were* hot, Blakey conceded — but necessary, if the Africans were to recognize what they were supposed to be and spread the word through the villages and hut clusters through which they were jarring and jolting, in a perpetual mist of dust, on the Massakori bus.

But was his function necessary? It had been easy in Washington and Vienna to give the assurances that had been demanded by the CIA Director. But cramped on a wooden seat, with animals and children scuffling at his feet and shyly smiling Africans using the shuddering movement of the vehicle as an excuse to touch him, the doubts crowded in upon him. It was largely the affect of the defoliation, Blakey decided. They had come upon the first swathe just outside the capital and another section that had obliterated a maize and cotton field near the last town they had passed. It was still too early for the chemical to have acted upon everything, so the affected areas drooped with decay. Another week, Blakey knew, and it would be utterly lifeless.

Until now, Blakey had never had to confront a moral conflict so openly. He had been on station in London and Rome and then, during the civil war, in Beirut and had never been required to do more than gather and communicate intelligence. There had been a certain cowardice in his refusal to face reality but he'd never thought of what he was doing as having any physical effect upon another human being. But now he would have to hurt people. He had to explain away the pestilence which had apparently fallen from an empty sky and then — as if that were not enough — he had personally to do things that would disable and even kill ... to destroy their crops and their livestock ... to cause starvation ... the baby clutching at this foot would never grow up to laugh and play as Samantha laughed and played in the well-fed safety of their Washington apartment. It might have been easier if he could have regarded them as enemies or opponents — people who would have injured him, if they'd got the chance. But they were innocent. The child groping at his foot, the tribally scarred woman sitting opposite or the wizened, crinkle-faced old man at his side hadn't had any responsiblity for allowing a rocket manufacturing complex into their country. But they had to suffer for it; they had to be maimed and crippled upon the orders of men in air-conditioned offices thousands of miles away, men who would have sneered at the Africans around him and called them savages for grunting chants to bring rain or a good harvest or a boy child instead of a girl. They talked of balances of power. And global responsibility. Who, wondered Blakey, were the greater savages?

It was late afternoon when they got to Massakori. The jeep had been arranged for them in advance by the American embassy in N'Djamena and hired in the name of the Catholic mission they were supposed to be representing. They loaded their stuff aboard and checked the additional fuel cans to ensure they had not been tampered with.

'Hope this will be more comfortable than the bus,' said Makovsky. The public vehicle had had adjustable slats instead of windows and they were both coated with a fine red dust.

'It will have achieved its purpose, spreading the news of our arrival,' said Blakey. Savagely he added, 'Just as the defoliant seems to have achieved its purpose.'

The Russian looked at him curiously. 'You knew it was going to happen,' he said.

'Being told in a luxury house in Vienna and then seeing it here on the ground are two very different things,' said the American.

'Don't let it be,' warned Makovsky.

They set off with Blakey driving, going back along the route for about a mile and then striking off north-westwards towards Lake Chad. They reached their destination — a hamlet about ten miles away from Massakori — an hour before darkness. The heat had gone out of the sun and the cicadas were chattering from the brush all around. The cooking fires were alight, trailing their white smoke into the darkening sky. It was very peaceful. The hamlet was small, hardly more than three streets, all radiating from a central market area. It was here that they parked. The elders were grouped in a half-circle beneath a baobab tree which had been stripped of its scales for about fifteen feet from the base.

'You are the priests?'

In the greyness which precedes the complete blackness of the African night, Blakey had difficulty in seeing who had spoken; at least French meant there would be no communication difficulties.

'Yes,' he said. 'We've come from N'Djamena.'

'We heard of your travelling.'

Blakey identified the spokesman. He had an upright, almost aristocratic demeanour. The looseness of the white body cloth hung around him, making it difficult to decide whether he was fat or thin, tall or short.

'I am Ndala,' said the man.

A Muslim, guessed Blakey, noting the name and the clothes.

'We seek rest in your town,' said Blakey, formally.

'Why do you come?'

'To spread the word of God,' said Blakey. Heaven forgive me for the hypocrisy, he thought.

Blakey had expected a question about their denomination, but instead the African said: 'You are welcome.'

How much he had wanted this unknown man to reject them; he wanted something — anything — to delay them.

'We are grateful.'

It was Makovsky who spoke and the American half turned, surprised at the Russian's accent: it was better than his.

'This is a humble place,' apologized Ndala, in advance.

'We are humble people who would be grateful for your kindness,' said Makovsky.

'And we would make few demands,' said Blakey, indicating their supply-laden jeep. 'We have food.'

'You are welcome,' repeated the African, 'both to the village and to my food.'

'Thank you,' said Blakey.

The man rose from among the other Africans. He was very tall, Blakey saw. As Ndala moved away, there was a movement from among those he left behind; they envied the man his ability to talk to strangers and to offer them hospitality, the American decided. Ndala walked awkwardly, his left leg stiff. Blakey wondered if the loose robe covered an artificial limb. It was unlikely, he thought.

'From where do you come?' asked the man, as they walked.

'Rome,' said Blakey.

'Is that far away?'

'Very far,' said Makovsky.

The rest house was a small, domed building. They had to stoop to enter. The only ventilation or light, apart from the door, came from an uncovered opening high to the left. It was warmer inside where the heat of the day had been trapped, and Blakey winced away from the mosquitoes. Ndala seemed untroubled. Seeing the American's reaction, Ndala said, 'It is the marshes. Now the lake is far away, but during the rains it develops a big belly.'

There was no furniture. Rushes covered the floor. They dumped their packs and then followed the man to a larger house about twenty yards away. There was a woman at the pots and when they saw Ndala and two strangers approaching her two children ran and hid behind her; one would have been about the same age as Samantha, guessed Blakey. Ndala spoke to the woman in dialect and she half rose, bowing nervously. Uncertainly, Blakey and the Russian bowed back to her. She said something and Ndala translated: 'She regrets the appalling food.'

She scooped mealie into bowls and handed it to them. There were no utensils so they ate with their fingers. Ndala made far less mess than the other two men. There was native beer, which tasted thick and sweet as if there were molasses in it.

'Where do you intend visiting?' asked Ndala.

Blakey gestured generally westwards, towards the lake. 'As far as possible.'

'To the north of the lake there are others,' said the man.

'Priests?' prompted Makovsky.

'Men of different colour,' qualified Ndala.

'Doing what?' asked Makovsky.

'Making stars,' said the African.

Bent over his mealie bowl, Blakey winced at the simplicity of the man's imagery.

'God makes stars, not man,' said Makovsky.

'There is fire, then stars,' insisted Ndala. He finished his beer and the woman appeared immediately from the darkness with a jug.

'Do you know these people?' asked Blakey.

Ndala shook his head. 'From Rig Rig and Mao some of the men go to work. Their buildings are of rock. Inside it is always cold, like the night ...'

He made a scrubbing motion with a food-flecked hand. 'There is much cleaning and the floors make pictures, like water.'

Blakey could see enough of the man's stiff leg to know that it was not false; he wondered how Ndala had sustained the injury.

'Perhaps we will visit them,' said Makovsky.

Ndala shook his head. 'There is a fence like silver, and those who work there have to make a mark against paper, every day, with their fingers which are dipped in mud. If they do not know your mark, you cannot enter.'

'Do people from this village go there?' asked Blakey.

'Some,' said Ndala. 'They camp, because it is too far to travel each day. They are treated well; there is good tobacco and much food.'

'How do the people feel about such a place?' asked Makovsky.

Ndala appeared surprised by the question. 'They are very happy,' he said simply. 'Good tobacco and much food. Without them, it would have been difficult. The harvests have not been good and last year the rains were short, so the lake did not get a big belly, as it normally does. Now, in many places, the crops and trees are dying.'

'My God says that no one should do his work or make statues of him,' said Blakey, needing to look again into his bowl as he spoke. 'Perhaps the gods are angry at others making stars.'

Again Ndala appeared surprised. 'Our wise men do not think that.'

'Perhaps they should consider again the reasons for it happening,' said Makovsky.

It was Makovsky who remembered the courtesy of tobacco, producing cigarettes at the end of the meal. Ndala accepted, holding the cigarette awkwardly with his palm upwards as he smoked.

'Are there many villages between here and the lake?' asked Blakey.

'They follow the waters, as they grow and get small. They are from the Sara tribe. Christians,' said Ndala.

'You?' queried Makovsky.

'Wadai' said Ndala proudly, as if he regarded himself as superior to the fishermen. 'We farm.'

'Is the farming good?'

Ndala made an uncertain gesture. 'The sands in which nothing will grow are gradually moving from the north; it is not easy. Now the crops die in the ground, for no reason.'

They smoked a second cigarette before rising from around the fire. Ndala walked back with them to the rest-house and watched, interestedly, while Makovsky lit the solid fuel lamp they carried in their packs. As soon as there was sufficient illumination, Blakey ignited the smoke flare to repel the mosquitoes. They waited for almost thirty minutes after the African's departure before signalling to Peterson aboard the *Arthur J. Grant*. While Blakey transmitted Makovsky remained at the doorway, attentive for any movement outside. It was a short message reporting their arrival and took only a few minutes to send.

Makovsky waited until the American had repacked the radio and then came further into the hut. The insect repellant was keeping the mosquitoes away.

'It was useful,' he judged. 'We can suggest the poor rains last season and the encroachment of the Sahara were caused by the complex.' He paused. 'And the defoliation,' he added.

'Yes,' said Blakey.

'Do you think Ndala will react to the thought that the gods might be angry at what's happening there?'

'Yes,' agreed Blakey again. 'It's unusual for two white men to stay in an African village like this; everything that was said tonight will have been repeated by now.'

'Did you notice anyone who could have been a witch-doctor among the group in the square when we arrived?'

'No,' said the American. 'But he was probably there; it would be his place, among the elders.'

Makovsky smiled suddenly at an apparent recollection. 'Wasn't

that food foul tonight?' he demanded. 'I never thought I'd manage
to get through it.'

'Because we ate, the woman and the children went without,' said
Blakey.

The Russian looked at him, curiously. 'Anything wrong?' he
demanded.

'Nothing,' said Blakey. Another lie, he thought.

It had taken a long time to make the discovery; so long, in fact, that
Walter Jones had begun to fear there was nothing in Flood's background that they could use to fight back. It was only when he'd
taken the enquiries beyond Harvard to the mid-West university
where Flood had held his first Chair in political science that the
break had come. The woman was married now, Jones noted —
well past thirty, in fact. Prettier than in the campus pictures.
There were two other children, both girls. Flood's child, which
had apparently been accepted by her insurance salesman husband,
would almost be a teenager. There was a picture of him, standing
in front of a typically middle-income house: wood frame and single
storey, two cars parked neatly in the background. He was holding
a baseball glove proudly in front of him — probably a birthday
present, Jones guessed. He was a tall boy, much bigger than his
stepsisters.

Jones sighed, uncomfortable about what he was going to do.
Properly presented, a professor abandoning his pregnant student,
it would create enough moral doubt to damage the chances of
Flood's political career. But it could wreck this family.

The Deputy Director put the picture and the reports aside, seeking justification. Flood had started the war, not them, he
remembered. They were being forced to protect themselves. It
was unfortunate but unavoidable. Perhaps it wouldn't affect the
family as badly as he feared. He reached out towards the
telephone.

CHAPTER 23

With such comparatively large parties, it was obviously judicious to separate the assault groups for their initial entry into the country, in case of accidental interception.

Sharakov's team parachuted directly into the country from the Tupalov, far to the north in the largely barren desert region. He had awakened them long before they reached the drop zone, to conduct his mid-air briefing. Trained as they were — and in awe of being led by such a man — there were still snatched glances among them at Sharakov's instructions. There was, of course, no questioning.

Bradley's group had dropped into the Cameroons, to make the border crossing on foot. There was a fail-safe margin of a further twelve hours built into the two days that had been allowed for the American and Russian soldiers to reach their co-ordinate, a thickly jungled swamp area just north-west of Lake Chad.

The Americans had a good drop without any mishaps, and despite the darkness they assembled quickly. Bradley star-sighted their position as the crooked finger of uninhabited territory in the north-easternmost part of the Cameroons. The Nigerian border would be about four miles to the east, with Marte and Dikwa the nearest towns.

'Good,' Bradley said to the sergeant, Richard Banks. 'Better than I had hoped.'

From his Washington meeting with Walter Jones, until the moment when they made their close-formation jump from the unlighted C-130, Bradley had had eight full days to mould his men into a unit. There were seven Green Berets and three Marines, all long-term soldiers who, even before the Azores briefing at which he had announced that they were to work with a Russian unit, sensed with professional soldiers' instincts that they had been selected for a difficult and perhaps unusual operation. They had

come together well and, after the Azores, with complete understanding. But it wasn't sufficient, Bradley had decided. He
allowed three hours rest, then had them back-packed and ready,
parachutes buried, an hour before dawn. Fires would have made
smoke detection possible, so they ate their rations cold. Around
them the forest remained black, but the sky began blooming a rose
pink and the birds and monkeys started screeching and chattering
with the excitement of a new day.

Bradley waited until it was almost light before giving the
briefing.

'There mustn't be any obvious reluctance,' he began. He still
burned with the humiliation of that warning in Vienna, in front of
the Russians; there was going to be no complaint about him holding back.

'It's been decided by the President, so it's an order,' he took up.
'It's an order that we completely liaise and completely co-operate
and so we will.'

He stared around at the faces; it was still difficult to discern all
the features completely.

'I want no antagonism ... no hostility. Understood?'

There was a variety of movements from the men grouped before
him.

'But there's something else I don't want,' said Bradley, reaching
the point of the talk. 'I don't want any failure. We're matching the
Soviets, man for man. But that's just in numbers. We're going to
be better — consistently better — than any of them. If there's a
foul-up, it's to be a Russian one. If a soldier can't stand the pace,
it's to be a Russian soldier. If we've got to penetrate the goddamned place to take out the rocket, then it's to be an American
shell or an American bullet or an American grenade that does it. I
make myself clear?'

There was more movement from the men and he detected a
smile from the sergeant.

'And so,' he said, 'the next thirty-six hours are going to be used
for further training ... ' He looked at the heavy Rolex, remembering fleetingly how the watch had become almost an identification
symbol for the Green Berets in Vietnam. 'We're scheduled to meet
with the Soviets at 16.00 tomorrow,' he said. 'At 16.00 I want us in

M.—H

position, packs and equipment ready for inspection, every man shaved and prepared ...' He smiled, happy at the impression he was making upon the men. 'I want us ready for anything,' he finished.

Bradley divided them carefully, a function decided for every man. Two were assigned as vanguard, alert for any native settlement or movement. Two more made up a rearguard, to move out an hour after everyone else and to ensure that in the area where they had rested there were as few signs as possible of their having been there.

It was precisely the moment of dawn when the remainder, with Bradley at the head, moved out between the protection of the forward and rear groups. Where the undergrowth permitted, he ran them at double time, able to test them in proper rather than simulated climatic conditions and aware that proper acclimatization was one of the first things he had to achieve if he were to avoid any physical collapse. After an hour he backtracked for a hundred yards, pointing at the crushed grass and broken branches and scuffed earth that showed their route. He made them erase as much as possible, then hurried them at a pace faster than he had used before, to catch up with the vanguard soldiers and stage a mock ambush. It failed because the scouts became aware of their approach and prepared an ambush of their own, intending to let them pass unhindered if they had been Africans and showing themselves only when they realized who the pursuers were.

It was four hours before Bradley permitted any break. He was greased with perspiration, his uniform black ringed under his arms and across his back. His shoulders and legs ached with the weight of equipment and weaponry he was carrying and the air seemed to burn the back of his throat when he breathed. Aware of his own fatigue, he studied each man in turn, alert for any indication of weakness. They were all slumped around, mostly just spread back against their packs; two had discarded the weight and sat hunched forward, heads between their knees.

'Attention!' he demanded, suddenly.

They came up immediately, even those who had kept their packs on and Bradley nodded, contentedly. It had been an extreme test, and he knew if he demanded another four hours, they could have done it.

'Thank you,' said Bradley, who believed in controlling men as much by persuasion as by command and was therefore rarely openly impolite: the inherent rudeness was kept in the mind. When he moved out, he continued the psychology, matching it with a physical awareness. For forced acclimatization, extreme exercise is necessary but it has to stop just before the point of final adjustment goes over into exhaustion. Bradley was aware of this and balanced his men carefully. He discarded the force marching, splitting them instead into two-man squads and despatching them at intervals, each to ambush the other within the confines of the forward guard unit, to avoid accidental encounters with any Africans. Bradley appointed himself as adjudicator, awarding points as in a war game, but doing it only for the satisfaction of his soldiers. It was an exercise for his benefit, not theirs: he wanted to test their junglecraft in real conditions, not the threadbare patches of scrub and forest which was all that had been possible in the short time available before they had left America. Vietnam had been a long time ago and it would have been easy to forget.

He concluded the exercise after an hour, as happy with that session as he had been with the earlier one of climate adjustment. At midday they had their first hot meal, beef from a K-ration pack that self-heated when a fuse was pulled. Bradley estimated that they were roughly at the Chad border. He watched attentively while the tins were buried and then radioed to the two men bringing up the rear, setting them the task of locating the hiding place. After a further hour, they came upon a small river not marked upon Bradley's maps. He decided it was a tributary or sub-stream from some larger source feeding into Lake Chad. He looked at his sweat-drenched men and waited for the first suggestion that they should bathe. They formed a disorganized group at the water's edge and then Banks pointed and said: 'There.'

Bradley concentrated on the spot and saw the ridged back of the crocodile almost completely hidden in a far mud-bank.

'And there,' said someone and Bradley saw two more, about three yards further along. From the side on which they were standing, Bradley heard the slithered splash as something entered the water but was unable to see what it was.

'Let's find where the others crossed,' he said.

'I think these are the tracks.' The speaker was a man named Logan, an angular, prominent-boned man who came from Kentucky and had a deep Southern accent. Bradley had already noted that no one in the group mocked him because of it.

Aware of how the footprints would have marked in the mud, the two soldiers sent ahead had trailed tree branches behind them, to disguise the marks as crocodile paths. It was possible, by bending close, to detect the sharpness of boot edges and once the pattern of a sole: Bradley noted it, for later criticism. He had the men find their own tree debris from the jungle floor, pointing out the earlier mistake to ensure it didn't happen again. It was difficult following the river edge. And dangerous, too, because the undergrowth was very thick near the ground. They had to ease their way through without being able to see below their knees, so they could never be sure of what they might be treading upon. Logan, who was the lead man, almost stumbled on to the crocodile nest. He had just started across a welcome clearing when he heard the hiss and turned to see the mother astride her eggs, mouth open in warning. He unslung the M-16, selecting automatic fire in readiness and gestured the others to cross behind him. The crocodile hiss became more frenzied and when they had almost crossed the gap it made a sudden, flurried movement, as if it were going to attack: the tail thrashed from side to side. It stopped about five yards from the nest and waited. Slowly, never turning away from it, Logan backed away to catch up with the rest of the unit. Bradley was waiting at the rim of the clearing. Sergeant Banks was standing braced and looking out to the river, guarding against another reptile coming out of the water behind the southerner.

'Wait until she goes to the nest,' warned Logan, with a backwoodsman's knowledge. ' 'Gators see a turned back as a weakness and they can run faster than we can. Reckon these are worse.'

The crocodile made one more feigned attack but slowly began retreating. It took fifteen minutes before resettling itself, covering the eggs. Logan still went backwards, until the clearing was no longer in view. They found the crossing-point about a hundred yards further on. A tree had come down across the river but had been prevented from going into it by a thatch of vines which held it up at an angle, like one half of a suspension bridge. Two men climbed the inclined trunk, forcing their weight down to test the strength of the vines. Then one of them continued on to the point at which it hung out furthest over the river and managed to secure a grappling line to another tree on the furthest bank. He threw the end back to the second soldier, to be attached to a more secure tree on the bank, then launched himself out and went hand over hand across the water. The rope jerked once, when the grappling iron shifted in the branch arc into which it had embedded itself, but it held. Safely ashore, the first soldier strengthened the rope on his side and they had a line stretched about fifteen feet above the river. Logan climbed out along the half-fallen tree and threw another rope across, which the waiting soldier tied to the base of the tree. One of the unit had climbed the securing tree on their side to fix the second rope much higher than the first. All the packs and weapon-webbing were fitted with clamped tubular pulleys for exactly this sort of transfer. Logan had lashed himself to the tree. The others thrust the equipment up to him, to be attached to the rope and then slid over the water to the first soldier across. Bradley led the way, remaining at the spot where he had dropped from the rope and back-pushing each of his men further into the jungle the moment they reached him. Logan was the last to cross. Both ropes had been tied with a release knot; each gave after a sharp tug, crashing into the water. The soldiers managed to retrieve them before any of the crocodiles reached the spot.

Banks was at Bradley's side when the colonel turned. The sergeant squinted up: the sun was almost obscured beyond the overhanging foliage. 'It'll be darker when the others get here; they'll be less able to see things than we were.'

Bradley nodded, pleased with the concern. While the men were reassembling their packs, he radioed the map position of the river and the tree crossing, giving a warning of the crocodile infestation.

Bradley had determined upon 16.00 as camp setting time, so he occupied the time insisting that the soldiers with him identify edible fauna and water-producing plants which might be useful in the event of severe survival conditions. The advance unit contacted him fifteen minutes before the designated time giving him the location of the camp site, and Bradley arrived ahead of time. It was an excellent site, a high rock outcrop to give them back cover and matted, almost impenetrable jungle on two sides. The men waited, expecting praise. Instead Bradley harangued them for leaving the trail at the river edge, glad of the opportunity to show some annoyance; he'd balanced the demands of an arduous day with politeness and now it was time to swing the pendulum again, let them know that he was harder-assed than any of them and would not put up with any bullshit.

They were approaching the outermost edge of the marshes and the ground was soft and spongy underfoot. By cats-cradling a series of linking lines, they were able to erect hammocks which would keep them dry and safe from snakes. It was almost dark when the rearguard arrived: Bradley had posted camp guards, of course, and was pleased that one recognized the other and that neither had the advantage of surprise.

'A problem,' announced the first soldier, immediately he entered the camp. Promulka, remembered Bradley: third generation Pole, from the steel area of Pittsburg. If a difficulty were to arise with the Russians, Promulka would be in the forefront, he guessed.

'What?'

'A nesting crocodile.'

'What happened?'

'Attacked just before we got across the clearing,' said the second man. His name was Sweetman, Bradley knew. Silver and purple heart in Vietnam and arrived home in Kansas to find his wife in bed with his brother. He'd broken both her legs as well as those of the man.

'We had to kill it,' said Promulka, 'Short burst — I don't think anyone would have heard.'

'What about the carcase?' demanded Bradley.

'Opened it up and put it into the river,' said Sweetman. 'We saw the other crocodiles attack.'

'So unless the noise was heard, we're OK?'

'We think so,' said Sweetman. 'We waited around for about an hour after we crossed. There was nothing.'

Bradley nodded, accepting the report. It created an uncertainty and he was a man who did not like uncertainties. But he was a realist, too. It was the only set-back, so far. And hardly even a set-back: he had little cause for concern.

'We didn't locate the mess tins,' said Promulko, unthinkingly adding to Bradley's confidence.

'Let's hope we can conceal them as successfully tonight,' said the colonel.

Denied the use of any light, they had to eat and assemble their bedrolls before nightfall. They used the self-heating tins again, lamb this time, buried them and then prepared to rest. Bradley established a three-hour guard rota. The mosquitoes were already swarming, so those who were to remain out of their sleeping bags put on the special head and hand nets, in addition to the repellant that they smeared on every exposed part of their bodies. Those getting into the hammocks covered their skins as well and then assembled over their sleeping bags the second mosquito nets with which they were equipped, a long gauze strip that encased them like cocoons. It was impossible to zip without trapping some of the insects and for almost an hour after they had settled down, there was the sound of shifting, grunting men trying to kill something that had got inside the netting.

They were highly trained professionals, engaged upon an operation and so none of them slept in the accepted sense of the word. Those unaffected by the changes were aware anyway of every guard rotation and of every jungle movement of anything larger than a bird or a monkey. It didn't rain, but the deepening coldness of the night after the heat of the day caused a build-up of condensation and so there was the constant drip and splash of water from the leaves and the vines. Towards dawn there was a sudden death scream of an animal, and everyone was immediately alert; Bradley counted six safety catches being released, but he guessed he had miscounted; there should have been more. It was another pre-dawn, cold food rising. Everyone was very wet and showed signs of the insect attacks during the night; Logan had a bite at the very tip of his nose and the swelling gave him a strange, almost clown-like appearance.

Bradley knew that the progress would not be as good as on the previous day. The approaching swamps meant they had to be cautious for water-snakes and crocodiles and also for the lake Africans, who lived from the contents of the water. The swamp grass and reeds were very high, taller than a man, and false-bottomed; what appeared to be firm ground was often just matted roots, with maybe a foot of water beneath. Although they were groping along, it was more arduous than the force marching. The reeds seemed to blanket the heat about them and the insects swarmed around them in clouding mists of flying things: Bradley felt a sting near his left eye and realized after a few moments that the lid was swelling closed. He kept squinting anxiously behind, aware of the marked path they were creating but unable to disguise it as they had been on firmer ground.

He wanted to call a halt, but knew it would be pointless just to stop and stand knee deep in water. So he urged them on, towards any one of the islands that the maps had marked as uninhabited. It was nearly midday before they got to one. Bradley was suddenly aware, above the reeds, of a scrappy tree-line, and gestured for caution. Although unsettled, the Africans sometimes grazed their stock on the islands and occasionally a cattle-minder or a goatherd camped alongside. He sent Sweetman to reconnoitre. The rest stood patiently in the water, seeming vaguely self-conscious, as if aware how odd they looked. Because they were so still they heard the splash. It was Banks who saw the snake first, just as he had been the one to see the crocodile. He pointed, without speaking. It was S-bending through the water, at an angle which would bring it very close to the soldier at the rear — Promulka, Bradley saw. The Pole waited, the M-16 ready.

'Knife,' ordered Bradley softly, to Banks who was standing behind him. The sergeant passed the message down the line. Without taking his eyes from the approaching snake, Promulka slung the rifle and unsheathed his knife from alongside the pack. Bradley knew the weight would unbalance the man, making it difficult for him to move quickly enough. Promulka spread his free hand, ready to make the grab. And then the snake changed course. It probably wouldn't have done, but Sweetman returned from the island and as he moved through the water he created a rippled wash which caught the snake and deflected it sideways, so that it passed two feet from beyond where Promulka stood ready, and disappeared into the reeds. There were no theatrical gestures of relief from any of the unit.

'Dry,' reported Sweetman. 'Lot of mosquitoes but nothing else to worry us. Not a great deal of cover. Saw some evidence of defoliation.'

They pushed on, bending low as they began finding the rising, drier ground, so that they would not appear as moving objects above the skyline. It was a squat nipple of land, at its peak hardly more than six feet above the water-line; during the rains it would be submerged, Bradley knew. The acacia were stunted bushes but they provided cover. The group examined the ground more thoroughly than Sweetman would have done, making sure it was safe before settling themselves. They automatically removed their boots and socks, dried their feet and then powdered them against infection. Bradley allowed cigarettes to burn the leeches off their legs and went from man to man, examining the insect bites. Jordan, a Marine who came from the Bronx and was among the oldest of the unit, had a badly swollen face. By some odd irony, the other worst affected was the youngest, a man named Krantz. Bradley's vision was obscured because of the bite over his eye, so from the medical kit he broke out three histamine injections. He gave one each to Jordan and Krantz, then administered one to himself to reduce the swelling. With the pack still open before him, Bradley counted the twenty inoculations left. Banks carried a duplicate supply: Bradley knew he had under-estimated the insect problem and hoped what they had would be sufficient.

He sat, waiting for the drug to take effect and ease the tightness from his skin. The sun was almost directly overhead, thrusting down upon them, but because they were still wet the discomfort was not an immediate problem. Bradley checked their compass position against his maps, estimating that they were about four miles from the meet-up point. Midday he saw, from his watch. It wouldn't be easy, arriving on time. Aware of the colonel's eye difficulty, Banks was using the field-glasses.

'Cattle on another island, about two miles away,' he said. 'No sign of any Africans with them. Way over by the horizon there appears to be a group of fisherman. They're too far away to see us. Defoliation on the shore-line to the west.'

He lowered the glasses, looking to Bradley. 'Known pleasanter places,' he said.

'They're holding up well,' praised Bradley, looking at the soldiers spread out in the sun; their combat uniforms were drying in cardboard-like, filth-covered stiffness.

'Still early days,' said the sergeant cautiously. 'I wonder if the Russians have had it easier.'

'Certainly drier,' said Bradley. He raised his voice, to the other soldiers. 'Eat now. We're moving out in thirty minutes.'

There was movement among the men for their ration packs.

Banks nodded in the direction of the fishermen it was not possible to see with the naked eye. 'There won't be a shortage of food, once we establish a camp,' he said.

'Food isn't my concern when we establish camp,' said Bradley.

'It isn't going to be easy, is it?' said Banks.

'I meant what I said,' warned Bradley. He looked again towards the soldiers: they'd all finished eating and were assembling their packs. 'Don't let them forget for a moment that we're going to be the better group.'

'I won't let them forget,' promised Banks.

A fog of insects swirled about them when they pushed back into the reeds, seemingly unaffected by the repellant they smeared upon themselves. Krantz put his head-net on and looked like an armed bee-keeper. Things moved and splashed in the grasses around them; snakes became a common sight, none near enough to cause any concern. Once Banks jerked away from what he thought to be a crocodile; it revolved at the sudden movement, proving to be a bulk of wood. The smell of the mud they disturbed rose about them, a stink of rot and decay.

To gain speed, Bradley ventured to the very edge of the swamp, to the harder ground, sending Sweetman and Logan ahead to scout for any African settlements. Despite the easier going, they were still half a mile short of the co-ordinate at the scheduled meeting time. Bradley tried to suppress the annoyance, recognizing it as irrational. Most commanders would have boasted at such an achievement, he knew.

The vanguard halted at the compass bearing he had given them, and by the time the main body caught up they had located a water-pool. It was almost stagnant, scummed over the top and clustered with water-flowers. They cleared it as much as they could, stripped and washed themselves in the brackish water. Because of the insect bites, Bradley decreed battery-operated electric rather than wet razors, not wanting to risk infection in even the smallest cut or abrasion. They changed their uniforms and repacked, standing while Bradley checked the webbing. It took fifteen minutes.

Bradley moved the unit out in the same formation as he had employed on the acclimatization march: vanguard, rearguard and main body between.

'If they're there, I want to suprise them,' he ordered flatly. 'Let's start as we intend to continue.'

It was another exercise, but this time there was a different determination. They were alert to everything, easing their way through the matted undergrowth with hardly any disturbance, using hand signals to communicate, to reduce noise to the minimum.

A hundred yards short of the co-ordinate they stopped completely, to allow Logan and Sweetman, who were in the lead, to scout the terrain thoroughly. It was a thick, overgrown area of jungle, creepers and vines latticed overhead, making the forest floor twilight dark. Giant fern and broad-leafed sucker plants grew taller than a man, and the birds and monkeys blurred among them, their colours muted by the gloom.

It was Sweetman who came back. 'It's very thick,' he said. 'And dark. But it looks as if we got here first.'

Bradley re-checked the compass reading, to ensure he had the correct location. 'Let's move up and dig in,' he said. There wasn't any annoyance now — just satisfaction.

It was so dark that Bradley was almost upon Logan before he saw the soldier.

'Bitch of a place,' said Logan.

Bradley was turning to the rest of the group when the movement came. It happened so quickly that Bradley later realized they must have practised the ambush several times to perfect the timing. The Russians just seemed to appear, so unexpectedly that Bradley jumped, involuntarily. They had dug in on three sides, covering the trenches with the topsoil that had been lifted with the care of a gardener cutting turf. The emplacements were expertly positioned, putting Bradley's team in the middle of a triangular field of fire. None of them would have survived the initial burst, Bradley accepted.

Sharakov emerged from the trench to Bradley's right; his combat fatigues were glued with mud and his face was filthy.

'You're dead,' said the Russian. He was smiling, very pleased with the trap.

Bradley was glad of the semi-darkness: it would prevent the Russian detecting the redness of anger suffusing his face.

'Bang! Bang!'

Sharakov jerked around at the shouts. Banks and Promulka, who had formed the rearguard, were lolling against trees either side of the approach path, M-16 rifles crooked in their arms.

'So are you,' Bradley said, to Sharakov.

The Russian's smile had gone when he turned back to Bradley.

'A draw,' judged Bradley. But it shouldn't have been; they hadn't been good enough.

Lucille looked up from the magazine every time someone entered the common room, even though Paul had followed up the telephone call to the duty nurse with a short note of apology for missing the visit. It was an article she wanted to read, about child care, but her eyes kept sliding over the words without understanding and at last she put it aside, accepting it would be impossible. Without something in her hands, she began to feel self-conscious. After a few minutes she got up, walked slowly from the communal area and started going towards her room. There was an intersection before her door, the corridor leading to the main exit. Without any positive intention, she turned down it, just able to detect the gatehouse through the open doors. As she left the hospital block and felt the gravel of the driveway under foot, she began to walk more purposefully, as if she were eager to get to some destination.

'Mrs Peterson.'

She stopped instantly, her body held in an attitude of guilt. She didn't look around.

'Mrs Peterson.'

She moved, reluctantly. Dr Harrap stood about ten feet away.

'I was just going for a walk,' said the woman defensively.

'Yes.'

'I wasn't leaving.'

Harrap didn't say anything.

'I didn't have any visitors today,' said Lucille — there was a petulance in her voice.

'Your son warned you. Wrote a letter even.'

'Everyone else had visitors.'

'He's had to go away on a trip. You know that.'

'I'm lonely.'

'You're the only person who can really help yourself, Mrs Peterson. We can only show you the way — you've got to want to do it.'

'Just a walk,' she insisted.

'Shall we go back inside now?'

She hesitated, and for a moment the doctor was unsure whether she was going to defy him. Then, her feet scuffing through the gravel, she started moving slowly back towards the building.

A thousand miles away, Paul got off the airport bus in Wichita Falls, squinting at the Texas sunlight; men really did wear stetsons and heeled boots, he saw. He hurried out of the depot, Beth's letter in his hand. Please God let her still he here, he thought.

CHAPTER 24

Gerda was already waiting in Dr Muller's suite when Bohler arrived. For the first time since they met, she was wearing her hair loose, falling to her shoulders. Bohler noticed the change and smiled across at her. She blushed, very slightly. Muller appeared unaware of the exchange.

'You slept well?' greeted the Director politely.

'Excellently,' said Bohler.

'So did Dr Lintz,' reported Muller.

Bohler looked at the woman again. It seemed strange, hearing Gerda referred to so formally. He didn't know why — it was a title for which she was qualified. Coffee was arranged on the table where the previous night there had been drinks. Bohler stared through the windows from which they had seen the sunset; even with the smoked glass, the countryside looked baked and arid. He felt favoured, protected by the air-conditioning; outside Africans were working in the gardens, weeding and cultivating. They were naked except for waistcloths, apparently unconcerned.

Muller, solicitous as ever, poured the coffee. 'Dr Bloor will be joining us shortly,' he said. 'I thought we could talk and then later visit the control area. Maybe even the silo itself.'

'Fine,' said Bohler.

'With the launch so near, you must be feeling some excitement?' said Gerda.

Muller nodded, an oddly reflective expression upon his face. 'There's always excitement, just before a launch,' he said, as if in memory.

Bohler was seeking the words that would encourage the older man to talk further when there was a sound behind him. He turned. A woman stood just inside the door.

'Dr Bloor,' said Muller, the mood of nostalgia gone 'Come in and meet our guests.'

Bohler rose, intent upon the woman as she moved further into the room. Short-haired, tall, probably a little under six feet, slim, but heavy-busted, her figure just discernible through the loose covering of her laboratory coat. He memorized the description for later transmission to Peterson. Muller fussed between them, completing introductions. There was a dampness about her hand, Bohler noted. She smiled, a formal expression. Bohler decided she was treating them absolutely neutrally, neither with the friendship that Muller was displaying, nor with any hostility at the imagined intrusion from Bonn. A very self-contained person, judged the American; maybe even a little conceited. And very attractive.

'Our coming must be a nuisance,' said Gerda.

Hannah took her coffee and stirred it before replying. 'Dr Muller regards it as necessary,' said said, not bothering with politeness.

'You must surely be able to appreciate the government's concern?' said Bohler, curious at the immediate change in her demeanour.

'Why should America and Russia have the monopoly in space exploration?' she demanded. It appeared a practised argument.

'Isn't there some point in asking if this sort of enterprise might not create a proliferation of satellites, each country trying to outdo the other?' prodded Bohler, intrigued at her defensiveness.

'We hope so!' Muller came in quickly, trying to reduce the antagonism that appeared to be developing in the room.

'What danger can there be in the peaceful development of space?' said Hannah, refusing the Director's attempt.

'None at all,' said Bohler easily. 'It's the possibility of it being turned to non-peaceful uses that is the concern in Bonn.'

'They're rather late worrying about that, aren't they?'

'I don't think it had been properly realized until now,' said Bohler. 'There's been anxiety shown by both America and the Soviet Union.'

'Anxious to maintain their monopoly,' said Hannah, as if Bohler had confirmed something.

'You must be near final assembly stage,' came in Gerda, repeating the earlier peace attempt of the Director.

Hannah nodded, replacing her empty cup upon the table. 'The

satellite will be put into position within seventy-two hours,' she said. 'From then on, it's countdown.'

'Geographically, this is an ideal launch spot,' said Gerda.

'Yes,' agreed Hannah. 'Although I'm confident the rocket would be powerful enough without the benefit of the earth's rotation thrust. But it's certainly an added advantage.'

'So it will be a synchronous orbit?' said Gerda.

Hannah frowned at the question. 'Of course,' she said. 'Would you have expected anything else this near the Equator?'

That would cause concern in Washington and Moscow, thought Bohler. A synchronous orbit meant that the twenty-four hours it would take the satellite to get into position would be cancelled out by the twenty-four hours of the earth's rotation — it would be positioned permanently on one spot. For as long as Libya wanted to pay the usage fees, the Arab countries would have an open window to anything that went on, not only along any of Israel's borders but within the country as well.

'I'm not here to *expect* anything,' said Gerda, refusing to be intimidated by the other woman. 'I'm here to make a full report to my government and, to prevent any mistakes in their report, I'm going to ask the most elementary questions. I want to know what you're going to do, not what I *think* you'll do.'

'I'm sorry,' said Hannah.

Bohler tried to catch Gerda's eyes, so that she would appreciate his approval of her rebuke, but the Russian did not look towards him.

'Shall we go?' invited Muller.

Muller and Dr Bloor were already wearing their identity plates, complete with photographs. As they rose, Muller handed one to Gerda, then another to Bohler.

'*Our* security,' he said, heavily.

Gerda brushed against him as she passed and he felt a different interest stir within him. It surprised him. Until that moment he hadn't thought of her sexually. Bohler stood back to allow the two women out behind Muller. They walked squeakily along the glittering corridor, halting at a door about fifty yards short of the junction with the living quarters. Muller inserted a plastic control card into a computer mouth and seconds later there was a hiss as the pneumatically operated doors released and then opened for them. It was steel-cored Bohler saw as he passed through: at least five inches thick. It appeared to have no function other than protection or security, because immediately beyond was a small vestibule, with lift doors set into the far wall. There was no indicator light, to show the depth from which the lift was rising. Hannah Bloor stared straight ahead as the lift descended, making no attempt at conversation.

'The favourite working place of everyone,' said Muller. 'The coolest part of the installation.'

The corridor was narrower than that which they had just left, making it difficult to walk more than two abreast. Muller and Bloor led, with Gerda and Bohler following. Bohler felt out, lightly touching Gerda's hand. He had intended nothing more than an encouraging squeeze but she tugged away. There was another sealed door, operated by the same card, and beyond that swing doors leading into the control area.

There were five Europeans there, all men. They looked up at the entry of the Director and Dr Bloor and there were shifts and movements of greeting. There was no effort made at introductions.

The launch room was smaller than any either Gerda or Bohler had known before. There were three padded chairs at the central control console, every lever and button overriding the larger, clearly designated and graded, function areas against the far wall. Ignition was on the far left, fuel control adjacent to that, then a separation mechanism in case there was any in-flight malfunction of the rocket motors, finally gyro adjustment for the satellite. To the right and ignored for the moment, because it had no immediate purpose, was the receiver section which would take and adjust the information sent back once the vehicle was in orbit. There were three television monitors and a separate camera to receive still pictures, with a feeder tray beneath it from which the developed photographs would be discharged. Beneath the radio was another print-out section, which would provide visual as well as audio record of any intercepted radio messages. Bohler curbed any outward show of his immediate concern; it was far more elaborate than any of the potential assessments he had seen prepared at Langley before he left.

Hannah Bloor immediately moved to her project group, leaving Muller to play the part of tour guide.

'There is what will make us all famous,' said the Director. He laughed, unable to contain his excitement and again Bohler was conscious of the man's boastfulness: there was a strange sadness about it, as if the man were unsure he would succeed.

Directly in front of them was a television screen in operation and focused upon the silo housing the rocket that was six days away from launch. The rocket was obviously at an angle to the lens, making an accurate gauge difficult, but Bohler estimated it would weigh between 1000 and 1500 lb. Upon that assessment, the payload would be about 300 lb. Bohler knew the silo head would be sealed, but even so there was a vague mist around the rocket base where the coolant was vaporizing.

'Dr Bloor,' called out the Director. 'Would you like to take us through it?'

With apparent reluctance, the woman came back to them. She began quickly, a schoolmistress unwilling to bother with obtuse pupils.

'Three-stage rocket,' she said, gesturing towards the screen. 'As I've already explained, the satellite will be in geostationary orbit. There'll obviously be slight perturbations, but those will be corrected inboard by a gyro operator station-keeping system. If there's a need for anything drastic, there's a motor, running off hydrazine.'

'Rocket is obviously solid fuelled?' said Gerda.

The other woman nodded agreement. 'Please,' she said, gesturing them through a linking door of which Bohler had until then been unaware. There was a short corridor and then another room similar to that which they had just left. There were only three technicians here and far fewer control systems. The satellite was supported upon a central dish, rubber tipped support struts splayed out like the arms of a spider's web to cushion it completely.

Once again Hannah adopted a lecturing voice. 'For ground control we will be using a tone digital standard, operating on VHF at about 150 megahertz. That will provide up to seventy different commands per tone ...'

'That's very impressive,' said Bohler, admiringly. And very

close to the standard to which he had been accustomed at NASA.

Hannah looked at him sharply, as if suspecting sarcasm. She started again. 'Its radio transmission to us will also be on VHF, obviously ...' She pointed to the antennae visible to them. 'Omnidirectional aerials,' she identified. 'We decided upon cross-dipole rather than turnstill.'

She shifted slightly, indicating a series of glass housings. 'Solar-powered, of course ...' Her hand moved on, towards the first of the cameras. 'We're going to employ a laser beam image producer, using helium and neon-laser, focused on unexposed film. There's an intensity modulator sending video signals through a ferro-electric crystal. The laser beam is scanned across the film and the film driven forward in synchronism, to produce an image and continuous picture.'

She turned to Bohler, smiling expectantly.

'Even more impressive,' he agreed. 'What about heat sensors?'

He had already identified them, but wanted her confirmation.

'Here,' she said, pointing to them. 'And here.'

To give Gerda the chance of having the technical discussion they had decided was her function, Bohler moved slightly away from the group towards the satellite. It was an almost standard construction, coned but hinged to open like a petal once in position. He got as close as the guard rail would permit, trying to identify the high modulus protective. Boron rather than carbon fibre, he decided.

Peterson would be very worried when he received today's transmission; he had every cause to be. Bohler knew they had all misjudged and therefore minimized the technical possibilities of the satellite: there was some US equipment in orbit now, still regarded as having a useful operational function, but far less advanced than this. God knows how Israel would respond, once it learned the degree of sophistication.

There was a walkway allowing complete access around the payload. Slowly he circled it, studying the display of the attachments. It was impossible to reach out to touch them properly. To do that, he would have had to go beyond the perimeter surround into the inner work area. Half-way around he glanced up: Hannah Bloor was studying him, intently.

He got back as the two women were discussing the inertial guidance system.

'Gyroscopes again,' Hannah was saying. She had obtained a pointer from somewhere and was indicating the adjusters with the stick.

'What about thrust misalignment?' queried Gerda.

Once again the baton flickered over the satellite housing, pointing out attachments. 'After final separation, it will be despun,' said Hannah.

'What ascent pattern?' queried Gerda.

'Hohmann transfer,' said the other woman.

'So there's an apogee motor then?'

'Of course.'

'Very sophisticated,' said Gerda.

'All this was known to Bonn,' said Hannah immediately.

'Of course,' said Gerda, equally quickly. 'I didn't mean my admiration for the development began from this moment.'

There was a hesitation, then Hannah smiled. 'It's going to be a very accurate device,' she said.

'Your customers should be very satisfied,' said Bohler, entering the conversation to take the pressure from the Russian girl.

The blond woman turned to him. 'We intend them to be,' she said.

With Muller still the attentive guide, they moved back along the subsidiary corridor to the main control room, studied the control mechanisms under Hannah's guidance once again and then moved back towards the lift. For the first time since his arrival in the country, Bohler shivered and Muller smiled at him, aware of the movement.

'Like I said,' repeated the older man. 'The favourite working area, because of the coolness.'

Had it been that? Bohler asked himself. Or the sudden awareness of how difficult it would be for them to affect the operation of the satellite seriously.

'I can understand,' he said, easily. He looked at Gerda. She was rigid faced.

They didn't go to the elevator that had brought them to the control room level, stopping instead at another to the right of the main shaft, which only took them what appeared to be a few feet higher. Bohler was conscious of the heat as they approached the silo.

They emerged on to a gantry walkway about half-way up the silo wall. Bohler instantly realized that he had under-estimated the size of the rocket — it had to be nearer 2000 lb, maybe even as much as 2500. He lagged behind the two women, watching Hannah gesture towards the stages that would separate in flight, panting up the single-file metal stairs to just beneath the silo ceiling and closing up to the others when the Project Director indicated the final assembly of the pay-load to the rocket head. There were two girdles holding the rocket upright and at two stages the fuel lines were already connected, like umbilical cords.

'Satisfied?' demanded Hannah.

There was a challenge in her voice and Bohler looked at her curiously. 'Satisfied?' he echoed.

'That we're not attaching anything other than the communications satellite for which we are contracted?'

'Who suggested otherwise?'

'I thought that might be the reason for your sudden arrival here.'

'I thought you knew from Dr Muller the reason for our coming,' said Bohler. 'There's been some concern about the function of your company and the government wanted to provide itself with a satisfactory answer to any criticism.'

The woman stood examining him uncertainly. 'So you don't imagine we're putting a nuclear warhead on to the rocket,' she said.

She meant it as sarcasm, Bohler knew, but he responded completely seriously. 'The United Nations General Assembly ratified a treaty as long ago as 1966, prohibiting the placing of any nuclear device whatsoever in space,' he said. 'Were I to believe for one moment that there was a chance of such a rocket being assembled here, then I would immediately report to Bonn, recommending that action be taken against every company forming part of this consortium. And that the West German government make known what it was doing.'

'Dr Bloor was not being serious!' said Muller, anxiously. 'It was a joke.'

Bohler remained apparently unrelenting. 'I don't believe this is a matter to joke about. Neither does Bonn. That is why they sent us here.'

'I appear to be in error,' said Hannah, conscious of the Director's bird-like apprehension. 'Of course I didn't mean to suggest for a moment that there was the possibility of us launching anything other than that which we are legally contracted to provide.'

'I'm glad of that undertaking,' said Bohler.

The Project Director appeared embarrassed.

'Shall we go back into the complex?' said Muller. His annoyance with the woman showed in his face: there were blaze marks of red upon either cheek, as if he had been slapped. Hannah Bloor was flushed too, fully aware of her mistake. Bohler led the way back down the single-file gantry steps and along to the exit on to the corridor leading to the lift. He purposely kept ahead, not wanting the discomfort between them to diminish.

In the elevator taking them to ground level, he said stiffly to Hannah, 'Thank you very much for sparing the time. My colleague and I are aware of the inconvenience it must have caused you.'

'You're welcome,' she said. 'It was no inconvenience.'

'Perhaps I misunderstood then,' said Bohler, increasing the tension.

There was discernible hostility in the way that Hannah regarded him. 'Perhaps you did,' she said.

At ground level, they grouped uncertainly around the lift exit.

'I have more work to do, if you will excuse me,' said the Project Director, breaking the impasse.

'Of course,' agreed Muller instantly, relieved.

They stood silently in the corridor, watching her walk away.

'I'm very sorry,' said Muller, when she was beyond hearing. He waved his arms, hopelessly. 'What can I say?'

'The emotion at the beginning of a launch,' reminded Gerda, recalling their discussion at the start of the day.

'You're very understanding,' said Muller.

'We're scientists,' said the girl. 'Perhaps employed differently from yourself and Dr Bloor. But scientists, nevertheless.'

'This hasn't been as I intended,' said the old man, apologetically. 'I would like there to be another meeting very soon with Dr Bloor. Tonight, in my suite perhaps. We'll eat there again, as we did last night.'

'We'd be very pleased to accept,' said Bohler, for both of them. Gerda nodded.

'Again,' said Muller, 'my apologies.'

'I don't consider that you have anything to regret,' said Bohler, the formality of his speech indicating otherwise. 'As Dr Lintz has already said, we understand perfectly.'

He turned, taking Gerda's arm, moving her away to maintain the Director's uneasiness. Without question this time she turned to the left, towards his quarters. Gerda managed to contain herself until they got into the suite and then she turned, seizing his hands with almost child-like excitement. 'You were magnificent!' she said. 'I don't know why you did it to her, but you were magnificent.'

'A card,' said Bohler, simply.

'Card?'

'The admission disc, into the launch area. Unless we have access, we might as well pack up and leave now. I reckon we've got Muller so edgy, he'll give us one without fully being aware of what he's doing.'

'That's very clever.' The enthusiasm had gone now; in its place was quiet admiration.

'The opportunity presented itself, so I took it,' he said, simply.

'I think she hates you,' said Gerda. There was satisfaction in her voice and Bohler smiled.

'I don't think she does,' he said. 'I think she was just overly defensive. I can understand it.'

'She's a bitch.'

'Nice body, though.'

Her face stiffened momentarily and she instantly tried to relax the expression, belatedly aware that he was mocking her. She tried to retreat behind her barrier and this time Bohler made it easier for her.

'Work,' he said, simply.

As she had done the previous day, Gerda moved to the door, to provide a warning of any unexpected entry. Bohler made no attempt to disguise the fact that he was writing out the information that they had discovered, putting it in the form of an official report of the sort that the authorities within the complex would imagine he had to compile. It took him almost an hour and then, silently, he offered it to Gerda. For a further thirty minutes, with Bohler at the door this time, she added the technical details she had learned from her separate discussions with Hannah Bloor and inserted in his account the gyro anti-spin fitment to the satellite which he had forgotten. It took a further fifteen minutes to dictate the report into the special radio and another five to transmit it. Bohler finally sat back in his chair, aware of the ache in his shoulders from the tension of what he had been doing. Needing no prompting this time, Gerda came further into the room.

'It isn't like they believed it would be, is it?' she said.

He frowned at her, not understanding.

'Who's in charge of whom,' she expanded. 'You've taken control.'

'It didn't happen consciously.'

'I didn't say I minded.'

'You spoke to Dr Bloor more than I did,' said Bohler. 'What's the most obvious sabotage?'

'Gyro settings,' said Gerda immediately.

Bohler shook his head. 'I got closer than you did to the satellite,' he said. 'They're already housed within the cone. There would never be sufficient time to locate them, unscrew the guard plates and re-set them.'

'Fuel then,' said Gerda. 'Try to make it misfire. Or burn up on launch.'

'What about the television monitor? The silo's under constant observation.'

'What's your idea?' demanded Gerda.

'Something far less ambitious,' said Bohler. 'It would only take a slight over-tightening of one of those protective plate screws and the satellite wouldn't open properly, once it was placed in orbit.'

'But it would still operate partially,' argued the girl. 'Surely we were told it had to malfunction completely.'

'What we were _told_ to do and what we _can_ do are two different things,' said Bohler.

'The satellite isn't closed yet,' reminded Gerda, accepting his argument. 'Could we misalign the omnidirectional aerials?'

'Probably,' said Bohler, doubtfully. 'It would probably be picked up during the final check through and corrected.'

'You're being very defeatist,' she protested suddenly.

'I'm trying to be objective,' insisted Bohler. 'We came here expecting fireworks in a tin shed. Not this degree of sophistication. To be effective, we should have got in here months ago, during the early construction stages.'

'But we didn't get here during the early construction stages,' said Gerda. 'And the satellite pictures didn't show tin sheds, either. They showed us what we've found.'

'OK,' agreed Bohler. 'So _I_ under-estimated.'

She indicated the radio. 'Shouldn't we warn them how difficult it's going to be?'

Bohler considered the suggestion. 'That _would_ be defeatist,' he said. 'Let's see if we can do something, first.'

'All right,' she said.

'I like your hair,' he said suddenly.

Instinctively her hand went to her head and she smiled and then flushed, as she had done in the Director's suite.

'I felt I had to meet the competition,' she said. She attempted to make it sound a joke, but Bohler knew she meant it seriously.

'What competition?' he said, going along with her mood.

'We hadn't met her then,' said Gerda, coquettishly.

This time she didn't remain still when he went to her. She reached out for him eagerly, pulling his mouth to hers, holding his head between her hands and kissing him again and again. He matched her frenzy, lifting her from the chair so that they were both standing, bodies close together. After a while they stopped, breathless, and he guided her unprotesting to the divan. He laid her down, gently, and began kissing her once more, more softly now. She lay with her eyes closed, one hand caressing his cheek, the other looped around his neck, as if she feared he might pull away. She moved her body, to make it easier when he began undressing her. He had expected her to be shy, but she lay naked before him almost proudly, one arm behind her head so that her breasts were lifted for examination. He bent, trapping a nipple between his teeth and she mewed and circled her hand around his neck, pressing him down upon her. He snailed his tongue lower and she opened her legs: her hand was firmer on his neck, guiding him to where she wanted him to go. It wasn't a mewing sound any longer. She was groaning, the emotion shuddering from her. Her body began to thrust into him, in urgent, arcing movements. Her nails were biting into his neck, holding him there. He was nervous of hurting her with his teeth, but she drove his head into her body until it was difficult for him to breathe, then she gave a tiny scream and the thrusting gradually subsided. He looked up. Gerda's face was flushed and her hair lank with sweat.

'You've still got your clothes on,' she complained. Her voice was thick.

'You didn't give me time.'

'I'm giving you time now.'

He hurried his clothes off, easing on to the bed beside her. She felt out for him, her fingers and mouth butterflying over his body.

'Now it's your turn,' she said, the words blurred against his stomach. She seemed to get as much enjoyment giving as receiving pleasure. He started to move very quickly and she straddled him, bearing down and groaning afresh when he entered her. She controlled their pace, hands pressed down against his shoulders, saying 'No, no,' when he tried to go too fast. They exploded together, clutching each other and she still kept moving, not wanting him to stop.

'My God!' he said. It was a disbelieving sound.

She pulled herself from his shoulder, holding her head just above his so that they were nose to nose. 'Was that a note of criticism, sir?' she said, lightly.

'That was *definitely* not criticism,' he said. She seemed very pleased with herself.

Her mood suddenly changed. 'I'm still very frightened, being here,' she said.

'But this wasn't because of nervousness?'

'No,' she agreed immediately. 'This was because I wanted to.'

'Why all the rejection, before?'

'Because I didn't want it to happen. I knew it would, but I wanted to avoid it.'

'I'm glad you didn't'.

'So am I.'

She was so close that he only had to move his lips to kiss her. 'Be very careful,' he said, tenderly. 'I don't want you getting hurt.'

'And you,' she insisted.

'We'll both be careful,' he said.

'For what?' she demanded, in sudden complete awareness.

'Let's not think about what might happen afterwards,' he pleaded hurriedly.

This time she kissed him. 'Wouldn't it be nice to stay in here forever, with the door locked?' she said.

'That wouldn't get a rocket off its axis.'

She got off him, grinning down. 'We destroyed one projectile pretty effectively,' she giggled. 'I wonder if that's an omen.'

The Israeli Premier entered the room with his customary fluster and David Levy wondered why the man constantly felt the need to indicate the pressure upon his time.

'Sorry to keep you,' said Weismann, automatically.

'I know you're busy,' said the Mossad Director.

Weismann indicated the file upon his desk. 'They've got an amazing amount of intelligence out of the installation,' he said.

'It's a very good operation,' agreed Levy.

'What about the other groups?'

'So far there's been no cause for them to be used. They're in position, according to the last report I got from Washington.'

'Are the Americans telling us everything?'

'I think so,' said Levy.

'What about our own group.'

'Fifty-five man unit,' reported Levy, immediately. 'I've had them training for a week. The desert area near Beersheba is sufficiently large for us to have built a complete mock-up of the installation, created to scale from the satellite reconnaissance the Americans provided.'

The Premier nodded. 'What about refuelling?'

For a moment, Levy appeared embarrassed by the answer. 'The Egyptians have given us permission to establish a fuel dump right on the border with Libya and the Sudan, about two hundred miles south east of the Dakhilah oasis.'

Weismann smiled, knowing the reason for Levy's discomfort. 'So there is a point for establishing treaties with Egypt, after all,' he mocked.

'They've been very helpful,' said Levy, stiffly. 'We're airlifting Sikorsky helicopters in, by C-130. We'll be able to refuel in mid-air, too. Logistically, we're in a much better position than we were in Uganda.'

'When do you go?'

'Not yet,' said Levy cautiously. 'Let's see what progress the Americans and the Russians make first. We might ruin everything by moving too quickly.'

CHAPTER 25

Across the other side of the hut, Makovsky slept with one arm over his face, as if he were protecting himself. Blakey stirred cautiously, concerned at the sound the rushes made and not wanting to awaken the Russian; they intended to get off early, before the heat of the day, but there was no reason to rouse him for another hour. The mosquito flare still burned and a lot of the vapour clung to the inside of the hut. It stung Blakey's eyes, making them water and he blinked against the discomfort. At least this was physical, something he could rectify. He wished it were as easy to resolve the doubts and uncertainties that had kept sleep beyond a dozing distance. It was not a new emotion, this stomach-emptying, numbed feeling of despair. Or even — yet — as bad as he had ever known it. At the seminary it had been far worse. A helplessness, he supposed. Certainly that was how he had identified it then, a helplessness to avoid hurting the fathers who had spent so much time preparing him, and his parents, who had sacrificed so much to keep him in the college. But hadn't the seminary been easier? he demanded of himself. He'd agonized over the disappointments he would cause — wept with them, even. But beneath it all he knew that the priests who had tried so hard and his parents, who had wanted so much, would learn in time to accept his decision. Respect him for it, maybe. But this was far worse: the helplessness this time was in setting out knowingly to harm and not being brave enough to prevent himself doing it. No one would understand and respect him for what he was about to do.

He eased the wallet from his rear pocket and then, from one of the rear recesses, took out the picture of Jane and Samantha. He stared down at it, rubbing it free of imagined dust. The child on yesterday's bus would have been a year older, perhaps a little more. Dear God, he prayed, what am I to do?

'What's that?'

Blakey jumped at Makovsky's question. 'I'm sorry. I didn't mean to awaken you.'

'You didn't. What's that?'

Blakey handed the photograph across the small hut. The Russian took it, gazing down expressionlessly. 'Yours?'

'Yes,' said Blakey proudly. 'Samantha is four. She can already read a few words.'

Makovsky returned the photograph. 'What's a Roman Catholic missionary doing with a wife and child?' he demanded.

'There's nothing identifying them as that. It could be any-one — my sister, for instance.' He was irritated not so much by the criticism as by the other man's apparent lack of interest.

'Jane — that's my wife — she's a kindergarten teacher.'

'Oh,' said Makovsky. He sat up, knocking the soles of his boots to clear them of anything that might have crawled in during the night.

'You married?' asked Blakey.

Makovsky looked up, frowning at the question. 'No,' he said. 'Never bothered.'

Blakey smiled at the man's phrase. 'It's not a bother, believe me.'

Makovsky was back at his boots, unwilling to continue the conversation.

Blakey suddenly remembered the information he had received back from the missile ship the previous night, after reporting their arrival. He looked across to the Russian, wondering if it provided the excuse.

'They've managed to penetrate the complex,' he said. 'And the commandos are in position.'

'You told me last night.'

'So we're almost superfluous,' suggested Blakey, hopefully.

'Superfluous?'

'If they're going to be able to sabotage the rocket from inside the complex, there doesn't seem a lot of point in our creating all this misery for the people outside.' He shuddered. 'That defoliation is terrible.'

Makovsky didn't reply immediately. Instead he pulled himself over the floor until he was sitting only a few feet from the American.

'What the hell are you talking about?' he demanded.

'Doesn't it upset you, the thought of what is being done?' asked Blakey, openly. The wetness of his eyes was still being caused by the mosquito vapour, he was sure.

'No,' said Makovsky. 'And it shouldn't upset you.'

'It does.'

Makovsky reached across the short distance between them, seizing Blakey's arm. 'It's too late for morals or conscience now,' he said sternly. 'If you had any doubts, you should have said so in Vienna.'

'I *did* argue,' insisted Blakey.

'For the sake of conscience, not conviction,' said the Russian presciently. 'You can't run away from it now; it's too late.'

'What we're doing isn't right.'

'You knew that in Vienna, too.'

'But it's unlikely to *achieve* anything. Except unnecessary hurt.'

'It just *might* cause the installation a problem,' said Makovsky. 'So therefore it's worth doing. Just because they're in the complex doesn't mean they're going to succeed in doing anything.'

Makovsky stood, nudging the American's water-bottle towards him with his foot. 'Take a drink,' he said. 'Then I'll go to the well and fill them both up before we set off.'

Blakey did as the Russian suggested, handing the man the bottle without comment. Alone in the hut, Blakey began filling the bags of his pack with belongings, then set out ration cans for their first meal. They were army supplies, but the containers were labelled with proprietary brand names. He had them opened by the time Makovsky returned. They put chlorine into the bottles to purify the water and then swilled down their malaria pills; Blakey grimaced at the metallic taste that the cleansing tablets had given the water.

'The villagers are up,' reported Makovsky. 'I saw Ndala. He asked if we wanted a guide and I said no. He's told me the best way to go.'

Blakey attempted to eat but found it impossible.

'What's the matter?'

'I'm not hungry.'

Makovsky made as if to speak again but shook his head instead; it seemed a gesture of disappointment.

The African headman approached as soon as he saw them at the doorway. 'I have told your friend the way to travel,' he said to Blakey. 'Always to where the sun rests.'

'Thank you,' said the American.

'Will you return?'

'I don't know. Probably.'

'You will be welcome.'

Beyond the African, Blakey saw the woman crouched again over the cooking fire. The children, with the safety of distance separating them, had grown bolder. They were standing in front of their mother staring at him and giggling at their bravery. Makovsky heaved his pack into the back of the jeep and pulled a securing strap across it to prevent it bouncing out when they travelled over rough terrain. Blakey did the same. Ndala was on the driver's side. Blakey extended his hand and the African took it.

'God be with you,' said the African.

Blakey swallowed, trying to reply.

'And with you,' said Makovsky, from the other side of the vehicle.

Blakey took the car slowly out of the village, watchful for children or any sudden flutter of chicken. Beyond the village, maize grew high along either side of the track. Makovsky screwed around in his seat, staring back to the village. 'Damn,' he said bitterly.

'What's the matter?' said Blakey, preparing to brake.

'The track is too straight: they'd see if I tried to poison any of this crop.'

Blakey winced, gripping the wheel tightly and taking his foot away from the pedal.

The Russian turned around, settling himself in the seat. Carefully he cleaned his sunglasses. 'It might have been too much anyway,' he said, reflectively.

'Too much?'

'To kill the crops, as well. When I got our water this morning I fixed a cyanide cap to the side of the well. It'll take most of the day for the adhesive to melt in the sun. Then it will contaminate the water.'

Blakey stopped the car, turning to the man beside him. 'Why?' he demanded, anguished. 'Why them? They looked after us, for God's sake.'

'Why not them?' rejected Makovsky angrily. 'Don't play the bloody hypocrite with me. It doesn't matter, don't you see? We've only got a short time, so we've got to hurt anyone who befriends us just as we have to hurt a village where we'll only stop for an hour.'

A feeling of positive nausea spread from Blakey's stomach and for several moments he feared he was going to vomit. The sun was not yet over the rim of the horizon, but the perspiration spread over his face as if he were fevered.

'Let's go on.' said Makovsky. He leaned across the dashboard, firing the ignition. Blakey engaged the gears and took the car forward again. They travelled without talking, each man encased in his misgivings about the other. The track was baked hard from the months of summer sun and Blakey was able to take the jeep faster than he had expected, despite the occasional teeth-snapping pothole. Sometimes the savannah grew higher than the vehicle, so that all they could see was the dark ribbon of road ahead, and when that happened the American slowed, not risking any sudden collision with an animal. For other long stretches, the grass was short and stunted and they could see for miles; the sun was drying out the overnight dampness, puddling milky-white mist in dips and depressions. On one of the open plains they came upon a pair of rhinos, quite near the road. The animals jerked up, startled by the vehicle and Blakey briefly wondered if they might charge; instead they turned and trotted leisurely away, occasionally looking behind to ensure there was no pursuit. It was an hour before they came to the next village and this time the road twisted through the maize and millet fields.

'Stop!' demanded Makovsky.

Blakey slowed but didn't brake.

'I said stop.'

The American halted the vehicle and remained staring straight ahead. 'Be quick,' he said.

'You.'

'What?' Blakey turned at last.

'You do it,' insisted Makovsky. He held out the canister of defoliant powder.

'I can't,' said Blakey, indifferent to the pleading tone in his voice.

'You're not free of responsibility, just because you don't actually do it,' said Makovsky. 'You're here, therefore you're guilty.'

'Yes,' agreed Blakey reluctantly.

'So do it.'

'No.'

'I shan't do everything, just to satisfy your conscience. Get out of this fucking vehicle and start doing what you were sent here to do.'

Slowly, holding the canister as if he were afraid it might explode, Blakey got from the jeep and edged his way into the crackling maize stalks. Dust and the inevitable flies rose about him. He ripped the seal away from the canister top and started spreading the powder with quick, twitching flicks of his wrist. He was very careful to keep the powder from coming into contact either with his clothes or skin. A parody of the Commandments forced its way into his mind; Thou shalt kill but not be killed. The law according to Henry Blakey and the superpowers. He covered a wide area in the middle of the field and then began making his way back to where the Russian sat waiting. The tears came when he had almost reached the road and he stopped, squeezing his eyes tightly closed, clenched fist tight against his teeth. He wouldn't pray for forgiveness; that would be the greatest hypocrisy of it all. What about Confession? Could he ever sit in a confessional, a missal in his lap, and admit to what he had done? Were there more or less Hail Marys for killing a child than for killing an old man? He shuddered, appalled at his own blasphemy.

He emerged unsteadily from the field, unable to keep a straight line. Makovsky watched unsympathetically.

'Give me the container,' demanded the Russian.

Blakey held it forward silently and Makovsky took it, testing its weight and then shaking it, to ensure it was empty.

'I did it!' said Blakey, suddenly angry at the disbelief.

'Makes you feel sick, doesn't it?' said the Russian.

Blakey looked across the jeep at the other man, curious at the softening of his attitude. 'Yes,' he said.

'I don't enjoy it either,' said Makovsky. 'I'd rather be doing something ... anything else, to damage the complex but this. But this is what I have been sent to do. And so I shall do it. I'll do it and for the rest of my life I'll wonder what sort of pain and hardship I caused these people.'

'I'm sorry ... .' Blakey moved his hands helplessly, as if he were physically trying to hold the words. 'I mean ... Oh shit ... .'

'I think you were right not to become a priest,' said Makovsky. 'You're far too selfish.'

Blakey restarted the jeep and drove slowly on towards the village. It was much smaller than the one where they had stayed the previous night, just a cluster of about ten conicle-roofed huts buttoned either side of the track. Half-way along was the plaited lean-to for midday shade, and next to it the well, marked by a tiny surround of rock and pebbles and a bent balancing arm, from which the rope and bucket were suspended. Bony cattle, ribs and haunches marked out through taut skin, were hobbled on the scrub grass. Children ran towards the jeep fearless, because they didn't know vehicles and were therefore unaware they could be dangerous. Kwashiorkor swelled their bellies and brought their navels out in hard protuberances, like accusing fingers.

'We've done enough here,' decreed Blakey.

'Yes,' accepted Makovsky immediately.

The men of the village were beneath the lean-to. Again Blakey and Makovsky found a bridge with French. They hunched in the shade, offering cigarettes and accepting the sweet beer in return. They let the conversation meander towards the complex and then insinuated the thoughts of the harm it might cause. After a while, Blakey realized that their arrival had not surprised the villagers; the bush telegraph would help them, he decided, spreading the word far faster than they could ever manage. It was too small and poor a hamlet to maintain its own witch-doctor, and the Africans digested the hints without any argument. Blakey was half aware of the children grouped respectfully beyond the lean-to and finally turned, conscious that there were several women there too. They appeared to be waiting patiently, and Blakey asked the men grouped before him what they wanted. At first the Africans appeared embarrassed to discuss it but gradually it became clear that they wanted help.

A child was at last pushed forward, his head held back for Blakey to see the eye discoloration. Each eyeball was inflamed and red. Conjunctivitis? wondered Blakey. Or the first indication of glaucoma? From his pack in the jeep he took a tube of anti-histamine eye cream and squirted ointment into the infected eyes. His hands were shaking, and several times he became frightened that he might cause more damage than the infection he was attempting to treat. Makovsky had pulled away, still talking to the men.

They left after two hours, continuing on in the general direction of the lake.

'See the signs of hunger in those kids?' said Blakey.

'Of course I did.'

'Nothing will grow in those crop areas,' said Blakey, as if he were realizing it for the first time. 'It will be poisoned now, for years.'

'I know the effects,' said the Russian.

'Christ!' said Blakey, in self-digust.

They stopped at an animal water-hole just before noon. Any animal which might have used it was far away in the shade, but a few birds were at the rim. They fluttered away as the men approached. The immediate surround was trodden and track-marked. Elephant impressions were clearly visible; about fifteen yards away there were the bleached rib-cage and leg bones of what must have been a zebra, obviously trapped by a lion while watering. The water was stained and dirty. The cyanide splashed in with a tiny plopping sound and within seconds was still again.

They erected the canvas hood for some protection against the sun and drove with the windscreen folded down on to the bonnet, so there was a constant inrush of air against their faces and bodies. The skin across Blakey's forehead and on his arms was tight and red; he glanced across to Makovsky. The Russian appeared to be tanning immediately without any initial discomfort. They ate as they drove, unwilling to sacrifice the breeze by stopping. It was mid-afternoon when they reached the lake edge. Along wide areas there were broad bands of carbonated sodium, blinding white in the sun.

'How about cleaning ourselves up?' suggested Makovsky.

They carefully checked the area for any crocodiles and then Makovsky undressed unashamedly, spreading his clothes out for the sweat to dry in the sun. The man was very hairy, not just upon his chest but over his back and shoulders. Blakey took off his clothes more slowly, feeling the embarrassment he had known from his very first arrival in the seminary at undressing in front of other men.

Lake Chad is an enormous area of water, covering four thousand square miles in the dry season and spreading out to twice that size when the rains come. But nowhere is it deeper than twenty feet. The shore area is extremely shallow and Makovsky had to walk out almost two hundred yards before there was sufficient water to immerse himself. Blakey hurried after him, seeking the covering of water. Completely naked, he felt curiously unprotected. He washed, gazing back towards their clothes and the jeep, as if he feared something might happen to them; his back was to the Russian, his genitals hidden. He was much smaller than the Russian.

He left the lake first, thrusting through the water. By the time he reached the edge, the water had dried upon his skin and he was already beginning to perspire again. There were isolated smears of sodium upon his skin and he wiped it off.

'That was good,' said Makovsky, from behind.

Blakey waited until his trousers were on before turning round. 'Yes,' he said. 'It was.'

They continued to drive north-west, with the lake to their left. Their progress was slower now. The track was less well defined and softer, because of its proximity to water. The undergrowth was thicker, too. Frequently they had to make a detour around some sudden brush outcrop or reed forest, and frequently Makovsky had to use the compass to confirm their direction. Several times they splashed through tiny streams feeding into the lake. They came upon the next village tucked into a corner made by the lake and one bank of a large stream. Seine nets were strung out on drying poles and there were dug-outs and fording rafts pulled up beyond the shore-line.

They were greeted with as much friendly courtesy as before. As well as beer they were given mealie mealie, mixed here with fish. They were offered a hut for the night but refused, anxious to cover more ground before nightfall. The conversation about the complex was easily managed, the confirmation coming quickly that four of the younger men had abandoned the fishing to go to work there. The innuendo was received impassively, and Blakey wondered at one stage whether they were explaining themselves sufficiently. Blakey was alert for the gathering of the women and children and this time there wasn't the same hesitation in the explanation. A very young mother, perhaps no older than twenty, her face open and trusting and her breasts still obviously milk-filled, offered him the baby.

'She wants a baptism,' Blakey said to Makovsky.

'Then give it to her.'

'I'm not ordained.'

'You don't have to be.'

The villagers grouped respectfully around him in a semicircle. Blakey used the chlorinated water from his drinking flask, poured into a gourd that the mother provided. He began mumbling the ritual, straining the words through a throat which felt tight and restricted, as if it were swollen. He completed the blessing and lifted the child to kiss it. As he did so, it began to scream and he quickly handed it back to the giggling woman. Makovsky recognized his emotion, taking over the conversation and sparing Blakey from any immediate need to join in the talk.

They left after an hour, still with some hours of daylight left. They had to drive inland along the rivulet edge to find the ford, about four hundred yards from the lake. Under the guise of checking a tyre, Makovsky got down from the jeep and waded into the water, concealed from the villagers by the vehicle. He embedded the cyanide canister into the river bottom; the cyanogen poison would be released over a regular period, as the movement of the water eroded the seals. They crossed and turned back towards the river. As they got near to the village again, the Africans waved to them: the woman with the newly baptized baby held it up, so they could see it had stopped crying. Half a mile further on, Blakey went into the water almost as far as they had waded when they bathed and implanted another canister in the lake.

They stopped an hour before sunset, on a sudden jut of high ground topped by trees. They erected the tent attachments from the rear of the jeep, then lit a vapour candle to fumigate it from insects. While they waited, Blakey radioed Peterson aboard the missile ship.

Without any risk of detection, he did so on an open channel, holding a two-way conversation with the CIA Director. Blakey reported their position, listened silently while Peterson reported on the activities of the other two groups and then wrote down and dictated back, for confirmation, the frequencies each would use in the event of an emergency. Peterson disclosed that they had established a weather satellite over the area, and that a build-up of cumulus was forecast. A B-52 had already taken off from the Azores, to seed the cloud with carbon dioxide, so in the subsequent encounters with Africans they had to predict an unexpected rainfall. Almost as an aside Peterson added that to make the trip really worthwhile, the aircraft was also going to be dropping more defoliant, stronger than the original, for a quicker effect. Blakey hesitantly recounted the damage they had already seen. His misgivings were obvious and Peterson's voice demanded, 'You sick?'

'Not physically.'

'I'm not reading you clearly,' protested Peterson. He appeared to be shouting into his transmitter.

'The damage is very widespread,' said Blakey.

'If it weren't evident before you visited the villages, then you'd be the prime suspects.'

'Is it necessary, to do any more?' attempted Blakey, aware of

Makovsky's surprise at his open opposition.

There was a pause and for a moment Blakey thought their connection had been broken. Then Peterson said firmly, 'If it weren't necessary, you wouldn't be there. You got that?'

'Yes,' capitulated Blakey.

'Don't forget it.'

The vapour was thick and sickly in the small space of the tent. They got into sleeping bags and then encased themselves in the cocoon of mosquito netting.

'That wasn't much of a protest,' said Makovsky, in the darkness.

'The channel was open for you to speak,' said Blakey.

Makovsky didn't reply.

'When I get back to Washington, I'm going to quit,' announced Blakey suddenly.

'That'll impress all these people we're hurting,' said Makovsky.

'It'll mean I'll never again have to harm anybody else.'

Again Makovsky was silent. Then he said, 'At least you can get out. I don't have the choice.'

On the missile destroyer, Peterson sat gazing at the receiver upon which he had just spoken to Henry Blakey. The argument shouldn't have surprised him after the protest in Vienna. And really the feeling wasn't surprise; it was irritation. He decided not to include the conversation in his report to Petrov. It showed the American apparently the weaker of the two men and Peterson didn't want that to be evident.

In the older area of Wichita Falls the stockyards and the warehouses were gradually being demolished. The buildings were condemned and boarded up and supposedly empty, but they had been discovered by derelicts with the instinct they have for such ghettoes where they can exist for a day or a week or maybe even a month, safe and undisturbed by any officialdom.

It took Paul two days to locate it, a building set back from the service alley and isolated among a cleared area of rubble and debris. Groups of people sat round two fires, kindled from the rafters and planks of buildings already destroyed. Separate from the others, a group of three were squatting in a lotus position, apparently meditating. From within the building came a shift of movement, hidden and secret. It was like a huge nest, thought Paul.

Apprehensively he moved from group to group, aware of their hostile wariness. At first he imagined it was because they regarded him as authority but then, with a stab of actual fear, he decided they were assessing him as a victim, trying to estimate the amount of money he might be carrying or the value his watch would bring at the nearest pawnshop. There were no longer any doors at the warehouse entrance, but it was dark inside. He edged in, trying to blink the sunlight from his eyes and focus. There were about twenty people spread about, some close together in occasional, mumbled conversation, others quite alone, isolated from everything.

'Whadya want?'

The question made him jump, echoing around the cavernous building. Knowing they'd sense any fear and try to use it, Paul immediately went to the largest group. About them clung the odour of urine and dust and body smells.

'Looking for a girl,' he said. 'Beth Peterson. Anyone here know Beth Peterson?'

There were four men and the fifth was probably a woman, although he wasn't sure. In the middle of their circle the neck of a bottle stuck out from a brown bag. They stared up at him sullenly, not answering.

'Beth Peterson,' he said again. Should he offer them money? Around him the nest moved and heaved. They'd rush him, if they openly saw money.

'My sister,' he tried again. 'I'm looking for my sister.'

A raincoated man, face streaked and ingrained with dirt, reached forward for the bottle, shaking his head. Paul was unsure whether it meant ignorance of the girl or rejection.

He moved on. A boy, hair streaming down his back, barefoot and wearing just jeans and T-shirt, watched bird-like as he approached.

'What have you got?' demanded the boy and Paul recognized the voice which had shouted, startling him.

'Got?'

'Coke? Horse maybe. How about grass? You got any grass?'

'I'm looking for my sister. Do you know a girl here called Beth Peterson?'

'You ain't got anything?' the boy seemed aggrieved.

'No,' said Paul, shortly. 'I haven't got anything.'

'Betcha got the money to buy something, though?' the boy leered, a cunning look.

Paul knew he could have defeated the boy easily enough, if he had made any sudden grab — he was emaciated, almost skeletal. But others would have joined in, the moment any fight began. He backed away, moving further along. Dotted about were odd scraps of furniture and bedding and occasionally a packing case, up-ended to form a table. Halfway along a metal stairway thrust up to nowhere, the floor to which it had once led long ago removed or collapsed. At its base was a side door and he was actually in front of the figure slumped there, about to ask his question, when he realized it was his sister. She was wrapped in a greasy, once-red-but-now-brown poncho. The jeans were frayed and tattered at her ankles and she wore sandals with no securing straps, just a small toe hook. Her hair was banded with dirt. Her face was smeared, too, and there were yellowing spots in the crease where her nose met her cheek and in the corners of her mouth. Her eyes were vacant and unfixed.

'Beth,' he said, going down on to his knees in front of her. 'Beth.'

Her mouth moved, in a haphazard smile. 'Hi,' she said, in a far-away voice.

She had not recognized him, Paul realized. He reached out into the folds of the poncho, trying to find her hands to squeeze some response from her.

'Beth,' he said again. 'It's me, Paul. I've come to take you home, Beth.'

He found her hands, pulling her forward eagerly. The movement shifted the poncho and he saw the black needle marks near the big vein in the bend of her arm. There were ridged bruises, too, where she'd hurried to tie the tourniquet and in several places, particularly on her left arm, some of the puncture marks were scabbed and festering.

'Jesus Christ!' he moaned.

She was blinking, squinting her eyes together at the growing awareness of someone before her.

'It's me, Beth. It's Paul. Come on; we're going home.'

With an effort, she concentrated upon him. 'Not my daddy,' she said, accusingly. 'You're not my daddy.'

'It's Paul,' he said, cupping her face and holding it in front of his, urging her to recognize him.

'Wanted my daddy. Wanted him to come.'

'He couldn't make it, not this time,' said Paul, bringing the girl to her feet. 'I came instead.'

This time the effort was so great that sweat broke out upon the girl's face. 'So glad you came,' she said. 'So glad.'

CHAPTER 26

Now that the Russians had washed away the dirt and camouflage of their ambush, Bradley could see how close they were to complete exhaustion and realized the pace at which Sharakov had forced them, to make this possible. He could have done it, the American decided. He could have forced his unit the previous day, after the initial acclimatization, and made the rendezvous first. But he'd consciously held back, to keep them properly fighting fit. And his had been the right decision: troops as drained as the Russians obviously were could perform no useful function. Without any embarrassment or reflection upon his own intentions, not three hours earlier, Bradley decided that Sharakov had managed a cheap advantage and gained nothing by it.

The Russians appeared to have realized it. Sharakov had openly shown the irritation and his men given indications of it as they had laboured to erase the traces of their trap under the gaze of the Americans. Sergeant Banks had intercepted Bradley's look and correctly assessed it; he'd let the men settle themselves. They sprawled and lounged against the trees and undergrowth, waiting with apparent patience while the Soviet group refilled their trenches, replaced the top covering, brushed the footprints away and then washed in a pool similar to that in which the Americans had cleaned up, a mile back along the track.

The Russians were slow reassembling. Their movements were unco-ordinated and they all appeared drooped and listless with fatigue. Bradley timed the moment perfectly. Just as they had managed some sort of assembly and were looking towards Sharakov for the order to rest, as the Americans had been doing for the past hour, Bradley moved forward with sudden urgency and said, 'Shall we move out then?'

There was just a moment of perceptible hesitation before Sharakov turned, to look at him.

'Move out?'

Bradley waved generally towards the dark overhanging jungle. 'This is no good for any sort of camp,' he said. 'And there's only three hours of daylight left.'

Bradley stared blankly at the Russian, waiting. There was no way that he could be challenged: it *was* a bad spot at which to remain and it *would* be dark in three hours.

Sharakov nodded, snapping a command without looking at his men. He stayed gazing at the American, an expression of baleful dislike.

'Man for man, front and rear?' said Bradley, appearing unaware of the other man's feelings.

Sharakov nodded, shouting again to his men without looking at them. Two men detached themselves from the group. Bradley gestured to Logan and Sweetman and the four men moved together; Logan nodded and smiled in a lopsided way and Sweetman appeared embarrassed. The two Russians stayed open-faced. Bradley singled Logan to set out first and Sharakov picked out a man to accompany him. Sweetman and the other Russian moved to the back of the clearing, waiting for the main group to file out ahead of them. There was a confused milling and Bradley realized the men were waiting to see how he and Sharakov would move out. The American strode to the head of the group without any consultation; Sharakov followed. Bradley consciously moved fast, setting the pace. Where the jungle growth permitted it, they walked side by side, but at the places where it closed in, making single file necessary, Bradley allowed almost elaborate courtesy, gesturing the Russian ahead of him. Every time it happened, Sharakov made a conscious effort to slow the speed of the march. They travelled without any conversation, the only sound apart from the shouts and screams of the jungle was the occasional creak of some loosely-tied webbing or the chink of improperly secured metal. Sweat engulfed them; Bradley could feel the wetness squashed against his back as his pack lifted with each step. He guessed it was the fear of ridicule by the Russians that prevented his men using their head-nets against insects.

It was Bradley who called the halt, after an hour. His men immediately spread themselves and so did one or two of the fitter

Russians, but the majority of the Soviet group merely halted, heads hung, as if they were unaware of the stop. Sharakov jerked a command at them and they seemed to pull themselves awake, then immediately slumped to the ground.

'Your men seem tired,' Bradley said to Sharakov.

'And yours careless,' came back Sharakov.

'You knew the co-ordinate,' argued Bradley. 'It was an easy ambush to set.'

'So were you aware: it should have been as easy to detect.'

'My men are working under orders to co-operate — we weren't anticipating amateur theatricals.' Bradley had intended sarcasm but it came out badly.

'You're in hostile country on a hostile mission,' Sharakov scored, easily. 'You should anticipate everything.'

Logan's Kentucky twang spurted out from the radio, sparing Bradley the difficulty of a reply. The camp site was about six hundred metres ahead, where a knoll had suddenly thrust up in some geological freak, creating an area that was both dry and easily guarded.

'Mah friends agreed it's good,' came Logan's voice, as if aware of Sharakov's attention to the transmission.

Bradley rose at once, knowing he had put himself at a disadvantage with Sharakov and unwilling to continue the discussion. The other Americans came up instantly, ready for a sudden movement and then the Russians dropped unsteadily into line. There was an anxiousness about the Soviet soldiers, an eagerness to reach some sanctuary, but unsure if their strength would last out until they got to it.

It was a good site, the best they had had since their parachute drop and Bradley nodded appreciatively towards Logan. The knoll rose up, a gradual sweep of dry, firm ground topped by a thatch of trees and undergrowth from which a sentry would be aware of any approach for over a hundred yards in any direction. The incline wasn't regular but broken in the middle, creating a cupped area of perfect protection between two small ridges.

Aware of the scrutiny, Logan nodded his head beyond one of the ridges and said, 'There's even a stream: water's fresh and good.'

Without any apparent intention and certainly without orders

from either Bradley or Sharakov, the Russian and American soldiers spread out over opposing ridges, like the formation of some biblical encounter. The Americans at once began erecting tents and cover sheets but the Russians sat dully on the grass, recovering. There was no conversation between them.

'Time to talk,' Bradley invited Sharakov.

The Russian nodded, following Bradley further up the slight hill. Bradley stopped where the two ridges joined, before climbing up on to the tiny coppice at the top. He turned, gazing down: the Russians were to the right, the Americans to the left. On higher ground, it was easy to detect the defoliation to the east.

'Your men should get their tents up,' said Bradley, squinting towards the sky; the sun had already gone beyond the tree-line and the shadows were spreading out towards them.

'Time enough,' said Sharakov.

Fearing that the Russian was going to resume their earlier dispute, Bradley began talking urgently, outlining what he had learned from his radio contact with Peterson in the Gulf of Guinea, with no way of knowing that he was merely providing a confirmation of what Sharakov had been told during his radio discussions with Petrov in Odessa. Sharakov listened intently, knowing of Peterson's honesty from the KGB's interception of the broadcast from the complex, and wondering whether Bradley would attempt to hold anything back. He didn't.

'They seem to be doing well, inside the complex,' judged Sharakov.

'Remarkably so.'

'A week isn't a lot of time — for any of us.'

'It's got to be,' said Bradley.

Below them there was movement from the Russian side as the soldiers began assembling their tents.

'Libyan officers commanding African irregulars shouldn't be much opposition, if we've got to go in,' said Sharakov.

'If we lost the element of surprise, they'd have an advantage with whatever firepower they've got established in those watchtowers and beyond, nearer the complex,' said Bradley cautiously. 'Bohler thought the approach might be mined and certainly the wire is electrified ...' He paused, thoughtfully. 'With that degree of protection, I think we should expect some other sort of electronic surveillance. Sensors maybe.'

'Sensors would make any sort of night-time reconnaissance difficult,' said Sharakov. 'And we'll have to establish an entry path, in case we've got to go in.'

'We'll have to do both,' suggested Bradley. 'Daytime, for sensors. And then nighttime, to get in close.'

Daylight was almost gone now; everything stretched before them in greys and blacks. Sergeant Banks had posted a sentry near the jungle edge from which they had emerged, and they were suddenly aware of the man gesturing into the camp, beckoning other men forward. As Bradley and Sharakov stood up, they saw Sweetman and the other rearguard Russian. Sweetman was carrying both packs and rifles and supporting the Russian's lolled, almost collapsed body. Americans and Russians moved from both sides to help. By the time the two commanders reached the spot, the Russian had already been laid out, his boot and sock removed and his trouser opened to the knee. It was so dark they had to use a flashlight to see the injury. The man's leg was swollen from ankle to knee and very inflamed; just above the ankle there was a contrasting patch of white about two inches in circumference. In the middle were two puncture marks. Between them was the incision which Sweetman had made with the scalpel from his first aid kit, and there was a perfect circle around the wound where he had clamped the extraction tube and immediately attempted to withdraw the poison by drawing the vacuumed plunger upwards.

'Snake?' said Bradley.

'Didn't see it,' said Sweetman. 'Thought I would have heard the sound of it moving away, at least.'

'Perhaps a spider?' suggested Sharakov.

The Russian soldier had not lost consciousness. He was staring up at them without any real focus, groaning occasionally. He looked frightened.

'Smelt what I got out of the bite,' said Sweetman. 'Couldn't recognize anything.'

A Russian edged through the group and began strapping a pre-medicated poultice over the mark: the soldier tensed, as if the pressure were causing him pain. Everyone pulled back and two

Russians lifted the man and carried him towards one of the tents. Sweetman handed the man's pack and AK-47 to a third Russian who nodded and smiled, as if expressing gratitude.

Bradley moved towards their side of the camp and congratulated Sweetman.

'Heavy son of a bitch,' said Sweetman, mildly. 'Apparently their colonel marched them right through the night without a stop. They're bushed, every one of them.'

'How do you know?'

'Speaks good English,' said Sweetman. 'Seemed a nice guy. None of them very keen on this, apparently. Suspicious of it.'

Bradley frowned at the intelligence. The day and night march didn't surprise him, from the condition of the Soviet troops. But their uncertainty did.

'Sure he wasn't bullshitting ... leading you on?' he demanded.

Sweetman shook his head. 'Just chatting,' he judged.

Bradley turned, aware of movement from the Russian side. Sharakov appeared through the darkness. He spoke to Bradley as military courtesy dictated, but looked twice towards Sweetman, nodding recognition.

'I'd like to thank you,' he said. 'From what I gather, your man was very quick and did everything he could to help. We appreciate it.'

Bradley nodded at the gratitude, disconcerted by it. He indicated Banks. 'I'll let my sergeant liaise with yours about guard duty.'

Sharakov gestured agreement, looking directly at Sweetman. 'Thank you,' he said again.

No one spoke for several minutes after Sharakov had moved away from them. Sergeant Banks got slowly to his feet and went to find the Russian sergeant. 'Seems almost as if he wanted to be friendly,' he said.

'The orders talk of co-operation,' insisted Bradley. 'They say nothing about friendliness.'

Walter Jones hesitated outside the President's office and instead of turning left, which would have taken him through the corridors to the exit, went instead to the right. He moved hesitantly because he had never before been to the office of the foreign affairs adviser. It was very close, which he supposed he should have expected. An aide smiled up as Jones entered and, before the Deputy Director could speak, the man said, 'Mr Flood told me to expect you. He asked if you would wait.'

Jones settled himself into the indicated chair and wondered about his pipe. It probably wouldn't light anyway, so he decided not to bother. The President appeared encouraged by the briefings, reflected Jones. And with every reason — so far the operation was going remarkably well. He decided they had been due for some luck; it had been a disastrous beginning. He was surprised that Peterson did not appear to be happier about it. There again, there was sufficient reason. He would feel very cut off, stuck in the middle of an ocean: he might appear the fulcrum for all the information, but Jones guessed Peterson would be anxious about what was going on, back here in Washington. He had tried to indicate that some opposition was being mounted, during their last radio conversation, but he was unsure whether Peterson had properly appreciated what he was attempting to convey. He had had to be very circumspect.

Jones guessed that after his briefing, Fowler would have had a meeting with the Secretary of State and Flood, so he was surprised when the foreign affairs adviser bustled through the door after only fifteen minutes.

Jones rose as the man entered and Flood threw an arm around his shoulders, propelling him into the inner office. Jones moved awkwardly, uncomfortable at the gesture.

'Good of you to stop by,' said Flood, as if the Deputy Director could have considered refusal.

'I had to brief the President,' said Jones, joining in the charade.

Flood made a tower with his arms against the desk and sat with his head propped upon his hands. 'Just seen him,' he confirmed.

Jones waited, wanting the other man to make an assessment first. 'The President seems pleased,' said Flood, avoiding any personal commitment.

'The amount of intelligence from inside the complex has been remarkable,' said Jones, irritated by the man's attitude but careful not to show it.

'There's still no guarantee we can abort the launch,' said Flood.

'I don't see how there could be, at this stage,' said the deputy.

'I didn't ask you to come to talk about Africa,' announced Flood unexpectedly.

Once more Jones waited.

'You've heard the stories?' demanded Flood.

'Stories?'

'The smears about me ... something that happened a long time ago.'

'They're pretty prevalent,' said Jones.

'It's filthy,' said the foreign affairs adviser, adamantly. 'It's a filthy, disgusting campaign ... someone's out to damage me.'

'Who?' said Jones, ingenuously.

Flood smiled, a conspiratorial expression.

'That's what I want you to find out,' he said.

'Me?'

'Who else? There's no other agency with the resources that you've got. And it's a personal thing — not a problem I could ask the FBI to involve themselves in.'

'It won't be easy, mounting something like this within the country,' said Jones, entering another charade.

'It won't be difficult at all,' refuted Flood, unoffended at the token objection. He smiled again. 'You know and I know that when I leave this office for the last time, it will not be to go back to some campus in Massachusetts. I'm going to be an important man in this city and anyone who links with me early enough is going to share in all the advantages that's going to mean...'

He took his hands away from his chin so he could lean forward urgently. 'Throw in with me now, Walt,' he urged. 'Show your loyalty by helping me with this thing and you'll not find me ungrateful.'

'I'm flattered,' said Jones, keeping any reaction from his face.

'You'll do it?'

'I'd like time to think about it.'

'Of course. But not too much time, Walt. I want to find the

bastard and I want slowly to strip his skin away and then nail it to the wall to dry. It'll be an example to anyone who imagines they can try to destroy Herbert Flood.'

With the properly thought-out responses, this approach meant they could have Flood rebounding from suspicion to suspicion like a bee ricochetted from the inside of a honey pot, decided the Deputy Director.

'I won't take long,' he promised.

'It's important for you to get it right,' said Flood. 'This could be one of the most important decisions you've ever made in your life.'

'I realize that,' said Jones.

'Be sure you do,' said Flood. 'Be very sure you do.'

As Jones stood, the foreign affairs adviser said, 'You know the thing that upsets me?'

'What?' said Jones.

'The unfairness of it,' said Flood. 'That's what it is, damned unfair. Why the hell would anyone want to mount a personal attack upon me?'

'Have you contacted the person with whom your name's being linked?' asked Jones, curiously.

Flood frowned up, as if he found the question difficult to understand. 'Of course not,' he said. 'Why ever should I have done?'

'Just wondered,' said Jones, moving towards the door.

CHAPTER 27

The atmosphere was discernible as soon as they entered Muller's apartments and Bohler looked curiously from the Director to Hannah Bloor. And then he remained looking at the project leader. The change in the woman was startling. He had guessed at her figure beneath the shapeless laboratory uniform and done it badly, he decided. She was quite remarkably attractive, heavy-busted but slim-hipped, her skin toasted to a chocolate milk brown and accentuated by the violet, halter-topped dress that she wore. Her hair didn't seem mannish now. It was perfect for the long ovalness of her face: for the first time, because of the dress perhaps, he became aware that her eyes were violet, too.

She shifted under his stare and he looked away, embarrassed. Gerda was regarding him steadily, her face unmoving.

Muller hurried to meet them, retaining Gerda's hand in his and leading her to the couch where Hannah sat. The German scientist smiled at the approach, moving as if to make room. Gerda didn't smile in return. Seeming not to notice, Hannah bent forward and began to talk, creating a perfect contrast between the two women. Gerda had kept her hair down, because she knew he liked it worn that way, but alongside the other woman it looked untidy and dis-arrayed: she appeared aware of it, constantly moving her hand to replace some escaping strand into position. When Bohler had met Gerda outside her room, he had thought the dress attractive, a cut-to-the-knee affair of muted greys. Next to Hannah's it appeared functional; one woman seemed dressed for a day at the office, the other for a sophisticated party.

Muller came between him and the women, breaking the compa-rison, offering a glass. Bohler took it, smiling his thanks.

'Satisfied with the day?' asked the old man.

'Very,' responded Bohler, honestly. 'I've spent a lot of the after-noon assembling my report.' He had left his transmission notes openly visible in the room, deciding that if any sort of security check were made, it would look more suspicious if there were no record of what he was being shown in evidence.

'Always so much paperwork,' sighed the Director, 'I seem to find so little time for practical research these days.'

'I am grateful for your kindness in allowing us the freedom of your establishment,' said Bohler. He glanced towards the couch. Both women seemed to be deep in conversation, paying no attention to him. 'It would be an inconvenience if we had to bother you constantly to escort us to the control room. Or ask Dr Bloor to come to the surface and admit us.'

Muller stood head to one side, frowning at his difficulty in recognizing Bohler's point.

'Would it be possible, I wonder,' said the American, 'for Dr Lintz or myself to be allowed one of the admission cards ... ?'

Muller went to speak and, anticipating refusal, Bohler hurried on: 'We would never approach the project area without Dr Bloor's express permission, of course. I'm thinking solely of the establishment and causing as little trouble as possible.'

Muller smiled. 'I'm aware of your security clearance from Bonn. It's as high as that of anyone here.'

Bohler felt the uncertainty begin to leave him and grinned back. 'Thank you,' he said.

Muller glanced up the room towards the office section, hesitated, and then, as if making a sudden decision, walked towards the small safe adjoining the desk. Hannah shifted slightly as the old man passed, half aware of his movement.

He returned with the square of serrated, index-punched card held out in his hand. 'I've recorded it against your name,' he said. 'There's no point in issuing two, is there?'

'One will be perfectly adequate,' he said. He knew Gerda had been aware of their immediate success in gaining access and tensed against any look from her which Hannah might have intercepted. The Russian continued talking, ignoring him. There was the ritual examination and admiration of the sunset and then Muller led them to the table. Bohler decided there was something incongruous about sitting down to such linen and crystal and plate in the middle of the African jungle. Muller positioned him immediately opposite the project leader. As he helped her into her seat and then moved around the table, he became aware that more than just her appearance had changed. There was none of the hostility that she had shown earlier in the day. She smiled openly across at him, showing small but very even teeth.

'Settling down?'

'I think so.'

'It takes time. I was homesick for months.'

'How long have you been here?'

'Dr Bloor was one of our pioneers,' intruded Muller. 'Almost four years.'

'Where's home?' said Gerda.

Bohler waited intently, admiring the Russian woman for the question. They could have been caught out attempting to lie about their own supposed home towns if, by coincidence, either of the Germans came from the same place.

'Berlin,' said Hannah, immediately.

'How often do you get back?' asked Bohler.

'There's home-leave allocation every three months,' said the woman.

'But Dr Bloor hasn't taken it for the past year,' said Muller, proudly. 'She claims the project is more important.'

She smiled fondly at the old man, unembarrassed that his customary pride had grown to include her. 'There'll be time enough for a vacation when the launch is completed,' she said.

Africans moved unobtrusively around the table, placing and removing courses: two of them were assigned exclusively to pour wine. Tonight there was Rhine as well as Moselle.

'You sound very confident,' said Gerda, to the other woman.

For the first time Hannah's smile faltered. 'I've no reason not to be,' she said positively. 'Nothing has been left to chance. Everytning has been checked, checked and checked again. It's as foolproof as it can ever be.'

The woman's sudden intensity was almost embarrassing, and for several moments no one spoke. Gerda broke the silence. 'When will you complete the satellite assembly?'

'Another thirty-six hours,' said the woman. 'I want to finish the fuelling first.'

'Worried about volatility in this heat?' said Bohler.

'It's one of the slight unpredictables,' conceded Hannah, withdrawing slightly from her earlier confidence.

'I'm sure it will be fine,' smiled Bohler.

The German woman looked up and their eyes held. She smiled back. 'Thank you,' she said.

Hannah shifted away from Bohler's stare, to include Gerda in her question. 'Will you return to Germany immediately after the launch?'

'I suppose so,' said Gerda.

'There might be cause to remain for a few days,' contradicted Bohler. 'The interest is in world reaction, remember.'

Gerda's head came up at the correction. 'Yes,' she mumbled. 'Perhaps we'll stay on for a few days.'

'Perhaps we might go on a camera safari together,' said Hannah, suddenly enthusiastic. 'It was something we did quite a lot in the early days. It's not uncomfortable at all, once you've adjusted to the climate. And there are some marvellous sights ... lion, elephant, rhinoceros, giraffe, ostrich ...' She was ticking the animals off against her fingers, anxious not to forget any.

'We'd like that,' said Bohler, matching her enthusiasm.

'There isn't any danger,' Hannah said to Gerda, as if she needed reassurance. 'We can take some Africans with us to scout the area and establish the camps. We've even got machines that provide something near to air-conditioning in the tents.'

'I'm sure it would be very interesting,' said Gerda. There was a tightness in her voice and, for a moment, Hannah looked at the other woman with the beginnings of curiosity.

'Why don't we agree to do that then?' said the German woman, speaking quickly, as if to cover some awkwardness. 'We could ask the Africans to start making arrangements.'

'Fine,' said Bohler. It would never happen, if they succeeded in destroying the launch. It would be an uncomfortable expedition if they were unable to interfere and *had* to go.

'The natives claim that the crocodiles near the lake are the biggest in Africa,' said Muller. 'The lake people are very expert at tracking them.'

Gerda shuddered slightly. 'I think I'd prefer the animals,' she said.

Whey they rose from the table, Muller paired with Gerda and Bohler was left to escort Hannah back to the wider living area.

'How long does it take to get a tan like that?' he said.

'You've got to be careful,' she warned. 'During my first three months I was one big blister.'

'The scars don't show.'

She laughed. 'It was sore at the time,' she said. 'The trick is to go out for the last three hours of the day and not to expose yourself for more than a few minutes at the beginning.'

'I don't think I'll have the time,' said Bohler. 'It seems quite a production, just to go brown.'

'Perhaps on the safari,' she said.

'Perhaps,' he agreed.

'Have I upset Dr Lintz?' asked the woman suddenly.

Bohler frowned at her. 'I don't know,' he said. 'I don't see how you could have done.'

Hannah shrugged. 'Neither do I,' she said. 'It was a passing impression I had.'

There were coffee and liqueurs arranged on the table and Muller selected some Beethoven tapes. When Bohler admired the Director's stereo-installation, the old man shook his head, indicating Hannah. 'That's the radio equipment you should see,' he said. 'Mine is practically a crystal set by comparison.'

'Dr Muller and I share an interest in music,' said Hannah. 'It's a way of relieving the inevitable boredom. It's different now, with the excitement of a launch so near, but there are times when it can be tedious.'

'I would have thought you could find enough to entertain you,' said Gerda.

Everyone turned to look at her, their faces mirroring different reactions to the remark. Gerda flushed, aware too late of its ineptness. 'Safari ... bathing ... things like that,' she attempted to recover.

For a moment Bohler thought Hannah was going to refuse the other woman her escape, prodding her into more embarrassment, but instead she smiled and said, 'You can't keep on animal-spotting. And sunbathing becomes a bit monotonous after a while.'

Bohler excused them early, leaving Hannah and the Director with their Beethoven. He and Gerda walked silently up the corridor towards the living accommodation, the woman appearing intent upon maintaining a certain distance between them.

At the junction she said, shortly, 'Goodnight.'

'I want to talk to you.'

'Well?'

'Not here. My room.'

'I don't want to come.'

'What the hell's wrong with you?'

'I thought of asking you the same question.'

'My room, Gerda,' he said, insistently. He thought she was going to refuse, but then she walked past him, towards the men's quarters. Again neither attempted any conversation until they got inside.

'OK,' he said. 'What is it?'

'What's what?'

'This attitude.'

'There's no attitude.'

From his pocket Bohler took the computer key for entry into the launch area, waving it before her. 'Within fifteen minutes of going into Muller's rooms tonight we get this,' he said. 'Dr Bloor starts to unbend and offers us courtesy, if not open friendship. And you come on like God knows what. I don't understand you.'

'There's nothing wrong with me.'

'There's *everything* wrong with you,' he said. 'There were times tonight when I thought you were openly setting out to screw the whole thing.'

She faltered under the pressure of his attack. 'Nothing wrong with me,' she repeated, less defiantly this time.

He reached out, taking her shoulders. She moved her head, refusing to look at him. 'I want to know what it is,' he said again, some of the anger leaving his voice. 'We're here to do a job and so far we're having a lot of success. I don't want it fouled up.'

'Flirted,' she said. She mumbled the word, awkward with it and still avoiding his eyes.

'What?' he said, genuinely not hearing her.

'Flirted,' she said again. 'You flirted with her.'

'Oh darling!' he said, astonished. He cupped her chin, bringing her face around to his. 'Don't be so *silly*.'

'You did,' insisted Gerda.

'I was *friendly*,' he corrected. 'She was making an effort and I responded to it. She's the Project Director, for Christ's sake. I want to get as much of her confidence as it's possible to get.'

'She's beautiful,' said Gerda.

'She's the Project Director,' repeated Bohler. 'That's how I look at her.'

'I saw how you looked at her!'

'You're being childish,' said Bohler. 'Whatever I did tonight I did for a purpose. And it's not the purpose you're imagining.'

She sniggered, despite her anger; she was close to tears, Bohler realised. He brought her face to his again, bending forward to kiss her lightly. She'd fallen in love with him, Bohler thought, recognizing the collapse of all the training. The awareness worried him.

'You've no cause for jealousy,' he said. 'No cause at all.'

'Not jealous,' she said petulantly.

'Yes you are,' said Bohler. 'And I'm flattered. And I'm worried, too. Nothing can get in the way of what we're trying to do.'

'I warned you it was an unnecessary complication,' she reminded him.

'Not if we're adult about it.'

'I'm sorry,' she capitulated, at last. 'I knew it was stupid, but it was as if I couldn't help myself.'

'It was very stupid.'

'I know. I'm sorry.'

He kissed her again. 'I mean it,' he said. 'There's no cause.'

She came nearer to him and he put his arms around her — she was trembling. 'Sorry,' she said. She looked up. 'This afternoon was so wonderful,' she said.

'Didn't you think it was for me?'

'I didn't know.'

'You do now.'

'Take me to bed,' she said.

She was as demanding as she had been earlier, maybe even more frenzied because of her doubts. She made love to him, devouring him with her mouth, and then moving astride him and arcing her body as if she were trying to pull him inside her. He tried desperately to keep pace with her, knowing that if he failed, her uncertainty would remain. He managed it, just. He collapsed, shuddering under her, panting against her neck. He realized he felt very sore. It was a long time before she moved and when she did, it was only to take her head slightly away from his, so that she could talk more easily.

'It'll have to be tomorrow,' she said. 'That'll be our best chance.' Her breathing was still uneven.

'Yes.'

'I think we should make two separate attempts, in case one fails.'

'Yes,' he said again. 'I intend trying to sabotage something in the satellite itself; it's still open.'

She nodded against his shoulder. 'I'll try to create some imbalance in the fuel: from what Hannah said tonight, that's where they expect a problem. A misfire would cause the least suspicion.'

'It's not going to be easy,' he said, more to himself than to the woman.

'I've thought about that,' she said, seizing the words.

'What?'

'There's a high degree of technology here.'

He pulled further away, curious at the point she was trying to establish.

'If we're caught ... if either of us are caught ... then they'll be able to break us easily enough. Scalpolamine or some other truth drug. I wouldn't want to, but I wouldn't be able to stop involving you as well.'

He put his hand against her shoulder, shaking her. 'Darling,' he said. 'What are you talking about?'

'We mustn't get caught,' she said urgently. 'If we're detected, we mustn't let ourselves be caught.'

He lay quietly, feeling her wet body against him, digesting what she had said. She was right about the impossibility of their being able to resist any sort of scientific interrogation.

'We'll just have to be careful,' he said. 'And make sure we aren't detected.'

It was too glib, Bohler knew; it wasn't the sort of response to satisfy her.

'Yes, my darling,' she said. 'Please be careful. Please be very, very careful.'

Bohler remained awake long after Gerda had drifted into a whimpering, occasionally twitching sleep, his mind occupied with what they had to attempt the following day. His thoughts drifted increasingly away from the sabotage he would attempt on the satellite head, towards the Project Director. Hannah Bloor was attractive, he thought — sensationally so.

Paul had bathed his sister in the Wichita Falls motel room, cleaning her of the filth with which she was encrusted, and in her purse he had found the heroin dose which had been sufficient to get her back to Washington. But that had been almost twelve hours ago and now she sat cross-legged at the foot of his bed, hollow-eyed and staring up at him beseechingly; she had her arms clasped around her, trying to contain herself against the pain which was feeling out for her body.

'Help me, Paul. Please *help* me!'

'How can I, for God's sake?'

'What do you mean, how can you? You know the places ... where to score. I've got to score, Paul. You don't know what's going on inside my head. I hurt. I really hurt. You have got to do something, to stop the hurt ... .'

'I don't know anyone ... don't have any contacts.'

'Bullshit, Paul. You're the great drugs lawyer in this town. Paul Peterson, the voice of freedom. Don't tell me you don't know the places ... use it yourself maybe.'

'Marijuana, Beth. Only marijuana. Not the sort of shit you've been pumping into yourself.'

A fresh spasm swept through her, stronger than the rest. She gripped at herself and whimpered, lips tight between her teeth. 'Please, Paul. *Please.*'

He jerked up from the bed, walking aimlessly around the room. Behind him she groaned again and he turned back eagerly. 'A doctor. I'll get Dad's doctor. He'll help.'

'That's bullshit, too. And you know it. No doctor will help me, not the way I want to be helped. It'll be a clinic and that'll take until tomorrow and I don't have until tomorrow. I don't have until anywhen.'

He fumbled for his address book, scrambling through it for names. There was a secretary at the drug rehabilitation centre but there was no reply when he tried her number. He saw the name of Rubie Weinhart, whom he'd twice defended for marijuana possession and managed an acquittal. But the third time, when the man was arrested for pushing cocaine around a school in a black area of the city, he'd refused to represent him.

'Oooh!' The agony gasped from his sister and he turned to see her doubled up, gripped by stomach cramps.

Weinhart answered on the third ring; there was music and the sound of people in the background. The pusher heard him out, sniggering towards the end, and Paul had the impression that the man had held the receiver away from his ear, so that others could hear the conversation.

'You jiving me, you mother?' demanded Weinhart.

'There's a reason ... a special reason,' said Paul desperately.

'Like setting poor old Rubie up for another bust.'

'I'm your defence attorney, for Christ's sake. Why should I set you up?'

'You *were* my lawyer,' qualified the man, 'until I needed you and then we got a set of rules we'd never heard of before and Rubie went to the slammer.'

'And you'd have gone to prison before that if I hadn't represented you. So you owe me.'

'I don't owe you shit, man. I paid the fee.'

'Just once. Help me just this once. I need help, very badly.' He was begging, Paul realized, uncaring. The man *was* holding the telephone so that others could hear; he detected the sound of muted laughter.

'There's a mark called Arnold,' said Weinhart. 'Puerto Rican dude who runs the Greyhound bus area, right in your patch. Ain't the best stuff, but if you're out in the rain, even a leaky umbrella is something.'

'Where do I find him?' demanded Paul, anxiously.

'Around,' said Weinhart, generally. 'There's a spic deli where he sometimes eats, down the block. And a bar called Maxi's, right opposite. If he ain't around, then the Lord who cares for junkies don't like you none.'

'Thanks,' said Paul.

'You ain't got nothing to thank me for,' said Weinhart. 'And I ain't got nothing to thank you for, mother.'

In the bedroom Beth had toppled sideways. She lay hunched up, knees almost to her chin. She was shaking as if she were very cold, but there was a sheen of perspiration on her face and when he touched her arm, it felt damp.

'It's all right,' he said, bending over her. 'I've got a score. It's going to be all right.'

Her teeth were tight together now and he saw that she had bitten her lip: blood wavered down her chin. He looked down at her, helplessly. He pulled the cover from the bed and put it over her, then ran from his apartment to the Volkswagen outside. He knew every shortcut to be taken and reached the station area in five minutes. Apart from the bus depot, it seemed quiet: the people on the streets were mostly black. He went to the delicatessen first, parking directly outside and hurrying in. He stopped, just beyond the doorway. He saw three men, one white and two negroes, at the food counter. He went further in, staring around in case the man was somewhere else in the shop. There was no one who could have been identified as a Puerto Rican.

He went to the first man at the counter, nudging at his arm.

'I'm looking for Arnold,' he said. 'He eats here a lot. Do you know a guy called Arnold?'

The negro turned slowly, examining him, then shook his head.

'Puerto Rican,' said Paul. 'Smart dresser.'

There was another headshake and the man turned back to his food.

Paul took the car back towards the bus depot. He had to park some way from the bar. He started walking fast towards it and finished at almost a run. It was a bar typical of major terminals,

large and dark: a place for strangers. There was a juke-box immediately inside the door, booths beyond, a long bar to the left and a
doorless telephone cubicle at the rear. Paul progressed slowly
along, head moving right and left. The barman came almost as
soon as he edged on to a stool and Paul fought against his
impatience, calmly ordering a beer; he'd been gone almost an
hour, he calculated. She had been bad when he left, so what
would she be like now? He held his hands together tightly before
him on the bar, aware that they were shaking. He offered a five
dollar note, indicating he didn't want a tab run up, and when the
man brought him his change Paul said, 'I'm looking for Arnold.'

The man shrugged. 'I'm Ray and I'm gay,' he chanted lightly.

'Puerto Rican guy. Uses this bar a lot.'

'You a friend of his?'

'I want to be.'

The barman ran his eyes as far down Paul's body as was possible
across the bar and then up again. 'There's friends and friends,' he
said.

'I want to see Arnold,' insisted Paul.

'He know you?'

'Not yet.'

'Perhaps he won't want to.'

Paul bit at the anxiety, knowing that if it showed he would lose
the chance. 'Why don't we give it a try?'

Paul had left his change on the counter. The barman picked it up
without a word and walked away. He took his time, serving several
people further along the bar and Paul clutched at the beer, feeling
it warm between his hands. His eyes were constantly upon the barman and then he looked beyond, to the telephone. Would she be
able to answer, if he called? Probably not. And what could she do,
other than scream for help — help that he wasn't able to give her.

He had expected to be able to detect the contact, perhaps see a
head jerk and then someone further along turn to look up at him.
When the approach came it was from the other side, from the
direction of the door and not from the barman at all. Paul felt pressure against him, as someone got on to the adjoining stool and then
the man said, 'You the guy who's looking for a friend?'

Paul jerked around. He wouldn't have thought the man was

Puerto Rican — the features were more negroid.

'You Arnold?'

'I'm many things to many men,' said the man.

'Arnold,' said Paul, positively.

'If we're making introductions, what's your name?'

'Paul. I need help.'

'And who told you that you'd get it from me, Paul?'

'Someone I know.'

'And unless I know him too, then we're just jiving here for nothing.'

'Rubie Weinhart.'

The Puerto Rican pulled back at the name and his face set in an expression of contempt. 'That's a cocksucker you got for a friend, Paul, and I don't think you and I got anything more to talk about.'

The man shifted, preparing to move away and Paul snatched out, holding his arm. There was something hard and ridged beneath the sleeve and Paul wondered if it were a knife.

'Wait,' he said, imploringly. 'Please wait. Don't go.'

The Puerto Rican looked down at the restraining hand. 'People lose fingers for doing things like that,' he said. 'Ever wondered how you wipe your ass without fingers?'

Paul took his hand away. 'Sorry,' he said.

'That's what the world's full of,' said Arnold, making to move again. 'Sad, sorry people.'

'I didn't say Weinhart was a friend of mine.'

'He sure as hell ain't a friend of mine.' The man was standing now, about to walk away.

'I'll pay anything. I must have something. It's for somebody who's sick — very sick.'

'People never care what it costs and they're always buying for someone else, never themselves,' said Arnold. 'World's just knee deep in good samaritans.'

Paul started to cry. He was unaware of it until he felt the wetness and then he rubbed his hand across his face, not caring that the man could see the breakdown. 'I've got a sister,' he said. 'I've got a sister who's so full of shit that she's coming unglued. If I don't get something for her, she's going to go out of her mind.'

'Sick people go to doctors,' said Arnold, unmoved.

'She needs something now, right now,' said Paul. He'd shouted and the Puerto Rican looked quickly around the bar, seeing what attention had been attracted.

'Easy boy,' he said. 'Easy.'

'A hundred dollars,' said Paul. 'Just one purchase, a hundred dollars. That's three times the rate.'

'Now how does an innocent boy buying goodies for his sister know what the rate is?'

'I know.'

The Puerto Rican stood looking at him for several moments. Then he said, 'Down by those telephones there's a men's room. Why don't you go and have a little pee-pee?'

Paul hesitated, then got down from the stool and walked the length of the bar. The barman saw him and smiled. As Paul went by he called 'There's piranha fish in the urinals. Maybe you'll be lucky.'

The lavatory smelt of sour urine and unflushed toilets. The wall was spidered with graffiti and telephone numbers and holes had been gouged in all the cubicle doors. The noise of occupation came from one of them and there was a man standing at one of the stalls. Paul walked to a stall at the end and tried to isolate the entrance from the window reflection. Two men came in, each going to a cubicle. The man further along the line zipped up his trousers and made towards the exit. As he left the door remained open and Arnold entered. He walked towards Paul, but stopped as he did so, looking beneath the cubicle doors to see if they were empty. He moved to the adjoining stall and raised a finger against his lips in warning against conversation, gesturing behind him. Paul had already counted out the money and had it ready in his pocket. He offered it immediately. The Puerto Rican took it, carefully checking the bills.

'What?' he said, softly.

'Heroin,' Paul whispered back.

From behind a flowered handkerchief in his top pocket the man took a cellophane sachet of crystalline powder, handing it across the separating barrier towards the younger man. At that very moment the two cubicle doors smashed open and a voice yelled, 'Hold it!'

The shout was the signal for others waiting outside. The door from the bar burst inwards and three other men came into the lavatory. The two in the cubicles were crouched down, both levelling guns.

'Motherfucker,' screamed the Puerto Rican. He swept out with his hand, striking Paul across the bridge of the nose and sending him stumbling backwards, blinded by tears. Through the blur he saw the man running at him to kick, and tried to roll himself into a ball. One of the men who had come through the door grabbed for Arnold's shoulder, off-balancing him, so instead of hitting his groin the kick caught Paul high on the thigh, numbing him. Then the two others got to him and, almost casually, one of them kneed the Puerto Rican between the legs and stood back, watching him collapse on to the floor. Paul was suddenly aware of the reek of what he was lying in and pulled himself upwards. As he did so, he felt himself being seized and spun against the wall.

'You know the way,' said a voice. 'Arms outstretched, legs apart. Try a smart-ass move and you won't have an ass to be smart with any more.'

Paul still couldn't see very well and his nose stayed numbed from the Puerto Rican's blow. 'There's an explanation,' he said; it sounded adenoidal.

'Jesus!' said a voice. 'There's always an explanation!'

The Puerto Rican made another grab for Paul, but now he was handcuffed and one of the detectives twisted the linking bar. The man jerked away in agony.

'He sure don't like you none,' the policeman who was searching him said to Paul.

'I said there's an explanation.'

'There always is. Never made a bust yet when the guy admitted to being an addict.'

Paul's vision began to clear, as his hands were swept behind him and cuffed: it hurt his shoulders and upper arms.

'Let's go and hear all about it,' said the drug squad officer, shoving Paul towards the door. There were more detectives in the bar and two uniformed men at the door, preventing any escape. As Paul went by, the barman glared at him sullenly. He was put into a different car from the Puerto Rican. It was difficult to sit, manacled the way he was and the pain increased. He had to perch forward on the edge of the seat.

'What's the time?' he asked the man next to him.

'We got all the time in the world,' said the man.

'Please,' said Paul. 'What's the time?'

'Nine-thirty,' said the detective. 'And if you got an appointment, you just missed it.'

Two hours, calculated Paul. He closed his eyes against the despair. Would she have become unconscious by now? Or been driven berserk by the withdrawal pains, crashing and falling around the apartment? There was no point in trying to argue in the car, he realized. Speed was all that mattered and it would be faster to wait until the precinct house, where he could see the sergeant or lieutenant or the captain in charge.

It was a dirty, much-used, institutionalized sort of a building: a tired ant-hill. Paul was jostled straight past the station sergeant, up a broad flight of stairs to the first floor and then along to the drugs room. It was an open area of several desks, with an arrest cage in one corner. Leading off it were two doors, which he assumed opened into offices occupied by senior officers. Both were ajar and the offices were empty. The Puerto Rican called Arnold was already there, twisting and jerking against the men who held him.

'Put him in the cage, for Christ's sake,' said the man in charge of Paul.

Arnold swung against the bars, as soon as he was thrust into the cell. 'This is entrapment, motherfuckers. And you know it. This is a frame, and by this time tomorrow I'll have writs out against every one of you.'

All the detectives studiously ignored the drug pusher, knowing it would increase his fury. It did. He pulled back and forth against the bars, screaming obscenities and threats. One detective unstrapped his gun from the waist holster and brought the butt against the man's fingers, sending him writhing back against the wall.

'Assault,' hissed Arnold, his face tight against the pain. 'Now I'll get you for assault too, mother.'

'Please,' said Paul, to the detective who had brought him in. 'I want to get this over with quickly. My name is Paul Peterson. I'm an attorney.'

There was a slight change in the man's attitude, but not that for which Paul had hoped. 'Then tonight just isn't your lucky night, is it?'

A second detective had heard the exchange and stared at Paul, curiously. 'The drug-taker's friend,' he said, in recognition.

Almost at once the attention switched from the Puerto Rican to Paul: the hostility was the same.

'Well, well,' said the man who had cracked the pusher's fingers. 'We got us the junkie's friend.'

The detective who had arrested him thrust his hand into Paul's jacket, extracted the billfold and gazed at the identification. 'That's what it says here,' he confirmed.

'We're going to be famous,' said another detective. 'After a year we get Arnold. And bag Peterson at the same time.'

The door behind them opened and from the change that went through the assembled detectives, Paul decided the man was of senior rank. Paul's arresting officer went immediately to him; there was much gesturing and head nodding and the newcomer began to smile, looking first at Arnold and then at Paul. The briefing finished, he went first to the cage.

'I got you, Arnold,' he called, through the bars. 'It's taken a year, but at last I've got you.'

'You ain't got shit,' said the Puerto Rican, still nursing his bruised hands. 'It's entrapment and you'll be kissing my ass when I get to my lawyer.'

'Thought you had a lawyer,' said the officer, turning to Paul.

'My name is Captain Vincenzi,' he said, as if that should instil respect. 'And I know all about you. Do you know what you've done, Peterson? You've cost us about thirty convictions in the past year.'

Paul suddenly realized that he was not going to be able to talk his way out of the situation. Until that very moment, confused as he was, he had believed that once he had explained what had happened he would have been set free. Now, suddenly, he knew that the men in the room felt almost as much hostility towards him as they did towards the Puerto Rican. There was a wall clock high up near the arrest cage. He'd been away from Beth for three hours.

He jerked his shoulders, wincing at the discomfort. 'There is no need for these handcuffs,' he said.

'I'm the one who decides the need for things here,' said Vincenzi.

'Then it's time for you to make a very important decision,' retorted Paul, forcing the demand into his voice and nodding to the wallet lying on the desk before him. 'In there you'll find an unlisted Langley number. It's the number of my father, who is Director of the CIA. You'll also find the number of the White House and if you call that you can get confirmation from the President's office ...'

He moved his shoulders again. 'I want these off, right now. And I want calls, first to the White House and then to Langley. The man you'll speak to is Walter Jones. He's the Deputy Director. Just tell him what's happened and then listen.'

There was a stir within the room. The detectives were uncomfortable at hearing their senior officer spoken to with such disrespect, and Vincenzi himself was filled with a mixture of anger and uncertainty. Paul knew his face was burning and hoped they would think it anger rather than the embarrassment it was. He had done it. He had done what he had vowed he would never do — invoked the power and the influence of his father. So what would there be to sneer at now? Was Beth and whatever state she might be in sufficient reason to discard his training in legality and run instead down the familiar Washington corridors: you fix for me and I'll fix for you?

Vincenzi remained standing before him for a long time, then nodded to the arresting officer who unlocked Paul's hands. The captain picked up the wallet and went without speaking into one of the side offices. Gauging his momentary advantage, Paul sat uninvited in a chair, trying to convey a calm he did not feel. His wrists were raw and he sat massaging them.

'How about me? What about me, for chrissake? Ain't I got rights?'

The detective with the gun went to the cage, unstrapping it again as he walked. 'You don't shut up, Arnold, and I'm going to

wack this right across your mouth and ruin all those holiday snap-
shots.'

The other detectives began to move around the room, behaving
almost as if Paul were not there. He sat watching the minute hand
slowly ascend and then descend the clock-face. Vincenzi's door
remained closed. Occasionally, from somewhere else in the building there came isolated shouts and once, from the street below,
there was the sudden blare of a police siren as a patrol car went
away on a call.

Paul had expected movement from Vincenzi's room, but instead
it came from the door leading in from the corridor. Walter Jones
entered almost unobtrusively but at the same time with a very
studied demeanour of control. It was such that there was no immediate challenge from the assembled detectives. Before they could
react, Jones had walked across to where Paul was sitting.

'You all right?'

Paul held out his chaffed wrists. 'Just a little sore.'

The Deputy Director looked up into the room. 'Where's
Captain Vincenzi?'

'In the office,' said the detective who had arrested Paul.

'Tell him I'm here.' He turned back to Paul. 'Is it Beth?'

'Yes.'

'How bad is she?'

'Very bad.'

'Where?'

'My apartment.'

The detective returned and said, 'He asks if you would go in.'

Jones moved, gesturing Paul to follow. None of the detectives
attempted to stop him. Jones put out his hand as he went into the
office and Vincenzi hesitantly took it.

'I'm sure this is a problem that we can resolve,' said Jones.

'I'm not,' said Vincenzi.

Jones paused at the rejection. 'The Director's away on assignment at the moment,' he said, 'but I know he would be very grateful for your understanding.'

So this was how it was done, thought Paul, listening to the
exchange. Quietly, calmly, using as many ambiguities as you
could.

'What do you need?' asked Vincenzi.

'Quite a lot,' said Jones, moving to anticipate the other man's protest.

'Like what?'

'It never happened,' said Jones, quietly, 'No reports filed, no charges made. It just never happened.'

'No,' refused Vincenzi.

'That's what I want.'

'I said no,' repeated the captain.

The two men were still talking very quietly: it could have been a discussion about a baseball game or some very minor, unimportant disagreement in a political argument.

'The Director would be extremely grateful,' repeated Jones. 'He'd make it personally clear to you as soon as he returns to this country.'

Vincenzi's control began to slip. He leaned across the desk, finger outstretched towards Paul. 'Without him,' he said, 'I haven't got that fucker out there in the cage. You any idea what that guy's responsible for? I've been staking him out for a year — a year in which he's pushed every sort of shit from sleeping pills to heroin into God knows how many kids. There are children ten years of age in psychiatric clinics because of what he's done. I *want* him.'

'It's a problem, I agree,' said Jones. His voice remained very even.

'Not my problem,' said Vincenzi. 'I'm sorry. I really am. If I could help I would.'

'You must,' said Jones, an edge of insistence in his voice.

'We're talking of favours,' said the policeman, warningly. 'You don't have any jurisdiction. No jurisdiction at all.'

Jones allowed a slight pause, as if the assessment were open to challenge.

'There are very special circumstances.' said Jones.

'I *know* the circumstances,' said Vincenzi. He looked at Paul. 'If he were the *President's* son I wouldn't help. I'm not going to lose that pusher.'

'The one in the cage out there?'

Vincenzi nodded. 'If I release him, he'd be back on the streets in an hour.' He gestured to a plastic possession bag lying on the desk, containing what had been taken from the Puerto Rican in the lavatory. 'Look at it,' he demanded. 'Amphetamines, coke. Eight ounces of heroin, at least.'

'You want him off the streets?' demanded Jones.

'For a long time.'

'How about forever?'

Both the policeman and Paul stared at the Deputy Director, confused by the question.

'What?' said Vincenzi.

'What's his nationality?' said Jones

'Puerto Rican.'

'Hold him overnight,' ordered Jones. 'By noon tomorrow he'll be a prohibited alien. My people will collect him from you so he'll have no time to contact anybody, collect anything. He'll go straight to a ship and be dumped within twenty-four hours — without money, papers or anything. We'll leave him stateless in Puerto Rico.'

Vincenzi sat back, exhaling slowly and trying to disguise his awe.

'I wouldn't get a public conviction,' he argued, weakly.

Jones looked at Paul. 'What have you got: one simple case of pushing? You'd be lucky to get two to four. He'd be back on the streets in eighteen months. My way it's permanent.'

'I'd like to think about it.'

'I said there were special circumstances. There isn't time.'

'You'd really do that to the bastard?'

'My word.'

Vincenzi nodded, shortly. He looked at Paul. 'I don't know what you thought you were doing,' he said. 'But you're a lucky son of a bitch.'

Once in Jones' car Paul gave the address of his apartment, and as they drove towards it the Deputy Director used the car telephone to arrange a clinic and ambulance. They still arrived first. The bedroom was disordered, not so much by any pain-induced frenzy but more as if Beth had tried to move about to relieve her discomfort and had collided with things. She had collapsed very near the spot where Paul had left her. Her bladder and bowels had given out and she lay in her own filth. Her face was waxed and shiny and her eyes half open. She was still shivering and groaning, but appeared unconscious when Paul tried to speak to her.

Paul covered her again with a blanket and stood to face Walter Jones.

'Thank you', he said, 'for all you did tonight. Thank you very much.'

'I promised your father I'd help.'

'Will you tell him about Beth?'

'Only that we've got her back. He's got a lot to worry about; this wouldn't help.'

The lobby bell sounded and Paul pressed the button to admit the ambulance men.

'You're quite a guy,' said Paul.

'There's really not a lot to admire,' said Jones and Paul knew the man was being honest without trying to attain any false modesty.

CHAPTER 28

Mosquitoes had got beneath Blakey's net during the night and feasted off him, particularly around his ankles. The skin was puffed and red and when he tried to walk, little spurts of pain went up into his legs, making him wince. Makovksy became aware of the other man's discomfort and did more than his own share of preparing their meal and then breaking camp. The final chore was to fill the petrol tanks from their reserve cans.

'Only two left,' warned the Russian.

'Mao then,' said Blakey. Fuel had been arranged for them there.

The Russian stared up at the sky and then, apparently dissatisfied, took field glasses from the jeep and looked again. 'Cloud's building up on the horizon, just like the forecast said.'

Blakey took the binoculars. In the half-light it was just possible to pick out a great foam of cumulus where the plain edge met the sky. 'More than I expected,' he said. 'Unusual, for the season.'

'That's what the Africans will think,' said Makovsky. 'Something else we can blame on the complex.'

'Shouldn't be difficult to achieve quite a rainfall from clouds like that.'

'Then that'll be enough, von't it?'

The American turned, curious at the suggestion from Makovsky. 'Yes,' he smiled. 'That'll be enough for today.'

Makovsky sighed and the tension seemed to leave his body.

'Surely you didn't think I'd argue,' said Blakey.

The Russian shrugged. 'I hoped you wouldn't. I didn't know.'

'The plane will be dropping defoliant as well,' reminded Blakey. 'But we won't.'

'Now who's using a strange sort of morality to avoid responsibility?' demanded Blakey. There was no animosity in the question.

'Had a grandfather who was a priest,' reflected Makovsky. 'Russian orthodox: thought it was a disadvantage and that I'd never get anywhere in the service. I actually *wanted* this.'

'And now?'

The Russian shook his head. 'You know how I feel now.'

The first rays of sun were creeping across the plain when they set out northwards. Makovsky drove because of the American's bites. To the west the mist was still capping the lake. For the first hour it was so cold that they repositioned the windscreen to keep the breeze off their faces and bodies. The heat was just getting into the day when they encountered a small encampment of Tubu; for the first time, word had not travelled ahead of their presence. Blakey supposed that being nomads, the Tubu had no links with the close, interlocking communications of the other villages and groups. The Africans had already parcelled up their tents and were moving out with their cattle when Blakey and Makovsky drove up. Only one man knew any French and he spoke it badly; the Africans stood around regarding them uneasily. Very early on in the conversation, Blakey discerned a reason for their apprehension. They talked almost immediately of the devastation through which they had travelled, further north — for two days now they had been unable to find even the minimal grazing for their animals. It led Blakey easily to the rocket installation and suggestion that it might be responsible for the troubles. The tribesmen had passed it a week before. Less accustomed to it than the more settled tribes, it had frightened them, even before Blakey's innuendo. And by now the clouds were ballooning in the sky, making it easy for the American to implant further fear.

'Made the biggest impression yet,' judged Makovsky, as they drove off. Spared the need to inflict harm physically, the Russian was in high spirits.

'With little point,' said Blakey. 'You saw what was happening. When they feel threatened, they move away. The opposition we want is from Africans who feel their homes are being endangered.'

The Russian's lightness waned. 'There'll be quite a few people imagining that, by now,' he said.

There was a very large village about fifty kilometres from Mao where for the first time they encountered a witch-doctor. The man appeared to have been expecting them. A leopard skin, complete with head, covered his shoulders and back, the animal's head arranged so that it made a cap. He wore several necklaces, made of animals' teeth, one certainly that of a lion, and his chest was patterned in unguents of red and white and a thick, almost purplish, blue. He carried a fly whisk in one hand and an enclosed gourd rattle in the other. His thighs were streaked with the blue colour and leaf fronds were tied around his legs, just below the knee. The man stood in the centre of what appeared to be a committee of elders.

Blakey and Makovsky parked some way off and approached respectfully on foot. All except the witch-doctor were shifting uncertainly.

'I am Asaph Miburu,' said the African. 'Your coming was known to me.'

Blakey wondered if the uneasiness of the other Africans arose from the shaman's forecast of their arrival.

'Why do you come?' asked Miburu.

'To talk,' said Makovsky.

'Of God?'

'Yes,' said Blakey reluctantly.

Overhead, the clouds were so thick that the village was only patched with sunlight. Most of the Africans were glancing frequently at the sky.

'Soon there will be rains,' said Blakey.

'It is not the time,' said the African.

Blakey noticed a cleared area beyond them and he guessed the African had been incanting spells before their arrival. There was a pattern of crossed sticks to which chicken feathers had been attached by what appeared to be blood. A series of lines had been inscribed in the dirt, all drawn towards a blackened area where something had apparently been burned.

'I have said there will be no rain,' said Miburu.

'I believe there will be,' said Makovsky. The stir among the other Africans showed that several of them understood French.

Miburu hesitated, then stood aside, gesturing them into the long hut in front of which he stood, clearly the village meeting house. Blakey and Makovsky entered. There were rush mats arranged in a circle, with a raised dais of earth set slightly back. Miburu went towards it as if by right, gesturing again for the two men to sit by him. Blakey and Makovsky squatted, waiting for the African's lead. The other villagers assembled respectfully on the mats.

'I have said it will not come,' repeated the man.

'There are moments when things happen that cannot be foreseen,' said the American. The witch-doctor would lose face if he were proved wrong.

'Here the seasons do not change.'

'Perhaps there are things to make them change,' said Makovsky. Blakey decided they were becoming very practised at guiding conversations.

Miburu looked from one to the other for several moments. He was about to speak when there was a sudden rustle from above them and rain began to fall upon the leafed roof of the hut. There was a stir of murmuring among the Africans and several looked accusingly at Miburu. Blakey remembered the briefing from the expert in African studies before he had left Langley; weather divination was widely practised by the wise men of the tribes, their accuracy enhancing their reputation. It took only minutes for Miburu to bring the conversation around to the complex and, despite his distaste at what he was having to do, Blakey felt a tinge of satisfaction as he realized how successful they had been in implanting doubts in the minds of the Africans. The African expert had insisted that in the beginning they should be seen as much as possible, but Blakey had never expected the stories about them to spread as widely and as quickly as they had done. He thought back to Makovsky's changed attitude and wondered if the Russian would agree that they had now succeeded sufficiently and did not need to inflict any more injury or hardship. As in all their encounters, Blakey and Makovsky were very careful to avoid voicing directly the suggestion that the installation could be the cause of harm, always allowing the thought to come from the African first, and then letting it become a conviction by refusing to argue against the possibility. During the rambling talk Makovsky produced cigarettes and the gesture was reciprocated with sweet beer. It was a long time before it emerged that over a dozen young men from the village worked in the complex, and even longer before Blakey realized why the Africans grouped around him were so easily susceptible to suggestions of evil: one of the men had returned home a week before, badly blistered by an accidental collision with the electrified fence. Miburu called it 'wire that burned'.

The rain had stopped by the time they left, but water was still dripping off the thatches and roofs, and the dust had become a slimy, sticky mud. Even with a four-wheel drive vehicle, Makovsky was conscious of the changed road conditions and drove slowly away from the village, cautious of skidding.

'They're convinced,' said Makovsky confidently.

'Yes,' said the American.

'We were very lucky.'

'I was wondering whether we'd done enough ... ' suggested Blakey hopefully, 'whether it wasn't enough now just to talk to people ... to spread the rumours.'

The Russian drove for several moments without any response. 'I'd like to think so,' he said.

Blakey waited for the other man to say more, but he had apparently stopped.

'Well?' said the American.

'Mao is one of the biggest towns near the complex. They must draw a lot of labour from there. We should do something.'

The Russian was right, Blakey accepted miserably. 'What?' he said.

'To poison the water supply would be most effective.'

'No more,' said Blakey insistently. 'After that, we stop.'

'Yes,' said the Russian. 'That will be enough.'

They found the supply river as they were driving away from the town. They filled their water-bottles and reserve cans, added their purifying pills and then implanted the slow release canisters in the river. Mao was just beginning to stir after the oppressive midday heat when they drove in. Their petrol was waiting where the American embassy had promised it would be, and they went through their duty meeting with the town's leaders. Blakey suspected that there was a resistance here to any suggestion of the BADRA installation causing harm and accepted that they should have expected people living in a town to be less influenced than those in a village. It was difficult to assess a figure, but Blakey supposed that a large number of men from Mao were employed by the Germans. Perhaps the momentary disadvantage would become a positive benefit when they began becoming ill. Blakey realized what he had thought and the sickness immediately bunched in his stomach. He'd thought it! He'd actually allowed his mind to consider things the way that Peterson and Petrov and everyone else in Washington or Moscow was prepared to think. It must have been obvious from his expression, because he was aware of Makovsky looking curiously across the headman's house at him. He tried to compose himself. The feeling of disgust remained deep in his stomach. There was the predictable invitation to stay overnight, which they refused; it would have meant sharing the food and the food would have been prepared with the poisoned water. Thou shalt kill but not be killed, thought Blakey again. This time there was no embarrassment at the blasphemy. He'd gone beyond blasphemy, he knew. There was no excuse, no pardon, no escape from perdition. He was damned, forever damned — perpetually, irredeemably, horrifyingly damned. He tried to recall the terrors of hell that had been used as a constant warning in the seminary and decided that any of these was too easy a retribution for the things he had perpetrated. He hurried the meeting to a close, cutting across the stylized courtesies that Makovsky and the African were exchanging before departure, anxious to get away from yet another place they had despoiled.

'What the hell's the matter?' demanded Makovsky, immediately he started the car moving from the township.

'Hell's the matter,' said Blakey.

'I don't understand.'

'It won't be enough to resign,' said the American. 'That's just something else for my conscience ... for me. That's no real atonement.'

'There isn't anything else.'

'There must be. Who do they think they are, these people who can determine sentences that we are being called upon to inflict?'

'That's stupid reasoning. And you know it.'

'It's my reasoning.'

'Then it's stupid, like I said.'

'People should know.'

Makovsky slowed the car, so that he could turn to look at the other man. 'What?' he demanded.

'They shouldn't be allowed to do it, Peterson and Petrov and whoever else it is in whose name they operate. People, ordinary people should know.'

Makovsky stopped the vehicle completely. 'They'd kill you,' he said, 'if they thought for a moment you were going to attempt some public exposure of what we're trying to do.' He snapped his fingers. 'Just like that.'

'They wouldn't know, until it was too late.'

Makovsky reached out, gripping his arm. When the American looked up, he saw a wetness about the other man's eyes. 'I haven't a country that's free, not like yours in free,' he said. 'I know the environment to which I will return. And I know better than you the sort of situation to which you will go back. You won't be free, not for a long time. They'll call it debriefing or processing or some other expression; our people, both our people, are very good at expressions which really mean things quite different from what they sound. You'll be kept away from Jane and from Samantha and you'll be studied and examined, and only when they're completely satisfied that you're not going to do anything which they would consider disloyal will you be set free. And the moment they think otherwise, then they'll kill you. Jane will get her pension and Samantha's schooling will be paid for and there'll be some story of your being brave upon an assignment and everyone will think you're a hero.'

Blakey shuddered, the physical movement vibrating through him. 'I could hide it,' he tried, stubbornly.

'No you couldn't,' insisted Makovsky. 'I looked across that hut back there and I could have told you, almost word for word, what you were thinking. I don't think I've ever known anyone whose emotions are more on the surface than yours.'

'Then what am I going to do?' demanded Blakey, his voice anguished.

'Nothing,' said Makovsky, simply. 'We've finished inflicting all the injury. Now we've just got to reinforce the suspicion, point them in the right direction. And after that we go back to

N'Djamena, and you and I might get drunk. Then we'll say good-bye forever and we'll go back to our homes and never speak another word of what we've done.'

'I don't think I'll be able to do that.'

'It's a simple choice,' said Makovsky. 'You either do that, or Jane will be a widow and Samantha an orphan.'

Blakey slumped against the seat, head thrown back. 'Oh my God!' he said, agonized.

'I don't think you've got one, not any more,' said the Russian.

Petrov had been very quick to gauge the advantage of the Jewish emigration from Russia to Israel, carefully choosing and infiltrating his agents over a long period and establishing cells in Tel Aviv and Jerusalem. It had been from one of his best established people that he had first learned the rumour of government concern about a rocket installation in Africa. The same man, an engineer who worked in the mistaken belief that success would guarantee the release of the rest of his family from the Soviet Union, informed the KGB chief of the mock-up near Beersheba. He immediately activated everyone he had in the country and within twenty-four hours had information about the commando training in the south and the fuel dump in Egypt.

Aboard the destroyer in the Gulf of Guinea, Peterson was experiencing the first feeling of relief at Walter Jones' news about Beth, when the contact came from the Russian. It was a secure line, with very little fade in the volume.

'They're planning their own operation?' said Peterson.

'That's the only inference,' said Petrov. 'Did you tell them what we were doing?'

'I said there was to be an atttempt. And asked Levy to hold his people in readiness in case we failed and there was a need for a second attempt.'

'My information is that they're not going to wait.'

'They'll ruin it.'

'Can you contact Levy? Get him to stop?'

'I can try,' said Peterson. 'But if there's been a decision made he'll ignore it. I'll get Washington to attempt to impose some pressure; there's an aid allocation which might work in our favour.'

'We'll have to warn everybody in Chad.'

'Yes,' agreed Peterson.

'And particularly the deep penetration group. That's what the Israelis will be attempting — a tactical assault.'

'Bastards!' said Peterson, vehemently.

'We'll have to kill them, if they make an attempt,' insisted Petrov. 'I'll try to impose what monitor I can, and if we learn there's been an incursion, then our men must be ordered to intercept and remove them.'

'How the hell could we do that, without alerting half the country?'

'The launch is just three days away,' reminded Petrov. 'We might not have time for such considerations.'

'It was going so well!' said Peterson, exasperated.

'And it's got to continue that way,' said the Russian. 'If the Israelis go in, they're to be destroyed.'

CHAPTER 29

The American and Russian commandos woke professionally, very quietly, both sides guarding against any unnecessary noise. There were still wraiths of mist across the jungle floor and through the coppice above them, and although the monkeys and birds were screeching and calling, the forest was not properly aroused. Any unfamiliar sound would have carried. Bradley got his men to the stream first; though it was still cold they stripped and washed. He judged them all sufficiently recovered from insect bites to shave. By the time the Russians straggled towards the water, the Americans were bent over their boots, clearing the soles of clotted undergrowth and buffing the uppers. Bradley was disappointed he could do nothing about the stained combat uniforms.

The Americans were breaking camp and clearing away all evidence of their presence when Sharakov approached. The Russian's face was sore from mosquitoes.

'The soldier who was bitten is still delirious,' said Sharakov.

'What are you going to do?'

'I would abandon him here, but there's the danger of his being discovered.'

Bradley nodded, unmoved by the callousness. 'It'll slow us down, having to carry him.'

'I regret it,' said Sharakov shortly and Bradley decided that the Soviet colonel regarded the problem as a weakness from his side and was irritated by it.

'It can't be helped,' said the American.

The Russians had made a pallet from fallen branches, extending them at either end so that a man could get between the shafts front and back to support the one in the middle. The soldier appeared to be unconscious when they lifted him on to the improvised stretcher. The bearers' packs were redistributed among the remainder of the troop.

Bradley timed the approach carefully, determined upon the maximum effect. Just as they were about to move and were sufficiently close together for everyone to hear, he said to Sharakov. 'We'll help with the carrying, if your men tire.'

'My men will not tire,' said Sharakov immediately.

'The equipment at least,' offered Bradley.

'That won't be necessary.'

Bradley nodded acceptance at the refusal, happy he had increased the other man's annoyance. They travelled as they had done the previous day, with front and rear guard, and the main body in the middle. Bradley was aware of Sharakov constantly urging his men on, determined to forestall any criticism for slowing the march towards the complex. There was no proper track, and so close were they to the lake and its irrigation that the jungle grew in a tangle of vines, creepers and trees. The stretcher was cumbersome to manoeuvre, frequently snagging on branches and trailing undergrowth. They changed carriers every hour, Sharakov moving impatiently around every transfer.

The warning came from the advance look-out after about two hours' marching. About five hundred yards ahead was a clearing near to the water's edge which the Sara tribe apparently used as a temporary camp while they were fishing. There were signs of recent occupation and some boats, about a mile offshore. The soldiers struck out east immediately, deeper into the jungle and away from the lake edge, to skirt the open area where they might have been seen.

'I wanted to attempt a daylight reconnaissance today,' said Bradley, careful to keep his voice neutral of any complaint.

'There'll be time.'

'We're still ten miles off.'

'The forest should thin out, as we get nearer.'

They stopped at noon, both sides instinctively moving apart when they settled to rest. The Americans ate their can-heated food, but Bradley noted that the Russian provisions were cold. He decided that the Russian group had recovered from their exhaustion of the previous day, and despite the additional burden of their unconscious colleague, they all looked remarkably fit.

Sergeant Banks approached Bradley just as the colonel finished eating.

'We going to make it in daylight?'

'We need to,' said Bradley. 'I don't want us blundering about in the dark, trying to discover what we're up against.'

'The priests should be somewhere around,' said the sergeant unexpectedly.

'Probably,' agreed Bradley.

'We going to make any contact?'

Bradley shook his head. 'No point,' he said. 'Orders were that we were to remain self-contained units.'

'Wonder how they've made out?'

Bradley shrugged, uninterested in the conversation. 'What do you think of the Russians?'

'Good men,' judged Banks, expertly. 'Know a lot of junglecraft.'

Bradley was about to order the Americans to their feet when he saw the Russians were grouping around the stretcher and that there was a sudden flurry of conversation. As he approached, Sharakov looked up. 'He's died,' he said.

'That's another thirty minutes delay, for burial,' said Bradley. It was an automatic remark and not calculated to irritate this time.

'Fifteen minutes,' promised Sharakov.

Bradley looked beyond the other man. Three soldiers were already carefully lifting topsoil for later unobtrusive replacement and two others were standing ready to start the dig. While they worked, others stripped the dead man's pack of food, water and ammunition and then sealed the corpse in a body bag. From across the separating gap the Americans watched in respectful silence. The body was interred and the grave covered in twelve minutes. The Americans rose expectantly and then appeared surprised when the Russians moved immediately away and started to prepare themselves to march.

'The Soviets have no religion,' reminded Bradley. 'Not officially, anyway. There won't be a service.'

'Still doesn't seem right,' complained Sweetman, in mild protest. 'He was a nice guy.'

'It saves us fifteen minutes,' said Bradley practically.

Even among soldiers, death still had its sobering affect. Bradley detected several nods of sympathy from his own men towards the Russians, and they stood around momentarily in head-bent, inward-looking stances.

For the first time since they had linked together, Bradley and Sharakov responded without trying to gain some psychological advantage, each hurrying his men into readiness and moving them out at speed, to prevent the mood of depressive uncertainty increasing. Freed of the difficulty with the stretcher, their progess improved immediately. Very quickly, as Sharakov had predicted, the jungle began to thin, with less obstructive undergrowth. After an hour there was even an area of plain, a bald geological discrepancy in the middle of the forest. Promulka, one of the advance guard, had warned them of it and advised that it was safe to cross without fear of any observation, but its size still surprised Bradley when they reached it. There was a hardened animal track through the savannah to a muddied water-hole, and they were able to jog across, making up even more time.

It was mid-afternoon when they reached the jungle fringe, and Bradley and Sharakov lay at the very rim, field-glasses shaded against any tell-tale reflection from the sun, and studied the rocket installation, two miles away.

'Effective protection,' said Sharakov.

'Probably machine-guns in those control towers.'

'Wood construction,' said Sharakov, critically. 'Easy to bring them down with an explosive charge.'

'Three miles from the perimeter to the rocket installation,' recalled Bradley, remembering the details of Bohler's first transmission. 'The noise of any attack won't travel that distance.'

'It's an advantage,' agreed Sharakov. 'But it means we've got to achieve complete surprise when we take out that watchtower. If they've a chance to raise an alarm, there's no way we will be able to cover that distance without serious interception.'

Both remained flat, wriggling backwards to the deeper protection of the trees before rising. Bradley selected Logan as the scout and Sharakov indicated the smallest man in his group, a thin wiry soldier whom he identified as Gribanov. The two men crouched before Bradley and Sharakov, excited at the prospect of some positive action. The quietness caused by that morning's death seemed to have disappeared completely.

'We guess that three men got this far,' lectured Bradley warningly. 'Three men as well trained as you. They got caught, which probably means electronics. That's all you're looking for — some scientific detection devices. There's a cleared area all round the complex, maybe over half a mile deep. Ignore it. We'll reconnoitre that later. Just go to the edge of the brush line then come back to report.'

Logan nodded understanding. Bradley turned to Sharakov, to see if the man wished to translate, but Gribanov said, in English, 'I understand.'

The men stripped off their kit and changed their rifles for handguns. Both carried knives. From one of the supply packs Bradley took an electronic detector, a slim, battery-operated wand fashioned upon the design of the detectors that beachcombers use, but modified to respond over a twenty-yard range not only to metal but to any electrical impulse.

'What happens if we come across any Africans?' asked Logan.

'Avoid them,' said Bradley.

'What if we're seen?' demanded Gribanov.

'I don't want you to be seen,' rejected Sharakov pointedly.

'And no conversation,' ruled Bradley. 'Just signals. We don't know what form any monitoring might take. Microphones are unlikely, with all the animal interference, but I don't want any chances taken at all. Understood?'

The soldiers nodded.

'Back an hour before sunset,' ordered Sharakov.

Logan and Gribanov crawled up to the forest edge and began studying the immediate savannah, seeking an undetectable point of entry. Dissatisfied with their current whereabouts, they moved parallel to the grassland until they came, with unknowing irony, to the animal track along which Edgar Williams had groped towards his death three weeks earlier.

They went in carefully, a pattern forming almost at once. Logan progressed with the detector outstretched before him, and his attention focused on the ground and nearby surroundings. The Russian concentrated on a wider area to give the American early warning of anything suspicious they might be approaching. As Williams had done before them, they travelled crouched, concealed below the grassline. Because it was positioned at ground level, Logan saw the first witchcraft symbol and stopped, so suddenly that Gribanov stumbled into him. Logan gestured towards the painted tortoise shell and then held the detector out towards it: there was no reading. The American went closer on his hands and knees, putting his face only inches from the object, and then he rose, skirting it carefully and continuing on. They came across two more in fairly close sequence and then, near the water-hole at which Williams had been staked out as an offering to the animals, Gribanov found the clay hyena figure. It was Gribanov, allowing his gaze to range further, who spotted the ostrich at the water-hole. Both men sank to the ground, waiting for the bird to finish, not wanting to send it off in any abrupt, attention-focusing run. It took a long time. Frequently it stopped, raising its head as if testing the occasional wind which stirred and rattled the grasses. Satisfied at last it poked about the mud hole, as if reluctant to quit, and then began coming back along the track where the two commandos were squatting. It stopped about twenty yards from them, its head coming up in a series of attentive jerks.

'Easy now,' said Logan, involuntarily. 'Easy.'

For several moments the bird appeared unsure of what to do. Then it turned sedately and high-stepped away from them, making its own pathway through the grass.

Logan and Gribanov eased upwards, continuing in the direction of the complex. The hyena symbols, the really bad muloi, were more frequent now. And then the detector blipped. They both froze, staring around. The track was quite wide here, sufficiently so for them to crouch side by side. Logan swept the detector back and forth in front of them. There were three separate registers, all faint. Logan made a cushioning action with his hand against the ground and Gribanov nodded, understanding that they should continue, kneeling now, testing each pressure before exerting it. Every third movement they stopped and shifted their concentration from the immediate terrain to the complex itself.

Gribanov found the first sensor. They were not difficult to detect, with sufficient care; upon close examination they didn't really resemble the grass stalks they were supposed to represent. The savannah stalks were bent and bowed by the weight of the seeds, but the sensors stood stiffly upright and were markedly more yellow than the faded dun colour of the real grass. There was an arrangement to the surveillance settings. They were patterned along the track edge, the most obvious approach to the complex, and Logan and Gribanov discovered more at the junction with minor animal trackways. Near the point where the grass had been erased to create the swept no man's land, the detector vibrated in a constant chatter of contact.

Logan turned, gesturing to Gribanov that they had learned enough. He remained crouched in the same position facing the complex, while he guided the Russian in his turn, careful that the man did not collide with any of the metal strips. It took a long time for them to get back to the water-hole at the slow speed at which they had to travel, and already the shadows were darkening around them. Gribanov jabbed his finger against his watch, showing that they risked a later return than that dictated by the Russian colonel. Logan bunched his hand with the exception of the middle finger and jerked it upwards in an up-his-ass movement. Gribanov grinned.

The American maintained his detector checks and, when the reading ceased, stretched gratefully from his crawling position and motioned to Gribanov that they could trot. It was not easy, bent as they were beneath the cover of the grass. There was already a heavy twilight by the time they got back to the protection of the jungle. Sweetman, one of the guards established at their resting spot, saw Logan approaching and whistled softly. Logan whistled back. The Russian sentry was alongside by the time Gribanov got to the spot. The two Russians nodded and smiled.

Apart from the sentries, both Americans and Russians grouped around Logan and Gribanov, making a circle around the two reporting to Bradley and Sharakov.

'Sensors!' exclaimed Bradley. 'So that's how the bastards got them.'

'From an installation as sophisticated as this clearly is, we should have expected it,' said Sharakov.

'But they've only been seeded in the most obvious places,' said

Logan. 'Along the paths and tracks, where an approach is most predictable. If we have to go in, then we'll have to make our own way through the grasses. If we do that, there isn't any risk until we get to the very edge of the savannah.'

'We've still got to discover if that cleared area is mined,' said Bradley. 'We've got to cross a sensor line sometime.'

'So how are we going to make a path which won't attract attention through the grass?' demanded the Russian.

Bradley smiled, glad of the chance of showing his superiority. 'We go hunting,' he said.

Walter Jones had responded the moment the alarm had come from the missile destroyer, managing to contact the Mossad chief in Jerusalem with surprisingly little delay.

He and Peterson had rehearsed the approach, alert to the dangers of antagonizing the Israeli; for a long time the conversation appeared to be Jones giving a situation report of what was happening in Africa. There was some impatience in Levy's voice when he finally cut across the Deputy Director. 'Why are you calling me?' he demanded.

'Because we are concerned,' replied Jones, honestly.

'About what?'

'The possibility of your mounting a separate incursion: the Director thought you and he had an understanding that any force you might be assembling would be held in readiness, in case we failed.'

The sneer was obvious when Levy laughed, even over the telephone line. 'Peterson might have regarded that as an understanding,' he said. 'I never did.'

'We think we can abort it,' said Jones, urgently. 'The operation is going perfectly and we've built in some fall-backs if there's a problem. Let us try without any interference. Please!'

'I made it clear to Peterson and I'll make it clear to you, Mr Jones,' said the Mossad leader, patiently. 'Israel has not got the slightest intention of sitting back and hoping that this problem is going to be solved by somebody else.'

'You could ruin *everything*!' pleaded Jones, desperately.

'Or ensure its success,' said Levy, unmoved by the anxiety in the other man's approach. 'No rocket is being placed in position over Israeli territory.'

'Give us time,' insisted Jones.

'The western world gave Hitler time, arguing that a house-painter could never become a dangerous world leader,' said Levy, manipulating history to support an argument. 'And in the end six million Jews died. I'm not giving anyone time. I'm not giving anyone anything. Except results.'

'What shall I tell the Director?' asked Jones, buffeted by the other man's implacable attitude.

'Tell him not to risk his soldiers getting in the way.'

CHAPTER 30

Bohler had tried to keep his nervousness from Gerda but was unsure whether or not he had succeeded; as they walked down the corridor towards the entry into the rocket control room she felt across for his hand, squeezing it encouragingly. In his pocket the small-shafted screwdriver seemed heavy and he kept looking down to see if its shape was conspicuous through his clothing; as he moved, it seemed to swing heavily against his leg.

'I meant what I said last night.'

He looked at her enquiringly.

'About getting caught.'

'I know.'

Hannah Bloor was already in the main project room, laboratory-coated and efficient again. As they entered she smiled up, continuing the friendliness of the previous night. Both Bohler and Gerda · had worked in rocket launch situations and were immediately aware of the tense excitement in the room; people were smiling just a little too quickly, and there was a controlled urgency about their movements.

Hannah was at the central console, the point of maximum control. The countdown had already commenced, the hours and minutes clicking away on a digital screen before her. There was a gauge showing the temperature of the fuel, an unmoving register like the one monitoring the pressure inside the silo. The meter recording the weight of fuel being pumped in flickered as the filling continued. Having smiled her greeting, Hannah had gone back to the console, continuing with the checks of electrical circuits and their back-ups. She was showing her emotions less than anyone else, talking quietly into the command microphone, her hand moving from dial to dial as each circuit was monitored. Constantly in view was the television picture of the rocket, a faint mist of condensation around the base.

Bohler and Gerda had rehearsed their attempt before leaving his room, trying to anticipate the difficulties. For a long time they remained quietly in the main chamber, wanting their presence to become accepted by everyone. Only when they were completely satisfied did they go into the smaller room housing the satellite. Bohler's immediate reaction was one of dismay. He supposed he should have anticipated it so close to final assembly, but there was a great deal more activity in the room than there had been during their first visit. The rocket tip still lay like an open flower in its pod, with all the control, communication and power devices clearly displayed, but around it there was a concentrated team of technicians, apparently cross-checking the final tests being carried out in the main chamber.

Bohler felt Gerda touch his hand again, but he made no response. Once more they stayed long enough for the attention to shift away from them and then returned towards the larger room.

'It's going to be impossible,' said Gerda, quietly, as they went along the corridor.

'It's not going to be easy,' said Bohler.

'Impossible,' she insisted.

Hannah moved away from the console as they entered. 'Transistor collapse in one of the command radios,' she reported.

'Serious?' asked Gerda.

The Project Director shook her head. 'We can replace it in a few hours.'

'I'm interested in the countdown checks,' said Gerda. The plan dictated that Gerda should occupy the other woman to give Bohler the opportunity to sabotage the satellite.

Hannah turned back to the console as they had hoped she would, gesturing the Russian closer. Bohler held back, listening as the technical discussion began but slowly withdrawing from it, turning at last and going back towards the other room. There was even more activity than there had been earlier, with technicians suspended on elevated steps to have better access to the satellite equipment. The command radio, remembered Bohler. He felt a slim burst of hope. He edged forward as far as he felt it was prudent, watching the men dissemble the faulty part. At a bench on the other side of the room, more men were preparing replacement valves and laying out the delicate assembly tools. Bohler edged away from the satellite, wondering if he would be able to interfere with the part about to be installed. As he had expected, the men at the bench were intent upon what was happening at the other side of the room: one of them nodded and smiled as he approached. His presence didn't seem to inspire any curiosity.

'Always a last minute problem,' he greeted.

There were more smiles but no other response. Behind them was a complete circuitry plan of the command equipment. The transistorized sections were laid alongside in an orderly pattern, each graded from the commencement of the plan so that the men could work consecutively through the radio, checking valve for valve until they located the faulty one. Bohler stared at the sections, just four feet away. The minutest scratch across one of those metalled print-outs would be sufficient to cause a malfunction. He put his hand into his pocket, locating the screwdriver and running his finger over the sharpened tip. He went closer, apparently to study the circuit plan, moving it slightly as if to obtain a better view. One of the technicians glanced casually across at him and then turned back to the satellite. The transistors were just two feet away now—near enough to stretch out and touch. There was a sudden burst of noise from the satellite pod as the broken radio was finally freed and men began trying to withdraw it without interfering with or damaging any of the nearby equipment. The attention of the technicians around Bohler was now completely occupied. Tentatively he reached out, an interested scientist idly picking up something with which he was familiar. He was looking not towards the transistors but to the men around him, alert for the beginning of any movement. And then he stopped, his fingers inches from the nearest section. There would be another circuit test, after the repair. So any interruption he caused would be discovered and replaced yet again. He would be risking a pointless sabotage, an interference that would achieve nothing. He withdrew his hand and moved away from the bench just as the radio was lifted clear and the attention shifted from the satellite towards the bench. He stood aside as the group moved across the room, leaving the satellite clearer of people than at any time since his entry that morning.

The support pod was in a series of divisions for easy removal, and because of the work that had just been carried out there were three gaps in the surround rail, as well as the steps still in position. One technician remained there, bent over the solar cell assembly that would provide power from the sunlight once the device was in position.

Bohler approached from the side furthest away from the man, intent on the most easily accessible pieces laid out before him. Two of the omnidirectional aerials jutted out and, as he looked beyond them, he felt another surge of hope. Not more than a foot away was the gyro housing that would despin the satellite after its final rifle-bullet spurt into orbit. It was a standard type of fitting, the gyrostat secure in its metal encasement bolted rigidly against a base plate. If he could loosen just one of those screws, it would make the gyro unstable, guaranteeing a malfunction that would destroy the satellite. And because it formed no part of any electrical system, there would be no way the scientists could discover the sabotage before launch. The screwdriver was intentionally small, concealed completely in his hand. He felt out, lightly touching one of the satellite petals, smiling across at the solar panel technician who looked up at the movement. The hand holding the tool was hidden beneath the opened panel.

'Dr Bloor is very pleased with the check-out,' said Bohler, wanting to establish himself as someone in contact with authority. 'The radio is the only problem.'

The man nodded, bending over his power assembly again. Bohler reached in, idly touching the aerials, intruding his body as far as possible to cover what he was going to attempt. Satisfied that there would be no protest from the man, he brought up the hand with the screwdriver still concealed. The holding bolts would be very secure, so he manoeuvred the tool until it was dagger-like in his palm, with the tip just inside the heel of his hand and his thumb capped over the handle, to give himself maximum leverage. He couldn't open his fingers to see the facing of the tiny instrument, so he had to work it into the bolt-head by trial and error. He tried twice and it slid away, unconnected. There was resistance on the third attempt and he tightened his hand against the handle, tensed with the sudden effort to unscrew. His knuckles whitened with the strain. The bolt remained unmoving. He breathed in, veins standing out along his arm as he tried to shift it. And then he heard Gerda's voice, over-loud in warning. He managed to get his hand away just as the two women emerged from the passageway, Hannah slightly in the lead. She started to look towards the work bench, in anticipation of what the technicians would be doing there, but stopped, frowning in curiosity at Bohler's closeness to the satellite.

'What is it?' she demanded, as though suspecting that he had found some other problem.

'Just getting a really close look,' said the American, confused.

For several moments she remained looking at him, as if uncertain. Then she came nearer. The technician made room for her and she stood slightly raised on one of the sets of steps, gazing in at the assembly. Her face was expressionless when she looked up from the check; he returned the stare, equally blank-faced.

'Well?' she said.

'A clever assembly,' Bohler improvised.

Aware of his difficulty, Gerda said, 'It seems they've been lucky in locating the fault.'

The Project Director turned at the noise from the work bench. A man was holding up a transistor section, indicating where the break had been.

'Shall we go across?' invited Hannah, coming back to him.

'Of course,' said Bohler. A feeling of frustration suffused him, bringing a physical weakness to his legs. He almost stumbled as he moved back out of the satellite pod to walk around to where the two women stood waiting. He avoided looking at Gerda.

By the time they reached the bench, work had already begun re-assembling the command equipment. Hannah had a brief conversation with the men and then turned back to them. 'Seems it won't take hours after all,' she said. Her excitement at the news was immediately apparent; she seemed to have lost any suspicion of Bohler.

While they were watching the radio being re-installed and the further electrical check run to establish there was no longer any malfunction, Dr Muller came into the room. He had a vague, distracted appearance and Hannah turned away from the satellite pod, towards him.

'What is it?'

He straightened, as if he were trying to discard the feeling physically. 'Some trouble with the Africans,' he said. 'It happened before in the early months here, but now it seems worse. Over a hundred have not reported for work today. The tribal elders are saying that this place is causing some evil.'

Bohler felt Gerda looking at him.

'What are you doing?' asked the Project Director.

'Sent the Africans who have remained loyal out into the villages to discover what the trouble is.' He smiled, apologetic at discussing administrative problems in front of strangers.

Hannah looked back towards the main chamber. 'I don't think there's any point in delaying the final assembly any longer,' she said.

'Then let's put the satellite into position,' agreed the Director.

The feeling of helplessness again swept through Bohler as he watched the metal petals closing over the operating equipment and the final piece of the rocket moving easily down the tracked runway towards the silo. They watched from the larger room as the television picked up its arrival in the storage vault. Technicians appeared ant-like on the screen as they operated the gantry cranes to swing the satellite into position to form the nose cone of the rocket.

When it was finally secured into position there was a smattering of applause and an isolated cheer in the control room. Muller patted Hannah Bloor's shoulder, a congratulatory gesture.

The Project Director looked at the digital countdown. 'Two days and twelve hours,' she recorded. The pride in her voice was very obvious.

'It's going to be a resounding success,' said Muller confidently.

It was a further two hours before Bohler and Gerda could get away from the control room and the closeness to Muller and Hannah Bloor. The American walked dejectedly to his room. Gerda followed, conscious of his despair. He entered ahead of her, appearing unaware of her presence and hunched immediately into a chair. She came to him, putting her arm around his shoulders.

'I failed,' said Bohler, pumping his hand against the chair arm in his frustration. 'I had the chance and I fouled the whole thing up.'

'You didn't,' argued the woman sympathetically. 'I said it would be impossible.'

Bohler took the screwdriver from his pocket, frowned at it and then cast it disgustedly upon the daybed.

'I was actually at the gyro!' he said, awash in exasperation. 'I had the damned thing located into a screw, but I wasn't strong enough to undo it!'

'It was probably power-inserted,' she said, trying to help him. 'If it were tightened with a machine, there would have been no way you could have got it out.'

'I was there!' said Bohler, appearing unaware of what she had said. 'If I had been able to loosen it, the spin wouldn't have corrected and it would have gone into a maverick orbit.'

'But you didn't,' she said. There was a change in Gerda's demeanour, a gradual refusal to go on accepting the self-pity.

'No,' he agreed. 'I didn't.'

'So now it's my turn.'

'You saw the number of people in the satellite room today,' said Bohler. 'What the hell do you think it's going to be like tomorrow, around the silo?'

'Difficult,' she said. 'But what other chances do we have to abort?'

'We should have been in here weeks ago. Maybe then we'd have had a proper opportunity.'

'Stop it!' she demanded, allowing her irritation to show. He looked up at her, suddenly aware of her feeling.

'You're being defeatist,' she said. 'Since we've been here we've done extraordinarily well. Today was our first attempt and it failed. So next time we've got to do better. And there is *some* success to report.'

'What?'

'The effect that the bogus priests appear to be having in the field. Muller said over a hundred Africans have stayed away.'

'I'm sorry,' he said, belatedly embarrassed. 'I was behaving like a child.'

'Yes,' she said unrelenting. 'You were.'

'Do you want to know something?'

'What?'

'The thing that worries me most is that now you've got to expose yourself.'

'It's the job we were sent here to do.'

'Why can't I attempt it?' he said unexpectedly.

'Do what?'

'Try to interfere with the fuel supply. Why must it be you at all?'

'Because Dr Bloor was suspicious.'

He shook his head. 'Initially, perhaps. But that was predictable. The feeling went, very quickly.'

'No,' she refused. 'She might have accepted something odd just once. If you start trying to enter the silo and are found around the fuel lines, then she'll blow the whistle.'

He reached out, finding her hand. 'You'll be as exposed as hell! The whole bloody area is televised.'

'There's nothing else that can obviously be attempted,' she reminded him.

He got up from the chair and pulled her close to him. She was about two inches shorter; her nose came level with his lips. He kissed it at the very tip and she moved her head back, wanting more. 'I don't want you taking any risks,' he said.

She laughed aloud at the illogicality of the words. 'Then what am I doing here?'

'You know what I mean,' he said, dismally.

'I know what is necessary,' she said. 'I know I've got to create some imbalance in that fuel. I know it won't be easy but I know it's our best chance, and I know I'm going to be terrified every single moment.'

'I want to do it,' he said, the determination surfacing.

'It wouldn't work, after today. And you know it....' She reached up to kiss him. 'You said we should be adult,' she said. 'That we couldn't allow what has happened to become a hindrance.'

'I know what I said.'

'Then let it remain as it is.'

'I don't want to lose you,' he said.

She smiled up at him. 'If we achieve the most spectacular

success here, we're still going to lose each other,' she said.

'Yes,' he accepted miserably.

'Do you think you love me?' she asked hopefully.

'I don't know,' he said honestly.

'I think I love you.'

'We're not going to win, whichever way it goes, are we?' he said.

'No,' she agreed. 'We can't win either way.'

There had been pictures of the woman, one clearer than the rest when the photographer had obviously surprised her; she had looked shocked and distraught and her husband, alongside, had appeared bewildered. Finally there had been an attempt at a television interview and they had responded to every question with a 'No comment'. Walter Jones had winced at this, because the questions were phrased precisely to elicit that sort of response, so that they appeared to confirm the suggestions that the foreign affairs adviser had had an affair with one of his teenage students.

It was two days after the television coverage that the Deputy Director met Herbert Flood, at the Sans Souci this time.

'I'm being hounded!' protested Flood, who had previously always co-operated with any press coverage. 'The bastards are camped outside my house ... they chase my wife to the market and photograph the kids on their way to school.'

'It can't be pleasant,' sympathized Jones.

'Pleasant!' echoed Flood. 'It's fucking agony.'

'I'm sorry for you.'

'I'm not interested in your sympathy. I want results. The President and the Party are getting anxious: I know they are.'

'It hasn't been easy,' said Jones.

'Nothing's easy,' answered Flood irritably. 'Who's behind it?'

'I'm not sure,' said the Deputy Director.

'What do you mean, you're not sure? With the facilities you have, you *must* know.'

'It's a clever campaign,' said Jones. He had watched the irony without any satisfaction; like a pendulum, the innuendo and suggestions about James Peterson had subsided in almost perfect balance to the stories about Flood.

'I think it's close to home,' ventured Jones cautiously.

'What's close to home?'

'There's no friendship between you and the Secretary of State, is there?' said Jones.

'Moore!' exclaimed Flood, stretching the word as if he had just received confirmation of something he already knew. 'The bastard. The unmitigated bastard.'

'I'm not saying it's him,' retreated Jones. 'There are just one or two pointers.'

'I'll fix him,' vowed Flood. 'I'll fix the son-of-a-bitch for this.'

'I'd be careful,' warned the Deputy Director. 'There isn't a scrap of proof.'

'Bugger proof. I'll fix him.' Flood sat at the table, the food before him forgotten. He roused himself. 'You got access to the IRS files?' he demanded.

'In certain circumstances,' said Jones. 'And this isn't one of them.'

'Make it so,' instructed the man. 'I want all the details of the tax returns he's made over the last ten years. He lives well—too well. There's bound to be a disparity. We'll get his figures and then get an accountant to check them out against his known sources of income.'

'I'll see what I can do,' promised Jones.

'I'll get him,' repeated Flood, with bitter vehemence. 'Christ how I'll get him.'

CHAPTER 31

They had established camp about ten miles east of Mao, towards Rig Rig. It had been an easier night than the previous one, because they had allowed more time for the insect vapour to clear the tent and then taken care with their mosquito netting. Blakey awoke to hear Makovsky humming. The Russian smiled at him through the tent flap, water already bubbling before him on a primus stove. Blakey crawled out and then perched on the bumper of the jeep, accepting the coffee that the other man handed him.

'We could drive on to Rig Rig,' suggested Makovsky.

The American shook his head. 'You heard what Peterson said on the radio last night: the Africans are refusing to go near the installation. We've done what we were sent to do.'

'Straight back to N'Djamena then?'

'Peterson said he wanted the villages we've been to visited again, to reinforce the fears,' reminded Blakey.

'I suppose it's necessary,' said the Russian reluctantly.

They packed slowly, each aware that today they would confront the effects of what they had been doing and wanting to postpone the moment. Blakey's legs were sufficiently recovered for him to drive, and Makovsky sat in the passenger seat, not talking. Occasionally he raised the field-glasses to his eyes, checking things that attracted his attention in the grass or scrub. Blakey navigated by the compass mounted in the dashboard, heading south to keep a distance from Mao and then after about ten miles turning west, to bring them to the village where they had encountered the witch-doctor.

Because he had the glasses to his face, Makovsky saw it first. 'Jesus Christ!' he said, drawing the expression out.

'What is it?' demanded Blakey.

For several moments Makovsky didn't reply, scanning left and right with the binoculars.

'What is it?' insisted the American, slowing the vehicle.

'Defoliation,' said Makovsky simply, handing the glasses across the vehicle.

The American fumbled to adjust them to his vision and then stared towards the village. It was the season when anything struggling for life was normally bleached and stunted by the sun, except immediately around the lake, but now the area ahead appeared seared, as if some enormous fire had swept across it. There was no breeze and therefore no movement and from a long way off everything looked desolate and empty.

Blakey handed back the binoculars without a word and began driving again. The defoliation was evident many miles from the village. Great swathes were cut through the savannah and the vegetation was so sparse that it was very easy, now they were closer, to see the birds and small animals rooting and poking through the dead area: they seemed disorientated and confused. Blakey stopped at the first outcrop of trees. Bark was already flaking off, like skin scorched from a bone. There was no foliage anywhere.

'It never grows again,' said Blakey softly. 'In Vietnam you could fly over the greenest, lushest jungle imaginable and then suddenly come upon something like this. I always thought of those places as a graveyard: a graveyard where all the space had been used up and abandoned.'

'They must have done it quite indiscriminately,' said Makovsky, as if he found it difficult to believe. 'Just up-ended the containers in some disposal device and let it pour out, as they flew over.'

The vehicle stopped. They could see the carcases of several small birds who had been directly deluged by the defoliant. They were almost atrophied blackness; the ants had already swarmed over what had died. By some freak of wind or flight-path, half the fields surrounding the village had been destroyed and half spared: the line across was almost mathematically accurate, as if it had been drawn by a ruler. Where the defoliant had fallen everything was dead — millet, sesame, even the crouched cotton bushes. The wailing was audible above the sound of the engine before they got to the village, the strange tongue-clicking yet gutteral lament of

the African in times of grief. As they drove past the first set of
hutments, they could see the womenfolk shuffling slowly around
the village square in a prayer-line. Some of them had put dust and
dirt over their hair and bodies, and where they were weeping there
were bright track marks down their faces.

'Dear God, what have we done,' murmured Blakey.

During their first visit there had been an arrogance obvious in
the witch-doctor, even when the rains he had forbidden had begun
to fall. Now, beneath the façade he was still attempting to maintain, there was a bewilderment about Miburu, a man whose function was to protect against evil, yet who was unable to comprehend
the evil that had befallen them.

Before he had waited for them to approach him, but today he
came from the shade of the long hut, eager to reach them. Blakey
detected two further squares for spells, in addition to that which
Miburu had created to repel the rain.

'There was a wetness from the sky after the rains,' said the African. 'Our crops began to die as we watched. Our skin was burned.'

Now that he was closer, Blakey could see sores upon the bodies
of the naked children and upon the exposed arms of some of the
men and women, where the defoliant had fallen directly upon
them. Cratered burn marks were forming; some were already
festering.

They entered the long hut and assembled as they had done
before, with Miburu squatting on his earth dais and the other
elders grouped about him. In a voice almost without inflection,
something like a chant, the African recited the destruction that had
occurred: from his account, it appeared that the defoliation was
very widespread. Men he had despatched to discover the extent of
the damage had still not returned, but stories bush-telegraphed
from village to village talked of it having no end. There were even
reports from Mao of the effect of their poisoning the water supply.
Miburu talked of many deaths before the awareness that they were
being caused by the river. Now the people living there were having
to rely upon animal water-holes, the nearest being two miles from
Mao itself. Both Blakey and Makovsky sat dully, listening to the
African speak. The American's reaction had gone beyond revulsion and horror. He had a light-headed hallucinatory feeling of

unreality: it was as if he were a spectator, aware but in no way responsible. Makovsky's control was just slightly better. He was talking, haltingly, but still managing words, promising to inform the authorities in N'Djamena and even, despite the self-disgust that was evident to Blakey, intruding the innuendo about the complex. As soon as the conversation touched upon the rocket installation Miburu's attitude altered, became more positive. The men who worked there had been ordered home. The messengers sent to recall them journeyed with a complete account of the devastation and Miburu's belief that the establishment was responsible. Other witch-doctors were preaching the same conviction.

They had antiseptic cream in their first-aid boxes and, before quitting the village, Makovsky and Blakey treated as many children as they could, conscious even as they applied the dressings that the medication they had would do little to help those who had been injured. They left repeating promises to get assistance sent from the capital. It was Makovsky who broke the silence in which they travelled for several miles.

'I mean it,' he said, with tight-lipped determination. 'We must get as much help for them as we can.'

'Yes,' agreed Blakey immediately.

'It's a very backward country,' said the Russian. 'There's no machinery or administration for dealing with disasters.'

'So very little will be done,' said Blakey.

'We'll probably get promises,' said Makovsky, with growing acceptance. 'And then after we've gone, nobody will bother to do anything.'

'If we're attempting to establish influence in this area, perhaps some United Nations aid might be possible,' suggested Blakey, in sudden hope.

'It would only take an expert a matter of hours to recognize the damage for what it is,' said the Russian objectively. 'Neither your country nor mine is going to allow that sort of risk: these people aren't going to get help from inside the country. Or from the outside, either.'

'Dear God,' said Blakey, in a sudden wash of despair.

'I don't want to go to any more of the villages we visited,' said the Russian insistently. 'I know we've been ordered to and I know it's cowardly, trying to avoid seeing what we've done. But I don't think I can go through this man-of-God charade any more. When I saw those children I thought I was going to be physically sick.'

'No more villages,' agreed Blakey instantly. 'I just want to get out. As quickly as I can.'

To the west, the shore-line of the lake was just visible. The defoliant sweep had missed the area and the constantly watered trees and shrubs flared out in a sudden rim of green along the horizon.

'I feel very dirty,' said Blakey. Bathing wouldn't help very much, he thought.

'Yes,' said Makovsky. 'I'd like to wash.'

The American turned the car, bumping and jolting over the undulating ground. Makovsky checked the compass bearing and then looked southwards. 'The village where we treated those kids' eyes is pretty close,' he said warningly.

'I'm keeping clear enough,' promised Blakey. He parked the jeep in a slight depression, getting out and stretching the cramp from his back and legs. They took the communications radio, field glasses, towels and change of clothing from the vehicle, dropping down from the harder ground and making their way through the deep screen of reeds towards the water. Burdened by guilt as they were, they still moved carefully, watching for crocodiles. Close to the water there was a sudden hump of land and they put their things down. This time there was none of the embarrassment that Blakey had felt earlier undressing in front of the Russian. He stripped, dropping his clothes carelessly and waded out about a hundred yards alongside Makovsky towards water deep enough for them both to submerge themselves. They scrubbed the sweat from their bodies and then swam in aimless circles. The water was very warm, almost shower-temperature and neither man was anxious to get out. It was over an hour before Blakey called across to the Russian, suggesting a move.

'We could get back to N'Djamena before nightfall, if we hurried,' he said, swimming towards the other man.

'I wonder if there would be a flight tomorrow.'

'There'll be a flight *somewhere*,' said Blakey. 'I don't care where: I'm going to be on it.'

'What if Peterson says we stay?'

Blakey was very close to the other man. He stood so that the water came up to his chest.

'I don't give a damn about anything Peterson says,' insisted the American. 'I'm not following his orders any more.'

'It's not his fault ... not personally, I mean,' said Makovsky, in an unexpected defence. 'Any more than it's Petrov's fault. They just represent the system.'

'They don't *have* to.'

Makovsky smiled, wrily. 'If it wasn't Peterson or Petrov, it would be other people,' he said. 'There's always someone.'

They began slowly to wade from the water, feeling the impact of the sun upon their bodies. Only the very bottom of their legs were still wet by the time they reached the hump of land. They stood there, waiting for the process to be completed. Makovsky was the taller of the two and so it was he who detected the movement, little more than a stir on their skyline. He picked up the binoculars, focusing on the spot. Their jeep came into vision. And then the Africans around it. Miburu still had the unguents about his body, so he was the first whom the Russian identified and, as he whispered the warning to Blakey, he isolated Ndala.

'They're going through the vehicle,' said Makovsky. As he spoke he saw Ndala withdraw a cyanide canister from one of the packs and hold it up for the inspection of the other Africans. Another held out a second canister for apparent comparison, and then the Russian realized it was one of the villagers from the fishing village in whose water supply they had implanted the poison.

He had been whispering a commentary of what was happening as the Africans searched. Now he took the glasses from his eyes, staring across at Blakey. 'The fishermen must have found the canister,' he said. He was grabbing at his clothes, thrusting them on. Blakey was dressed first. When he looked through the binoculars there were more Africans than he had expected grouped around the vehicle. There appeared to be a discussion in progress and then they began staring out towards the lake and the reeds behind which Blakey and Makovsky were temporarily hidden.

'What are we going to do?'
'Run.'

The first twenty-four hours had been the worst. Until they had
sedated her towards the very end, Beth had been jerked and thrust
by convulsions, some so forced that Paul had worried she might
break an arm or a leg. Even rendered deeply unconscious, it had
still been necessary to secure the girl to her cot. Her real relief had
begun with the administration of the transfer drug, methadone.
Paul had slept little during the return flight from Texas and not at
all during the night of his arrest. His sister's hospitalization and
the subsequent twenty-four hours of pain had given him little
respite; he had sat in the chair alongside her bed and cried for her
agony.

She blinked rapidly back into consciousness, gazing around at
first confused and then frightened by her surroundings. At last she
fixed upon him, blinked some more and then smiled in recognition. It was a very brief expression, because almost immediately
she became serious and said, surprised, 'Christ, you look awful.
What's happened to you?'

Despite what he had endured and the cotton-wool feeling in his
head, Paul laughed. 'I've been through a rough time,' he said.

'I believe you,' said the girl, still not fully aware.

'You're in hospital,' said Paul.

'Yes.'

'They're trying to make you better.'

'Is that possible?'

Paul hesitated, unsure of the psychology. 'I don't know,' he said.
'I hope so.'

'I do, too. You know that's the worst part, knowing you're killing yourself and not being able to stop it?'

'We'll make it possible,' he said. In his tiredness, it was difficult
to get any conviction into his voice.

She tried to reach for his hand, but the securing straps swung
her arm back on to the bed. 'Just like the real madhouse,' she said.
She tried to fight against it, but there was no resistance and she
started to cry.

He felt out for her hand — she was very cold. 'You're going to get better, baby!' he said desperately. 'Really better.'

'Where are they?' she demanded.

'Who?'

'Mummy and Daddy.'

He stroked her hand, wishing there were not so much disorder in his mind. 'Dad's abroad, on a special assignment,' he said. 'He was ready to come to get you. But then there was a crisis. He asked me to come instead.'

She looked at him steadily, doubtful even through her drug-induced lethargy. 'Where's Mummy?'

Again he struggled for the explanation that would cause her the least distress. 'She's not well,' he said, wondering why there were not better words.

She managed to stop the crying, stirring against her bindings. 'What's wrong?' The concern in her voice was very evident.

He tried to find the euphemism, but nothing would come and so he said, 'She's taking a cure, Beth. She's become an alcoholic,' but that's going to get better, too.'

She slumped back against her pillow, for the first time appearing completely aware of her surroundings and the conversation they were having. 'Holy Mary!' she said. 'We're just one fucked-up family, aren't we?'

'Not any more,' said the boy, urgently. 'It's going to get better. You're going to get it together and Mother's going to get it together, and a year from now it's going to seem like some dreadful dream that didn't really happen.'

She struggled to maintain the alertness, glancing once around the room before locating him. 'Wouldn't you really like to believe that?' she demanded.

'Yes,' said Paul, exhausted. 'I'd really like to believe that.'

CHAPTER 32

Bradley knew the Russian had tried to find faults with his proposal, so the satisfaction was increased when Sharakov had finally been forced to admit it was workable. The animal hunt could have developed into an immediate challenge between them, but Bradley anticipated that, too, determined not to lose his advantage. He reminded the Russian of the pairing orders and Sharakov had to concede his idea of the two groups setting out separately.

After they had divided, American for Russian, Bradley led the briefing, insisting that for the minefield check to work, they had to capture the same sort of animals and not return with a Noah's Ark selection. It was an hour before nightfall when they set out, both sides armed with the modern crossbows which form a standard part of commando equipment; the steel bolts were carefully coated with a combination of etorphine hydrochloride and acepromazine maleate to render the animals unconscious.

The majority moved back deeper into the jungle but Logan, who had been linked again with Gribanov, jerked his head towards Sweetman who smiled, indicated Gribanov to his Russian companion and followed Logan's lead northwards, parallel to the jungle line. Because they were moving within the forest to avoid any chance identification from the complex perimeter, it took them longer than Logan had expected to reach the animal track leading through the savannah to the water-hole. As soon as Sweetman saw the choice he smiled and reached forward, patting Logan admiringly on the back. The men divided again, Logan and Gribanov remaining on one side and Sweetman and the other Russian going on to form a crossfire pattern. Almost immediately there were animal movements and the soldiers stiffened expectantly. The first was a hyena, shuffling along alone and therefore useless for their purpose. An ostrich was next, sedate but nervous in its approach; Logan wondered if it were the same bird they had seen earlier. The pigs came just as the half-dark was forming, a squealing, grunting pack. The noise preceded them, giving the soldiers time to take the tension of their crossbows and reduce the risk of killing rather than stunning the animals. There were eight of them, and so quick were the soldiers that they managed to stun four with the first volley and then actually reload and bring two more down before the screeching pigs scurried away.

When they got to the animals, they found that one had been killed by the force of the bolt, but that five were still breathing. Logan bent over the bodies, carefully extracting the darts. Gribanov and the other Russian went from one to another, taping their snouts so that they could not make any noise but were still able to breathe. Then they bound the legs and Sweetman located two more or less straight branches to slide through the hind and front quarters, so that they could be carried.

It was almost completely dark when they returned to the camp. Two more pigs had been caught by other groups and, in desperation, a Russian had captured a hyena. When they saw Logan's catch, Sharakov ordered the hyena to be released. They split branches to form a latticed pen in which they set the pigs free, careful to provide the water they had been on their way to find.

Even though they were so far away, Bradley and Sharakov ordered the minimum of talking. Anything metal was handled very carefully to avoid noise. They didn't use the tents, because of the sound that might have carried from their erection, but stretched canvas from branches to provide a makeshift covering and then encased themselves in their mosquito cocoons. They were awake long before daybreak, needing to get to the edge of no man's land in darkness. The pigs were bound again and this time one animal was allocated to each man who was to make the incursion. Bradley whispered a final briefing, co-ordinated their watches so there would be no premature release, and then squatted with Sharakov alongside and watched them disappear in the darkness. Sergeant Banks was already waiting, pencil and paper ready. Sharakov also had his man prepared.

The soldiers pushed through the grass without any attempt at concealment, careful only to remain in file so that the pathway would not appear too wide. Promulka was leading, the electronic detector stretched in front, and only when there was a register did he gesture them down, below the savannah cover. It was still dark, so they settled as comfortably as possible, waiting for the sky to lighten. Promulka sat with his arm outstretched, checking off the time. The indeterminate greyness was settling over the landscape when Promulka withdrew his knife; first he slit the tape away from the animal's snout and then cut its legs free. Behind him he heard the scrape of metal against sheath as other knives came out. The sudden squealing seemed very loud in the pre-dawn quiet. Promulka covered the last six feet to the very edge of the cleared area, not bothering to move softly against the sensors' detection. Through the grass he could see the lighted perimeter fence and two of the watchtowers. So far there appeared no response to their presence. Promulka thrust his animal out into the cleared area, reaching back and taking the next as the pigs were chain-ganged forward. For a moment they milled haphazardly at the grass-edge so Promulka risked the noise, shooing them further into the cleared area and then turned, scurrying back along the track. He heard the siren after he had covered about twenty yards and then the first explosion, as a pig stumbled on to a mine. Three mines went off in very quick succession and another siren blared out, louder this time. They were still a long way from the jungle edge, running awkwardly as they were. After half a mile, obedient to their instructions, they slumped down, so no movement would be detectable in the shifting grasses.

Back under the cover of the scrub, Bradley and Sharakov bunched forward, watching the guard assembly beyond the wire. The area was being swept with field-glasses by officers in the watchtowers who were communicating with one another by radio. After about fifteen minutes one of the smaller gates set into the wire was swung open and a squad moved carefully out, six Africans and two Arab officers. One of the officers held the mine-field map. He remained near the wire, shouting directions to the other men. They moved in a patterned line through the no man's land, and Bradley and Sharakov dictated the directions of their progress to their waiting sergeants, creating their own maps from the guidance being unwittingly provided. There was isolated laughter and shrugs when the carcases were found. The group stared through the grass at the track they believed the pigs had made and then moved back through the minefield, their path providing a confirmation of the plan that the commandos now had before them. The first of the incursion team was just slipping from the grassed area into the jungle, when there was fresh movement from the complex. Another unit moved out carrying replacement mines, and Bradley and Sharakov watched as they were carefully sunk into the ground and then activated.

It was midday before the last of the group returned to the safe concealment of the jungle. Immediately they were assembled, Bradley and Sharakov moved their men even further away from the complex, no longer needing to remain close, thus risking discovery. They found a cleared area with a sufficiently close water supply and raised camp: as before, the Americans settled on one side and the Russians on the other. With time to kill, both commanders ordered their men to clean and repair their equipment and then established a sleep rota, so everyone could get the maximum amount of rest. Both sides produced several copies of the minefield map and distributed them for study among the soldiers.

The evening meal was being prepared when Sharakov crossed the divide between their encampments towards Bradley. 'Knowing the mine placings, we could get through that field to the wire before the sensor alarm was properly raised,' he said.

'The fence is still electrified,' reminded the American.

'We'd be close enough to shoot out the junction boxes,' dismissed Sharakov.

Bradley nodded, accepting the correction. 'If we're called upon to go in, I don't really imagine too many difficulties,' he said.

'No,' agreed Sharakov. 'Very little trouble at all.'

As he spoke, fifteen miles to the west, Blakey and Makovsky had already been fleeing for an hour from the pursuing Africans, blundering and panting through the sucking mud of the lake edge.

With the encouragement of every report from Africa, Fowler's good humour had been constant for several days and Walter Jones realized that quite a lot of personal advantage was accruing from his close proximity to the man. They finished their promenade in the Rose Garden and turned back towards the open French windows.

'Make it clear to the Director how grateful I am,' instructed Fowler. Hurriedly he added, 'It mustn't appear a direct message, of course.'

'I understand,' said the deputy.

'I must admit that there were times when I didn't think it was going to go as well as this.'

They were only about twenty yards from the Oval Office and Jones knew that he would have to say it soon, if he were going to say it at all. He slowed, uncertainly, running his tongue over his dry mouth.

'May I speak to you about something, Mr President?' He stopped, bringing Fowler to a halt. Fowler frowned, waiting.

'It's somewhat of an embarrassment,' continued Jones, forcing the rehearsed words into his mind. 'But I think it's a situation of which you should be aware.'

'What?' demanded the President.

'There's been a request made to the Agency ... one that I fear is improper.'

'Go on.'

'We've been asked to investigate the tax affairs of the Secretary of State.'

Surprise flared in Fowler's face. Very quickly he controlled it.

'Who?'

'Mr Flood.'

Fowler snorted, a disbelieving sound. 'I would have thought he was in enough shit as it was,' he said, almost to himself.

'It would be very embarrassing for the agency if Mr Flood discovered how you came to learn of the request,' said Jones. He paused, just sufficiently. 'As embarrassing as if your awareness of the African operation were to become public knowledge.'

The President looked up sharply, alert for any threat. The Deputy Director gazed back, innocently.

'No fear of my not showing discretion,' promised Fowler. 'And you were quite right to bring it to my attention. It *is* improper — damned improper.'

'I've not taken any action, of course,' said Jones.

'Of course not,' agreed the President.

CHAPTER 33

For the first time Gerda had remained in his room throughout the night, clinging to him. They had slept very little, just occasionally lapsing off into a doze; he'd moved to make love to her when they had first got into bed, but she had refused him.

'I'm sorry.'

'It doesn't matter.'

'I'm very frightened, Michael.'

He had tried to find something to say but, when nothing came, pulled her even closer to him.

They breakfasted in the cafeteria, nodding to the technicians and scientists whom they had come to recognize, but talking little between themselves. Gerda ate nothing.

'Be careful,' he said.

'I'll try.'

'Promise.'

She looked up from her coffee, holding his eyes. 'I won't get caught.'

He began to smile, then remembered her concern at being made to disclose everything if they were detained. 'I didn't mean that,' he said.

'I know you didn't,' she said. 'I did.'

They were approaching the door to the launch room when they encountered Dr Muller. He had a worried, distracted look about him, and it was not until they were very close that he recognized them at all. Bohler thought that for the first time he looked like an old man.

'What's the matter?' asked the American.

The Director shrugged, appearing unsure whether to tell them. Then he said, 'The Libyans are insisting upon increasing the security, now that the launch is so near. I've protested to Bonn and been told to allow them the facilities they want ...'

He stared at Bohler, watery-eyed. 'If this weren't so important to me I would consider resigning,' he said.

'A successful launch would strengthen your position,' said Bohler, easily. 'Why not wait until then before making any serious protest.'

Muller nodded. 'Perhaps you're right.'

They used the Director's card for entry into the secured area, and entered the lift silently. As Muller reached out for the indicator button, Gerda said, 'I thought I might look at the silo area.'

Locked in his own thoughts, Muller made an absent-minded movement and pressed the selector for the first stage. It was a very short drop and Gerda showed just the slightest hesitation when the doors hissed open and the corridor appeared before them.

'I'll see you in a moment,' she said to Bohler.

'Yes.'

At the corridor edge she paused again and the automatic doors started to close, so that she had to push out to make them retract again.

'In a moment,' she repeated, then turned and started walking towards the silo.

Pressed back, the doors remained open for several seconds and Bohler stared after her. She was walking slowly but resolutely; she must have known the lift was still there, but she didn't look back. Impatiently Muller pressed the 'closed' button and the elevator plunged deeper. Bohler stood respectfully aside for the Director to precede him into the control room. As soon as he entered, he realized the cause of Muller's distress. At the back of the room, not interfering with any of the work but very obvious by their presence were two uniformed officers; the resentment was discernible in the chamber. Hannah Bloor turned at their entry, her face mirroring the general irritation. She ignored Bohler, looking at Dr Muller.

'Well?' she said.

'They say they must remain.'

Bohler realized that Bonn's decision had only just been made, and that Muller had left the room to complain to Germany and encountered them in the corridor on his return.

'This is like another time, when the military imagined they could control everything,' said the woman, bitterly.

342

'I don't need reminding,' said Muller. 'I was there.'

At last she looked to the American, smiling automatically. 'Where's Dr Lintz?'

'She thought she'd look at the silo area,' said Bohler. They had planned a reversal of the previous day's roles: she would make the sabotage attempt while he made himself conspicuous in the control room, talking and asking questions that would distract any concentrated attention to the television screen. Almost immediately, Bohler recognized the difficulty. Prevented from following what was happening in the room because of their lack of German, the Arabs were staring fixedly at the television screen: worse still, an operator had been seated directly before the screen, beneath which another set of indicators recording the final hours of fuel loading and pressure had been activated.

'She'll find quite a crowd,' said the woman.

As she spoke, Bohler looked up at the monitor and saw the blur as Gerda emerged from the corridor on to one of the gantry stepways. But his concentration was not immediately upon her; looking properly for the first time he saw soldiers at every level. There must have been at least six of them, in addition to the technicians carrying out the final inspection. With a numbing, empty feeling of despair, Bohler knew that what Gerda intended to do was impossible.

'It's monstrous,' protested Muller, for his own benefit. 'How can people be expected to work with such interference.'

There was only one fixed camera trained upon the silo, so that it was not possible to see what everyone was actually doing within the launch area. Figures kept entering the picture and then leaving it again, like actors performing silently upon a stage. Bohler gazed unblinking at the diminutive figure of Gerda, watching her look around the silo and guessing her thoughts at seeing the increased number of guards. He had expected her to make a token gesture, perhaps involve herself in a brief talk with some of the on-site technicians and then withdraw, accepting the impracticability of any interference. There were some technicians nearby and for a moment she did engage in conversation with them but then, instead of turning back into the corridor as he had anticipated, she began walking towards the gantry link that would take her to the rocket's second-stage level, into which the liquid fuel was still being loaded, and he realized, horrified, that she intended to attempt to go through with it. She disappeared, obscured from the camera lens by the bulk of the rocket itself and when she next appeared she was halfway up the catwalk. Above her, beyond the second-stage landing at a mid-level console assembly was another group of technicians. By their side were two soldiers. At the very top, near the satellite housing were two more uniformed Libyans, looking down upon everything.

Bohler became aware that both the Director and Hannah were watching the monitor and desperately forced himself to begin talking, to fulfil his part of the plan. As he spoke, he moved about, trying to insinuate himself between the two officers at the back of the room and the television screen, conscious as he did so that it was ridiculous. Every time he remained in their way for more than a few seconds, they moved slightly and without protest either right or left, so they could see again. Muller and the Project Director responded to him, looking away from the screen, and involving themselves in conversation about entry windows into the atmosphere, weather forecasts which might impede any launch and checks subsequent to that which had discovered the electrical fault in the commmand radio the previous day. Like an alcoholic trying to prevent himself going towards an open bottle on a convenient table, Bohler pulled his eyes away from the television, forcing his concentration upon what Muller and Hannah Bloor were saying so that his questions did not show the anxiety with which he was gripped.

It was the operator who had been placed before the screen who shouted the alarm, bringing them all back to the television. The sentries at the very top of the silo were obviously shouting, gesturing to those beneath them and Gerda suddenly broke from the concealment of the rocket, near the spot where the fuel line snaked in. The technicians were about thirty feet above her, at the mid-level assembly. As he watched, his body frozen, Bohler saw them turn and stare down. He thought one may have shouted, but it was difficult to be sure. The other soldiers were hurrying from the lower levels and, at the speed they were moving, Bohler could imagine how the sound of their boots against metal would have been very loud within the silo. Gerda was trapped between the ascending soldiers and the scientists above her. Her arm thrust out in some indefinable movement and then she began clambering up the tiny ladder towards them. Later Bohler was to accept that even committing suicide, Gerda had tried to make the explanation easy for him. Halfway up, she appeared to stumble, then miss her footing completely. Her arms came up, nearly too much a motion of panic, and she seemed to grab for the support rail and miss.

'Oh God, no!' screamed Hannah, hunched in her seat before Bohler.

There was a second of arm-waving, frenzied attempts to grab the rail and then, in agonizing slow-motion, Gerda went over the rail and plunged down into the well of the silo. Her body seemed weightless and the fall endlessly long. She flopped like a rag doll, once striking the gantry housing and rebounding off against the very well of the silo.

'Oh no,' said Hannah, again. She screwed around in her seat, looking up towards Bohler.

The American stood rigid-faced, unable to get any movement into his body. He realized for the first time how cleverly she had made it appear an accident, to protect him. And then with that thought came another recollection.

'... If we're caught ... if either of us are caught ... then they'll be able to break us easily enough ... we mustn't get caught ... if we're detected, we mustn't let ourselves be caught ...'

Gerda's words: her fear of failing him. The night she had become jealous, imagining he was attracted to Hannah Bloor so soon after they had become lovers.

'This is terrible ... awful.'

Bohler became aware of Dr Muller tugging at his arm, and he looked around at the old man.

'Appalling,' he agreed, needing the other man's words. 'What in the name of God can have happened?'

He moved at last, thrusting out of the control chamber towards the corridor from which he could get into the silo. As he left, he was aware that the two Arabs had stayed unmoving at the rear of the chamber. And that Hannah Bloor was remaining head-bent and shocked at her desk, not following either. By the time they reached the silo, everyone had clambered to the very bottom and grouped around the crushed, pulped body of Gerda Lintz. Bohler stared down, finding it hard to recognize her as the woman he'd held in his arms only two hours before.

The Libyan soldiers stood to one side, one of the officers in conversation with the technician.

'What happened?' demanded Muller.

'The soldiers thought they saw Dr Lintz interfering with a fuel line,' said a bespectacled man whom Bohler recognized from the breakfast cafeteria that morning. 'When I looked down Dr Lintz shouted that there was an imbalance and started climbing the ladder towards me. She seemed confused by the soldiers and stumbled ...'

With an enormous effort, Bohler forced himself into some reaction, fully appreciating how quickly Gerda had moved to cover her failed attempt at sabotage.

'It's outrageous,' he yelled, matching Muller's earlier protests. 'Dr Lintz actually *warned* you of a problem and was harassed to her death by this preposterous security.'

Behind them, medical attendants from the complex infirmary were moving with difficulty down the steel ladders, with a stretcher.

Muller turned to him, his face a mixture of anger and uncertainty. 'I am so sorry,' he said. 'So deeply sorry. This is a dreadful tragedy.'

'And one that was quite unnecessary,' said Bohler, maintaining his attitude. 'I shall make the strongest protest to Bonn.'

'With my full and complete backing,' promised Muller. 'I protested to Germany about it: I really did.'

The attendants were trying to manoeuvre Gerda's body on to the stretcher: Bohler looked for several seconds then turned away, shuddering. 'I'm going to my room, to prepare a full report,' he said.

He managed to retain his control until he got to ground level. The shuddering began just before he got to the door of his quarters. He entered before anyone noticed it. Inside, the shock seized him completely, the emotion jerking through him. He stood pressed back against the door, arms across his chest, gripping himself as if to resist the shaking. It took a long time to subside and when it did he considered it, wondering about the reason. Was it because he had loved her? Or because he was frightened at how near his discovery had been? And still might be? His own fear, he recognized, honestly. He had been lulled by their apparent success and had not realized how deep his apprehension was. He could not have been as brave as Gerda. He would not have been able to think as quickly as she had, providing so acceptable an explanation. Or done what she had done, to protect him. Had he loved her? He demanded the question of himself once more, trying to find a truthful answer. Had he loved her or had the need been for someone to help with the newly accepted fear? The fear, he decided again. He waited for the guilt, but none came. Had she loved him? Or had her need for him been the same as his for her? He would never know. He thought back to the near desperation in which she had held him during the night, and remembered her words as they had entered the lift with Dr Muller. He would never truly know, but he thought he could guess.

He moved at last, aware of the danger of the reverie. He recorded a full account of what had happened and warned Peterson to get Bock fully alerted at the Foreign Ministry to intercept the protest when he sent it from the complex. He had just transmitted the message at speed and returned the radio to its apparently real purpose when the tap came lightly on the door. Bohler tensed, half-crouched at his table, staring open-eyed towards the corridor, concerned that the transmission might have been overheard. The knock came again, slightly more insistent than before. Apprehensively he went towards the door, initially opening it little more than a few inches. Hannah Bloor stood in the corridor. Bohler looked at her without speaking for several moments, then stood back.

She came into the room slowly and he watched her intently, alert for any reaction to the radio. She appeared not to notice it.

'I heard what happened from Dr Muller,' said the project leader. 'I wanted to say how very sorry I was.'

'Thank you,' said Bohler.

'She was right,' said Hannah.

'Right?'

'She shouted up to the technicians about a fuel imbalance. For some reason we can't discover, the hydrazine flow had been reduced. The satellite would have malfunctioned during the last stages.'

'And because she tried to tell you, she died,' said Bohler. So Gerda had succeeded. If there hadn't been the additional security within the silo, they would have managed what they had been infiltrated to achieve.

'We're very sorry,' she repeated.

'The responsibility wasn't yours or Dr Muller's,' accepted Bohler, reducing the bitterness.

'Were you very close?'

'Close?'

'Dr Lintz and yourself. I got the impression that you were quite close.'

'Colleagues, that's all,' insisted Bohler.

The woman looked at him curiously. 'Still upsetting,' she said.

'Yes.'

'Had you known her long?'

'Until this visit, I had not met her before,' said Bohler, honestly.

'She was a very talented scientist.'

'Yes.'

'And an attractive woman.'

'That too,' agreed Bohler, unsure why the woman was pressing the conversation.

'Dr Muller has put staff on stand-by in the cable room.'

'I've hardly considered the report yet,' said Bohler.

'There will be people there, whenever you're ready,' promised the woman.

'Perhaps two hours.'

Hannah looked around his room, apparently examining it for the first time. 'Had she any family?' she asked suddenly.

'I don't know,' said Bohler, honest again. Had there been a fiancé in Russia? A husband even. Throughout their time together she had told him nothing of herself, nor asked anything about his background.

The woman stirred, moving towards the door. 'I must get back to the control room,' she said. 'So near the launch, there's a great deal to be done.'

'Of course.'

At the door she turned, looking back towards him. 'The launch is going to be overshadowed by this tragedy,' she said.

'All the checks concluded?'

She nodded. 'Everything done. We're into final countdown. There's nothing that can go wrong.'

The woman was right, accepted Bohler.

Petrov was surprised that Litvinov should travel from Moscow to Odessa, and the curiosity increased when the Politburo member arrived. Litvinov was very subdued, with little of his customary arrogance or animosity. Petrov guessed that the success of the combined operation had undermined the other man's attacks upon him, reducing his credibility with the ruling body. Wanting to increase the other man's uncertainty, Petrov spent most of the first day recounting in minute detail what was being achieved in Africa, deciding as he talked that he would send a similar report to Moscow while Litvinov was in no position to interfere with or obstruct it.

'Very impressive,' conceded Litvinov at the end of the first day.

'Thank you,' said the KGB chief.

'You didn't expect this visit?'

'No,' admitted Petrov.

'The Politburo decided it was necessary,' disclosed Litvinov, and for the first time there was an indication of his customary attitude. 'They want an unequivocal guarantee of success.'

'An *unequivocal* guarantee isn't possible,' disputed Petrov, unconcerned. 'But I see no reason for any fears about the ultimate outcome.'

At the very moment that Petrov was giving the undertaking, Peterson was hunched in the radio room of the missile ship, listening to Bohler's account of Gerda Lintz's death. He was just about to alert Petrov at the Black Sea command post when the second emergency signal came in. Blakey and Makovsky had been on the run for almost four hours and were crouched, near exhaustion, in the bole of a huge msasa tree. Believing themselves sufficiently ahead of their pursuers, they had decided it was safe to report their discovery by the Africans.

CHAPTER 34

He had hoped at first they were animal sounds. But with animal movements through the jungle there is always other noise, however muted: grunting or snuffling or snorted, open-nostril breathing. And this was just movement. Makovsky, whose turn it was to remain awake while Blakey attempted some sort of rest, reached across for the American, awakening him with a warning hand across his mouth. Blakey had not been sound asleep and became alert immediately, staring pointlessly down into the deep blackness below him. Back in the jeep were infra-red night-glasses through which he could have identified them — and the compass, too, which might have given him some idea where they were. Blakey felt the despair go through him, a nauseous feeling, and fought against it; to allow it was as pointless as gazing down into the forest below, trying to isolate the Africans who were pursuing them. Worse, if he let the fear take control then he increased the chances of their capture. And he couldn't be captured. He felt into his pocket for the familiar section of his wallet holding the photograph of Jane and Samantha: he couldn't leave them alone. Jane was too young, too innocent. Samantha was a baby who would one day grow up into a child needing the support and guidance of a father. He couldn't be captured.

His body began aching from the tensed, fixed position in which he held himself and, without relaxing his attention to what was happening down below on the jungle floor, Blakey eased himself back against one of the branches of the tree. So intently was he concentrating, in fact, that the rustling and twig-snapping for which he was listening merged into the other jungle noise and very quickly he felt a euphoria: there had been a mistake and there were no Africans down there at all. At first light they'd set off, fully rested, get a position fix from their radio and be able to walk out to a pick-up spot somewhere. Blakey screwed his clenched fists into his eyes, trying to drive away the euphoria as he had moments before suppressed the fear. There *were* Africans down there; there were Africans whose families he had maimed and whose crops he had destroyed and who would destroy him, if he allowed the exhaustion to take control of reasoning.

He started at sudden, unexpected closeness. Makovsky had moved through the tree tangle and reached out for him again, as if aware of the American's need. He squeezed Blakey's arm reassuringly several times and the American felt out and returned the pressure, gratefully. He wouldn't give in, Blakey determined; he'd keep control, whatever happened. He'd keep control and get out: once again he felt for the wallet and the photograph of his family.

The dripping dampness of a jungle at night wrapped itself around them, soaking their clothing and chilling their bodies. They hunched one beside the other, each trying to push back the fatigue and each, periodically, failing — until the sudden slump of tiredness jerked them awake once more. It seemed a night without end and they both stirred, thankfully, at the first signs of greyness. They were cramped and unrested and wet.

In the growing light, they peered down into the jungle, trying to see the Africans. Fronds and leaves shuddered under the weight of the birds and the monkeys and the dampness still dripped, undried as yet by any sun. Makovsky looked curiously across at the other man: Blakey humped his shoulders uncertainly.

They waited until it was fully light, and still there was no indication of any human life below them. Makovsky looked again and Blakey nodded. His body felt weighted and heavy. He was trying to concentrate upon any movement below him, but other images forced their way into his mind: children with bellies bloated from under-nourishment and Samantha in her favourite red dress with white stars on the collar; great gaps of ruined crops and under-growth, like the first workings on a six-lane highway; and village elders, looking at them with implicit trust. '*Do you come to talk of God?*'

Blakey felt the pressure against his shoulder and turned to see the Russian gesturing that they should move. Blakey tried to concentrate again, looping the radio around his body and stretching out, to get the cramp from his body. He dropped to the ground too quickly, before there was sufficient strength in his legs to support him, and rolled sideways in a ball. Within seconds, Makovsky was beside him, supporting his back.

'What is it?' asked the Russian worriedly.

'Just numb,' assured Blakey.

They stayed crouched, suddenly aware of the restrictions of their vision.

'We'll have to be careful,' said Makovsky.

'Bloody careful.'

They moved off cautiously, both tensing and pressing the life back into their arms and legs, twitching at any sudden screech or movement around them. It seemed a long time before they got to a clearing sufficiently large for them to gauge the position of the sun and decide upon a direction.

'Would Peterson risk any sort of helicopter pick-up from the missile ship?' said Makovsky.

Blakey shrugged. 'There probably isn't a machine with the range, anyway.'

'N'Djamena then?'

Blakey stared at the other man, then at himself. Their clothes hung in sweat and jungle slime, their shirts and trousers ripped in several places. Makovsky was hollow-eyed with tiredness, his face unshaven and criss-crossed with scratches. Blakey realized he probably looked even worse.

'What if the villagers have reported back to the authorities?' he said. 'They must know about the poisoning in Mao, at least.'

'What then?' demanded Makovsky.

'Attempt to cross the Cameroons border?' suggested Blakey, without any conviction.

'Without food or water or compass or any weapons?' dismissed Makovsky.

'You're right,' said Blakey. 'That was a ridiculous suggestion.'

The Russian looked at the radio slung across Blakey's back.

'Peterson could set something up for us in N'Djamena, in advance.'

'Yes,' agreed Blakey. 'N'Djamena is the only way to go.'

Both men remained immobile at the edge of the jungle clearing. 'Which way?' said Blakey. 'And how far?'

Now Makovsky looked disconcerted. 'I don't know,' he said. He squinted up at the sun, then gestured vaguely in what he thought to be a south-easterly direction. 'It's only a guess.'

'I can't do any better,' said Blakey.

'We should broadcast,' said the Russian. 'Give a position report at least.'

Blakey looked nervously around the forest, unwilling to spare the time, then unslung the set and assembled the aerial from the tree against which they were standing. They used an open line and immediately Peterson's voice came back to them, strained and uneven through the static. The Director asked their position several times, complaining of bad reception, before fully assimilating Blakey's inability to give it. He agreed upon N'Djamena and ordered Blakey to transmit news of any further trouble on the emergency wavelength. He promised that by nightfall he would have arranged shelter, fresh clothing and the earliest transportation out of the country.

'Best of luck,' he said.

'We're going to need it,' said Blakey. 'We're virtually lost.'

'Keep in contact on the emergency wavelength.'

'We will.'

Blakey closed down the transmission and looked to the Russian. Makovsky had squatted against another tree, his arms ringed around his bent legs and his head lolled forward. His eyes appeared open, but Blakey didn't think he was fully awake.

'Did you hear?' he asked.

Makovsky pulled upwards. 'Enough.'

'He's going to set something up in N'Djamena.'

'*If* we get to N'Djamena,' qualified Makovsky.

'We're not going to do it sitting around here.'

Reluctantly Makovsky pulled himself upright and helped Blakey set the radio comfortably across his shoulders. The Russian took the field-glasses and the water-bottles. He shook the bottles, testing the contents.

'About half full,' he said.

'And we don't have any more purifying tablets.'

'So we'll have to ration.'

Makovsky led, making a path for the other man and the bulky

equipment. They moved without any conversation, scuffing their feet through the undergrowth, arms raised ready to ward off the cutting, snatching branches. At first they were intent upon everything around them but gradually the exhaustion bore down upon them, and very soon they stumbled in head-bent unison, conscious only of the obstructing tree or sudden gully immediately before them. It was Blakey who called the halt, gasping out for Makovsky to stop. The Russian appeared not to hear him and the American grabbed out, pulling at the other man's shirt and gesturing him to the ground. They squatted, panting; the amount they allowed themselves from the water-bottles seemed to worsen rather than relieve their thirst.

After several moments, Makovsky looked back through the jungle.

'We're leaving a hell of a trail,' he said.

Blakey looked back, dully. 'When we get out of the jungle, we've got the open plains,' he said. He released a sudden sob, tried to disguise it as a cough, and failed.

'Dear God!' he said, giving way to the hopelessness. It was instinctive to pray, but he stopped himself. He had no right, not any more.

They felt their bodies settling and pushed onwards again. This time Makovsky shouldered the radio and Blakey the bottles and binoculars. They plodded on, the American leading now. The sun was quite high, trapping the heat among the trees and undergrowth. Sweat streamed from them and mosquitoes and insects were everywhere. It was too much trouble to flick them away and soon the bites stopped irritating. Blakey moved in a half-consciousness, the discordant imagery of the Africans they had encountered and the wife and daughter he loved so much swirling through his mind until they became intermingled, and Samantha was one of the babies with the red-pooled eyes and defoliant burns and Jane one of the bare-breasted women ululating her grief in a perpetual prayer-line. He was only vaguely aware of Makovsky's hand against his shoulder, held there by one of the water-bottle straps, as the Russian groped for guidance, like a blind man.

Again it was Blakey who decided the stop. Makovsky came down unprotesting beside him.

'It must be almost twenty-four hours since we've had anything to eat,' said Makovsky.

'Yes.'

'Are you hungry?'

'I don't think so,' said the American. Until that moment, he hadn't considered food.

Makovsky looked around, as if expecting to find something within arm's length. 'Nothing seems to grow here — nothing that we could obviously eat, anyway.'

'It would be dangerous, unless we knew what it was.'

Had they been walking, they would probably not have heard it, because for a long time they had been struggling, careless not only of their tracks but of any sound they might be making. But they were motionless and close to the ground and so they detected it. Like those they had heard during the night, the movement was different from the other jungle noises — a regular, unhurried pad of something confidently in pursuit. Blakey's head came up and he stared at the Russian, a disbelieving look upon his face.

'Oh no. Please no.' The plea whimpered out.

'Run,' said Makovsky, thrusting up.

Fear coursed through them, driving the lassitude before it. Blakey led, crashing wildly through bushes and vines, his mind blank of any thought except the need to get away from those behind. Breath was coming from him in wincing, mewing sounds. Once, far behind, he thought he heard something that sounded like a war-cry, a shout of triumph at least, and he tried to run faster, but the matted creeper and fern seemed thatched all around him and he ripped and tore at it in his frustration.

The break came suddenly in front of them, without any thinning that would have warned them. It was a lush, grassy area, the sort of place where they would have rested gratefully: maybe even bathed in the stream that coiled through and disappeared into the renewed jungle thickness about forty yards away.

Blakey came to a nervous halt, staring wildly around. 'The stream,' he said. 'We can wade along it: it'll be easier and with luck there will be no tracks.'

'What about crocodiles?'

'Too shallow,' judged the American. He turned, looking fully at the other man. 'And I'm more frightened by the certainty of being caught than I am by crocodiles.'

Blakey stumbled on, thrusting through the water and making what appeared to be a path into the jungle beyond, then carefully retraced his steps and entered the water. He shivered at the sudden, surprising coldness, testing the bottom and nodding at the firmness. The water came to just below his knees, making walking comparatively easy.

'Downstream,' he said. 'It'll drain into the lake. We can clear the jungle that way.'

Makovsky stepped in behind him and together they strained out against the water, immediately aware of the additional difficulty in walking. But the obstruction was far less, even where overhanging branches met and intertwined over the waterway. Only once did it threaten to become dangerously deep and that only lasted for a few feet. Once sufficiently far away from the clearing, Blakey looked back, satisfying himself that any sediment trail which would have pointed to their direction had cleared from the water. Makovsky was holding his shoulder again and almost involuntarily he squeezed it, one of his encouraging gestures.

They were making good progress now, far better than they had done in the jungle. Blakey waded along alert for any reptiles, despite the assurance he had given the Russian.

'We should broadcast,' said Makovsky, from behind. 'They should be warned.'

'No time,' gasped Blakey.

'If I kept the radio on my back, we could do it as we walked,' said Makovsky.

Blakey hesitated, accepting the other man's advice. They reached out, holding each other's shoulders and then manoeuvred around, so that Makovsky was in front and the American behind. Blakey had reached out for the transmitter and tuned to the emergency frequency when the sound came from behind, the splashing of many men moving through water. Blakey and Makovsky urged themselves forward, actually trying to run in the places where the stream shallowed out to cover little more than their ankles. Blakey seemed to discover the microphone in his hand and it triggered his terror. Without any attempt at coherence he babbled out their pursuit and the closeness of the Africans behind them and then, all control nearly gone, shouted: 'Help. For God's sake help us!'

Six miles away Bradley and Sharakov leaned towards the radio. Hours before they had tuned to the emergency frequency upon Peterson's instructions and they now heard the plea.

'Jesus!' said Bradley softly, stirred by the near hysteria in Blakey's voice. The Green Beret colonel nodded to the men around him and the Americans began to assemble.

'What do you think you're doing?' demanded Sharakov as Bradley stood up.

'What do you mean, what am I doing! Going to get them out of it, of course!'

Although the Americans had been gathering their kit, it was the Russians who appeared more readily prepared. At Sharakov's movement the AK-47s came up and there was a slightly unsynchronized sound of safety catches being released. Bradley and his group stopped in mid-action, gazing disbelievingly at the guns being pointed at them.

'Help,' came a distant, slightly distorted sound from the radio lying between them.

'We don't know where they are,' Sharakov began, talking slowly. 'We could blunder about in this jungle for days and they could be only a hundred yards away and we'd still miss them. We know that the girl inside the installation is dead. We know that your man failed. So there's only us left. All we'd be doing, trying to find them, would be chancing discovery; and to avoid that was the very first order that either of us received ...'

'You wouldn't shoot,' insisted Bradley, shifting slightly. The muzzles of two rifles moved with him.

'I would,' said Sharakov. 'I'd kill you all and attempt whatever we're ordered to do with a reduced group, and I'd be fully supported in any subsequent enquiry that your people might hold.'

'I'll kill you,' Bradley promised simply. 'For this, I'll kill you.'

'You'll probably try,' accepted Sharakov, without any apparent concern.

Cautiously Bradley made a gesture, ordering his men down. It was repeated by Sergeant Banks and, reluctantly, the Americans threw off their kit and settled on the ground again. Because there was nowhere else to look, everyone stared at the radio. There was no transmission, just the grunting, whimpering sound of the bogus priests trying to escape.

It went on for several minutes and then Banks said suddenly, 'It's stopped.'

Makovsky had slipped out of the shoulder supports and cast the radio aside, swinging it wide into the jungle in a desperate attempt to delay its discovery. Seeing the man's attempt to make the going easier, Blakey dropped first the binoculars and then, without thought, took off the water-bottles and let them go. They were beyond speech now, beyond almost everything. Neither was properly conscious; they were aware only of their left-foot, right-foot stumble through the water. First Makovsky and then Blakey fell, splashing full length into the shallow stream. The coldness revived them, initially making them want to stay there, in the relaxed, comforting wetness, then sufficient to make them struggle upwards again, to continue running. It was just after he'd fallen that Blakey felt the sudden hardness against his ankle, below the water where he couldn't see. He screamed, believing an attack from a crocodile he hadn't identified, and tried to pull himself away, instead forcing his foot even further into the wedge of a submerged tree root. When he fell this time, his leg was held almost in an upright position and he screamed once more, as the pain seared through him. Makovsky stopped at the noise, turning as Blakey thrust up from the water, swivelling into a sitting position so that he could see his ankle. Already it was ballooning up, the flesh tight and whitely pinched by his sock and boot.

The Russian waded back and for a moment stood looking down at the crippled American. Then he reached down, attempting to pull him upright on to his one good leg.

'I can't walk,' protested Blakey.

'I'll carry you.'

For a moment Blakey came up level with the other man, their eyes meeting, and forced the confusion from his mind. 'Don't be ridiculous.'

Makovsky stooped, attempting to get the American across his

shoulders. Blakey refused to bend. 'I said don't be ridiculous.'

From his crouched position Makovsky didn't bother to speak, just drove his fist into Blakey's groin, doubling him up to fall naturally across his back. It was a near impossible attempt. The Russian was at the very tip of exhaustion and his knees would not straighten properly under Blakey's weight. His feet went deeper into the bed of the stream, increasing the effort needed to drag himself along. The veins corded in his head and neck. He fell, inevitably, after only a few yards, and this time there was no groaning, strained effort to rise again. Makovsky lay face down, his head just against the bank; Blakey was on his side, propped gasping with his mouth at the water-line, looking backwards. And so he saw them first.

The Africans were moving quite steadily, confident of their quarry. Blakey attempted to cry out but no sound came. He tried to crawl backwards through the stream, dragging his useless leg behind him but the water was too deep, gushing into his mouth and nose and choking him. He snatched out to warn the Russian, but Makovsky just grunted, trying to escape the clawing fingers with a shrugging motion. The Africans stopped warily, about fifty yards away. There were a few rifles, mostly Second World War Lee Enfields and even an ornately-butted muzzle-loader which had obviously found its way down from the Sahara. There were also spears and knives. Blakey watched, fully conscious in his fear of the grunted conference. He saw some of the men break away either side of the stream into the jungle, and then the main group edged forward again, crouched against any sudden defence from the two prostrate men.

'No, please not,' moaned Blakey. 'Not me ... didn't want to ... please not ...'

The Africans were getting bolder as they realized that there would be no resistance. Blakey could see Ndala and Miburu and thought he recognized some of the men from the fishing village, but he couldn't be sure. Behind, both to the left and right, there was the crash of sudden spurted movement through the jungle and Blakey knew they were surrounded.

He tensed, waiting for the first burst of pain, his eyes clenched almost closed, but nothing came and when he opened them again he saw Ndala and Miburu only feet away. Miburu's body was smeared with unguents, but otherwise there was no indication of his being a witch-doctor.

'... I'm sorry ... so very sorry ...' said Blakey.

He shuddered at a sudden movement to his right and felt the pain at last, in his head. Then he saw something fall into the water in front of his face and realized that one of the fishermen had thrown the empty cyanide can into his face: he felt a stickiness as the salt of the blood trickled into his mouth. Around him there was a burst of Chadic dialect, and then someone whom Blakey could not see began prodding the Russian with a spear-point. When there was no reaction, he drove the point firmly into Makovsky's shoulder, until the pain slowly turned the Russian over on to his back. Makovsky lay there, staring up unseeingly. There was another brief discussion and then the Africans were upon them. Blakey screamed out, in advance of the pain, but initially there was none. He felt his body being moved and turned, and then a spurt of agony as hands gripped his injured ankle. He just managed to snatch some air before he was submerged and became aware that the Africans had strapped their legs to the shaft of a spear and were hauling them face down, through the water. It was a terrifying torture. Their faces grated and thumped over the stream bed and hidden stumps and branches and every time they tried to support themselves from the water on their arms, to catch fresh breath, they were pulled forward with their mouths open, so that the choking started all over again. They were both semi-conscious when it stopped, and so they were unaware of the other preparations for a long time. Blakey recovered, vomiting from his mouth and nose. They were in a small clearing with a ring of Africans around them; others were lopping branches from two of the more firmly established trees, clearing an area about twelve feet from the ground. Some were crouched over the detritus, selecting branches and then slashing at them with their knives. It was the shape that was being created from the trees that gave Blakey the first warning and at first he couldn't believe it, his mind refusing the comprehension. Then he saw that around the men selecting the branches there was a growing pile of stakes, and he reached out, warningly, for Makovsky. A deep groan came from the

Russian and Blakey knew the realization had come to him, too. So deep was their terror that they did not see that Miburu and Ndala were standing before them. The headman who had first befriended them said sneeringly, 'You came as men of God.'

'No,' babbled Blakey. 'Not priests ... really not priests ...'

'Priests of the devil,' insisted Miburu.

'No!' wailed Makovsky, as the Africans reached down for them. 'No!'

Blakey tried to brace his feet against the ground, to prevent himself being dragged towards the cross-shape that had been fashioned from the trees. The pain from his damaged ankle burst through him. He still attempted to force his foot against the ground, to prevent it happening, but there were too many and they dragged him easily, laughing when his bowels gave out in fear. Makovsky tried to fight and they laughed at him, too, jeering as they brushed aside his feeble blows.

It takes a very long time for a sacrificed man to die. Before death, most of the bones are disjointed and, to prevent the stakes tearing away from the hands and feet, the arms have to be roped to the cross. Before they finally became still, both Blakey and Makovsky had gone insane.

Petrov had learned of the Dakhilah staging post from his carefully implanted Israeli spies and had managed to position a satellite monitor over the area, so he knew immediately the C-130s began arriving in Egypt. He alerted Peterson, who managed a direct telephone link from the Gulf of Guinea to the Mossad chief in Jerusalem, at first pleading as his deputy had done, and then demanding that no incursion be made.

'Can you guarantee the launch won't happen?' demanded Levy.

Peterson hesitated. 'I'm sending an assault group in, within hours.'

'So everything else you've attempted has failed?'

There was another hesitation from the American. 'Yes,' he conceded, finally.

'I thought I made it clear to you in Washington that Israel had no intention of letting this thing be positioned anywhere over its territory,' said Levy. 'You fouled up; now it's our turn.'

The Russian monitor detected the midnight take-off and within an hour, Peterson was in radio contact with Bradley. The attack instruction had already been given and the Russian and American soldiers were grouped at the forest edge, faces blackened for night assault, all their weaponry checked and greased.

'You've no idea where they'll drop?' queried Bradley.

'No.'

'They could come down miles from where we are.'

'If they do, then it's not a problem.'

'If we locate them, we're to intercept and eliminate?'

'You're the last chance,' said the CIA Director. 'Nothing must get in the way of you destroying that rocket.'

Bradley disconnected the transmission and looked across at Sharakov.

'I told you we would be needed,' reminded the Russian.

CHAPTER 35

The assault had been timed for first light, around four-thirty. They heard the sound of the aircraft two hours before, droning in on a low, steady drop run. It seemed very far away.

'Shit,' said Bradley softly.

'Several miles,' judged Sharakov expertly.

'No chance of interception then,' agreed the American. So close to positive action, his animosity towards the Russian appeared to be lessening.

'Not if we're to keep to time.'

'And we've got to,' insisted Bradley. 'We've got three miles to go beyond that perimeter.'

Sharakov settled against a tree, attempting to assess the situation. 'The plane was throttling up, so the drop is over,' he said. 'Let's say they've been on the ground an hour: that doesn't give them much time to assemble into a very cohesive unit.'

'They would have been that before they left Israel,' argued Bradley. 'In Entebbe it took them thirty minutes.'

'On an open airfield, the plans of which they knew. The planes brought them to within yards of the target. This is altogether different.'

'I hope you're right.'

Around them the commandos were shifting and stirring with that nervousness that comes so close to an action, even from men as highly trained and professional as these were; there was an eager readiness to smile at things barely amusing and an anxiousness to help with each other's equipment. As with the commanders, the reserve between the American and Russian soldiers had lessened.

Bradley sat crouched forward, his arm against his knee so that he could count off the time. At three-fifteen he looked across at Sharakov again. Sharakov nodded and together they gestured their men up. Sure of the protection devices, they went swiftly through the scrub and then the savannah, careless of the tracks. They moved in a wedge-shape, lightly armed men on the fringe around those carrying the heavy equipment with which they hoped to immobilize the silo and make the rocket launch impossible. There were four bazookas very near the apex of the wedge, because the control towers had to be brought down very quickly. On either side were two flame throwers, included more for the psychological terror they would create among any opposition than for the practical damage they might cause. Behind this line came the rocket launchers, wire-controlled to ensure accuracy and then the mortars which would establish a line at the grass edge and lob the shells over the heads of the main force. Each man had been issued with six grenades, both percussion and shard-fragmented, the anti-personnel type which spewed out hundreds of metal darts upon explosion. Bradley and Sharakov were in the centre from which they had maximum command. Logan, who had carried out the first reconnaissance, was at the very tip of the group and, obeying the orders that had been issued before they set out, he halted them about twenty yards from the sensors at the commencement of the no man's land to avoid their advance being detected. The perimeter was perfectly targetted in the floodlights installed for its own protection. Bradley silently checked the group's minefield maps, one between two men. He and Sharakov moved up to lead the attack. The Russian was already stooped facing the installation, counting off the minutes. The two commanders brought their arms down together in perfect unified command, and they swept forward as a co-ordinated fighting unit. The immediate need, once they had activated the sensors, was for speed, because they could only move through the minefield single file, with no attack formation. Sharakov was first, Bradley following; they were about twenty yards in, moving well, when the American thought he heard some sort of distant alarm bell ahead. Behind them came the recognizable chink of metal assembling as the mortars were set up. Bradley snatched a look over his shoulder, smiling at the tight, zig-zag conformity of the men moving through the explosives.

They were almost in the very centre of the minefield, Sharakov about 150 yards from the perimeter wire and the last man in the line 100 yards clear of the grass when the first shot came. As if it were a signal to commence the assault, there was an immediate flurry of firing and then, from their left, a sudden staggering explosion as something, probably a rocket, fell into the no man's land and set off first one and then another mine. Bradley's first impression was that someone in the mortar line had fired prematurely and short. He jerked around, bringing the radio to his face and he saw the movement, far to his left, and then with sickening awareness, soldiers grouped much closer. As he watched there was a flash of further rocket launchings. One burst just beyond the wire and two more fell short: one activated another mine and, from somewhere within their own group, Bradley heard a scream as shrapnel scythed into them.

'The Israelis,' Bradley shouted, to Sharakov.

From the complex behind, the klaxons blared out and there was the hurried scurry of half-dressed figures from the barrack area. Bradley was on one knee, operating the radio now, ordering the mortar unit to direct their fire sideways into the Israeli group. He passed the order along the line: those at the very rear were to turn and fire at will.

'We can't fight from here: not in the very centre of a minefield,' yelled Sharakov.

'We haven't got a choice,' Bradley bellowed back.

Firing began from the complex, bullets wasping about them. Bradley tried to ease the men past him, to create a firing line. He gestured for the bazooka unit to spread out and they moved obediently. The furthermost man almost immediately trod on to a mine and was thrown screaming and maimed into the air, the explosion injuring another man, directly behind. It was Promulka, Bradley saw. The bazooka operator was writhing about legless twenty feet away and exploded another mine which killed him.

The Israelis were responding to the attack, firing not into the complex but at the American and Russian soldiers, who were pinned like funfair targets in the middle of a completely open, brilliantly lit area. Two bazookas hissed away close behind Bradley, but both fell harmlessly short of the control towers. Their rifle and machine-gun fire was scrappy and without co-ordination, and Bradley knew from its lightness that a lot of the men had been hit.

'It's no good,' Sharakov called. 'We haven't got the surprise: we couldn't possibly get into the installation.' The Russian was prostrate and had dragged an AK-47 from one of his dead soldiers, firing carefully into the complex. Two of the guided rockets burst into the Israeli advance, illuminating them momentarily in a flash of stark whiteness. Someone at the rear of their line lost control, leaping up in an attempt to throw a grenade and was cut down at the moment of hurling it, so that it exploded far short of the second assault group, bursting another mine.

'Retreat,' commanded Bradley, loudly.

The firing from the complex was now far more accurate, machine-gun fire sweeping across the cleared ground. As they grunted past each unmoving soldier, first Bradley and then Sharakov tried to check to ensure they were dead. It was not possible to detect Sergeant Banks' wounds, but he'd died in staring-eyed shock. Sweetman had a gaping hole in his chest and Gribanov a massive wound to the head. Bradley paused, once, glancing over his shoulder: the installation guards were against the wire, free-firing at them. He shouted an order to the mortar bank and within minutes a shell landed close to the guards, scattering them: there were a lot of dead and injured, Bradley saw.

There were only two mortar men still alive when they got to the savannah. Logan ran from the no man's land just ahead and only Sharakov came behind him.

'Disaster,' said the Russian bitterly. 'Because of the Israelis it's been a disaster.'

He gazed back into the minefield. The dead men of the combined group lay like a wavering, accusing finger.

'No damage,' agreed Bradley, as if he couldn't comprehend the failure. 'We caused no damage at all.'

'Let's get the bastards,' decided Sharakov, rising in the direction from which the Israelis were now directing their fire towards the complex. They were hopelessly short of range and causing little damage.

'No!'

The Russian jerked around, staring down at the M-16 rifle that Bradley was directing at him.

'Our attack has failed,' said Bradley. 'And so has the Israelis'.

They outnumber us, enormously. And if we're not killed in some futile attack, then we stand a chance of being captured by men from the complex. And that might mean some sort of show trial: neither your people nor mine want that sort of smear in Africa.'

Sharakov remained tensed, as if still expecting Bradley to shoot. 'They've got the proof, from the bodies out there,' he said at last, moving his head towards their dead soldiers.

'Not if we destroy them.'

'Holy Christ,' said Logan softly, from the protection of the grass.

Sharakov slowly sank to the ground. 'You're right,' he said.

They set up a mortar barrage against both the Israelis and the complex, and beneath its cover Bradley and Sharakov carefully hurled the grenades among the men they had an hour before led into battle, attempting to confuse identification as much as possible. It was fifteen minutes before they were satisfied and then, doubled up below the screen of the grasses, they fled back towards the jungle. They were almost at once out of range of the complex and encountered none of the Israeli commandos. They had established a base and supply camp well beyond the jungle edge and did not stop until they reached it. There they halted, panting. Bradley heard the sound of someone being sick. He saw it was Logan and wondered why, suddenly, he was unconcerned that one of his men was showing such emotion in front of the Russian. They stopped only long enough for sufficient provisions to be assembled for the march back through the jungle to the Cameroons border. As they moved out, they heard the sound of helicopters.

'Spotters, from the complex,' judged Sharakov.

Bradley nodded. 'They won't detect us in the jungle.'

They had travelled for several hours before Sharakov pulled up level with the American.

'You didn't do it,' said the Russian.

Bradley looked at him curiously.

'When you had the chance, you didn't kill me.'

Bradley smiled, an expression of embarrassment. 'It didn't seem important any more.'

So complete was the army's failure that there had been no point in an extensive radio conversation with Bradley. Peterson agreed the pick-up co-ordinates and then for a long time remained slumped in the chair in the radio room, staring down at the report files which had begun so well and which now recorded a gradual culmination in complete disaster. He had to force movement into himself, encoding a message to Petrov and then to Washington.

After he had sent the messages, Peterson stayed on in the radio room, almost comatosed by a peculiar feeling of uncertainty. He tried to pull himself out of it, attempting to convince himself that there could be little other response to the domino-like collapse of everything he had attempted. He was scarcely aware of Captain Ridley entering the shack, blinking recognition only when the destroyer captain offered him coffee.

'Can I ask what happened?' said Riley.

Peterson concentrated fully upon the man. 'I failed,' he said simply. 'I failed in everything I set out to do.'

There was a sudden movement from the duty operator, who turned towards Peterson within minutes. 'It's for you sir,' he reported. 'It says you're to return to Washington immediately.'

EPILOGUE

The observation room for the actual launch was above ground, a circular building with windows giving a 180-degree view of the silos from which Dr Muller expected one day to launch more rockets. From where he stood, Bohler could see the slight discoloration in the ground, marking where the silo covering had been removed, in preparation for blast-off.

Muller was to his right, immediately behind Hannah Bloor. The Project Director was at a control console linked to the underground chamber into which they had seen Gerda fall to her death the previous day. Everyone's attention was locked on to the digital countdown and when it came down to seconds, Hannah involuntarily began moving her lips in time with the figures flickering before her and then, at the very end, counted out loud.

Even through the concrete protection of the chamber they felt the vibration of ignition. Smoke and exhaust gases spewed up from the silo, and then from the middle of the clouds came the rocket, rising upwards in perfect trajectory.

Everyone in the room crowded forward against the windows. For several seconds the rocket was perfectly visible and then it was marked by exhaust flames and vapour gases and finally just the vapour. By the time Bohler turned back to the control panel, Hannah was already before it, counting now the time to first stage separation. It came precisely on time, without any fault. Muller's hand went out to her shoulder, resting there lightly. The second-stage booster came away ten minutes later, with the satellite perfectly on course. It was as if everyone in the room had been connected to an electrical current which had suddenly been turned off: they all slumped at the same moment, as the tension of possible failure left them. Hannah rose from her chair and Muller seized her hand, pumping it excitedly. Those from the project team who were not in the underground chamber crowded around her. She was very flushed and excited.

Muller had champagne in readiness on a side table. The Director poured it himself, clumsily, so a lot of the wine was spilled, and then carelessly handed it around. The exuberance faltered when he came to Bohler. Hannah appeared to become aware of him at the same moment and her smile also became uncertain.

Muller completed the movement he had started, handing Bohler a glass. Bohler took it. 'Congratulations,' he said.

'I wish the occasion hadn't been marred by the death of Dr Lintz,' said Muller sincerely.

Bohler looked beyond the Director to the woman, slightly raising his glass in a toast. 'You've had an overwhelming success,' he said. 'You must be very proud.'

'Yes,' she said. 'I am.'

Muller turned back to the others in the room, smiling again. 'A triumph, gentlemen,' he said. 'We've achieved a resounding triumph.'

Russian and American satellites detected the launch at once. In Moscow the Politburo convened an immediate meeting. Litvinov was entrusted with recalling Petrov from Odessa. In Washington, the President had a meeting with Henry Moore and Herbert Flood and decided that Israel had to be informed of their satellite monitor. By the time the message was received in Jerusalem, Fowler was already chairing a meeting of the National Security Council.

It was from Israel that there came the public announcement of the launch. An emergency session of the Knesset was scheduled and the army, navy and air force were put on twenty-four hour alert.

The first pronouncement from any leader came from the Israeli Premier. Before the Knesset meeting, Shimeon Weismann made a television address to the nation. Not since the 1976 war had his country faced a greater challenge, he said.

He added: 'Peace, which once seemed so close, is now in doubt again.'

BOOK THREE

O, what a tangled web we weave
When first we practise to deceive.

Sir Walter Scott

Peterson paused at the exit from the aircraft, curiously reassured by the dishevelled figure of Walter Jones awaiting him. The deputy was huddled in the familiar, seemingly over-large overcoat and Peterson shivered in the cold — a bitter contrast to the weather he had known off the African coast during the previous week. The CIA Director hurried towards the waiting car, extending his hand to the other man as he approached. Jones took it. Neither man smiled nor spoke.

Peterson entered first and waited until Jones had followed and the door was closed, 'How does it look?' he demanded.

'Bad.'

'I tried to raise the White House three times from the plane. I was blocked off every time.'

Jones nodded. 'The President is being very cautious, waiting to see which way it's going to fall. If what we attempted becomes public, the Agency would be a big embarrassment.'

'Anything so far?'

'Not about us, no. Or the Soviets.'

'What *has* happened?'

'Israel is keeping the tension up, with some ambiguous statements. Syria, Iraq and Jordan have their armies on stand-by. Egypt is appealing for calm, but they've begun specialized mobilization. Libya has claimed full credit: Gadaffi even appeared on television. There've been messages of support for him from Saudi Arabia and the Gulf states.'

'Quite a coup,' conceded Peterson bitterly.

'But not for us.'

'Any response at all from Fowler?'

'Just that you be recalled immediately. And that we hold ourselves in readiness for any summons.'

'What about Flood?'

'Nothing from him either. But he's the biggest danger. The moment he fears the criticism is getting personal, there's the risk he'll start to leak.'

'How well have we undermined him?'

Jones shrugged, setting out in fuller detail than had been possible in his messages to the ship the counter-attack that had been made upon the foreign affairs adviser. Peterson sat with his lips pursed, occasionally nodding at some point that the deputy made.

'Does Moore know of the income tax suggestion?'

'Not unless the President has told him.'

'It's a good ace in the hole,' assessed Peterson. On the public highway, the vehicle was being slowed down by other traffic. The Director stared out, recognizing familiar landmarks: once he had felt an excitement in isolating them, but not any more.

He looked back into the car. 'Have you set up a liaison with Bohler?'

'Fixed-time transmission, every night,' confirmed Jones. 'Do you want him brought out?'

'No,' said the Director immediately. 'Let's learn how effective that damned satellite is.'

'Does it matter?'

'It might,' said Peterson.

'There's something I didn't tell you about fully on the ship,' said the deputy, unexpectedly. 'About Beth.'

'What about Beth?'

'She's ill ... very ill ...'

Peterson flushed at the realization that he had not enquired after his family. 'Why didn't you ...?'

'You had enough to think about,' said Jones, cutting off the protest. 'She's a heroin addict. She's suffering from hepatitis, from some past injection or other. And there's evidence of some venereal infection.'

'Oh Jesus!' said Peterson.

'I told Paul you were home today; he's waiting for your call.'

'What about Lucille?'

'No problems, as far as I know. Paul's the one who has maintained direct contact with the clinic.'

'Does she know ... about Beth, I mean?'

'I don't know,' said Jones.

The limousine swept into the CIA headquarters and Peterson was already opening the door before the driver managed to get to it. Jones had set up a large work-table alongside his main desk; every report was assembled chronologically and cross-referenced to other information upon which it had had a cause or effect. Although he had been in the control centre and the conduit for most of the intelligence, it was the first opportunity the Director had had to consider it in its entirety. He went again through the whole operation, re-reading every message from within the African complex, then from the bogus priests and finally from Bradley, comparing them first separately and then together. Jones had added the President's assessment as the affair had progressed and introduced Petrov's reaction from Odessa, also his one contact with Levy in Jerusalem.

Peterson took two hours to re-assimilate all the facts, and he was frowning when he finally turned away from the work-bench. 'What's wrong with that?' he demanded, jerking his head back towards the files and folders.

'Wrong?' echoed Jones, confused. 'It didn't work, that's what's wrong.'

Peterson shook his head, reflectively. 'Not that,' he said. 'Something else.'

'I don't know what you mean,' said the other man.

'Neither do I, not yet,' said Peterson obtusely. He sat down at his desk, but continued to stare at the records of the operation. 'But there's something we haven't got right.'

Now Jones frowned. 'I could recite almost every word printed over there,' he said. 'I've checked it and I've cross-referenced it and I've collated it; if there were any inconsistency, I would have seen it.'

'I wonder,' said Peterson doubtfully. 'I wonder if we both shouldn't have seen it.'

Peterson straightened, casting off the uncertainty. 'I'm going to see my family,' he said, conscious as he spoke that he was making it sound like a pronouncement.

Paul was waiting at the entrance to his apartment when Peterson's car arrived. The boy hurried out immediately and got in beside his father. There was none of the customary antagonism between them and both seemed to want to acknowledge the other with some affection, but was unsure how to do it.

'Thank you,' said Peterson. 'I gather you got Beth away from something pretty bad.'

'It's going to take a long time,' said Paul. 'A very long time. Methadone is addictive, too.'

'What about the other things?'

'Curable, in time.'

'Was she whoring, to earn it?'

'I guess so,' said the younger man, unconcerned. 'I haven't asked her.'

'Poor Beth.'

'She's going to need a lot more than sympathy.'

'Then let's see if we can provide it,' said Peterson, as the car turned into the grounds of the clinic. Paul entered familiarly and Peterson followed, conscious for the first time that his son had shaved off the drooping moustache. Peterson was introduced to the administrator and promised an interview with the physician and psychiatrist in charge of Beth's case. Paul took the lead again, going into the ward section.

The girl had been moved from the admission area, where the security was strongest. Her room was brightly painted, almost garish. Beyond the mesh the windows were open. There were flowers on a side table and a bedside cabinet, a television set in one corner and a radio that worked through pillow-phones. There was none in evidence, but the cot was equipped with fittings for restraining equipment.

Peterson had expected to find his daughter in bed, but she was sitting out in a lounging chair alongside. She wore an all-enveloping Terry robe and pumps with pink feathers at the instep. Her hair seemed freshly washed and plaited, little-girl style. She wore no make-up, and her face and even the skin of her hands was yellowed with the liver infection from which she was suffering. Peterson realized the dressing-gown looked large because Beth was so thin; what he could see of her arms and legs looked almost skeletal.

Peterson stopped just inside the door, unsure. Beth dropped the magazine she had been reading into her lap and gazed up at him, and Peterson had the impression that she was frightened. He forced the smile to his face, hurrying towards her. She made as if to stand, then changed her mind, going back into the seat again. He leaned forward, hands against the chair arms, to kiss her. She threw her arms around his neck, clinging to him.

'Daddy,' she said, in a tight whisper. 'Oh Daddy.'

'Hello Beth.' His shoulders began to ache in the odd position in which he was standing, yet to put an arm around her would risk his collapsing on top of her. Slowly he lowered himself until he was kneeling before the girl and could reach out to hold her. He could feel the bones beneath the cloth. It was a long time before she released him and when she did, he remained crouched before her, guessing she didn't want him to move away. Close to, he saw her eyes were pouched in blackness and that they darted from spot to spot in a nervous vibration he had never known before. Her fingers were stained with nicotine. She reached out, touching his face as if she needed physical reassurance of his presence: both were uncomfortable with the tongue-tied awkwardness of hospital-visiting.

'How are you?' he said.

'All right.'

'I hear you're sick.'

'Apparently.'

'But you'll get better.'

'I hope so.'

'We'll see it happens.'

'Will you, Daddy?'

'I promise.'

Her hands came up to his face again, imploringly. 'I could do it, if you helped me,' she said. 'I could really do it.'

He covered her hand with his, turning his head slightly to kiss her palm.

'I'll help you,' he said.

She started to cry and then, although he tried to prevent it, so did Peterson. He thrust his handkerchief towards Beth and then realized he needed one for himself. She offered it back, giggling through her tears. He blew his nose and wiped his eyes.

'I'm sorry,' he said.

'You ashamed, for crying in front of me?'

'Yes,' he said.

'Why?'

He made an uncertain movement, uncomfortable at her questions. 'Fathers aren't supposed to cry.'

'I'm glad you did.'

'Why?'

'It showed you cared.'

'Doesn't it always show, that I care?'

'No.'

He blew his nose again.

'Have you seen Mummy?' asked the girl.

'Not yet.'

'Will she get better?'

'Of course.'

'You can't be very proud of us ... it's a mess, isn't it?'

'I *am* proud of you,' he said, trying to push the feeling into his voice.

'You mustn't lie, Daddy. I'm not anyone to be proud of. Not now.'

'You will be, when you get better.'

'Perhaps,' she said. 'When I get better. The doctors say I can ... that I've got the determination.'

'Of course you have!'

'Will you help me, Daddy?' She was very close to tears again.

'I promise,' repeated Peterson.

'Really promise?'

'Really promise.' Peterson remembered his son and turned to where Paul had remained standing, just beyond the door. 'And there's Paul to help us, too.'

'Hi, big brother,' said the girl.

'Hi,'

'Know what I think?' she said.

'What?'

'That we finally might be getting it together,' she said.

They remained with the girl for another hour and the interview with the physician and psychiatrist in charge lasted a similar time. The man was guarded in his prognosis. Beth had built up a heavy dependency and been with them too short a time to enable an accurate forecast of a complete cure; even now she was inclined towards unpredictable responses to certain situations.

'You were right,' Peterson said to Paul, as they re-entered the car. 'It's going to take a long time.'

'Can you allow enough?' asked the boy pointedly.

'Yes,' said Peterson. 'I can allow enough time.'

'You're looking very tanned.'

'I've been in the sun a lot.'

'Successful trip?'

Peterson turned sideways to the boy. 'No,' he said. 'A disaster.'

At that moment the car telephone sounded. The President had summoned him to a meeting at eight; it meant he would have only fifteen minutes for Lucille.

'Trouble?' asked Paul, as his father replaced the instrument in its securing clip.

'Probably,' said Peterson. 'It usually is. I'll have to drop you at a bus stop.'

There was an air of anti-climax about the rocket installation, despite the monitoring of information that had commenced within twenty-six hours of launch. With unrestricted access, Bohler was able to see nearly everything that came in; when the first pictures started to arrive, Muller actually summoned him, to boast of their clarity. They were as good as any the American had ever seen at either Houston or Cape Canaveral; the quality of some of the television transmission was even better. Even without the benefit of proper analysis, Bohler could identify the troop movements in the Negev and Sinai deserts and on the Golan Heights. He knew of the world response from easily obtainable newscasts, and guessed that his reports to Langley over the once-a-night radio link-up would increase the anxiety in Washington.

He was by the swimming pool, actually assembling the report in his mind, when he heard a sound and turned to see Hannah Bloor approaching. She was wearing the briefest of bikinis beneath a silk wrap and the American felt a stir of excitement.

'Any news of your recall yet?' she said, choosing a reclining bed beside him.

'No,' said Bohler. 'There's a lot of reaction. I'm probably still regarded as useful here.'

'More reaction than I anticipated,' agreed Hannah. 'Perhaps I've been cut off here for too long.'

'The satellite is proving remarkably effective.'

'Better than I'd dared hope,' said the woman.

'Should bring you more customers,' encouraged Bohler, seeking additional material for his report.

'Too soon to guess,' she said. 'I'd hope so.'

She slowly covered her body with suntan-oil, looking up suddenly and smiling at his embarrassment at being caught watching her do it.

'If you're kept on, perhaps there will be time,' she said.

'Time?'

'For the camera safari we talked about.'

'Yes,' agreed Bohler slowly. 'Perhaps there would be time.' Could it only be four days ago that Gerda had died?

CHAPTER 37

Dimitri Petrov managed almost a casual entrance into the cabinet room, completely concealing his unaccustomed nervousness. The débâcle in Africa was the first traceable mistake of his career. And pragmatic as always, he accepted that it would provide the focus for all the resentment and dislike which had for so long been directed towards him by those offended by his refusal to conform to the pattern of the Kremlin hierarchy.

The Politburo committee had already assembled, waiting for him. It had been several weeks since he had seen Boris Dorensky, but he had been aware of the rumours. The chairman sat whey-faced and unmoving, his eyes frequently unfocused and a palsied shake in his left hand. Ivan Borrosuba was to his left, neat and precise as always, note-pad before him as if he were about to take a deposition of some crime. Litvinov was to the left and, as he approached the table, Petrov detected a slight smirk of satisfaction. At the KGB chief's approach, Dorensky made a conscious effort to compose himself, gesturing the man towards a seat that would put him immediately before them.

'We were assured, both by yourself and by Comrade Litvinov after his visit to you in Odessa, that the African operation would be successful,' accused Dorensky. There was a slight blur in his voice, as if he were finding difficulty in pronunciation.

'The death of Dr Lintz was a tragedy,' said Petrov. 'And the assault was impeded by an Israeli commando attack that we were unable to prevent.'

'*Unable* to prevent,' attacked Litvinov immediately. 'Are you telling us that a unit as highly trained and as expert as ours was unable to defeat a rabble of Israeli and Arab soldiery?'

'The Israeli soldiery is not rabble,' said Petrov, getting an advantage from the other man's extravagance. 'At the very moment of attack, our people were disclosed by their independent action. We lost the benefit of surprise and were caught in crossfire: there was nothing they could do but withdraw.'

'The history of this miserable affair seems to be that of your telling us there was nothing you could do,' interrupted Borrosuba.

'That is a gross exaggeration,' fought back Petrov. 'An operation was mounted and achieved a very high degree of success ...'

'... and then a very low level of failure,' cut off Litvinov. 'The point was to prevent the launch of a satellite over the Middle East. That satellite is now in position, and once again the Soviet Union is being drawn to the point of confrontation with the United States of America. Where's the success in that?'

The way in which Litvinov and Borrosuba were conducting the attack was almost rehearsed, thought Petrov. Having lost so much, it was difficult to provide any sort of defence.

'I was not attempting to argue that there had been any ultimate success,' said the KGB Director. 'I was attempting to balance the affair by pointing out the considerable success in the initial stages.'

'The only point of which was to abort the launch. And it wasn't aborted,' retorted Dorensky, making the opposition to Petrov absolute.

'Something of which I am very well aware and deeply regret,' said Petrov. As always, he found humility very difficult.

'What proposals do you have for exposing the American presence in Africa, to get some slight advantage out of the whole thing?' demanded Litvinov, over-confidently.

'None,' said Petrov, immediately aware of the advantage. 'Surely I don't have to remind you that there is an operative still undetected within the installation!'

'An American,' said Litvinov, trying to retreat.

'There is still contact between myself and the Director of the CIA,' said Petrov. He hesitated, aware that Litvinov was still unbalanced and waiting to increase the awkwardness. Stressing the sarcasm, he went on, 'And surely there is no need either for me to point out that the satellite is still controlled from within the complex.'

'You don't have to tell us that,' agreed Borrosuba, coming to his colleague's rescue. 'But you do have to tell us if there's the slightest chance of the man still being able to interfere with the operation of the satellite ...'

'... and let me make it clear,' said Dorensky, before Petrov could make any response, 'that we want a very accurate and considered reply. Because whatever action the Soviet Union takes in the event of some clash between Israel and the Arab nations may well depend upon it.'

Petrov stared back at them uncertainly. The assurance might give him a temporary respite from their pressure, but if they did gauge their response from it and Bohler failed, then there would be no way that Litvinov would allow him to survive.

'I still hope there is a possibility of his causing it to malfunction,' said Petrov.

'You *hope* there's a *possibility*,' sneered Litvinov at once. 'Oh come, Comrade General! It's becoming increasingly difficult for me to believe that you comprehend the gravity of what's happening.'

'It's because I'm fully aware of the gravity that I made the reply I did,' said Petrov. 'The fact that the man still in Africa is American is quite immaterial: from our liaison, we know that the United States is as anxious as we are for this launch to fail. We have to look upon him as the best possibility still available of causing some kind of problem with the satellite.'

'Look maybe,' said Litvinov. 'But not rely.'

'May I ask what other proposals are being considered?' said Petrov, without sufficient thought.

Instantly Litvinov came back at him, making the relegation very obvious. 'No, Comrade General, you may not. The Politburo gave you the opportunity and you failed. There would be no point in involving you in any further discussion.'

Petrov felt the flush burn through him and regretted that they would be able to see his reaction to the dismissal. 'I do not yet consider that I have completely failed,' he said, hoping they would not discern the desperation in the protest.

'Are you asking us to allow any policy decision we might take to be affected by the presence of that one man? And an American, at that?' said Dorensky.

'I am asking you not to overlook his presence,' said Petrov.

'And how long must we sit and hope?' said Borrosuba.

He'd been forced into a cul-de-sac, Petrov recognized. 'I cannot properly answer that question until I have further contact with the CIA Director,' said Petrov, aware of how weak it sounded.

'Magnificent!' said Litvinov. 'Now we are being asked not only to depend upon an American in Africa, but to accept guidance from an enemy's intelligence organization before making a policy decision.'

'That's a very wrong interpretation of what I said,' protested Petrov.

'Provide another,' challenged Borrosuba.

'Permit me contact,' pleaded Petrov. 'Permit me time to consult and let there be another meeting, at which I hope to tell you more.'

Litvinov stared across the table, without any pity. 'How much time?' he said.

The man intended to allow him no escape, Petrov recognized. 'Twenty-four hours,' he said urgently. 'Just allow me twenty-four hours.'

Dorensky looked at the two men sitting either side of him and then gave a curt nod. 'A day,' he agreed. 'But let me warn you, Comrade General, that by that time we shall want positive answers to positive questions. We do not intend to make any more mistakes.'

'I repeat what I said earlier,' assured Petrov. 'I fully understand how this matter might seriously affect the country.'

'And not just the country,' said Litvinov, unable to stop himself. 'Don't forget how it might affect you, Comrade Petrov.'

The omission of his rank was intentional, the KGB chief decided, back in his office in Dzerzhinsky Square. The first indication that a purge was underway. Petrov decided he wouldn't concede anything — certainly not to people like Litvinov and Borrobusa. Would they attempt a show trial? It would be the sort of humiliation that Litvinov would enjoy. He would be too proud to stand in the dock and parrot a list of supposed crimes, Petrov knew. What then? There was only suicide.

The idea of defection came to him with startling suddenness. He could do it, he knew. It would be particularly easy, with the contact he still had with Peterson. America would give him

anything he wanted. Protection. A new identity. Enough money
to live for the rest of his life. And Irena was in America. Then he
shook himself, a physical movement. The pride that would
prevent him appearing before any mock judgement would also
prevent him becoming a traitor to his country. And there was
more than just the refusal to betray Russia. No matter what protection the Americans gave him, his own service would trace him, in a
month or a year or maybe two years: it was inconceivable that they
could allow their controller to escape, unpunished. And if Irena
were with him, then she would be punished too. Petrov sighed,
irritated at the direction in which his mind had wandered. There
was no escape for him.

Dr Harrap had been waiting for him, so Peterson's meeting with
Lucille was foreshortened even more than he had feared it would
be. As soon as he entered the ward he was conscious of the
improvement about which the doctor had spoken. Lucille had lost
her attitude of furtive awkwardness: she looked directly at him
now, not letting her eyes slide nervously away, as she had done
before. She rose to greet him and he kissed her spontaneously. She
seemed surprised.

'You look well,' he said.

'I feel fine. You look fit, too.'

'I've been in the sun.'

'And now you're back.'

'Yes.'

'For how long?' Before, there would have been a challenge in the
question, but not now.

'A long time, I hope.'

'Did it go well?'

'No.'

'I'm sorry.'

'Beth is back,' declared Peterson abruptly. Would Dr Harrap be
behind the one-way mirror, assessing the reaction of the
announcement upon the woman? It had been the physician's idea
and Peterson suddenly accepted that he was taking part in an
experiment upon his wife. Lucille was blinking, nervously; she

glanced instinctively over his shoulder, as if she expected the girl to be waiting in the corridor outside.

'Where?'

'Here, in Washington.'

'Then why isn't she ...?'

'She's ill, Lucille. Very ill.'

She came up half out of her chair, her eyes flooding. 'What's the matter with her?'

As succinctly as possible, Peterson told her of how their daughter had been found and of the medical diagnosis that had been made. Towards the end she began to wince at his words, as if they physically hurt her, and Peterson wondered at Dr Harrap's insistence that she be told everything so brutally.

'Oh my God,' she said.

'But we've got her back,' said Peterson urgently. 'We've got her back with us and she's under expert care. We're going to make her better.'

She tried to smile at his attempted reassurance but it came out as a crooked expression. 'How long?'

'A long time,' he said. 'She's going to need a great deal of help ...'

Peterson paused, unsure. Harrap insisted that the interview be conducted this way and that he be the one to do it.

'... and the person who's going to have to help her most is you, Lucille.'

'No!' The woman cringed before the demand.

'We're all going to be here, you and me and Paul. But when she's discharged you'll be the person with whom she's going to have to spend most of the time.'

'But I'm not ... I can't ...'

'Yes you can, Lucille. You can because you've got to. Beth isn't strong enough, not by herself. She's going to need you.'

The woman seemed to quieten, looking at him steadily. 'What you're telling me is no more booze.'

'I'm not telling you that,' said Peterson. 'Dr Harrap and the other counsellors tell you that. I'm telling you what there is for you to do when you get out of here.'

'Caring for Beth again,' said Lucille, wistfully. 'It will have been such a long time.'

'And it won't be like before — it won't be easy.'

'No,' accepted the woman, still distant. 'It won't be easy.'

Peterson turned at movement behind him. His driver was standing, expectantly. 'The White House,' the man reminded.

Peterson rose immediately and when he looked back, Lucille's attitude had changed. ' "... we're all going to be here," ' she quoted, accusingly.

'I meant it,' insisted Peterson.

'Until something more important comes up,' she said disbelievingly. 'Until you're too busy.'

'Honestly, Lucille. It won't be like before.'

A few feet away the chauffeur shifted impatiently.

'You hadn't better keep them waiting,' she said.

'I'll see you tomorrow,' he promised.

'I won't hold my breath until you arrive.' It was little-girl cynicism and both were embarrassed by it.

He leaned forward to kiss her again and this time the movement was stilted. She half pulled away and their noses collided.

'Tomorrow,' he repeated, turning away from her. Dr Harrap had been wrong, he decided. The intention had been to give Lucille an awareness of responsibility — a purpose for which to be discharged. The last impression Peterson had had of his wife as he turned to leave was of the furtive awkwardness again: the furtive awkwardness that had always been obvious when she was going towards her first drink of the day.

CHAPTER 38

It was an uncomfortable feeling, a numbing uneasiness. It came as Peterson approached the White House, staring from the car windows across the park to the illuminated doric columns, and he frowned, trying to identify the cause. Apprehension, at the coming confrontation with the President? Reason enough, certainly. But he did not think it stemmed from that. Distress at what he had just found: one hospital visit after another, seeing one sick member of his family after another? Maybe a contributory factor. But nothing more. What then? Without any positive calling to mind, he thought again of his complete analysis of the African operation and the amorphous, ungraspable impression that somewhere, somehow, something had happened which he had failed to recognize. There *was* something: the conviction was increasing in strength without his having the remotest idea of what it was. It was a belief he would have to keep to himself, or share only with Walter Jones, so that he would have a sounding board. He definitely could not introduce it at the forthcoming meeting. His credibility would be under enough strain, without attempting to introduce vague impressions when he was unable to explain what they were or even provide grounds for any doubt.

The limousine halted at the gate check and then continued on to one of the side doors from which there was easier access to the President's working quarters. Peterson walked steadily behind the usher, returned the nod of greeting to the appointments secretary and was shown into the Oval Office. Everyone whom he expected to be there was already in the room, waiting. Fowler sat behind the huge rectangular desk, with Moore and Flood in their accustomed seats; they all turned, as he entered. Only from the President was there any other movement. He jerked his head in an odd, pecking motion and gestured the CIA Director to a chair which placed him like a witness before a tribunal. Peterson supposed that was how they regarded him. He seated himself carefully, positioned the brief-case beside the chair and looked up, waiting for Fowler's lead.

'It didn't work,' said the President. He made it sound like an accusation.

There was no longer to be any Rose Garden protection, realized the CIA Director. Everyone — the President, the Secretary of State and the foreign affairs adviser — was taking out publicly proveable insurance. He had no reason for surprise; the President had warned him.

'No,' he agreed. 'We achieved a lot, but in the end it didn't work.'

'So it was ill conceived?' tried Flood.

'I don't consider it was,' defended the Director. 'I think it was a properly considered operation which failed for reasons which could not be anticipated.'

'So now we're dangling with our balls on a hook,' complained Fowler.

'There's a problem, unquestionably,' said Peterson. He felt curiously calm against their criticism, like an anaesthetized patient moments before going down for an operation: he was aware of the preparation but felt no pain.

'It's been seventy-two hours since the fuck-up,' said Fowler, swearing now not for folksy affectation but from anger.

'Yes,' accepted Peterson.

'There's been no announcement ... no protest from Chad. Why not?'

Peterson humped his shoulders, startlingly aware that he was in a room with people as frightened as he was. No, he corrected: not as frightened. More nervous even. Inexplicably it gave him a feeling of superiority.

'The Chad government is getting a lot of financial support, officially and otherwise, from the consortium. And in return they get virtual autonomy over the area occupied by the complex: it's practically a German state. They want to sell rockets. To make a public announcement about a foreign incursion, even one that failed, wouldn't be very good business, would it?' he said.

'That's my guess,' intruded Moore. 'At the moment, the consortium has got an incredible international reputation for what it's doing; they're not likely to frighten away future customers by disclosing what happened, are they?'

'We hope,' sneered Flood.

'It's been three days,' reiterated Peterson, 'If they were going to do it, they should have done it by now. We mustn't forget, either, that the perimeter is miles away from the actual complex. Bohler said that no one appeared to be aware of the attack. Don't overlook the absolute control that the Libyans were given over security.'

'Why should they want to suppress it?' demanded Flood.

'For every reason,' Peterson argued, enjoying the new feeling of confidence. 'Gadaffi has made an overwhelming international coup: his first. Why cloud it with some failed effort to stop it?'

'So we might have got away with it ... the risk of exposure, you mean?' said the President. The hope was obvious. Peterson was surprised Fowler let his control go, aware as he must have been of the recording equipment.

'I think it's too soon to be certain of that,' said Flood.

For the first time Peterson looked directly at the man who had started the destruction campaign against him. In appearance Flood was still the rumpled, haphazard academic, but Peterson thought he detected less of the aggressiveness that had been present at their earlier encounters.

'What about the Soviets?' demanded Fowler. 'Any risk from them?'

'I don't think so,' said Peterson. 'At the moment, it's a contained failure. There would only be advantage to Moscow if there had been any public difficulties.'

'I think it's too soon to be certain of that, as well,' disputed Flood. 'They might just be waiting, like we are.'

'That's a thought,' said Fowler, eagerly. 'Why don't we try to incriminate them?'

'In what?' demanded Peterson, concerned at the President's lack of projection. 'There's *been* no public announcement, either by the German firm or by Chad or by Libya. The protection we took was precisely that — protection. It was not to attack ...'

He paused, hoping for their attention. 'And we still have a man inside,' he reminded them. 'How long do you think he would survive if we started a smear campaign?'

The President appeared to become aware of his ill-considered haste. 'As an operation, it was still a disaster,' he complained, almost petulantly.

'I was entrusted with control and therefore I must accept responsibility,' admitted Peterson formally. 'I still think we might have stood some chance in the final stage if there hadn't been the Israeli interference.'

'Bastards!' said Fowler bitterly. 'Have you had any contact with them since?'

'No, not yet.'

'The Premier has refused three requests for a meeting with our ambassador,' disclosed Fowler. 'No one is getting through; Weismann is saying they're going to make their decision without any outside influence.'

'They'll want to fight,' insisted Flood, attempting an appeal to the President's frontiersman attitude. 'And if they do that, we've got them by the balls: they're dependent upon us for re-supply. We could exert some pressure by letting them know there won't be any.'

'Try that,' said Moore, 'and Jerusalem would leak the threat within hours. It would be played back here on every television network and in every newspaper and we'd lose the Jewish vote. And without the Jewish vote, what chance would the President have for re-election?'

The put-down was so brilliant that for several seconds no one apart from Flood seemed to realize the extent to which his suggestion had been exposed.

Fowler recovered first, turning to the foreign affairs adviser. 'That was a pretty dumb-assed idea,' he said brutally.

'I wasn't suggesting outright pressure,' the man tried to recover. 'Just making the position clear.'

'I think the position could be a great deal clearer and less potentially dangerous if we began discussion about the additional arms supply and loan applications their delegation made here a few weeks ago. That's where the hints should be made. And made in a way that they *are* hints, not threats. Israel wants the additional arms and — more importantly — it needs the additional money. That's where our strength lies,' said Moore.

'I agree,' said Fowler.

Peterson knew he had no place in the exchange and remained quiet. The hostility which Walter Jones had managed to inculcate between the men during his absence was relieving him of the unremitting criticism.

'And Egypt is important,' said Moore, hurrying on to complete victory. 'Since the peace agreement, nearly all the Arab countries have withdrawn their financial support. I think we should open immediate talks with Cairo and offer to make up more of the shortfall than we have promised at present. It won't prevent a Middle East war; but if Egypt stays neutral, it'll fragment any Arab action.'

'Good idea,' decided the President. 'Get on that today.'

Peterson was bemused by the anxiety that Fowler was allowing to show. There had been previous occasions when Peterson had wondered how the public would regard the private behaviour of their leaders, whom they believed possessed abilities beyond normal man; on this occasion it would be with shocked amazement, he decided.

'There's still the satellite,' said Flood, trying to move back into the discussion. 'While that thing stays where it is, we've got a priority crisis on our hands.'

The President turned back to Peterson, involving him again. 'We've still got the man inside?'

'Yes sir.'

'Can he create a malfunction, even now?'

'We've a radio patch established late tonight our time. I shan't know the answer to that until I speak to him.'

'What if he can't?' demanded Flood, recovering by the minute. 'What are you going to do then?'

Peterson looked to each of the other men, allowing his surprise at the question to register. 'Then he'll remain there,' he said, introducing a tone of patience into his voice. 'He's still incredibly valuable if he can tell us the effectiveness of the satellite. And perhaps give us some idea of the Third World interest ... a purchase, even.'

'You missed the point of the question,' resisted Flood determinedly. 'I meant the satellite. How do we get that bloody thing out of the sky?'

'What about our particle beam development?' said Peterson. He was extending the function of his office, but the other three seemed anxious for suggestions.

'That's hardly more than experimental,' protested Flood, aware of his bad performance.

'It's developed further than that,' rejected Peterson. 'The army's Sipapu project is sufficiently advanced for them to be able to project the proton beam from an orbiting space vehicle.'

The President worriedly wiped his hand across his forehead. 'It's too extreme,' he protested. 'The media have already called it the Domesday weapon, or the thing that makes nuclear warheads obsolete. Can you imagine world reaction, if it were ever discovered we were operating one of those things over their heads!'

'We could be considering a way to stop a war,' pointed out Peterson.

'We *are* talking about how to stop a war,' agreed the President. He looked to the Secretary of State. 'What about the Soviets?'

'I'm seeing the ambassador later.'

'Who's request?'

'Theirs.'

'Stress our concern, our determination to do everything to avoid any conflict. They shouldn't need much convincing, after what we've just attempted.'

'The Knesset should reach a decision soon,' reminded Flood.

'Summon the Israeli ambassador,' instructed Fowler, speaking to the Secretary of State. 'Talk about the additional aid programme ... hint we're sympathetic and then come on strong about our concern at any open conflict ...'

He stopped, looking at each of them. 'I think we're in real trouble,' he said seriously. 'And I can't see any way of resolving it.'

Peterson decided it was a worrying thought that this harassed, anxious man theoretically had the power to press a button and start a nuclear holocaust.

'Any ideas?' said the President.

There were shifts of uncertainty from all three men before him. No one spoke.

'We're in the shit,' announced Fowler, shortly. He stirred at his desk. 'I've got an all-party delegation from Congress and the Senate to talk about it. I want all three of you on immediate stand-by, for consultation.'

Everyone rose, but Fowler called out, stopping Peterson as he approached the door. The CIA Director returned to his chair, perching upon the edge expectantly.

'How sure are you there won't be any official protest ... seventy-two hours, after all?' said the President.

Peterson controlled the wince at the plea in the man's voice. 'I can't be sure,' he said, refusing the assurance. 'But after that length of time, I'm hopeful.'

'Why the hell didn't the operation work?' exclaimed Fowler, irrationally.

'It still might,' tried the Director, wanting to help the other man. 'We shouldn't dismiss Bohler completely.'

'Estimate his chances,' insisted the President.

Peterson hesitated. 'Fifty to one,' he said, well aware of the exaggeration.

'Then we might as well dismiss him,' said Fowler instantly. 'Like I said, it's an insoluble problem.'

'I came here today expecting you to ask for my resignation,' admitted Peterson.

'The shit hasn't really hit the fan yet,' said the President. 'I still might.'

Peterson looked sadly at Fowler, curious at his own lack of concern at the repeated threat. Why the hell did the man covet the job so much, he wondered. He shifted in his chair, caught by his own question. But then again, why did any of them?

By the time Peterson got back to Langley, the warning of Petrov's wish for direct consultation had already come through the Vienna route. Peterson alerted their own switchboard and then, as an extra precaution, warned their section of the White Plains receiver. The KGB General came on the line at precisely the time he had stipulated. The reception was extremely clear and Peterson was able to gauge the concern in the Russian's voice; as in the Oval Office, Peterson again experienced the sensation of superiority. He listened without interruption as Petrov sought assurances that Bohler was still operative, and detected the depression in the other man when he refused to give any sort of guarantee.

'I never imagined when I learned from my people in Israel about this complex not six weeks ago that it would have reduced me to this level of inability,' complained Petrov.

'I heard about it at the same time,' sympathized Peterson. 'I didn't see it as a problem either.'

'Do you think you can survive it?' asked the Russian Director unexpectedly.

It was a spontaneous question, without any artifice, decided Peterson. 'I don't know,' he said. 'You?'

'I don't know either,' said Petrov, in a voice that indicated that he did.

Long after the conversation with Moscow, Peterson sat staring over his desk at the specially installed table holding everything he knew about the Overcrowd Operation. The uncertainty was with him again and then suddenly he recalled something that Petrov had just said. Peterson pulled a cable form towards him and began writing a lengthy query to the American embassy in N'Djamena.

CHAPTER 39

There was no pretence today about conflicting appointments or pressure of work. Shimeon Weismann was waiting in his office when David Levy arrived and as the Mossad leader entered, the Premier called his secretary on the intercom and instructed that there should be no interruptions. Weismann was very controlled and grave-faced, but there was a tenseness about the man; it was not nervousness, decided Levy, rather excitement. A map-board had been moved into the office, with marker pins indicating the mobilization positions of Syrian, Iraqi and Jordanian troops, and the placing of the Israeli divisions and battalions which had been assembled to confront them. Egypt was unmarked.

Remarking Levy's attention to the map, Weismann said, 'I'm giving an off-the-record briefing to foreign correspondents before the Knesset meeting. It should make a good backdrop.'

'They're not the locations of our troops?' said Levy, immediately concerned.

'Of course not,' said the Premier. 'Sometimes you under-estimate me, David. I think it wise to indicate we're not taking the Egyptian call-up as a threat, don't you?'

Levy smiled back, knowing there was no offence in the man's correction. 'What's happening?' he said.

'Gadaffi's making another television appearance; he's responding exactly as we thought he would in the circumstances. Syria and Iraq are on full mobilization and they seem to be dragging Jordan along with them, rather reluctantly. Saudi Arabia and Abu Dhabi have committed troops, re-supply and whatever financial aid might be necessary ...'

'Pretty formidable,' said Levy. The military intelligence concurred exactly with his. 'So Gadaffi's got his moment as an Arab leader at last?'

'He's pledged his full army to whatever conflict arises, to fight alongside any of the bordering Arab countries.'

'What about diplomatic activity?'

'The Secretary of State summoned our Washington ambassador. It took almost two hours to get him to say that we could have the extra M-60 tanks, the guarantee of oil shipments at unfluctuating prices and the billion dollar aid programme if we didn't go to war.'

'No threat on re-supply?'

'Not yet.'

'It's a good negotiating position for them to adopt,' said Levy. 'What about Russia?'

'Their Washington ambassador followed our man into a meeting with Moore.'

Levy tilted back slightly in his chair, reflecting on a thought that had just occurred to him. 'Moore could be our channel through to Moscow?' he said.

'Of course.'

'Why don't we attempt a little benefit?'

'What do you mean?'

'Why don't we get our ambassador to seek another meeting with the Secretary of State ... the excuse can be created easily enough. Clarification for the aid programme, for instance. And then make it clear that any agreement we might consider would be greatly increased if there were a publicly committed announcement from Moscow of how many Jews they would allow to emigrate in the next year or two.'

Weismann brought his hands down together on the table, a gesture of enthusiasm. 'That's a brilliant idea!' he said.

'It must be a public declaration,' insisted the Mossad chief, pleased with the praise. 'Then it could be monitored, to ensure they were keeping their word.'

'Of course,' accepted Weismann. He paused, then said, 'What were the casualties among the people we sent into Africa?'

'Surprisingly light,' said Levy. 'The Americans and Russians turned on them. But we came upon them in a minefield, so only a mortar emplacement caused any real problem. No one was killed; a lieutenant lost a leg and one man was blinded.'

'Did they all get out?'

'We fitted long-range tanks to the Sikorsky helicopters. They went in an hour behind the Hercules transporter, so we were able to pick them up the moment the attack failed.'

'We were lucky, not to lose any people,' reflected Weismann. 'Very lucky.'

'What about the Americans?'

'I haven't had any contact since it happened.'

'I need to send a delegation,' said Weismann. 'The Deputy Premier will head it; I'd like you to go as well.'

'If you think it necessary,' agreed Levy.

'It is,' said Weismann. 'Everything must go just right.'

'I know that,' said Levy. 'And I would like to know the quality of information being relayed from the satellite. They might have learned something from the man they've still got inside.'

'I've arranged a cabinet meeting before the Knesset session,' disclosed Weismann. 'I'm putting that as the first item on the agenda. Do you think Peterson will tell you?'

Levy shrugged, doubtfully. 'He won't want to,' he said. 'But they're anxious to keep us from any open conflict: it gives me a lever.'

'If the information is extensive, he might feel it would give us a reason to *start* a conflict,' pointed out Weismann.

'Yes,' agreed Levy. 'It'll be a tricky one. How do you see the Knesset debate going?'

'I'm giving an all-party briefing, in private, before the open session,' said Weismann. 'That won't stop the Likud from demanding war, of course. And there'll be a lot of support.'

'It'll be difficult to control,' said Levy sympathetically.

Weismann leaned across the table to emphasize what he was about to say. 'Everything is at a very critical state, David. One wrong, ill-considered move and we could be facing one of the biggest crises since 1948.'

'I know,' said the Mossad chief solemnly.

'Over the next three or four days we must be more careful than we've ever been in our lives.'

'I know that, too.'

Weismann smiled, an unexpected expression. 'I don't envy you, confronting Peterson.'

'It won't be easy,' agreed Levy. 'But then nothing has been easy, from the start.'

Two-way communication meant that the transmission to Langley took much longer, and Bohler signed off drained and damp with perspiration from the tension of half-listening to any sounds from the corridor outside. He supposed the Director's demand that he attempt to do something to the control system to make the satellite malfunction was predictable—particularly after the information that the quality of the intelligence being relayed back was so high. But the order still unsettled him, adding to the nervousness of open radio links. He showered and changed and remained in his quarters, trying to calm himself. It was almost an hour after his conversation with Langley before he felt sufficiently recovered to move towards the control chamber. Gerda had possessed far more courage than he did, Bohler decided. The despair, such a frequent feeling during the last four or five days, came to him as soon as he entered. At every control section sat an operator, assigned solely to that particular function. Directly behind them were liaison technicians, assessing the operation and performance of the satellite as a whole. And there were more Libyans than there had been immediately after the launch, at least five assembled at various spots around the room; Bohler glanced along the corridor to the smaller room which had once held the satellite and thought he detected more soldiers there as well.

Bohler strolled in, answering nods of greeting. It would have been intrusive of him to attempt to get anywhere near the operating mechanism of the satellite; to attempt some sort of sabotage would be utterly impossible. He felt a curious relief at the realization and again thought how much braver Gerda had been.

He remained in the control room long enough to avoid the visit appearing unusual, then took the lift back up to the ground level. There was an internal telephone system, but Hannah Bloor did not respond when he called her quarters. He found her beside the pool.

She squinted up at his approach and then, once she had identified him, smiled. 'Wondered if you'd come out today,' she said.

'Thought I might find you in the control room.'

'I'm doing the early evening shift.'

'Maintaining a twenty-four hour monitor?' said the American.

She frowned up, at the question rather than the sun. 'Of course,' she said.

'Lot of Libyans around,' said Bohler.

'Everything has gone so well I suppose we should expect it,' said Hannah. 'I gather there might even be some sort of official government visit in the next few days. And there have been some enquiries from elsewhere.'

'Oh?' said Bohler, guessing the woman would not need too much prompting.

'From somewhere in Asia, according to Dr Muller.'

'To purchase time in this one. Or have another?'

'Another,' said Hannah. 'I believe Libya intends increasing the time they've purchased on this rocket for a further six months.'

More intelligence to worry Peterson, Bohler knew. There would be increased demands that he attempt something with the controls.

'Put some oil on my back,' demanded the woman suddenly.

Bohler stooped beside her, applying the protection. Her skin was soft but very firm.

'Undo the strap,' she said, 'otherwise there will be a line.'

'That's nice,' she said drowsily.

He massaged from her shoulders down to the small of her back, aware of what was happening and enjoying it.

Unexpectedly she moved on to her side, careless that it showed the ripeness of her breasts. 'I finish at about nine tonight. Why don't we eat together, late?'

'I'd like that,' he said.

'Yes,' she said, holding his eyes. 'I think I would too.'

She turned back on to her stomach. 'Don't stop rubbing,' she commanded.

CHAPTER 40

Dr Harrap had stressed the importance of the outing for Lucille and Peterson had determined there would be no disappointment. And then Bohler had made the unexpected transmission, very early their time, and the Director had judged it sufficiently important for him to detour to Langley before going to the clinic.

'Asia,' said Walter Jones incredulously, looking up from the transcript of Bohler's message. 'Can you imagine the President's response to that! It'll be Vietnam, all over again.'

'I wonder which country it is,' said Peterson.

'I can guess any one of three or four who might want a satellite,' said Jones. 'But I wouldn't have thought any of them had the money.'

'What if it isn't their money?'

'What do you mean?'

'What if they're fronting for China?' demanded the Director.

Jones physically shuddered. 'You're frightening the ass off me,' he said seriously.

'And it's going to frighten the ass off Fowler: he started his re-election moves a month ago.'

The Deputy Director went back to Bohler's intelligence. 'And he's not going to be happy at Bohler's insistence there's nothing he can do to screw the satellite.'

'It's coming very close to getting out of hand, isn't it?' said the Director, remembering the President's behaviour at their last meeting.

'It's not good,' agreed Jones.

Peterson stood up from his desk, an abrupt movement. 'I want a hold on this,' he ordered, gesturing to the latest intelligence report. 'I don't want it to go to the White House for three hours, and when it does, attach the request for an immediate meeting with the President. You can get me in the car.'

Jones sat regarding him doubtfully. 'What happens if someone demands all the details ... the time of the transmission, for instance?'

'We were seeking clarification before making any sort of scare announcement,' answered Peterson easily. He returned Jones' look. 'Fuck them all,' he said, in sudden vehemence. 'I've made a promise to Lucille and I've made a promise to Beth. And for once I'm going to keep them. Three hours isn't going to make any difference. They'll still be running around like chickens with their heads cut off, not knowing what to do.'

'You don't sound very impressed,' said Jones.

'I'm not.'

'And they're not very impressed with us,' reflected the deputy.

'So the disappointment is mutual.'

'I hope they're getting on OK ... Lucille and Beth, I mean,' said Jones.

'Yes,' said Peterson sincerely. 'So do I.'

He was two hours late at the clinic. Lucille was waiting on the very edge of a chair in the communal room, hands gripped against her legs, her handbag beside her. Her morning dress seemed freshly pressed and she wore a hat which suited her. She was lightly and very carefully made up. The furtiveness was still there.

'Something came up,' she anticipated, not looking directly at him.

'I'm sorry. I called Dr Harrap.'

'He told me.'

'Shall we go?'

He helped her from the chair and, as they started to walk from the ward, he felt her hand against his arm, holding him tightly. He pressed it against his side in reassurance. There was no conversation until they got into the car and then Lucille said, 'I'm very frightened, James.'

'What of?'

'Myself. How I'll behave, when I see her.'

He turned towards her to impress the importance of what he was saying. 'You mustn't collapse, Lucille. Beth is more ill than you, far more ill. And she'll go backwards if she realizes she can't rely upon you.'

'I'm not strong enough,' protested the woman weakly. 'Not well ... not better ...'

Peterson reached out, squeezing her hand. 'You've got to be,' he said. 'Dr Harrap says you can do it and I think you can do it. You've got to think of Beth now, that's all.'

She looked at him, damp-eyed and accusingly. 'Who are you going to think of?'

'Both of you,' he said. 'I've made you the promise and I don't intend to break it.'

The car pulled up at the clinic entrance and the driver opened the door on Lucille's side. She remained sitting where she was, staring straight ahead.

'We're here, Lucille.'

'I can't.'

'Yes you can.'

'No.'

'Get out of the car!'

'Please, James.'

'Beth is waiting ... she's waiting for you.'

The woman stayed rigid for only a few seconds, but it seemed much longer. Then, falteringly, she left the vehicle, turning immediately to Peterson and reaching out for his arm. He waited while she prepared herself, and then they slowly walked towards the building. She stayed withdrawn and aloof from the admission procedure, almost as if she were unaware of its happening, but when they started out towards Beth's room he felt her pinching at his arm in her nervousness. He halted outside the door.

'Ready?'

She nodded, her lips hard together, her gaze fixed straight ahead again.

Beth was in the chair in which she had been sitting when Peterson had made his first visit, but she'd changed from the towelling robe. She'd given her dress size to Paul unthinkingly, and because of her thinness it draped around her, accentuating the emaciation. Peterson noticed immediately that his son had had the forethought to buy something with long sleeves, so that the needle scars were covered. Beth's hair was plaited, as it had been before. She wore no make-up.

Lucille stopped, resisting Peterson's pressure to go further into the room, so that they bunched together awkwardly in the doorway. Beth was trying hard to keep any emotion from her face, but Peterson was aware of the flicker of disappointment.

'I'm not contagious, Mummy.'

Peterson felt a sudden swamping of anger and was about to thrust past the obstructing figure of his wife when she moved hesitantly into the room. She stopped, as Peterson had done that first day, a few feet away, unsure what to do. Inevitably, the greetings were banal.

'Hello Beth.'

'Hello Mother.' The girl looked beyond Lucille, smiling to her father. Peterson thought that her teeth seemed bad and was reminded of the photograph of his daughter at Paul's graduation. She'd worn a brace then, he recalled again. Two years ago. She looked much older now — almost as old as Lucille. Careworn and used, too, like someone who had known only a life of drudgery.

Lucille went towards the girl in a sudden rush, the sobbing bursting from her, and Beth reached out to receive her and began to cry as well. The two women clung together, weeping unashamedly and Peterson shifted self-consciously, feeling the intruder. When they parted after several minutes, Beth was red-eyed and Lucille's make-up was streaked and smeared. Each looked into the other's face and laughed, embarrassed.

'You look awful,' Beth said to her mother.

'So do you,' said Lucille and they laughed again, less nervously this time.

'I'm sorry you've been ill,' said the girl.

'I'm sorry, too. About you I mean.' Lucille became aware of the yellowness of hepatitis about Beth's skin for the first time and touched her face curiously.

'I can get better,' said Beth, hopefully. 'They say I can get better.'

'I know, my darling.'

'It'll take a long time, though.'

Peterson remained on one side, detecting the switchback of his daughter's moods, one moment confidence, the next doubt.

'There's all the time in the world,' assured Lucille.

'I'm sorry,' said Beth, contrite now. 'It was very selfish of me to do what I did. Selfish and stupid and I wish to God I'd been stronger ...'

She started crying again and Lucille reached out for her, pulling Beth's face against her shoulder. 'Stop it, darling. Stop it! It's all over now, all over. Just get better — that's all that's important. Getting better.'

Beth drew away, sniffing. 'I want that,' she said. 'I want that very much.'

'We'll have to help each other,' said Lucille. 'It isn't going to be easy for me, either.' Lucille took her daughter's face between her hands and kissed her, tenderly. 'We'll do it together,' she said. 'You and me. Together.'

'I love you so much,' said Beth.

'And I love you.'

'I've done some dreadful things, Mummy.'

Lucille put her fingers to her daughter's lips. 'I said it's all over. Talk about it if you want to, but not because you feel you have to. And not now. Later.'

The girl put her head against the older woman, so that her words were muffled. 'I didn't think you wanted me back,' she mumbled. 'When Daddy didn't come to Arizona I thought you didn't want me any more.'

Lucille looked at her husband over their daughter's head and Peterson was shocked at the look of dislike.

'He was coming,' said Lucille. 'You left too quickly.'

Why had she spared him? Peterson wondered. Then he realized it was not him she'd spared, but Beth.

'I decided on one last try,' continued the girl. 'The letter to Paul ... if he hadn't come, I was going to kill myself.'

Beth spoke so matter-of-factly that initially Peterson didn't fully comprehend what she had said. When he did, he shivered. Lucille was holding the girl to her, eyes clamped shut against any breakdown.

'Shush, my darling,' said Lucille. 'Don't say such things.'

'I mean it,' insisted the girl calmly. 'I'd worked it out ... decided the way. Didn't want to live, not any more.'

'You're back with us now,' said her mother. 'You're back with us and you're safe.'

Beth pulled back, so that she could look up into her mother's face. 'Look after me, Mummy. Please keep me safe.'

'You know I will.'

'And Daddy?' said Beth, looking over her mother's shoulder.

Peterson moved closer to them, edging on to the bed and reaching out to take her outstretched fingers. 'You know I will, darling,' he said.

'You don't hate me?'

He was very near tears again, Peterson realized. 'Why should I hate you?'

Beth made an uncertain movement. 'For everything,' she said.

'We don't hate you,' said Peterson urgently. 'We love you.'

The three of them clung together like participants in some disjointed seance, and Peterson was seized by an overwhelming impression of failure. There was so little in which he had succeeded.

They let each other loose after a while and almost immediately the talk began to embarrass them, each bursting out with sudden, desperate topics of conversation which would not touch upon either Lucille or Beth's reason for hospitalization and stumbling almost immediately to a halt because the attempts were so obvious. Peterson decided that the encounter had drained both his wife and daughter and moved gently to end it. They parted at last, Lucille promising to come on the next release day from her clinic and Peterson undertaking to visit the following day with Paul.

Lucille clung to him as desperately as before as they left the hospital and entered the waiting car.

'She looks as if she's dying,' said Lucille.

'It's the drugs. And the illness,' said Peterson. 'I've spoken to the doctors. It's curable.'

Beside him his wife twitched convulsively and Peterson looked at her curiously. 'It was awful,' she said.

'Yes.'

She returned his look. 'And it's our fault.'

'Yes,' he said again.

'It was very difficult for me,' confessed Lucille.

'Difficult?'

'I didn't ...' she stopped, bringing her hands to her mouth and biting at her fingers. 'Christ, Jamie, what sort of mother am I? I didn't want to touch her; she disgusted me. I didn't want to comfort my own, sick daughter!'

Peterson tried to keep any reaction from his face, but was unsure whether he had succeeded. 'Shock,' he said. 'It was bound to be a shock.'

She shook her head, reluctantly. 'I'm not sure,' she admitted. 'I don't think so.'

She looked steadfastly away from him out of the window, and Peterson guessed she was crying, although there was no movement in her body. The vehicle began picking up the route back to her clinic and after a while she said, 'I don't have to be back until nine tonight.'

'What?'

'I've got a complete day. Thought we could have lunch — dinner maybe.' She'd turned away from the window and was looking at him hopefully.

'I ...' he started, then broke off. He opened his mouth to speak again but the car telephone purred, saving him. The President had agreed to a meeting immediately after receiving Bohler's report.

'The White House,' he said, to Lucille. 'The President.'

'Yes,' she accepted.

'Why don't we try Paul?' Peterson made an effort to sound enthusiastic.

'He's got a job to do,' she dismissed immediately. 'He's taken enough time off, as it is.'

'I'll take a whole day on your next release,' he said.

'Sure.'

'I promise.'

She smiled, sadly. 'It's a new expression, to go with "I'm very busy".'

He frowned, not understanding the attempt at sarcasm.

' "I promise",' she explained.

'I mean it.'

'I'm sure you do, Jamie. At the time, I'm sure you mean everything you say.'

They completed the last mile in silence. He helped her solicitously from the car, and she smiled with almost exaggerated gratitude. He walked her back into the clinic and kissed her on the cheek at the entrance to her room.

'I'll see you tomorrow,' he said.

'Yes.'

'Everything is going to be all right, Lucille.'

'So you keep telling me.'

'You must believe me.'

'Yes,' she agreed. 'I must try to believe you.'

On his way to the White House Peterson contacted Jones at Langley to update himself on any new developments, and learned that an Israeli delegation, including David Levy, had arrived at Dulles airport before noon. There had already been an approach from the Israeli embassy on Levy's behalf for a meeting, and Jones had agreed on three o'clock that afternoon. There had been another approach through Vienna: Petrov wanted further contact.

Peterson arrived at the Oval Office at the same time as the Secretary of State and they entered the room together. Fowler was not sitting at his desk but striding up and down behind it beneath the draped American flag. He stopped pacing at Peterson's entrance, but didn't sit down.

'Anything new?' he demanded.

'You know about the Israeli arrival?'

The President nodded, almost irritably.

'David Levy is with them. I'm meeting him this afternoon. And there's been another approach from Petrov,' said Peterson.

'Could the Russians be the financial backers for this Asian rocket?' asked Moore, taking his usual chair.

'They could be,' accepted Peterson.

'What are you doing?'

'All stations alert throughout Asia,' said Peterson. 'I'm hoping Bohler will learn more.'

'Why the hell can't he bring down the satellite?' demanded Flood.

'Because the control room is crawling with guards and technicians twenty-four hours of every day,' snapped back Peterson. 'The man is working near miracles as it is.'

'I'm sure it wasn't intended as criticism,' placated the President immediately. 'I don't think it's going to help if we start losing our tempers.'

The rebuke was intended for the foreign affairs adviser, not him, Peterson realized.

'I think that what's happened in the Middle East and what might be happening in Asia justifies my going to Bonn,' said Moore positively. 'I don't think the German government can evade responsibility any longer.'

'I agree,' said Fowler at once. 'Lean on the bastards. If they'd taken the proper attitude when we first raised it with them, we wouldn't be facing this now.'

'What about Chad?' said Flood. 'Can't we get more heavily involved there with foreign aid, create a dependence and then get control?'

'In time,' agreed Moore. 'And I certainly think it's worth the approach. But that isn't going to help us with the immediate problem.'

The President sat down at last, leaning forward over his desk towards Peterson. 'I'm seeing the Israeli people this afternoon,' he disclosed. 'I'm going to have their ass for what they did in Africa.'

'It's interesting that they've bothered to come,' said Moore, the better diplomat. 'Why would they consider allowing the Deputy Premier to leave the country at the moment of crisis like this?'

'Because they know that there might not have been a crisis at all if they hadn't interfered,' said Flood.

'I don't think it's as simple as that,' said Moore. 'They're not people given to apologies.'

'Perhaps they haven't come to apologize,' said the President. 'Perhaps they've come in an effort to get that additional aid — *that's* worth the journey, crisis or no crisis. And if there's war, they'll need the tanks.'

'Perhaps,' said Moore uncertainly.

'Bohler talks about a Libyan government visit,' remembered Flood, gesturing with the CIA report that he held in his lap. 'We going to do anything about that?'

The President moved uncomfortably and Peterson realized he was nervous at the recording devices in the room registering any interception or assassination attempt.

'Perhaps we could discuss that if I learned some more details,' he said quickly. 'At the moment, it's only a suggestion.'

'According to the Soviet ambassador, Russia is going to raise the matter at the United Nations,' said Moore.

'What did you promise?' asked the President.

'Our support,' said Moore. 'We've also got the undertaking from Great Britain and France. And Israel has tabled a motion.'

'It'll give the impression of action,' said Fowler, cynically. He stood and began pacing behind the desk again. 'I'm not going to allow any goddamned rocket in Asia,' he said positively. 'Whatever it costs, I'm going to take that installation out of Africa. I'm scheduling a meeting tonight of the National Security Council and I'm having every chief of staff there. I'm going to initiate contingency plans and, if there's confirmation from Bohler, then I'm going to authorize them.'

'We'll need congressional approval,' reminded Moore hesitantly.

The President moved to speak, then bit back the words. 'I'm going to get contingency plans prepared,' he repeated defiantly. 'By the time they're asked for approval, we could have a full-scale conflict in the Middle East.'

The President thrust out his hand towards the Secretary of State. 'I want you on a plane to Bonn by tonight,' he ordered. He moved his hand, stopping at Peterson. 'I want you monitoring everything from Africa, maintaining contact with Petrov and screwing Levy for everything you can get.' The hand moved on, to Flood. 'I want position papers and updates on every eventuality, both in the Middle East and Asia, ready for me an hour before the National Security Council meeting ....' He paused, for any reaction. None of the other men in the room spoke.

'... and I think I'm going to speak to Moscow, direct.' He looked back to Moore. 'Call in the Soviet ambassador to give them warning.'

The Secretary of State nodded.

Fowler went back to Flood, apparently making a decision. 'And on your position papers, for discussion with the joint chiefs of staff, I want debating notes on the proton beam capability. If there's no other solution, then we'll take the satellite out that way.'

Moore lingered as they moved out of the room, and Peterson decided that the man wanted some conversation in the corridor. He caught up, falling into step with the Secretary of State. Henry Flood was striding on ahead, out of hearing.

'I gather there was recently an improper approach made to your Agency,' said the lawyer, nodding along the corridor to the foreign affairs adviser. 'Something involving my personal affairs.'

'I understand there was,' said Peterson cautiously.

'I want to thank your people, for the correct and proper way they reacted.'

'There was no other way I would have had them respond,' assured the Director.

Again Moore gestured to the hurrying figure ahead of them. 'Were you aware he had political ambitions?'

'I had heard suggestions,' said Peterson.

'He's going to find it very difficult,' said the Secretary of State. 'Very difficult indeed.'

'Does he know yet?'

'Not yet,' said Moore. 'He hasn't sought adoption anywhere yet. It won't be long, though.'

Otto Bock had already been near to breaking point, before Gerda Lintz's death. But when that had happened, there had come the demands that he remain in the computer room to intercept the messages from Africa. He was to adjust the records and respond according to the instructions which Klaus' friends had urgently rehearsed with him, insisting upon the proper answers without any mistakes and frequently slapping his face when he stumbled or forgot. And Klaus laughed at him now. Worse still, he sneered and ridiculed, letting him know that the whole thing had been a deceit, that there had never been any love or even affection.

Bock had prepared it very carefully, because his insurance policies were nullified if suicide could be proved, and he wanted Gretal and the children to be cared for, because he loved them. Really loved them — not like it was with sex. Sex was disgusting now: filthy and repulsive and something he could never do again. Sex had destroyed him. God, how he wished he could have emasculated himself, or had a simple brain operation, or a glandular adjustment. But it was hopeless to wish. Or to grieve. He had to kill himself and hope that his death created as much anguish and harm as others had caused him. But in a way that protected Gretal and the children.

It had taken him several evenings to find the roadworks, on a side road leading down to one of the Rhine's most attractive beauty spots, and then slightly longer to establish the departure time of the workmen and the traffic flow. There had to be no chance of rescue.

Bock felt an unexpected calm, driving out to die. He had expected to be frightened: sad at least, needing to stop perhaps, to cry or to reinforce his courage. But it didn't happen. There was no light-headedness, no sensation of drugged euphoria. He was aware of the road along which he was driving and the scenery through which he was travelling. He obeyed all the traffic signs and did not exceed the speed limit and once, seeing a flower stall along the highway, actually started to brake, to buy a bouquet for Gretal, before he realized that he wasn't going home to Gretal any more. Even that didn't cause any collapse. It just increased the determination to succeed.

He would so have liked to leave a note. Not a note: a long explanatory letter, setting out in a limited way what he knew was happening and what evil people were attempting to achieve. But a letter of intent would prove suicide and destroy the chances of any better life for Gretal and the children. So he had to die without any accusation. He just hoped — dear God in whatever Heaven You occupy, deeply and fervently and sincerely he hoped — that the very fact of his death would wreck whatever it was they were hoping to make work.

The repair area was deserted when he got to it, as he had been confident it would be. It was a warm evening, with swifts and swallows diving and darting into the bunches of insects. Far away, maybe two miles, the Rhine eased its way between the hills and meadows. Nearer the water, he could see river houses and pleasure boats and activity. Gretal would be at home with the boys preparing the meal that she expected him to eat, probably considering the television programmes they would watch. She'd have the ice and the whisky all ready, because she knew he liked whisky, even though it cost a little more, being imported.

He stopped some way from the roadworks, getting out and checking something of which he was already sure. There had been a slight subsidence against the hill edge where the winter rains had caused a gully. Someone mistaking a turn, which is what he intended it to appear, would naturally skid and pull away from the hurdles towards the river's edge. He stood at the lip, gazing down. It had to be a hundred feet, maybe more, to the water. He stood there, staring into the slow, oily progress of the river, wondering when the fear would come. Perhaps with the pain — and there would be pain. It had to be painful, trapped inside a tumbling car, bouncing and rolling down the hillside. But it would not come now. His only emotion was one of relief, the knowledge that soon, within minutes even, he was going to escape. To escape was worth any pain.

He went slowly back along the road, deciding when to enforce the brakes to make the skid marks, so that the authorities would judge it an accident. He could do it, Otto knew. Do it easily.

Inside the car again he steadied himself, breathing deeply. Forty yards away the barriers were arraigned before him and the warning lights automatically blipped on and off.

He reached for the ignition key and then screamed in fright as a hand came across in front of him, taking the key from the lock.

'Can't kill yourself, Otto,' said a voice, and the German looked up at the big man who'd been waiting for him that night in Klaus' apartment.

'No,' said Bock, whining. 'Please no.'

'We'll decide when you can die, Otto,' said the man, jingling the keys from one hand to another. 'Trust me. When we're through, you can kill yourself any time you want.'

Bock fell forward against the steering wheel, his head cushioned by his hands.

'And don't try it again, Otto,' warned the Russian. 'You could kill yourself, without our being able to stop it. We know that. But listen to me very carefully. If you commit suicide before we've finished with you, we'll kill Gretal and the boys. And painfully, too. So stay alive, Otto. Stay alive and keep your family safe.'

CHAPTER 41

David Levy walked aggressively into Peterson's office, defying any criticism from the CIA Director. Peterson did not rise to greet him, nor relax his face into any welcoming expression. The Israeli hesitated at the work-bench which Walter Jones had established, looking first at the indexed arrangements of documents and then at the marked map showing the abortive penetration attempt. The portly, diminutive man gave an almost imperceptible sigh and continued on towards the Director. He extended his hand and Peterson pointedly regarded it before responding perfunctorily to the gesture.

'Isn't it hypocritical to behave as friends?' said Peterson.

'I'll concede an error of judgement.'

'Because of which we're facing a war situation.'

'That's an exaggeration,' said Levy. 'Your people might have got through the wire, but there was still three miles to cover beyond that. They could never have remained undetected.'

'Then why did *you* try?' rejected Peterson at once. 'It was a viable operation, and you know it. Just as you know that your crass interference ruined it.'

'I regret what happened,' said Levy.

'If there's any sort of conflict, a proportion of the blame will lie with you.'

'That's another exaggeration,' refused Levy calmly. 'No one's started shooting yet.'

'How long will it be?' said Peterson.

'My parliament are still talking.'

'Talking isn't going to bring that satellite out of the sky.'

'What about the man you've still got inside?'

'He's providing brilliant intelligence,' said Peterson. 'But he can't get anywhere near the controls.'

'I gather the Secretary of State has flown to Bonn.'

'Yes,' said Peterson. The decision to make the visit public had been taken to increase the pressure upon the German government.

'Do you think they will respond?'

Peterson shrugged. 'They've been unwilling to do anything so far.'

'We haven't been so near a crisis before.'

'They might move against any further development. That won't help the present situation.'

'No,' agreed Levy. 'It won't help the present situation.'

'Why have you come?' said Peterson, careless of the rudeness.

'I felt there was some fence building to do,' said Levy. He hesitated. 'And at this moment, more than any other, I need access to everything you're getting out of Africa,' he added honestly.

'Christ you're arrogant!' exclaimed Peterson.

'It's not arrogance: it's realism,' contradicted Levy. 'I've admitted a mistake and I've apologized for it. I want to repair whatever damage has been caused between us.'

'Just like that!' said Peterson, snapping his fingers contemptuously.

'Yes,' said Levy, refusing to respond. 'Just like that.'

Peterson shifted, exasperated at the other man's attitude. He was behaving badly, Peterson knew. Childishly almost. In Levy's position, he would have mounted a duplicate operation exactly as Levy had done. The only difference would have been that he would have hoped for more success.

'What are the chances of your country deciding to trust international pressure rather than go to war?' asked Peterson.

Levy moved his face into a doubtful expression. 'Very slight, I would guess.'

'Is it a guess?' insisted Peterson.

The Mossad chief smiled. 'I'm not admitted to the cabinet discussions,' he said gently. 'You know about our troop mobilization ....' He stopped, then added bitterly. 'Everyone knows about our troop mobilization!'

'You don't need admission to cabinet meetings,' insisted Peterson. 'You know which way the arguments are going.'

Levy nodded slowly. 'I see,' he said. 'It's a trade.'

'Any reason why it shouldn't be?'

'I suppose not,' conceded the Israeli. 'You've an advantage over me, though. You know the value of my information. I don't know what you're getting out of Africa.'

'You wouldn't have flown six thousand miles if you hadn't thought it worthwhile,' argued Peterson. It pleased him to be in a position of control and know he could force concessions from the other man.

'The Likud party are pressing to go to war,' said Levy.

'That's not intelligence,' said Peterson, irritably. 'That's a matter of common assessment; the Likud are always hawkish.'

'They've got a lot of support from the Labour Party.'

'What about Weismann? And the rest of the cabinet?'

Levy made a to-and-fro balancing motion with his hand. 'Equally divided,' he said.

Peterson sighed, wondering if the other man were being honest with him. 'What would tilt the balance?'

'It's difficult to say.'

'No it's not,' refuted Peterson. 'Not for you it isn't.'

Levy hesitated, a man making a decision. 'We want to be sure of our friends,' he said. 'America — and therefore the West — is being asked to make a positive choice, more positive than ever before. It's the oil-producing states, with Gadaffi as the spokesman for once. Or it's Israel. Which way is *your* balance going to tilt?'

'Israel has never wanted for friendship from America,' insisted Peterson.

'Since Iran, the West is starved of oil,' reminded Levy. 'It would become a weapon again in any war. We'd understand the practical reasoning behind any US shift of stance. We want to know it won't happen.'

The Mossad chief might want to know the intelligence from Africa, Peterson conceded. But that was not the primary reason for his having come to Washington. Peterson realized the man had made the journey to have precisely this sort of conversation and to use him as a conduit to the President. And the Israeli Deputy Premier was here to seek and give reassurances officially, once the American administration had digested the information. The CIA Director was unoffended at the manipulation: again, it was the sort of thing he would have done in Levy's position.

Peterson rose from his desk and went to the bench containing all the files. Walter Jones' system was so efficient that it took only seconds to locate the reports that had come from Bohler since the satellite had been launched. He handed them to Levy and then returned to his seat silently, intent upon the Israeli as he read them. It didn't take very long. When he looked up from the folders, there was a gravity about Levy: more, he seemed pressed down in his chair, as if suddenly feeling the pressure of some heavy weight.

'I didn't anticipate it would be as bad as this,' he said. 'The quality and accuracy of the information they're getting about us is frightening.'

'Yes,' admitted Peterson. 'It is.'

'Unless there is some international action soon ... and effective action, there would be no way the moderates in my country could argue against military action.'

'Once before I asked you to hold back from a course of action. You ignored the request, with disastrous results. Now I'm asking you again: delay until there's been a chance for proper consultation and negotiations.'

'That's not a decision for me to make,' pointed out Levy.

'You've got influence,' persisted Peterson. 'People listen to you; they accept your judgement. You know I'll pass on this conversation — that's the whole point of our having it. I expect you to repeat it, too.'

'I'm part of a delegation,' said Levy. 'Quite obviously there will be discussion between us.'

'When can we expect your government to announce its decision?' pressed Peterson.

'Tomorrow night,' said Levy immediately.

'That doesn't give us a lot of time,' protested Peterson.

'Time is something we haven't had for several weeks now,' reminded Levy.

An hour after Levy had left his office, the reply to Peterson's cable to N'Djamena arrived, and he felt the uncertainty beginning to lift.

M.—O

Petrov's interview followed a full session of the thirteen-man Politburo, and as he entered the committee room, the KGB chief recognized that for the moment the three men were still more occupied with the meeting they had just had than that which they were about to begin. Dorensky even appeared surprised to see him when he looked up. The party chairman seemed more alert than usual but his features were flushed, as if he were excited or under some sort of medication. As his attention shifted, so did that of the other two men and once again Petrov got the impression of being on trial. Unexpectedly, it was Dorensky who began the attack.

'We are having to make concessions,' he announced. 'In the hope of getting some Israeli agreement, we are having to make a public commitment of Jewish emigration.'

'Without any guarantees,' took up Borrosuba. 'We're being led by the nose, like some circus act.'

'You were allowed twenty-four hours,' completed Litvinov. 'Twenty-four hours to find a guarantee to resolve this affair.'

'Yes,' agreed Petrov.

'Well?' demanded Litvinov.

It was a conscious decision for Petrov to say what he did. After his conversation with Peterson the previous day, the KGB chief had studied every aspect and detail of what had happened in Africa, seeking an escape. And failed. And with the acceptance of failure had come an awareness of which he had never before been conscious. He was frightened of losing his position: a physical, sick-making fear like the fear he had known all those years ago in Stalingrad, on the occasions when he had thought the Nazi bombardment of the city might succeed, and that if he didn't get killed in the final assault he would be consigned to spend the rest of his existence in a slave camp.

'The Americans are confident that their man can cause some malfunction,' he lied.

It was a juvenile thing to do — like a bankrupt gambler putting the deeds to his house upon the last spin of the wheel. Litvinov's retribution would be terrible, he guessed. But at that moment any suffering would have been worthwhile to achieve the look of startled despair that settled upon Litvinov's face at the thought of being outmanoeuvred when he had been so close to causing Petrov's destruction.

At the moment when Petrov made his hopeless promise, six thousand five hundred miles away in Washington, Peterson was ending his briefing with the President in which he had outlined everything that Levy had said during their meeting. With the Secretary of State on his mission to Bonn, Flood was the only other person in the room.

'Will a commitment of friendship be enough?' wondered the President, aloud.

'And can we make it, so openly?' said Flood, returning the rhetoric. 'The oil states are unified this time. It won't be as easy as the last war. We had Iran then.'

'I'll lose the Jewish vote if I appear to prevaricate,' said Fowler. 'Whichever way I go, I'm trapped.'

'Levy said the Israeli cabinet were making their announcement tomorrow,' remembered Peterson.

'The aid,' said Fowler suddenly. 'I can positively commit us on the aid and the additional M-60 tanks without risking a break with any of the Arab states. It's already public that we've been considering that. It wouldn't indicate any sort of escalation.'

'Israel wants an oil assurance as well,' recalled Flood. 'How can we guarantee their oil when we can't guarantee our own?'

'We can blur around that,' insisted Fowler hurriedly. 'It'll look like some positive action, and that's what is important now. The impression of positive action.'

'How did Dorensky sound, when you spoke to him?' Flood asked the President.

Fowler didn't reply immediately. Then he said, 'Like a man without one good idea in his head. And in Moscow I must have sounded exactly the same to him!'

CHAPTER 42

Muammar Gadaffi made an airport speech about Arab solidarity before flying with the troops being airlifted into Iraq, and it was this that dominated television news early on the day of the Knesset debate. An hour before it was due to commence, Saudi Arabia issued a public condemnation of Egypt for failing to abrogate its treaty arrangements with Israel, and there were more television pictures of anti-Egyptian street demonstrations in Baghdad, Damascus and Jeddah. Shortly after the announcement that the United Nations in New York would convene for an emergency debate, there was isolated shelling from the Syrian side of the Golan Heights, in which five people from a border kibbutz were killed. In response, Israeli jets flew close to the border but there was no penetration into Syrian air space. A Palestinian commando group tried to take advantage of the tension by infiltrating from the Lebanon, near Hanita, but were detected by an Israeli patrol; four Palestinians were killed in the fighting and another was captured. He immediately confessed to being part of a guerilla emplacement near the Lebanese port of Tyre, but there was a cabinet decision not to follow the usual practice of straffing the area with air attacks, for fear of the other Arab countries using it as an excuse to claim that Israel was the aggressor who had begun the war.

Journalists from all over the world descended upon Israel. The film of Gadaffi leaving Tripoli was matched by extended coverage of hysterical street demonstrations in Tel Aviv and Jerusalem, demanding that the cabinet declare war. From Washington and Moscow, President Fowler and Praesidium Chairman Dorensky both issued appeals for restraint.

In America, Britain, France and Germany, television coverage of the Knesset debate was carried live, with simultaneous voice-over-translation from Hebrew. As Weismann had predicted in his conversation with Levy, the Likud party were unanimous in their demands for war, and there was unexpectedly strong support from the Labour Party. When Weismann took the microphone and it became clear from his speech that he was arguing against the general demands, there was uproar in the Israeli parliament. Several members tried to shout him down and one MP walked across the chamber, threw his order papers in the Premier's face and stormed out in disgust.

The session ended earlier than anyone had anticipated. Almost immediately there was an announcement from the Premier's office that a press statement would be delivered personally by Weismann.

NBC in New York and the BBC in London re-scheduled their programmes to carry it live, as did several radio services. Weismann entered the conference room exactly on time, confronting what was later estimated to be two hundred journalists. The Israeli Premier had the exhausted, almost distracted appearance of a worried man who has remained sleepless, attempting to resolve a problem. Five members of the cabinet accompanied him, spreading themselves out on either side on a slightly raised dais. There was a slight pause as Weismann appeared to have difficulty with his notes and then he coughed, indicating he was ready to begin. There was only a slight lessening of the hubbub and the room did not properly quieten until a government press officer asked for silence.

'Israel is a nation of long tradition but short personal history,' began Weismann. His voice was soft and unsure and the sound recordists grouped in front of the table scurried to improve the voice level.

'... but in that short history, it has too many times been brought to war by the hostility of countries at its every border ....' He cleared his throat, his voice strengthening as he got into his prepared speech. 'On every occasion Israel has confronted that hostility and defeated its aggressors ....'

The Premier paused, looking up towards the banked cameras and the reporters beyond, unseen in the glare of lights. 'For two thousand years, the ambition of the Jews was to have a homeland of their own. For just over sixty years, since the Balfour

Declaration established the Jewish right to that homeland, the ambition has been to exist peacefully within it ....'

The man stopped again, to sip from a glass of water.

'The treaty that exists between this country and Egypt', he took up again, 'was seen as the first step towards the fulfilment of that ambition. Its negotiation was difficult, the obstacles against its signing many and varied. But it was signed. Egypt, for so long an enemy, became a friend. But too many enemies remained ....'

Weismann coughed again and removed his glasses, now sufficiently aware of his words to be able to dispense with written reminders. '... and now we are confronted by enemies again. There is, positioned over Israel, an information satellite communicating intelligence to one of those enemies. Israel has no security any more. Every movement of its army, every movement of its air force, every movement of its navy is immediately available to those who would use that information to achieve the destruction of the rightful heritage of the Jewish people — a homeland of their own ....'

He sipped some water again, theatrically dabbing at his lips with a handkerchief.

'... on every occasion in the past, when confronted with aggression, we have matched it with aggression. And now the demands and the pressures are upon us again, to enter the battlefields and suffer the carnage and the destruction and the horrors of warfare ... a war whose effects would risk extending far beyond the Middle East ....'

The hesitation this time was to stress an obvious point, and there was a shift of expectation throughout the room.

'... in ending the enmity with Egypt, Israel declared itself a country intent upon peace. It remains a country intent upon peace. It remains a country determined to find peace. And to prove that determination, the government has today decided, following the Knesset debate, against placing its armed forces upon full war footing ....'

There was a burst of sound from the room, at the announcement of the very opposite of what had been anticipated.

Weismann had to resume in a louder voice to make himself heard. 'It is in the interests of peace that I shall be flying to New

York immediately I have concluded this statement. There I will appear before the United Nations to ask them to provide a peace-keeping force along our borders to resist this new aggression which is facing us. Israel will not drag the world into another war — so the world must guarantee our safety by removing the spy satellite and guaranteeing against any such action ever happening again ....'

Peterson and Jones had been watching the live transmission on a television set in the Director's office. The deputy responded first, swinging around in his chair and shouting excitedly, 'They're not going to do it! They've held off!'

Peterson showed no excitement. 'When everyone here and in Moscow and everywhere else thought they'd do the opposite,' he said reflectively.

'What's the matter?' demanded Jones, deflated by Peterson's reaction. 'The heat's been taken out of the crisis! We've got a breathing space.'

'Yes,' agreed Peterson, still locked in thought. 'A breathing space.'

The internal telephone rasped upon Peterson's desk and he picked it up, nodding at the message.

'Colonel Bradley's just arrived from the airport,' he said to Jones, as he replaced the receiver. 'He's on his way up.'

'Did you think this might happen?' said Hannah.
'I thought it might. You?' said Bohler.
'I hoped it would.'
'You're very beautiful.'
'And you're very tender. No, not yet!'
'What then?'
'Your tongue. I want your tongue.'
'Like this?'
'Yes. Just like that.'
'I'll want it too.'
'I promise. That's very nice.'
'I'm glad you're satisfied.'

'I didn't say that. I said it was very nice. Now your hand — very slowly. Your hand. Both ways.'

'I'll hurt you.'

'No. Do it.'

'I can't wait much longer.'

'I want you to.'

'You're unbelievable.'

'Better than her?'

'Her?'

'Dr Lintz. You were having an affair with her, weren't you?'

'No.'

'I was sure you were.'

'No.'

'Don't stop. I didn't tell you to stop. Didn't you like her?'

'She was a fine colleague.'

'Sexually, I mean.'

'I never thought about it.'

'I think she did, of you. Harder now: really hard.'

'I was never aware of it.'

'Now you. Now it's your turn.'

They shifted positions on the bed, momentarily face to face. He kissed her in small nibbling kisses, and she bit back at him hungrily.

'Glad it happened?'

'Very.'

'I think I could become very fond of you.'

Bohler opened his mouth to reply, then shut it again. It was absurd to say he loved her, but those were the words that had thrust themselves into his mind. To cover the moment, he kissed her again.

CHAPTER 43

Peterson arrived at the Sans Souci early, determined that everything would be right. He wanted his son to appreciate his gratitude for what he had done in bringing Beth back. He had the reserved table changed for another he favoured more and the wine put into a cooler, and refused a drink while he waited. Paul arrived exactly on time and, as Peterson rose to greet him, he thought how pleased he was to see his son; he felt like he had when the boy had still been at school and came to him for pocket money and called him 'sir'. Peterson was very glad that the hostility that had been a barrier between them for so long no longer existed.

'How did the meeting with Beth go?' asked Paul immediately.

'Not easy. But better than I expected.'

'How was Mother?'

'She's not sure she can do it.'

'Did you discuss it with Dr Harrap?'

'He said it was a predictable response — that I shouldn't worry too much about it.'

'I hope he's right.'

'So do I.'

The conversation stopped while they ordered and, when the waiter had gone, Paul said, 'Was it this Middle East thing that you were involved in?'

Peterson hesitated, an instinctive reaction against discussing anything he did with outsiders and then said, 'Yes.'

'Christ!' said Paul and Peterson smiled. There had been admiration in his son's voice, Peterson recognized.

'A lot of things went wrong,' admitted Peterson. He was surprised at wanting to impress his son, to boast even. Pity there wasn't more to boast about.

'Israel has withdrawn from any war declaration,' said the younger man.

'It's only a temporary respite,' judged Peterson.

Paul cupped his wine glass in front of him between both hands and spoke looking into it. 'I don't know how you do it,' he said. 'I thought about it a lot, particularly after what Mr Jones did when I got arrested. I don't know how you can become involved in it all and dispassionately do the things that will affect the lives of hundreds or maybe thousands of people, and then ....' He took one hand from the glass, spreading it out to indicate the restaurant, '... sit down in an ordinary restaurant like an ordinary person and behave ... well, normally.'

Peterson smiled again. 'The trick is not to think of it like that at all.'

'Doesn't it frighten you?'

'It didn't, once. Now it does.'

'Why do you *want* to do it?'

'I used to think it was important ... that I was contributing something,' said Peterson. The conversation was unsettling him, opening doors that he thought he had locked securely.

'*Used* to,' picked up Paul. 'You mean you don't think so now?'

'Sometimes I'm not sure any more.'

'You must be unusual ... special, I suppose,' groped the younger man. 'It's funny, I never thought of you like that before. Do you feel different from everybody else?' The admiration was more evident than it had been earlier, and Peterson experienced a vague sensation of embarrassment.

'No,' he said. 'No different at all.'

'But the *power*!' stressed Paul. 'Haven't you ever sat down and worked out all the things you could do and make happen, in one maverick hour?'

Peterson laughed aloud. 'Directors of the CIA never go maverick,' he said, consciously self-mocking. 'They remain level-headed at all times, correctly assessing everything and making the right decisions.'

Peterson knew that for too long now he had not been correctly assessing everything that had happened in Africa. But he thought he was beginning to, after the debriefing of Colonel Bradley. Before leaving Langley he had asked Walter Jones to carry out a complete re-analysis of all the files and to scrutinize with particular care all Bohler's reports of the equipment at the complex. He thought he knew what the man would find.

'I guess I should apologize,' said Paul.

'Apologize?'

Paul made an uncertain movement. 'For all the crap ... all the arguing.'

'Forget it' said Peterson. 'We both made mistakes. I'm glad we're not making them any more.'

'So am I,' said Paul sincerely.

Peterson was looking up to get the bill when he saw Walter Jones enter the restaurant behind the waiter. The deputy looked around and then saw Peterson's raised hand.

'I seem to make a habit of interrupting you,' apologized Jones, when he reached the table.

'What is it?' said Peterson. Inexplicably, a hollow nervousness had settled in his stomach.

'You've been summoned for a trip,' said the deputy. 'The President has decided to fly to New York to give a personal welcome to the Israeli Premier. The campaign managers have already come up with the slogan — The Man of Peace meets the Man of Peace.'

'The work of genius,' said Peterson cynically. 'We're going to visit Beth.'

'You're due aboard Air Force One at Andrews in two hours,' said Jones.

'I'll explain,' promised Paul. 'I'll see she understands.'

'She ran away before because I didn't have time,' said Peterson. 'The doctors say the feeling of rejection is the thing we've got to guard against most.'

'Fowler was very insistent,' warned Jones.

'You could be back by tomorrow,' said Paul.

Peterson looked enquiringly at his deputy. Jones shrugged and said, 'I wasn't given any timing; the President is staying overnight at the Waldorf Astoria, but I guess he'll come back some time tomorrow. There's talk of a weekend meeting with Weismann at Camp David.'

'Tell her I'm sorry,' said Peterson to his son. 'Tell her I'll be there tomorrow.'

'Sure.'

They drove to the airport in Peterson's car, the Director hunched in the corner almost sulkily and Jones regarding him curiously.

'I'm not going to let that girl down again,' said Peterson, as they began to clear the city. It sounded like a promise made to himself.

'It isn't going to be easy.'

'I might quit.' Peterson made the statement without thought. Immediately he straightened in the seat, as if surprised at having said it.

'To do what?'

The Director gave a shrug of uncertainty. 'I haven't thought it out,' he admitted.

'Perhaps Fowler would give you an ambassadorship — there's precedent.'

'No,' said Peterson at once. 'I want right out.'

A very special man, Paul had said. He didn't feel special, decided Peterson. He felt old and tired and unsure. And disillusioned. The awareness came suddenly. He had been honest with his son about the difficulty of making dispassionate decisions and he'd spent a long time that morning looking at the pictures of Henry Blakey's wife and child. He had personally written the letter of condolence and issued instructions to the accounting department that, upon his authority, all the pensions and allowances to the dependents of the soldiers killed in the abortive incursion and the agents who had been detected in the initial attempts to penetrate the Chad complex should begin immediately. There would be protests from the Accounts Director, Peterson knew. They didn't like deviations from established routine. He decided he didn't give a damn.

'Did you finish going through the files?' he asked Jones.

'Not yet.'

'It's important.'

'I'll call you in New York.'

Peterson was accustomed to travelling with an entourage of baggage handlers, helpers, secretaries and assistants, but the organization surrounding the movements of the President always bemused him; it was like entering a nest in which the worker ants were trying to work harder than they normally did. Although he was known and recognized as the CIA Director, he had to go through the customary security check, have his photograph taken and wait patiently for his seat allocation. It came with the reservation that had been made in his name at the Waldorf Astoria in New York. It was an open booking, he saw, worriedly, remembering the undertaking which Paul would be giving to his daughter at that moment. He was assigned a guide from the White House travel department and personally conducted to the aircraft; from the activity among the FBI agents, Peterson guessed the President would shortly be arriving.

He found Herbert Flood already waiting in the rear lounge of the aircraft, working in shirtsleeves with two speech-writers. The foreign affairs adviser looked up and nodded at his entry and Peterson nodded back, moving to the other side of the aircraft to the seat that had his name efficiently labelled on the head-rest protector. Immediately he sat down he closed his eyes against the bustle all round, trying to separate himself from it. Had he meant what he said in the car about quitting? He had spoken without any forethought or consideration, almost like a man responding from his sub-conscious under the effects of a truth drug. If he remained Director, then it would be difficult to give the attention to Beth that the doctors and psychiatrists insisted was necessary. And he had *really* meant it when he had told Jones he didn't intend failing her a second time. He opened his eyes, concentrating upon everything around him. Was he really sickened by the sycophancy and the compromises and the deceits and the manoeuvres? Or was the depression an over-response to a failed operation which would reflect personally upon him, because he had been in direct control? There was a brief announcement through the plane's public address system, and Peterson rose at the President's arrival aboard. He didn't know the answer, Peterson accepted, as Fowler strode towards him, beaming his politician's smile. He wondered how long it would take to make the decision.

'Glad you could make it,' said Fowler, as if there had been a choice. 'The entire Israeli delegation has gone up, so I figured you should be along. I plan to appear at the United Nations right after Weismann, supporting the call for international action. Already got an assurance from Moscow that they won't oppose.'

'I gather the Russians have made a positive commitment to Jewish emigration,' said Peterson.

'And during my speech I'll pledge all the additional aid, support and oil supplies they've asked for.'

'But the satellite is still there.'

Fowler looked around the aircraft, then pulled Peterson further away from where the speech-writers were gathered. 'The proton beam idea of yours was a good one,' he said heavily.

'When?'

'The army say it will take a few days: they're confident they can do it.'

'Have you told the Soviets? It might create an over-reaction from them.'

'Not yet,' said Fowler. 'But I intend to, a few hours before we activate.'

The President looked across and Flood managed to catch his attention. 'Speech-writers want me,' said Fowler, moving away.

Peterson resumed his seat and belted himself in for take-off. Fowler didn't bother to sit for the departure, leaning forward in earnest conversation with the foreign affairs adviser, a draft of the United Nations speech between them. Stewards circulated with drinks, but Peterson drank only club soda. The President took bourbon, he saw. The presidential plane was equipped for mid-air television reception and, on a set in the after-lounge, they all watched the New York arrival of Shimeon Weismann. The Israeli Premier seemed less fatigued than when he had appeared before the Jerusalem press conference. He made a brief statement at the airport, repeating his desire for peace and for world support. The only unexpected part of his speech was to welcome the Soviet undertaking guaranteeing Jewish emigration.

'Fine man,' judged Fowler, when the coverage ended. A few days earlier the President had called him a son-of-a-bitch, remembered Peterson.

Before the arrival at Kennedy, Fowler went forward to his private quarters on the plane to rehearse the speech he had agreed upon with Flood and change his clothes.

Shortly before touch-down, Flood crossed over and settled in a vacant seat alongside the CIA Director.

'The Secretary of State isn't having much luck in Germany,' he said.

'The pressure upon Bonn will increase after today's speeches,' predicted Peterson. He supposed Flood saw some personal advantage in Moore's failure in Bonn. He wondered how much longer it would be before the foreign affairs adviser made his bid for some political acceptance and realized he'd been blocked.

'I think we're going to avoid a crisis over this,' said Flood. 'It's becoming manageable.'

'We hope,' said Peterson, unconvinced.

The Washington departure efficiency was repeated on arrival in New York. Everyone remained in the aircraft for the President's disembarkation and airport speech and then guides led them off to limousines that had been brought right to the plane. Peterson was glad he had been allocated a vehicle of his own. He sat staring out at the traffic along the Van Wyck Expressway, letting his mind drift. How difficult would it be for him to adjust to handling his own baggage and going through immigration and customs procedures like everyone else, if he resigned the Directorship? He tried to think of any friends or acquaintances sufficiently well placed in businesses to be able to offer him a job. He didn't know any, he realized. Could he risk a resignation, in the hope that there might be an approach from some corporation? Lucille would have to remain in the clinic for another month at least. And then have out-patient treatment, probably. And Beth would be hospitalized for much longer. He had not fully calculated the cost, but it would be considerable: certainly more than any insurance cover. How much did he have in his bank? Twenty thousand; maybe a little less. Not enough to last a year, with his present commitments. He would certainly have to find something positive before he considered quitting. It would be irresponsible to do anything otherwise: there were more ways in which he could fail Lucille and Beth than by not being there every time they wanted him. Peterson shifted, looking at his watch. Paul would still be with Beth. He wondered how the girl had reacted to his absence? He'd telephone Paul, he decided, after the United Nations session.

At the Waldorf he found he had been assigned a suite and felt uncomfortable with so much room; it was loneliness, he accepted, surprised. It was fortunate the schedule was so tight that he wouldn't have to be there at any length. He checked and found that Levy was also booked into the hotel, but when he tried the room there was no reply.

Peterson was in the last car in the President's motorcade on the police-cleared route to the United Nations skyscraper overlooking the East River. The only congestion was that caused by the number of cars comprising it. The CIA Director went into the building about five minutes after the main party and so he was not immediately aware of the excitement. The President and Flood were looking impatiently towards the door when he entered; the foyer was crowded with people and just beyond their own group, Peterson caught sight of David Levy. Then he became aware of Fowler's irritated gesture and hurried forward.

'Something has happened to the satellite,' said the President. 'The Israelis say it's malfunctioning. Get on to our people; find out what the hell's happening.'

Peterson thrust his way through the bustle to a public kiosk, warning Walter Jones immediately the deputy replied that it was not a secure line.

'It's gone completely haywire,' reported Jones, his voice mirroring the excitement that everyone else was showing. 'It seems to be collapsing out of orbit; we're monitoring it, obviously, but our people calculate it'll start to burn up on re-entry into the atmosphere.'

'Bohler?' demanded Peterson.

'No,' said the deputy. 'I managed contact as soon as we got word of what was happening. He still hasn't been able to get near any of the controls. And there's something else.'

'What?'

'I finished reading all Bohler's information. And then checked with him again, when I was talking about the malfunctioning. You were right.'

'It's taking shape,' said Peterson. 'At last it's taking shape.'

Bohler made his entry into the operations room appear as casual as possible, to guard against hinting at any foreknowledge of what was happening, but it was an unnecessary precaution because everyone's attention was on the command console. Hannah was hunched forward over it, going from dial to dial, snapping out orders and course corrections to the technicians grouped in front of her. Dr Muller was standing rigidly behind the Project Director, hands gripped white against the back of her chair. As he approached, Bohler heard the instruction for the satellite rocket to be fired, in an effort to correct the course misalignment, then there was a shout from one of the white-coated men as the control dials almost immediately registered a worsening of pitch.

'The gyro,' he heard Hannah say to Muller. 'We can't correct the imbalance of the gyro!' She punched her fist against the console table, exasperated at her inability to rectify the fault.

'The motor,' said Muller urgently. 'Try the motor again.'

'You saw what happened last time,' she said.

'We must do something. It can't fail. It *can't.*'

The woman paused, then gave the order, limiting the burn to three seconds. It took a further minute for the effect to manifest itself, and a shout came from the technician who had given the earlier warning.

'It's going,' he shouted. 'I've no control ... it's descending into the atmosphere.'

'No!' said Muller, the word whimpering from him. 'It can't fail ... can't ....'

Everyone was gazing hypnotically at the needles of the dial, jerking and waving chaotically across the calibrated facings and then, abruptly, they simultaneously stopped registering.

Bohler realized that Hannah's head was bent low over her chest. She jumped up and, when she turned to leave the room, he saw she was crying. She went past him without appearing to be aware of his presence and he made no move to intercept her. There was complete silence in the chamber — a deadness about everything.

Bohler gave Hannah an hour to recover. He knocked lightly upon her door and it was a long time before she responded. She opened it a few inches, saw it was him, and then held it wider for him to enter. She walked ahead of him into the room, slumping down into a chair. He edged on to the arm and pulled her head against his chest. The movement seemed to release a fresh burst of emotion. She clung to him, sobbing. She pulled away at last, gazing up at him with reddened eyes. 'It'll be the end of us here,' she said. 'No one will take us seriously any more ... want to buy anything we build. There won't be any orders from Asia. There won't be any orders from anywhere.'

'I'm very sorry,' said Bohler. Illogically, he realized that he meant it.

CHAPTER 44

Peterson stood unobtrusively and quite alone at the side of the chamber, watching the Israeli Premier at the podium and admiring the performance. The debate had been postponed twice, until there could be confirmation of the failure of the satellite, and now Weismann had the world stage from which to deride the countries who had been so quick to mobilize against Israel.

'... let the world see the responsibility, the statesmanship of these countries. Unmitigated aggressors, they massed for war because they believed they had Israel impotent before the first shot was fired ... let the world see the efficiency of their gadgetry and how, without it, they will now have to slink away into the night ....'

The majority of the Arab delegations were absent, Peterson saw. Only Egypt had any major representation.

'... Israel did not want war. Israel did not intend war. We came here to demand international protection against it being forced upon us and we now invite this chamber to identify and publicly condemn those countries prepared to conduct themselves in such a way ....'

On the far side of the chamber, Peterson thought he detected the figure of David Levy: he'd already asked several of the FBI men to help locate the Mossad chief's whereabouts.

'... must this stupidity go on? Can't there ever be a time when our neighbours decide the time has come to stop: to treat us as friends and not enemies ....'

Peterson recognized that the Israeli leader was fully exploiting his advantages. But, very cleverly, the man was just refraining from using a tone of arrogance which might have antagonized the listening diplomats. The temptation to sneer openly must have been very strong, yet Weismann was resisting it. And he'd been very careful to avoid identifying by name the Arab nations who had rushed into preparations for war.

'... before the malfunction of the satellite over our country, Israel had demonstrated to the world its determination to have peace. I emphasize, as I will never tire of emphasizing, that determination. We ask for nothing, except safe and secure borders. We seek nothing, except friendship ....'

The abrupt ending of Weismann's speech seemed to surprise many of the delegates. The Premier remained at the podium for a few seconds, and it was not until he turned to leave that they realized it was over. There was a thunder of appreciation, bank upon bank of the assembled diplomats waving order papers of support. Peterson watched it all unmoved, letting the doubts parade themselves in his mind, a jigsaw puzzle of a thousand pieces and a gradually emerging picture.

The US President followed the Israeli. Fowler's hastily re-written speech was as well conceived as Weismann's had been. While Weismann had allowed himself hyperbole and rhetoric, Fowler had decided upon simplicity, the words of a far-seeing statesman looking beyond an immediate problem. The world had been confronted with a crisis, but now the crisis was past. Hasty decisions had been made and they were regretted. Now was the time to forgive, if not forget. Israel had proved itself a country of sensible, world-conscious leaders. America was proud to consider itself a friend. It would do everything in its power to work for the peace Israel so fervently desired.

Peterson saw Levy as the President was coming to the conclusion of his address and moved quickly around the circular corridor, anxious to reach the Mossad leader. Levy saw him approaching and smiled. 'I want to thank you,' he said as Peterson reached him. 'And your man, for what he did. I hope we can forget the differences that arose between us.'

'It wasn't us,' said Peterson.

'What!'

'We've already checked. Our man had nothing to do with it.'

The Israeli held out his hands in a vaguely uncertain gesture. 'But I thought ....'

'Yes,' said Peterson. 'That's what everyone thinks. But it isn't so.'

'Then how?'

'We haven't had a report on that yet.'

Levy smiled, a sad expression. 'You mean we did everything we did and it would have happened anyway, without interference?'

'That's the way it seems.'

'Incredible.'

'Yes,' said Peterson. 'Incredible. I wondered if we might meet later on; somewhere more private?'

Levy indicated some members of the Israeli delegation, a few yards away. 'Difficult to commit myself, with half a government here.'

'It's important.'

Levy regarded him curiously. 'Where?'

'We're both staying at the Waldorf. Why not there? Say in an hour?'

Levy's doubt seemed to increase. 'An hour,' he agreed.

The President appeared as excited about the satellite as Weismann was. During the Assembly meeting he had ordered that a reception should be prepared at the Waldorf and insisted, when Peterson asked to be excused, that the CIA Director attend. Peterson left ahead of the main American party, sure he could keep the appointment with Levy and still get to the celebration.

In his suite he sat at the bureau, listing the points to clarify them in his mind before the meeting, and driving the pencil into the paper in his bitterness. It was difficult, but he had managed to subdue his anger by the time Levy's knock came at the door.

'There's a reception,' said Levy, as he entered.

'I'm going, in a little while,' said Peterson. The Israeli had already been drinking, he guessed.

'What's all the mystery?' enquired Levy. 'Surely it's a time for celebration.'

'There isn't a mystery, not any more,' said Peterson. 'But there has been, for quite a long time.'

The other man's smile went. 'That remark might be clear to you,' he said. 'But it isn't to me.'

'Russia worked with us very closely over this,' said Peterson. 'Made a lot of reports available ....'

Levy was impassive now, head alertly to one side as Peterson spoke.

'I'd been troubled for a long time that there was something I'd missed ... some denominator I should have noticed. And then I thought back to the very beginning, to the first indication we had of what was happening in Africa ....'

'From me,' said Levy.

'Right,' accepted Peterson. 'From you, in Israel. And then I checked and found that the Russian alert came from Israel, from Soviet agents infiltrated in with the dissidents from the Soviet Union, which is a useful way of controlling information, if you know who they are. And then I thought of the first positive indications that it might be Chad. From Israel again ....'

'I still don't understand ....' Levy started to protest, but Peterson talked on. 'Several of the reports from the two supposed priests we sent in spoke of people appearing to expect them: I thought at the time that it was African bush telegraph, but then I decided that not even that would have been quick enough to assemble all the natives on the day they were caught. So I went back to our people in N'Djamena and they checked the airport arrivals and the passenger lists and then we made the bribe big enough for a local official to go out and make enquiries for us. And learned about the people who'd gone ahead of our two men. And who had travelled around behind them, practically in their footsteps ....'

Levy sat, shaking his head as if he still couldn't understand what the American was saying.

'When I debriefed Colonel Bradley, he said they'd heard helicopters from the complex, searching for them immediately after the assault went wrong. So I checked that, too. And discovered that although it has aircraft and an airstrip, there are not any helicopters there at the moment.' Peterson paused, waiting, but Levy did not speak.

'Not one of your party was killed,' reminded Peterson. 'And all of them were fortunately helicoptered out to safety. And I wondered how it was that you knew that you would be needing the helicopters so quickly. And how it was that with a vast complex covering something like 70,000 square kilometres, your people actually came to land and made an assault within two hundred yards of where a combined American-Soviet entry was being made. And not just made it at the same spot, but at the same time ....'

Peterson stopped again, but Levy still did not respond.

'It's been an amazing affair for Israel, hasn't it?' persisted Peterson. 'Your Premier has just finished convincing the world — to a standing ovation — that Israel is a responsible, statesman-like nation. You've got a public commitment from the Soviet Union of Jewish emigration. From America you've got all the money and all the tanks and all the oil you asked for. And every Arab country hostile to you has been ridiculed and humiliated. Gadaffi has been shown up yet again, and this time in such a way that the Arab countries won't trust him any more ... and a rocket installation that might have been a problem is disgraced.'

'This is all a very wild piece of conjecture,' broke in Levy.

'Oh no,' refuted Peterson. 'No it's not. It's got a logic about it. You set us up. You set America up and you set the Soviet Union up and I want to know how that rocket came down.'

Levy shook his head. There was no lightness about the man now, nor any indication that he had had any celebration drinks before coming to Peterson's suite. 'I don't know what you're talking about,' he said.

'Then you'd better think it out,' said Peterson, threateningly. 'Your aid and your tanks and your oil are promised. That's all, just promised. There's no agreement. You know what sort of a man Fowler is: a shotgun over his arm and a horse to ride off into the West. He hates being made to look a fool. And he's just left the United Nations having been completely deceived by this. Unless you tell me what it's about, I'll set it out piece for piece and convince him it's true and you won't get a damned thing. And then I'll let Moscow know what happened and you won't get another Jew out of that country for the next fifteen years.'

'Bastard,' said Levy.

'It's a necessity of the business,' said Peterson, careless of the abuse. 'You know me, David. You know I'll do it.'

'You'd have done the same,' defended Levy, clumsily. 'In fact I'm sure you *have* done the same, in the past.'

'What?'

'I had to evolve a foolproof way of keeping our own person in the installation free from suspicion. And she *would* have become a suspect, if there had not been so many diversions. It really didn't matter who mounted them, you or Russia. I was sure one of you would try. Combining, as you did, made it a bonus. Now she's got years of operational life left. Hannah Bloor is really a most remarkable woman: one of the most dedicated in our service. I couldn't possibly risk losing her.'

'As project leader, she could actually time the malfunction, so you could orchestrate the whole thing ... even the Premier's appearance at the right time, here tonight?'

'We planned it very carefully,' said Levy, allowing the conceit to show.

'You were prepared to commit hundreds of thousands of dollars and God knows how many lives, for one woman!'

'Of course,' said Levy, surprised at Peterson's outrage. 'She was in a unique position: she had to be protected.'

Peterson thought again of the photographs of Henry Blakey's wife and child, and the pictures of the mutilated agents he'd despatched in the beginning. 'And you regard it as an overwhelming success?'

'Absolutely,' said Levy. 'It worked perfectly, didn't it?'

'Yes,' agreed Peterson. 'I suppose it did.'

'Are you going to try to interfere with the aid agreement? Or emigration from Russia?'

Peterson considered the question. 'There wouldn't seem to be a lot of point,' he admitted.

'No,' smiled Levy, with obvious relief. 'There wouldn't, would there?' He made a pretence of looking at his watch. 'The reception has started. Why don't we have a celebration drink. We've come out even, you and I.'

'Yes,' said Peterson. 'Why don't we have a celebration drink?'

Soon they would be leaving the pool-side and going to her room to make love, Bohler knew. There was an unspoken awareness between them, like an aphrodisiac. Bohler stirred and put the towel over his lap and she saw the movement and smiled. Bohler was glad the depression was lifting and she was beginning to smile again.

'What will you do now?' he said.

She shrugged. 'Return to Germany eventually, I suppose. You?'

'I suppose I'll be going in a few days.' Bohler wondered if he would get the instructions that night. There seemed no need to remain any longer.

'I'd have liked it to have lasted longer,' she said.

'So would I,' said Bohler. He was surprised at his feelings, confused by them. It had been nervousness that had brought him and Gerda together, he knew. But he did not think it was nervousness with this woman. Was it possible to fall in love in a matter of days with someone about whom he knew nothing and whom he was supposed to be opposing? It seemed a ludicrous conjecture, yet Bohler was unsure of the answer. Certainly he felt differently about Hannah Bloor than he had felt about all the other women he had known.

'Would it be possible?' she said.

'I don't know,' said Bohler. 'Perhaps.'

She began gathering her towels and suntan-oil. 'Let's go back to my room,' she said.

He didn't want to leave her, Bohler realized. It was illogical and impractical and insane, but he didn't want to quit the complex knowing that he would never see her again.

Petrov knew there was no way the Politburo could learn that it was not the American who had caused the satellite to malfunction, and that he was therefore safe in his bluff. A consummate Kremlin strategist, he concealed his satisfaction from the other men in the room, enjoying the shift of attack upon Litvinov; it would be a long time before anyone else felt strong enough to mount any sort of challenge against him.

'It would seem that we owe you an apology,' said Dorensky.

'I never took any remarks to be directed personally against me,' lied Petrov.

'There were times when the lack of support was clear,' said the chairman. 'For that, on behalf of everyone, I apologize. As always, Comrade General, you have concluded the matter very satisfactorily and with the minimal amount of difficulty for us. I congratulate you.'

'Thank you,' said Petrov, staring pointedly at Litvinov and waiting.

'Congratulations,' said Litvinov, at last.

Back in his office, with the ugly view of the Kremlin complex, Petrov remained at his desk for a long time, considering his escape. He had been lucky. Amazingly so. He could not expect it to happen again. Which meant insurance. He pulled the file that had been assembled upon Sergei Litvinov towards him and for an hour he sat making notation marks in margins, to remind him of operations to initiate against the man, until he had sufficient material to insinuate a purge into the minds of Dorensky or some other member of the Politburo.

Finally he stretched away from the papers, his mind still occupied with protection. There was only one thing outstanding which might create a problem, he calculated, reaching out for the telephone.

Two hours later, the frightened, twitching figure of Otto Bock emerged from the side entrance of the West German Foreign Office in Bonn and started across the road. He was only aware of the Mercedes in the last few seconds, managing to half turn towards it before it struck him with a force that sent him arcing into the air, to thump down, by some obscene irony, on to the parked car towards which he had been heading. Otto Bock was dead upon arrival at hospital. The post mortem disclosed his homosexual tendencies, but at the inquest, at which the police admitted failure in every attempt to find the hit-and-run driver, the evidence was not produced, to spare the feelings of an already distraught wife.

CHAPTER 45

Peterson had caught one of the earliest shuttles back to Washington, ahead of the presidential party, summoning Walter Jones as soon as he arrived at Langley. The deputy remained silent as Peterson disclosed what the Israelis had done, just occasionally shaking his head in disbelief.

'Jesus!' he said finally, when the Director finished.

'They suckered us, all the way along the line,' said Peterson.

'Did you tell the President?'

'No. As far as he's concerned it was Bohler, so the credit goes to us. That puts Flood deeper into the shit, for the opposition he mounted.'

'What did you do, after Levy had admitted it?'

'We went and had a celebratory drink together at the President's reception.'

'You drank with the bastard!'

'We even toasted each other.'

'I'd have found it difficult,' said Jones.

'I didn't,' said Peterson. 'I wanted him to remember the moment later.'

'Why?'

'He cost us God knows how much money and a lot of people. He almost cost me my job. Do you think I'm going to take that?'

Jones smiled for the first time. 'No,' he said. 'I don't guess you are.'

'Can we get Bohler?'

'I hasn't been too difficult so far.'

'Then get him,' ordered Peterson. 'One quick message.'

'Saying what?'

'Kill Hannah Bloor.'

'Just that?'

'Just that,' echoed Peterson. 'I'll not have an Agency of which

I'm the Director behaving like trained dogs for the Mossad and David Levy. He thinks he's been as clever as hell. I'm going to show him how wrong he is.'

Because of the time difference between America and Africa, it was still early in the morning when the contact came. Bohler became immediately aware of the transmission light glowing on what appeared to be the station selector screen and hesitated before reaching out to adjust the set. It would be his recall, he guessed: the recall from Hannah. And he didn't want that. It would have to happen, but he didn't want it today. Or tomorrow. Just a few more days, that was all. Perhaps he could stall — argue that it was insecure to quit immediately and that it would take a little while to ease himself out. He smiled at the decision, reaching out to adjust the set and clip the miniature receiver into his ear.

There was the insistence for his identification code and Bohler gave it almost impatiently, then stared incredulously at the set as the message was relayed and the acknowledgement demanded from him.

'Acknowledge,' repeated the static-crowded voice from the Langley communications room.

'Repeat,' said Bohler, the request croaking from him.

'Kill Hannah Bloor.'

'I want clarification.'

'There's no back-up instruction,' said the operator. 'This transmission should be concluded.'

'No! I want clarification ... someone in authority.'

'I repeat, we should conclude. The message is kill Hannah Bloor.'

'Please!' said the American. 'I can't ... I want to know ....'

'This is against standard instructions ... you're in a detectable situation ....'

'I want ...' started Bohler, but he never completed the sentence. Behind him the door to his room splintered off its hinges and he swivelled round to see the Libyan guards at the very moment they thrust through. He half rose from the chair, but the headset threw him off balance and he fell towards the bureau. The first shots missed him and he screamed, initially in fright and then in pain as

the second burst from the Kalashnikov scythed into him, so fierce
that it lifted his body over the divan and into the window. It didn't
break and he bounced back lifeless into the room.

Dr Muller was still very shocked. His face was chalky and his
hand, when he lifted the brandy goblet, shook so that some of the
liqueur spilled down the front of his coat.

'It's still difficult to comprehend,' he said, his voice uneven. 'I
never ....' he stopped, shuddering. 'It's frightening,' he said.

'Yes,' agreed Hannah. 'Frightening.'

'You had become friendly?'

'I thought so.'

'Yet you had no idea?'

'How can you ask that of me!' protested Hannah, immediately
affronted.

'I'm sorry,' apologized Muller at once, raising his hands before
him in a placating gesture. 'If you hadn't gone to his door ....' He
let the sentence trail away, as if the idea were unthinkable.

Hannah excused herself quickly from the meeting with Muller,
her arms tight against her sides. Inside her room she secured the
door and then stood uncertainly in the middle of the room. Her
attention gradually fixed upon her complicated radio equipment.
Curiously she adjusted it to the wavelength to which it had been
tuned since the arrival in the complex of Michael Bohler and
Gerda Lintz. She waited and after a few seconds she heard the
American operator's voice, the alarm very obvious despite the dis-
tortion of distance. 'Acknowledge,' it said. 'Acknowledge.'

She spun the dial, losing the transmission, then sat down heavily
upon the bed only hours before he had occupied with her. Would
he have done it? she wondered. At last her control went and she fell
forward, sobbing.

EPILOGUE

Peterson had expected the tension, so he was not concerned by it. Lucille kept moving around the room, adjusting things that needed no adjustment and then going to the table, re-arranging the cutlery and the crockery. Paul tried humorous stories which he told badly in his nervousness, having to prompt responses from Beth and his mother by leading the laughing. For once Peterson would have welcomed a drink, but decided against having one. Dr Harrap had decreed there should be wine with the meal to test Lucille's control, but Peterson decided that was as much as he would risk.

'A family again,' he said, proudly, leading them to the table.

'Until we have to go back, at six o'clock,' said Lucille.

'Next month there'll be day releases every week.'

Peterson poured wine for himself and Paul, conscious of Lucille's eyes watching the movement.

'Will there be lots of meals like this ... all of us together?' said Beth, anxiously. She still looked very ill.

'Yes,' promised Peterson. 'A lot.'

'Ever thought of trying another job?' asked Paul.

Peterson looked sharply at his son, then realized there had been no intended point to the question. 'Sometimes,' he said.

'Why don't you?' asked Beth. 'There must be dozens of things you could do ... there'd be a queue of people wanting you ....'

Peterson smiled at her pride in his ability. 'Maybe sometime in the future, when I get fed up with what I'm doing. Not yet though.'

The phone jarred abruptly into the room and Lucille, who was the most nervous, jumped.

'Damn!' said Peterson. He got up quickly. 'Excuse me,' he said.

He took the call in the study, among the unread books and photographs of old friends, immediately recognizing Jones' voice.

'Sorry to interrupt you,' said the deputy. 'I thought you'd want to know.'

'What?'

'A message from Jerusalem ... from Levy.'

'Read it.'

'It says "Thanks for responding as I hoped you would." What does it mean?'

Peterson fought against the frustration, biting his teeth into his lip. 'It means I was meant to guess it,' he said bitterly. 'That it wouldn't have worked completely if I hadn't.'

'I'm not sure I understand,' protested Jones.

'They won,' said Peterson. 'In the end the bastards won completely.'

AUTHOR'S NOTE

The Domesday weapon exists. Near the city of Semipalatinsk, north-east of Tashkent and not far from the Chinese border, the Russians have created their most secret scientific installation to perfect the beam weapon. The device is triggered by a controlled nuclear explosion from which giant electrical energy is generated. This is stored for several seconds, then electrons of high energy and intensity are injected into a collective accelerator which takes the pulsed stream of electrons, mixed with heavier protons, and then accelerates the protons with such velocity that a lightning bolt is created.

All three branches of the American armed forces have been working on the development of a beam weapon. The greatest progress has been made at the New Mexico laboratories at Los Alamos, where the atom bomb that destroyed Hiroshima and Nagasaki was made. The project — code-named Sipapu — has almost reached the point where a space vehicle can be launched and a proton beam fired in outer space.

The effect of both the Russian and American weapons would be to eviscerate anything at which they were pointed.

Up to the time of writing, no rocket has been successfully launched from the African installation to which I referred in the introduction to this book. The Soviet spy satellites are still positioned over the area.